A CAINE & FERRARO NOVEL

BURNING CAINE

JANET OPPEDISANO

Burning Caine

ISBN Digital: 978-1-7778856-1-8

ISBN Paperback: 978-1-7778856-0-1

Copyright © 2022

Cover Art Copyright © 2022

Chapter 1

Samantha

There were days I thought my job title should be Professional Lie Detector. I crested the top of the ladder and stepped onto the roof. Sure enough, within ten seconds, I knew it was one of those days.

Frowning, I knelt and ran a gloved hand across one of the golf-ball-sized dents in the reinforced metal. One among dozens. There was no way hail had caused this damage. I snapped several pictures with my phone, using a tape measure to document the roof's condition.

My phone buzzed before I could finish, displaying Cliff's name. My boss. What did he want?

"Samantha Caine speaking."

"Sam, system says you checked in at Clark Orchards for an estimate on the machine shed. That accurate?"

"Yeah."

"Status?"

"It's the worst hail damage I've ever seen." I rolled my eyes and walked the length of the thirty-foot shed, mentally cataloging each dent. "Looks like a hundred-year storm opened up right above the building and then vanished into the night."

"Come again?"

I took off my ball cap to wipe the sweat from my brow while I scanned the orchard. The blossoms on the apple trees had long since faded, and the fruit was just big enough to see. No apples on the ground or signs of damage. I closed my eyes and inhaled the fresh country air deeply, imagining I was back out on the road instead of stuck in small-town Michigan again. Dealing with my fifth fraudulent claim since I'd moved home a month ago didn't help.

Tucking my long ponytail under the hat when I put it back on, I let go of the sarcasm. "The house roof, gutters, and downspouts are all fine. The machine shed roof, on the other hand, is covered in indentations one inch in diameter. One inch. Cliff, every single dent is exactly the same size."

"Another fraud?"

"Looks like. Policyholder says he hasn't gotten up here to look at it—afraid of heights. Contractor came by to tell him he was doing roofs in the area after the hailstorm and that the shed was banged up. I'd bet a month's pay someone went to town with a ball-peen hammer. So, the insured's lying, the contractor did it, or both. Either way, I'm sending it to the Special Investigations Unit."

"Good call. How much longer you need?"

"I have to finish my inspection, talk to the insured, and update the system. Shouldn't be more than another hour. Maybe hour and a half max."

"Pretend you're lazy for a minute," he said, and I suppressed a laugh. "Do the bare minimum and skip the system till you're in the office."

Something was up. Postponing work, especially updates in the claims management software system, wasn't like Cliff.

"I need you off that claim ASAP. The old man called about a friend of his—had a house fire this morning. Mike already picked up the property portion, but there's a specialty artwork claim on a high-value painting by someone named Chah-gull."

Chagall, I mouthed, shaking my head.

"Name of the painting's not English. I'm not gonna try to say it. Sounds like the artwork loss will top the dwelling and contents losses."

I bit my lip to keep quiet. If Cliff was calling because Roger Foster, president of Foster Mutual, wanted me on this, it was going to be something interesting. Something I could dig my hungry teeth into. Paintings by Chagall could run from the tens or hundreds of thousands, and sometimes even north of a million dollars. It had been too long since I'd handled something juicy. I made my way to the ladder; I'd completed enough for the referral to SIU.

"You've got the expertise, so I want you over there when the fire investigator and medical examiner leave. I'll send you the details, but the police should be ready for you in thirty."

He hung up before I could say anything else, so I pocketed my phone and headed down the ladder. This claim was going to be a big deal. An M.E. meant there'd been a death.

I stored my gear in the truck and grabbed one of my business cards. As I rang the doorbell, my phone buzzed, likely Cliff's details on the Chagall claim.

The homeowner opened the door. "All done?" He didn't step into the house to imply I was welcome, and I didn't try to enter.

"Yes, Mr. Clark, I'm done," I said. "I'm afraid the damage on the machine shed roof is inconsistent with what I was expecting to see. I'll have to forward it over to our Special Investigations Unit for some additional attention. You can expect to hear from one of our team within the next two business days."

His eyebrows knit together as he processed what I'd said. "So, you aren't going to replace the roof?"

"In the meantime," I said as I offered my business card, which he didn't reach for. "My contact information is on my card, so you can call with any questions you may have about my visit. The general claims support line is on the back in case you want to speak with someone about any further steps we'll be taking."

"My neighbor had his shed roof replaced after the storm." He pointed to his right, likely to his neighbor's house. This response was relatively common under the circumstances, and the suspicious voice in my head always questioned the person's motives. He was either the guilty party, thought I was accusing him, or disappointed I'd snatched away his windfall. He was confused, not angry, so number three was my guess.

"Mr. Clark, the decision is out of my hands. Our SIU will be in touch with you about the next steps."

I held out my card again, and he stared at me for another moment, searching for a way around this. Then he slammed the door, almost taking my hand off in the process.

I shrugged it off and stuck the card in the door, then headed back to my truck, my giant F-150 Raptor. I opened the door and climbed up on the running boards before sliding into the driver's seat. The beautiful behemoth was an effort to get into, but the size was valuable when navigating over debris or washed out roads after a big storm. The engine roared to life as I hit the ignition.

I drove a half-mile down the road, so I wasn't working in Mr. Clark's driveway, until my curiosity got the better of me and I pulled over. As I shifted into my backseat mobile office, my laptop sprang to life, and I called up the claim details. Skimming through the policy document until I got to the correct section, my breath caught.

Cliff had assigned me to a claim for Marc Chagall's *Les amoureux dans le ciel*. I knew this painting. It had been twenty years since I'd last stood in front of it with its owner, Bobby Scott. Twenty years since he set me on a life path I ended up abandoning.

And now, according to the claim details, Bobby was dead and the painting was destroyed.

I ran a shaky hand over my face. This wasn't the kind of interesting I'd been expecting.

Chapter 2

Samantha

Oak Street was in a quiet residential neighborhood in Brenton, Michigan, which had probably never seen so much activity. Firetrucks, ambulance, police cars, and unmarked vehicles clogged the street, not to mention the gawkers and a departing news truck.

"Fire team's all done and we've finished our sweep for evidence collection." Officer Jimmy Slater walked up the driveway with me, casual as always, as though we weren't approaching the scene of a recent death. An old friend from college I hadn't seen in a decade, he was a lanky man who wore his cap high on his forehead, emphasizing the size of his nose and the early gray in his sideburns. "M.E. already took Mr. Scott's body out, too."

My throat tightened at the reminder. The only time I'd met Bobby Scott, I was ten and visiting with my mother who was here with legal paperwork for his business. He'd made such an impression, I never forgot him. Now he was gone, and I was climbing his driveway, coming for the painting he'd introduced me to all those years ago.

A tent was erected on the front lawn, just before the driveway curved to the left. It shaded a working table, where six people remained deep in conversation. Brenton Police officers mingled with firefighters and a few people in white Tyvek jumpsuits to match my own.

The closer we got, the stronger the memories became. The sprawling ranch house, its red brick, and gardens. It was a private residence on a crowded street, a unique property along this part of Oak Street. It stretched two lots deep, all the way to the road along the river.

But the broken front window, overturned urns, and trampled flowers told a different story. As did the black smoke streak staining the front and roof.

An ebony-skinned female officer with buzz-cut hair stood by the door, speaking with a firefighter. When she turned around, my instincts told me to run.

Janelle Williams. Another face I hadn't seen in forever. My best friend growing up, turned—in her mind, at least—bitter enemy.

She was a hair taller than me and, even in her formless white coveralls, carried herself like she had enough muscle on her five-foot-ten frame she could have thrown me across the property. Her skin glistened with sweat from having to wear the extra layers over her uniform, but she seemed unphased.

"You remember Janelle from school, right?" Jimmy smiled, but it slipped when he looked from me to her. "Sorry, Sammy, I forgot about—"

"You're the insurance adjuster?" The corner of her lip curled.

"I am." I clenched my jaw and took a calming breath. We could be professional after all these years. "There was a painting hanging in the living room. I need to find it and evaluate its condition."

She stared, then yanked her hood up and did an abrupt about-face without a word. Words failed me, too. There were so many I wanted to say to her, despite the irritation bubbling inside. *Sorry. Forgive me. I miss you.*

I gave Jimmy a tight smile and followed Janelle, a few paces behind her.

Work. This was work. Calculate the damage. Brickwork to repair. Window replaced. Need to check the roof. But no, that was Mike's job. I had to find the painting and get out.

As we entered through the smashed front double doors, the scent of smoke hit me first, chased by the pungent odor of burned flesh. I zipped up my jumpsuit and pulled on my respirator and goggles, which blunted the stench and stemmed the stinging in my eyes.

Ahead of me, Janelle did the same, not sparing a second to glance in my direction.

I scanned the foyer. Other than the darkened ceiling, it was the same. Twenty years had passed and the grandfather clock was still in the corner. The small chandelier, bench, and the Tiffany lamps were no different, other than a wing missing from one of the dragonflies. It was once a gleaming wood-paneled room which smelled of lemon oil. Now, covered in a combination of dust and ash, it smelled of death.

Janelle gestured down the short hallway to the right. "Fire was over that way, in the living room."

The door to the home office was open in the hallway. A quick peek as we passed showed the same desk, same shelving, same floor and walls. I'd expected changes after all this time—new furniture, new rugs, new paint, something —but everything was the same.

As a claims adjuster, I'd witnessed the aftermath of many fires, from small ones that didn't meet the deductible to the utter destruction of whole neighborhoods during wildfire season. The living room would be a complete loss, everything scorched to some degree, and needing repairs to the structure itself.

"Fire team did a good job." Janelle walked through the living room, past the burned remains at the center of the room, to the broken picture window at the back. "They got the blaze down fast and stopped it from spreading past this room."

There was something peculiar about the burn pattern. The sofa and chair backs were blackened frames and springs, but the seat pans and legs had survived—like the fire started at the top.

I walked over to the remains of a love seat, and my hand hovered over the frame. Why was it crammed against the other love seat and the sofa? And was it the same sofa as twenty years ago? Same tables, same chairs, same baby grand? "The furniture's not right."

"What?"

I gestured to the love seats. "Those were over there." I pointed to where they'd been before, by the front windows. "The piano should be in the corner. And the wing chairs should be over by the fireplace."

"How do you know?"

"I was here before." On the east wall, a painting hung above the fireplace mantle. It was darkened from the soot, but I knew the size and shape of the frame. Trees on a hill, focused around a man and woman having a picnic. Nice, but nothing special.

And hanging over a fireplace would have meant it was probably filthy to begin with. Serious cleaning required.

"When?" Her voice was thick with skepticism. Of course, it was. She didn't want to be there any more than I did.

Don't bother with the details. She doesn't actually care. "A long time ago."

Janelle looked at me for a moment, gloved hand touching her hooded head, the way she always used to when she was frustrated. "There was a crew of painters prepping for some touch-ups. They moved everything to the center of the room and covered it with a canvas tarp."

The fire must have traveled along the cover, burning the furniture from the top down.

She beckoned me to the far side of the room, next to the rear windows. Behind the remains of the couch, on the ground, she pointed to a long, narrow swath of raw canvas, six feet in length, with a dark stain on it. It was the only part of the room untouched by the fire. "This is where they found Mr. Scott."

Mr. Robert Scott. AKA Bobby Scott, owner of Bobby's Books. But more importantly, the man who'd kindled my love of art. He'd shown me each painting in the living room and office, one standing out far above the others: Marc Chagall's *Les amoureux dans le ciel,* French for "Lovers in the sky."

I'd compared it to a dream, all fuzzy shapes and imagination. He'd told me I had a good eye and should consider a career in art. That moment had inspired so much.

Janelle snapped her fingers in front of my face. "Earth to Samantha."

I took a steadying breath. *Don't let her see you upset.* "Is there a theory yet?"

"It's early. We have to wait for the report, but the initial impression is that it doesn't look suspicious."

"I'm guessing the dark spot is blood?" I squatted next to the area she'd indicated and touched where he'd died. Two feet away, the shattered remnants of a glass table sat. "Probably from hitting his head?"

"Seems reasonable."

"So, he was either dead or lying here when the fire got going?"

"Looks like." She folded her arms, cocking her head to telegraph her displeasure at being there. Why hadn't she called over one of the other officers to escort me in? "Bit of a step down, isn't it?"

"What's that?" I closed my eyes in a silent moment for Bobby.

"FBI Art Crimes star recruit—" The venom dripped off her words. "—to insurance adjuster."

So few words, so many years of anger and regret tied up in them. More than a decade of not speaking should have tempered some of that. But she'd always been stubborn. Even more so than me.

I lifted my hand off the canvas on the floor and stood. Time to get to work, not waste time with petty squabbles.

"The First Notice of Loss says the painting is in this room." I walked toward the front window, where the piano had originally been. "If it was hanging in the same place it was when I was here before, it should be here."

I stopped by the wall where the painting had hung twenty years ago. There was no Chagall, but the hanger was still there. I looked at the piano, lying flat on the floor, its legs burned and cracked in the fire, and back to the wall.

I could still see it, clear as the day I'd been here. Vibrant blue background, a vase of flowers taking up most of the right side, and two faces in the top left. Just floating heads, one man and one woman. The red and yellow flowers were surrounded by greenery, all green smudges with a few defined leaves. A small table with a bowl of fruit and a violin. The thick frame was gold, edged with beads, leaves, and rosettes.

Janelle came next to me. "Now what?"

It couldn't have gone far. I scanned from the wall to the floor to the…There was something under the fallen piano. Kneeling, I felt the hard corner of an object stuck in the thin layer of sludge.

"Can you tilt the piano a bit?" I pointed to the end of the shell, where it narrowed, and she could get a good grip. I knew she had the strength to tip it, despite it weighing hundreds of pounds. Probably over her head if she was angry enough.

She hefted it, and I took a few photos for evidence before lifting the corner of the object to feel its underside. The frame of a painting, with rows of beads and flowers. This was what I was looking for.

"Hurry up," she grunted. As I pulled it out carefully, ensuring it wasn't caught on anything, I backed away, and she let the piano down, surprisingly gently.

"It must have fallen under the piano before the legs broke." About three-quarters of the painting was missing, burned to ash—one million dollars of ash. The frame was fully intact, though.

"The piano must have protected some of it." Janelle reached to turn it over, and I batted her hand. Instead, I shook it at an angle, so the soot covering the back fell away, and I lifted it over my head to check the front.

"Moving any of the debris around on it, including the soot and slurry, can damage it further."

"There's hardly any of it left––why does that matter?"

"Because this painting is worth a million dollars to Foster Mutual Insurance." I ran my eyes over what was left. "Before we can pay out, we need to make sure it's the right one. Standard procedure on something this valuable. Do you have any evidence bags we can put this in? And something sturdy to put under it?"

She rolled her eyes but left anyway. Hopefully, to get that bag.

On the front, the frame was blackened, with a few small glints of gold leaf remaining on the highest points. A portion of the painting remained along the bottom and a few other strips in the middle, creeping out like fingers from the left side. Some soot fell on my goggles, but I wiped it away.

Was that part of the signature at the bottom right corner? If so, it would be a big help in verification.

Janelle returned a few minutes later with a bag and a sheet of cardboard to brace the painting. She tagged it with the standard evidence information, including the chain of custody. From me to her. Not the other way around.

"You're taking this?" How could I do my job if I didn't have the painting?

"You know how this works. With a death in the fire, it's a homicide until we're confident it's not. All the teams have already gone through here, but this feels like evidence."

She was right, but the slight wrinkling at the corner of her dark eyes told me there was a smile behind her gear. It gave her more than a hint of satisfaction to make my life more difficult.

"Once we're done, we'll turn it over to you."

I took a few photos to confirm I'd found it and the state it was in when the police took it. "Indicate no one should turn it over or brush the surface dirt away."

She rolled her shoulders, narrowing her eyes. "I know my job, Sam."

With that, she spun on her heel and headed for the door, handling the painting more gingerly than her tone would have implied.

Work was done. I should have clamped my mouth shut and left, moving on to the next claim. That was the safe approach. But instead, I blurted out, "I'm still sorry, Janelle."

She paused, her shoulders heaving with a deep breath, not turning back to me. "And sorry still doesn't cut it."

My stomach dropped, and I rubbed a hand over my face, hitting cheek and respirator. Great. Whatever the soot from the painting missed was now covered. "I'm only in town for eight more months. Maybe we can grab a coffee or—"

"Friends don't do the shit you did," she muttered, words sharp as a knife in my gut. She stalked off toward the door, not looking over her shoulder. "Let Jimmy know you're leaving."

What was left to say? I let out a long, shaky breath and followed her out, our words done.

••••••••••

The midsummer sun hit me when I exited the house, and I closed my eyes, tilting my face up. Deep breath in, deep breath out. Relax. But it was no use. For eleven years, my best friend had shut me out. Why did I think that could change?

I shoved my goggles to my forehead and tore the respirator down to my neck, blinking away a piece of ash which fell onto my eyelash. Damn Janelle Williams. And this fire. And Bobby's death. And that painting. This day couldn't get any worse.

Thank god I was only in this forsaken town for the short term.

Find Jimmy. Then leave.

Janelle was talking to the officers set up under the tent, still holding the painting. Fortunately, none of them were him, so I could avoid her. I yanked the coverings off my boots and started down the curved driveway, reviewing the plan in my head.

A good art restorer might be able to clean away enough of the debris to run some tests. Less than a quarter of the canvas remained, but the signature and a section through the middle flowers survived. The frame was intact and a chemical analysis could be done on the paints underneath the rabbet, if nothing else.

Oak Street gradually came into view through the mature trees and thick bushes of the Scotts' yard. Firefighters packed up their truck, a K-9 and handler headed to a vehicle, and a medical examiner's van was pulling out.

A line of police tape stretched across the bottom of the driveway. Jimmy stood on the other side, speaking with a man in a short-sleeved shirt whose back was to me. As I approached, Jimmy pointed toward the house and the other man turned to follow his finger.

I scuffed my boot on the pavement, almost tripping over nothing. He was the most gorgeous man I'd ever seen. Heat flushed through my cheeks, inspiring an overwhelming desire to pull my goggles and respirator back into place to hide the blush I knew was there.

Tall and broad, deep olive complexion, and thick dark brown-almost black hair with a slight wave and obvious widow's peak. Just long enough on top to run your fingers through. His eyes drifted down from the house and met with mine, a tight smile creasing his face.

He looked expensive. From the polish of his cognac leather shoes to the perfectly tailored gray slacks, all the way to his navy polo which moved like it was made of silk. Lawyer, maybe? Already looking for a payout? Good. Give me handsome at work any day of the week—a gallery executive who thought insurance wasn't important, a contractor trying to pull a fast one, a slippery lawyer—and I could control the situation.

Just don't give me handsome anywhere else. I ran a hand over my cheek to calm the blush, but it scratched. Right. My filthy gloves were still on. Now my face was fully streaked with soot. Great first impression.

Jimmy let out a laugh, interrupting his conversation with the man. "You're gonna need a bath after that!"

"Yeah, no kidding." I blew out sharply and addressed the stranger as I paused next to them. "Sorry, I'll just be a sec."

He nodded, smiling politely.

The trees above us swayed in a slight breeze, the sun breaking through the leaves enough to glint over his chiseled face, flecks of gold sparkling in his brown eyes.

Good heavens. Quick check—no ring.

Stop it, Sam.

I folded my arms. "Janelle told me to check in with you before I left. She took my stuff into custody, so I'll drop by the station when she's done."

"You're in luck!" Jimmy flicked his cap an inch higher and rocked back on his heels. "I'm in charge of the investigation, so I'll make sure they put a rush on it for you."

"Thanks." I smiled at both of them.

"Sì, I should be going, as well." The stranger's voice was deep, reverberating inside my chest. But it was the thick Italian accent which sent shivers up my spine, memories washing over me. Cafés for breakfast, winding cobblestone streets, day trips to Rome and Florence. The view from the duomo.

"Roman?" The word was out of my mouth before I thought enough to stop myself.

A smirk tugged at his perfectly bowed lips. "American, but raised in Roma. You have a very good ear, officer."

"I'm not—"

"Slater!" We all turned to see Janelle stalking in our direction. She hooked a thumb over her shoulder to where a uniformed man stood. "Fire marshal wants to talk to you."

Things hadn't gone well between her and me. Time to skulk off and lick my wounds. I nodded to the men and slipped between them, toward my truck down the road.

The smell of smoke and burned electrical was still heavy in the air, but I caught a hint of something underneath it. Vanilla and amber, coming off the stranger. I held my breath, savoring the lingering scent.

Once that breath was done, the smoke from my suit and face overwhelmed me again. The clomp of my thick-soled work boots on the pavement. The indistinct chatter of a dozen voices working the scene.

But over it all, I heard the stranger's final words to Jimmy. "Grazie mille, Officer Slater."

A jumble of energy formed in my stomach, and I fought the urge to turn around. Maybe I should have introduced myself. With that silly idea, came more flashes of memory. Scooters and summer dresses and ancient frescoes. Italian pastries and big meals with lots of laughs. Throwing coins into the Trevi Fountain.

And a man who professed his eternal love, then stopped calling. Who swore he'd move to the States to be with me.

Heartache.

Yeah.

Good thing I didn't introduce myself.

CHAPTER 3

ANTONIO

I shifted the car into park and pressed a button to put the top up, music humming in the background. Anyone who knew me would ask what was wrong if I was listening to something so quietly. I turned the stereo off and closed my eyes, focusing on the vibration of the engine in my chest. This day was not going according to plan.

Bobby Scott had texted me yesterday about evaluating some artwork he was considering selling, which may have needed cleaning prior to auction. His collection was small, but well-curated. He had an excellent eye.

And now he no longer did.

It was not as if we were friends, but I was shaken. Getting back to work would help.

None of my three co-workers in the main studio budged as I slipped in through the back door. The space was airy and industrial with six ten-foot long, wheeled tables in the main area. Each was open underneath with space for various tools of our art conservation and restoration trade. To the left, the small wood shop; to the right, the kitchen. Large overhead lights added to the brightness from the skylights and rear windows.

I wound my way between the tables, passing Zander and his giant headphones, stopping to put a hand on Alice's back before I continued. "Do you need a hand with anything?"

She was a petite blond who carried what she called an extra thirty pounds, although I thought they suited her perfectly. She looked up and shook her head. In front of her, a wood-backed trompe-l'oeil of a snake winding around a tree. Her gels, solvents, and cotton balls surrounded the painting. "Frank helped me."

My cousin Gianfranco sat at the table next to her. Dark hair and olive skin like me, he also claimed to carry an extra thirty pounds, but refused to join me at the gym. He smiled without taking his eyes off the painting in front of him. "We had to give up on removing all the overpaint. It's so old some of it's cross-linked, so we'll just glaze over it."

I nodded and continued toward the lab, where my father stood over the hot table. Dominico was five inches shorter than me, but with a personality which barely fit in any room.

He turned as I neared, a beaming smile on his face, as usual. "Antonio!"

"Is my painting done yet?" I stopped next to him at the large table, running a hand over the warmed layer of mylar film covering the painting I was conserving. Heat soaked through my hand but was unable to warm the chill which had settled inside me.

"What are you doing back so soon? Did Bobby cancel?"

I flipped the heat off. "He passed away."

Papa sucked in a quick breath and clutched my arm. "He what?"

"This morning. House fire."

We stood silently for a moment, the only noise the gentle hum of the vacuum on the table, keeping the painting sandwiched tight until it cooled.

"You shouldn't be here." Papa's voice snapped me out of my reverie.

"I barely knew him. I don't need time off."

"That's not what I meant." He touched a light hand to my upper arm. "To be honest, Bobby's death is a reminder not to ignore what's important. I've been thinking about your future a lot, and I want to talk about. Working with me isn't what you trained for, my boy. All your years in school, your research, your brilliant dissertation...you wanted to do postdoctoral work. Why are you here?"

"I love working with you." I turned to face him, clasping him by the upper arms, and he held my elbows. "And Sofia and everyone else. Europe is too far away from you all. That's what's important."

"Frank will finish school soon enough. He can take over for me when I retire. Or one of your cousins in Roma can move here. Don't feel like you need to stay for that." He furrowed his brow. "You seem...unfulfilled here."

I shook my head and released him, running a hand over the film again. He was right in many ways, but I spent six years in Italia and almost as many in Delaware. A decade away from my family was too long. "I love working in restoration."

"But your studies?"

Holding up a hand, it was my turn to shake my head. "Compromise. If I promise to plan a few months with Mario in Napoli next year, will that make you happy?"

My cousin Mario worked at the Pompeii Archaeological Park, where I had done a great deal of my research. Surely they would welcome me back as a visitor, if not a temporary worker. Or perhaps he was right, and I could resume my research.

"Perfetto!" The smile returned, but softer than when I first joined him. "Exactly what I was hoping for."

My phone buzzed in my pocket, and I slid it out to peek at the screen. Victoria was returning my call. "Scusi, Papa. I have to take this."

He nodded, passing through the main studio toward his office.

I bowed my head, lowering my voice as I walked toward my own office. "Ciao, Victoria."

"Hey, hot stuff." Her voice, per usual for the last month, was a low purr. "I got your message. Change of plans for tonight?"

"Sì, I have a last-minute committee meeting tonight for the hospital gala and have to reschedule our dinner to tomorrow."

There was no response on the other end, other than a slow inhale of breath.

"Victoria? Are you free tomorrow night?"

"That's August first." Gone was the purr, replaced by a sound akin to her normal voice, which grew in speed and pitch as she continued. "Are you serious? I made it into August? Oh my god, Mae's never going to believe this! Wait until you see what I'm wearing to the gala!"

What was she talking about? Made it into August? "So, this is a yes?"

"Are you kidding? Of course! Text me the details!" She made a high-pitched squealing type noise as she hung up. For a grown woman, she reminded me far too much of a schoolgirl. Why was I going on another date with her?

Because my rule was three. Always three.

I sent her the reservation details and slipped the phone back into my pocket.

Lost Beneath the Stars stared back at me from the table under the mylar. In the painting, a rowboat crested a wave, three men huddled in the middle, no oars to be seen. The blue-green of the churning water reminded me of the officer's eyes from Bobby's house. They had popped against the dark soot covering her filthy face, practically glowing like the aurora. Tall for a woman, she moved with an athletic grace belied by the formless white coveralls she wore.

And she recognized my accent. Not just Italian, but she knew it was Roman. There was something about her. Something familiar I couldn't put my finger on. Perhaps it was déjà vu or wishful thinking. I should have introduced myself, but she was gone before I had a chance.

Who was she?

CHAPTER 4

SAMANTHA

I texted my sister as I sat in my truck outside the restaurant Saturday night. *Cass, I can't believe you talked me into this.*

Have fun! she texted back.

I pulled down the visor mirror for a pre-date check. Hair was good, a loose ponytail draped over my shoulder to complement my blue one-shoulder top. Make-up was light but satisfactory. Teeth clean.

Cass had sent me enough information about him to get me to the restaurant for this stupid date. Cameron Parker. Kind of cute, short blond hair, artist. Dinner at Caruther's in Lansing. I shook my head and rolled my shoulders. Why the hell was I doing this, other than because I loved her?

The hostess showed me to a booth, dropped off two menus, and let me know the server would be there soon. The lights in the restaurant were dim, and each table had a few small candles providing ambiance. Lots of oak furniture and walls decorated with hundreds of small black and white photos. The red cushioned booth was reasonably private and comfortable, so I sat back and waited.

The server arrived at 8:00, took my order for a glass of the house red, and poured water for the table. I let her know the rest of my party would be arriving any minute, so I would wait before ordering anything else.

When she got back at 8:05 with my wine, I thanked her and got out my phone. I texted Cass, *Five minutes late.*

She texted back. *You or him?*

Him, but the house red is pretty good.

LOL

I put my phone away and took the cutlery out of the napkin. I was about to place it on my lap but I'd be getting up to shake Cameron's hand when he arrived, so I left it on the table.

8:10

You gave me the right date and time, right?

She didn't text back right away. Hopefully she was double-checking. *Yeah - Sat Aug 1 8pm Caruthers*

Is there more than one Caruthers?

No - I'm sure he'll be there soon

At 8:15, the server returned, asking if she could interest me in an appetizer. Smiling as politely as possible, I ordered bruschetta, something so classic it would be an easy win when he arrived. If he arrived.

I was supposed to be in Yosemite that weekend. Me and my rock-climbing guide doing a two-day ascent of El Capitan. It would have been my best time. But instead, I was sitting in a booth by myself, waiting for a blind date who was fifteen minutes late. Because my sister thought controlling my life would make her feel like she had control over her own. As if I hadn't already given up everything to move home and help her, she thought throwing me in front of men was the best plan. Like I'd fall in love and never leave Brenton again.

8:20

Why did I go along with it? Placate her. Make her happy. Relieve some of her stress. But it was stressing me out.

People arrived, people left, people enjoyed their meals. And I sat alone. The way I preferred life. Except I'd rather be alone at home.

A laugh caught my attention. Two men at a table nearby regaled each other with funny stories while the women at the table talked quietly. I watched them for a moment when someone walked behind their table, and my eyes moved to him.

Tall, broad-shouldered, wearing dress pants and a button-front shirt, all black. The Italian lawyer from the fire site yesterday? Somehow looking even more astonishing tonight. Heat rose in my cheeks just watching the way he walked. Stalked? No, he strode. One of the women at the table with the laughing men nudged her friend and the two of them watched him go by. I couldn't blame them, and they weren't the only ones. I wouldn't mind if *he* were a half hour late.

I lost track of him when the server arrived with the bruschetta. 8:30. Still no Cameron. I sighed, my shoulders sagging. I cast a look around to spot the hot lawyer for a momentary distraction, but he was nowhere to be found. Probably in a private booth, talking in that deep, velvety voice to some gorgeous woman. Not stood up, for sure.

Half hour, I texted Cass.

WTF?

Guess I'm eating alone tonight!

As I took the first bite, a piece of tomato fell on my lap. Perfect. I picked it up, placed the napkin I'd forgotten about on my lap, and Cameron arrived. Also perfect.

"Sorry I'm so late," he said.

I stood to offer my hand, the napkin fell to the floor, and he sat opposite me without a second glance. He was shorter than me by a couple inches, with shoulder-length dirty blond hair and a goatee. His face was haggard, as though he'd been working too hard and not sleeping well. He was thin and wore torn jeans and a T-shirt reading "Stay calm and paint on."

I was overdressed. No, a two-second scan of the other patrons was enough. My date was underdressed.

"Hi, I'm Sam." I held out my hand again, which he shook and introduced himself. It was a loose shake, like wilted celery, and there was something strange about the way he said Cameron. "Sorry, how do you pronounce that?"

"It's hyphenated. Cam, then Ron. Not Cameron. Cam-ron Parker."

"Okay." I hesitated, but I rolled with it. "I ordered an appetizer. I haven't looked at the menu otherwise."

I pushed the plate of bruschetta toward the middle of the table to offer him some, but he put up a hand.

"I'm vegan. There's butter and cheese."

"Oh, sorry. I didn't know." This wasn't going well. Par for the course for my non-existent love life.

"I must have forgotten to include that on my profile. Doesn't matter anyway, you go ahead and order. I've already had dinner."

I paused mid-reach for the menu. "You already ate?"

"Yeah, about an hour ago. That's why I'm late."

"But, we have a dinner date?"

"Don't worry about it—I'll just have some beer." He pulled the drink menu closer.

Don't worry about it? Talking about the food was the saving grace of a dinner date. It gave you something to talk about if you didn't have anything in common. Or something to share if it went well.

Alright, next up, we had a love of art in common.

"I understand you're an artist?"

He hesitated a moment, eyes still on the drink list. "Painter. Mostly oil."

"What style do you prefer? Impressionism is my favorite, particularly Monet and Renoir."

"Haystacks, flowers, and picnics. The Impressionists were so monotonous! Easy and simple." He took a sip of his water and looked out at the people in the restaurant. He barely looked at me while he talked, as though the guy who was a half hour late didn't think I was important enough or pretty enough to look at.

"So, what style do you do?"

"A bit of everything, but I prefer abstract expressionism. You know, Jackson Pollock and Mark Rothko. Real meditative stuff."

I'd studied art history in college, and while I could appreciate how abstract art required the viewer to meld their own experiences into interpreting it, becoming part of it, it wasn't my taste. What next?

I should have left when he was fifteen minutes late. I snatched the menu and looked through to choose some food. Just because Cameron, rather Cam-ron, had already eaten didn't change the empty feeling in my stomach.

"What do you do?" he asked. "Your profile listed you as a contractor."

"I work for an insurance company."

"Doing what?" He remained more focused on the people in the restaurant than on me.

"I'm a claims adjuster. Basically, I—"

"Screw people out of the money they deserve when something bad happens?" He finally looked at me, head tilted.

Asshole.

"No, I help people get the money and the assistance they need when something bad happens."

The server arrived to take our orders. I had originally planned on ordering the fettuccine alfredo. It was petty, but instead I ordered a New York Strip, medium rare.

Cam-ron ordered a pint of an IPA from a local microbrewery, and that would be enough for him. The server hesitated for a moment, expecting a joke, but with none coming, she left.

"You know steak'll give you cancer," he said, not even looking at me, inspecting his cutlery.

I balled my fists in my lap instead of hitting him. "What the hell is your problem?"

"Rude much?"

"You arrive a half hour late, you've already eaten when you show up for a dinner date, you insult my favorite art style, and you insult my career. And then you imply I'm the one at this table with the bad manners?" I huffed, rolled my eyes, then flagged down our server. "I'm sorry, but something's come up, and I want to cancel my entrée. Is it too late?"

"Let me check." She headed to the back while I stood and waited next to the table.

"You're leaving?" The guy was oblivious.

The server returned after cancelling my order. Thank god. I put fifty dollars in her hand and apologized. "That's to cover my appetizer and wine, his beer, and the time we wasted at this table." I grabbed the bruschetta and my wine. "I'm eating this at the bar with another glass of wine."

I stomped to a free stool and dropped the plate on the bar, gulped what was left in my glass, and gathered enough self-control to put it down lightly. I tore my phone out of my purse and texted Cass.

I'm done dating for the rest of my life

He showed? came her immediate response.

Yes. And no, I'm not talking about it

The server spoke to the bartender, who poured me some more wine, while I moved the bruschetta aimlessly around on the plate. It was August first. Cass's treatments were supposed to be done by the end of March. Eight more months. Then I'd be out of this damn town again. Away from best friends who didn't talk to me anymore and men who were thirty minutes late for dinner.

CHAPTER 5

ANTONIO

I slid into the booth next to my date, smiling. "Mi scusi, it was work."

"On a Saturday evening?" Victoria was a beautiful woman with dark hair, big eyes, and a curvaceous body. She was a reporter, and I'd expected she would be fascinated by the world around her, with riveting stories to share. But her favorite story was herself.

"Papa doesn't understand evenings and weekends." I shrugged, looking at her plate, half the food still on it. "Are you finished?"

"Actually," she said, moving closer and putting a hand on my lap. "I didn't want to sate my appetite."

"You are propositioning me, sì?"

"God, that accent turns me on." She squeezed my thigh and inched her hand upward. I stopped her. She licked her lips, a clear sign of her intentions. "And yes, I am."

"Victoria—"

She dropped her voice to a husky whisper and leaned closer. "Yes?"

"What's my favorite pastime?"

She sat up straighter, brow furrowed. "What?"

I removed her hand from my lap, and it hovered there.

She tilted her head, speaking slowly. "It's our third date. August means I'm home-free, right?"

"Home-free? You said this yesterday. What are you talking about?"

The hand landed on my lap again, higher than where I had removed it, which I did again.

"Victoria, the answer is no."

"Maybe you don't understand the question."

As she reached for me again, I moved out of the booth and stood. "I think it's best if we don't see each other again."

She leaned back, as though I had slapped her. Her pretty face contorted. "You're kidding me! You are fucking kidding me!"

"I'm not, and please don't make a scene."

"A scene? You're breaking up with me in this shithole and you think I'm not making a scene?" She threw her phone into her bag and hauled herself out of the booth, straightening her dress as she stood. Shithole? The restaurant had been a test. A test she failed.

"Victoria, this was only our third date. It's not a 'break up' after only—"

"You're supposed to take me to expensive restaurants! Dress in a fucking suit! Take me back to your place and bang the shit out of me!" She poked me in the chest, her voice raising in pitch and volume.

I clenched my jaw and bore the brunt of her fury, relieved I had discovered her true self. My money, my body. All she cared about. That was all they ever cared about.

"I should have listened to Mae! She warned me about this! But oh, no, I thought I'd be the one to conquer

Brenton's Casanova!" The finger rose to point in my face. "Fuck you and your little Calendar Club!"

She stormed out of the restaurant as I shook my head. Who was Mae? And what was the Calendar Club?

I sagged to the edge of the booth seat, waiting for the server to return, and I closed my eyes to find my center. Her face was as clear as the day I had fallen for her. We only met once, and I never learned her name, but she was my anchor, my shelter from the storm. Every heart break, every rejection, every moment I thought about giving up, she was there. Her long brown hair, always in a ponytail or braid, and her pale eyes.

Last semester at MSU. Last class of Roman Art and Archeology. She scanned the class as she gave her end-of-semester presentation, blushing furiously, despite her calm and commanding demeanor. Brilliant and beautiful.

She had stuck out, always sitting in the front row, asking questions so quietly I couldn't hear from my seat in the back. She had passions in common with me, even though she turned me down the one time I asked. Still, the memory gave me hope there was someone out there I belonged with.

If only I knew her name, then I could find her. Instead, I held that image in my head for eleven years. For a time, I chose beauty and willingness over everything else, and her memory faded. But the last four years, she had become more persistent. I saw her in crowds, in my dreams, in the eyes of the officer at Bobby's house. Always giving me strength to continue and not go back to my old ways.

"Would you like your check?" asked the server.

"I'm heading to the bar for a drink. Send it over there." I needed a glass of wine.

Put on the public smile, nod to the people as I walked by, and breathe. One of these days, I would find a woman who cared about more than my surface. Who understood me and cared about who I was. Victoria Meyers was not that woman.

There were two empty high-backed stools at the bar, next to each other. On the left, beside a large man in a tweed jacket. On the right, beside a woman in a cerulean one-shoulder blouse. After Victoria, the tweed jacket felt like the right choice, but his girth took up a portion of the spare stool, so I chose the blouse.

Nice shoulder. Lean, muscular arm, but still feminine. Long caramel-colored hair over her left shoulder. Head bowed. This was a person who needed a laugh. Or a hug. Perhaps cheering her up would make me feel better.

I placed my hands on the back of the bar stool and leaned forward to get her attention. "Is this seat taken?"

She looked over absently, face toward the bar. "No." Her voice was restrained, as though masking anger, not sadness. Perhaps irritation. Her jaw clenched, highlighting a remarkable cheekbone.

I took the seat and ordered my wine from the bartender. The woman stared at a plate of bruschetta, barely touched, holding the foot of her wine glass. She rubbed a hand over her face, shielding it from me, which raised my curiosity.

"You look like your evening has gone about as well as mine has." I leaned an elbow on the bar, propping my head up.

She stiffened and sank deeper into her hand. "Worse, trust me."

"Would you like to talk about it?"

"No."

I evaluated the length of her. Tall for a woman, with a physique half-way between athlete and goddess. With an aura which said to leave her alone. Probably 'the fuck' alone. All the same, I dove in. "You know, I heard a rumor."

Silence.

"About the butter."

Silence, but her eyes flicked in my direction behind her splayed fingers.

"I shouldn't be spreading it."

Her shoulder shook with quiet laughter, but the hand remained in place.

I was feeling lighter already. "What did the fish say when it swam into the wall?"

Her hand dragged down to her chin and she looked at me askance, pretending to frown. My heart skipped. Her eyes were the palest shade of blue-green, like the Aegean Sea. Like *Lost Beneath the Stars*. Like the officer from Bobby's house? Marone! Tall. Athletic. Barely looking at me as she spoke. What were the odds I would see her twice in two days?

And why was she not saying something about it? Surely I was not that forgettable? Or perhaps she just met a great number of people.

As I paused, she raised an eyebrow. Her full lips curved up ever so slightly, like she was trying to keep her smile suppressed.

"I don't know, what did it say?"

"Dam."

She laughed and the hand went up again, covering her mouth and cheek, but leaving the eyes so I could lose myself in them. "You tell really bad jokes."

"Sì, I do."

Her eyes fell back to the plate, her laughter dying. "My date had already eaten and then he insulted me." She sighed. "What was so bad about your evening?"

"My date tried to seduce me."

She laughed again, both hands covering her face. It was musical, enchanting, and all I wanted to do was spend all night making her laugh. She revealed her striking eyes again, covering the cheek. "What man complains about that?"

I shrugged, holding my growing smile to a smirk. "Long story."

"I wanted to hit him. Badly." She rubbed her free hand on her leg. There was a small tremor as she moved it. She was nervous. That explained the hand on the face. She was attracted to me and the hand likely hid her blush.

I narrowed my eyes and ran a thumb across my pursed lips. She followed the movement, pupils dilating, and took a quick breath as she shifted her gaze to her wine glass. She was mine if I wanted her. Sexual attraction was easy. Everything else was difficult. All the important things, like connection, things in common, love. All the things which eluded me.

"Is he still here? I can take care of him for you."

She chuckled and looked at me from the corner of her eyes. "Trust me, I can handle that part just fine."

My eyes trailed from her face, down the strong arm and body, sure she was right about that. Perhaps she should be my next attempt at love.

"No one should be so rude to a woman as beautiful as you."

She rolled her eyes and groaned. "I was pretty sure I was done with dating forever, but your ridiculous lines are really sealing the deal." She reached to the back of her bar stool and turned to scan the restaurant. The pose highlighted her form, her breasts, her narrow waist. And her neck. Her long, elegant neck. As she turned back to me, the hand didn't cover her face and the ponytail fell from her shoulder to her back. She faced me directly and with a slight grimace said, "Yeah, he's still here."

But the words didn't matter. The hair, the blush, the squared posture. The serious expression. Her eyes. Goosebumps traveled up my arms and my heart began to thud so loud she must have heard it. I was twenty-one years old again, sitting at the back of class, transfixed by the girl giving her presentation. That's why she seemed so familiar yesterday.

It was her. Roman Art Girl.

My anchor.

She furrowed her brow at me. I continued leaning against the bar, calm and playful as always to the outside world, but inside my brain was racing. What came next? What was I supposed to say? Wine. I took a sip of my wine and leaned back in the bar stool, while she turned to her plate, the hand covering her blush again.

"If you are done dating, why were you on a date?"

She deflated, eyes closing, shoulders sagging. "Long story."

"Was it a...serious relationship?"

"I'm normally a private person." She took a sip from her glass, then another. "But it's been a shitty few days."

Her eyes glistened, and I wanted to put an arm around her, make her feel better. I wanted to hug her and tell her everything would be alright. Instead, I remained quiet, giving her time to talk.

"Thursday, my sister had her second round of chemo."

"I'm so sorry."

She nodded and took another sip from her wine. "Yesterday, I found out someone important to me died."

"Not Bobby Scott?"

Her eyes snapped up to mine, then shot back down to her glass. "You knew him?" She did remember me.

"Not well. He was important, you say?"

Again, she nodded and pulled her wine glass to her lips, remaining silent for long seconds.

I gripped the edge of the bar stool to stop from distracting her. This was about getting things off her chest, not about me.

"Then tonight..." She ran both hands over her face as she stared at the lights over the bar, blinking rapidly. She sighed, sitting up straighter and rolling her neck. "I moved home for nine months while my sister gets her treatments. Six three-week cycles of chemo, followed by a mastectomy, radiation, and reconstruction. She's in a rough spot. Setting me up on a few dates made her feel better, so I went along with it. But I'm done now. I've indulged her, and I'm just done."

"This is unfortunate."

"Unfortunate?"

"Sì, I had been thinking about asking you on a date."

She narrowed her eyes and tightened her jaw. "That's your response to everything I just said?"

I couldn't keep the smirk at bay while I waved a dismissive hand. "I said I was thinking about it, not doing it."

She continued to frown for the slightest moment, then laughed again.

"But here is the important question," I said. "Do you feel better than when you left the table with your evil, nasty, ugly, wart-faced date?"

She rolled her eyes again and shook her head slowly. "Yeah, I do. Thanks."

I extended a hand into the small space between us. "You are most welcome. My name is—"

She held up her hand instead of meeting mine. "No."

"No?"

"You're nice and you're funny. But I have enough friends already, and I'm not interested in more." She laid the hand against her diaphragm, taking in a deep breath. "Like I said, I'm only in town for eight more months anyway. So, there you go."

Unexpected. I was not accustomed to rejections anymore, especially not when there was such delectable chemistry. Her sister was encouraging her to date, so she was not in a committed relationship. Her attraction to me was clear. Maybe she was shy.

I grabbed my wine glass and raised it between us. "How about a compromise?"

She tilted her head but didn't pick up her glass.

I inclined my head toward it. "It's rude to refuse a toast. You and I have both suffered enough rudeness for today."

Suppressing another smile, she moved her glass toward me, holding the stem while it remained on the bar. Likely to hide the tremble.

"To fate. If it brings us together again within the month, you will owe me a date."

She stared at her glass, while mine hovered between us. Her jaw clenched and unclenched a few times. What was running through her head? Was the date idea too much?

"Or drinks. Or coffee. Anything."

The corner of her mouth twitched. She met my glass with hers and took a sip. "To anything."

She slid out of her chair and I did the same, close enough our bodies nearly touched. Almost as tall as me in her low heels. Statuesque. She looked at the floor, then back to me for the briefest moment, smiling. She rubbed her palms over her pant legs one more time. So nervous. So beautiful. So close I could almost taste her.

"Thanks for cheering me up." She tilted her head up to me again and time stalled.

It could only have been a breath or two, but there was a feeling of rightness to the moment. Being there with her, my universe rediscovered its axis. Papa had been correct about my life being unfulfilled. But standing there with her —with Roman Art Girl after all these years—everything changed.

And then she walked away, unphased by a moment apparently only I was having.

I stared after her, mesmerized. Ten feet away, she stood taller, moving like a predator. Strong, confident, head sweeping from side to side, taking in her surroundings. She said she could have handled hitting him and the way she moved echoed her words.

I had to talk to someone. Now. Tell them about her. I dialed my sister, unable to calm the smile making my cheeks hurt.

"Antonio, I'm just putting Nico to bed. What do you want?"

"I met her!" My heart was practically leaping out of my chest, prepared to follow her out the door.

"Who?"

"My wife!"

She huffed and spoke to my brother-in-law. "He says he's met his wife."

Pietro's laugh sounded in the background. "Again?"

"Exactly," she said. "What's this one's name?"

"I have no idea!" I laughed, a giddy energy consuming me.

"Oh my god, Antonio! Good night!" She hung up, but I didn't care.

I had to track this woman down. I was not leaving it up to fate. I couldn't wait eleven more years to see her again.

Chapter 6

Samantha

I downshifted coming around the corner of Sherwood Street, slowing as I approached my destination. The motorcycle engine purred, as only a Ducati did, and I pulled into the driveway. The Italian from the night before was stubbornly not fading into the background, but a visit with my sister would distract me.

The house was a two-story colonial, brick and white vinyl, sporting a porch the full width of the house. Every time I came, I remembered double Dutch in the driveway during summer vacation and swinging in the tire that used to hang from the oak tree by the road.

My brother-in-law, Kevin Hunter, was at the mailbox, tying a half-dozen pink and white helium balloons to it.

"Hey, Kevin! Just the five of us?"

"Six, until two o'clock. Want to swap? You can hang out with the hordes of three-year-old princesses, and I'll take the bike out?" He was slightly taller than me, with brown hair and an athletic build. He'd moved from California to play baseball for Michigan State, where he and Cass met. They graduated together, he took a job as a software developer with Foster Mutual, and they married soon after. He was like a big brother to me.

"In your dreams." I nudged down the kickstand, gave the motor one short rev to announce my arrival, and shut her off. "Who's the sixth?"

He grinned. "It's a surprise."

Great. Probably another set-up. I took off my helmet and dismounted, my black leather suit creaking. "How's Cass doing?"

"She's herself." He shrugged. "The house looks like a unicorn threw up all over it."

"Lovely."

"Yeah. Wait until you see the cake."

"She's pushing herself too hard."

"Preaching to the choir, Sam. Her first round was so easy on her, she thinks she'll be able to make it all the way to the end without taking any time off work." Hands on his hips, he sighed. "Speaking of work, Matt stopped by my office Friday. Asked where you've been."

I unlocked the top case on my bike and swapped my helmet for the package wrapped in pink paper, with its squashed bow. "Seriously?"

"Yeah, he seems to think working for the same company would mean he'd see you every now and again."

"Right. How often do you see me there?"

"Never." He shoved my arm. "Exactly what I told him."

· · · ● ● · ● ● ● · ·

True enough, the foyer was covered in balloons and streamers in pastel shades, and the curved staircase had pink fabric woven through the railing. Emma and Logan were not the pitter-patter type, and they thundered down the stairs to squeals of "Auntie Sammy!" They both jumped me for big hugs and were off again in a flash. After taking off my boots, I made my way through the center of the house to find my sister.

"Don't tell me that racket was you," she said as I entered the kitchen.

"You know it! Want to borrow it sometime?"

"Not likely."

We hugged, and I pulled back to look at her. Her straight brown hair was cut to her shoulders like our mother used to wear, her face and body were thin, and she had bags under her brown eyes. The bright white kitchen made her look even more washed out than Thursday, when I'd brought her home after chemo.

"You need sleep."

She turned away and went back to work at the counter. "I have a lot going on right now with Emma's party."

I pointed at the cake. "That's actually a cake that looks like you cut a watermelon in half, right? I mean, it's not an actual watermelon?"

She frowned and stood back up straight. "It's coconut whipped cream on an actual watermelon, yes. I've made this for Emma before, and she loved it."

"Does she know her birthday cake isn't a cake?"

Before Cass could argue further about healthy life choices and how I didn't take good enough care of myself, the front door opened.

"Knock, knock!" The voice was so familiar, I knew who it was instantly, Kevin's best friend and my other big brother stand-in, Nathan. So much better than another matchmaking attempt.

Cass stopped working on the cake and smiled at me. "Surprise!"

The kids stormed down the stairs, yelling, "Uncle Nathan!"

I deposited Emma's present on the breakfast table and headed to the front door, in time to see him swinging the birthday girl into the air.

I imitated the kids as he put her down. "Uncle Nathan!"

He grinned and wrapped me in a bear hug, kissing me soundly on the cheek. "Do you have any idea how creepy it sounds when you say that?"

"Why do you think I say it?"

He shoved me playfully, then put an arm around my shoulders as we walked to the kitchen.

"Look who I found!" I announced to Cass, like she hadn't heard.

Nathan released me and crossed the kitchen to Cass, whom he also hugged and kissed on the cheek.

Tall, blond, polished, with eyes a shade of blue like the deep end of a pool. I used to think Nathan's eyes were the most amazing, until I got a glimpse of those brown ones Friday. And again yesterday. Deep brown with the flecks of gold when the sun hit them right. Breathtaking. And his deep, soothing, Italian-accented voice. It was lyrical, all the extra 'uh' sounds rolling his words together, curling my toes the whole time we were talking.

I could start in Brenton's Italian neighborhood. It was small enough I could hit a few cafes or something, maybe pop into a deli or bakery, and see if we crossed paths. If he was from Brenton, that might work. Lansing was too big to track him down unless fate really stepped in. The promise of a date from our toast expired the end of August. I had another twenty-nine days. I could find him if I tried.

Fate had already brought us together twice, hadn't it?

"Wake up," said Nathan, snapping his fingers in front of my face.

"What?"

"I was asking about your hot date last night."

I exaggerated a shudder and crossed to a stool opposite where Cass was working, Nathan sitting next to me.

"I can't believe I've been home for a whole month—" I put a fist on my hip and glared at him. "—and this is the first time I've seen you!"

He grinned and knocked the hand off my hip. "Assistant prosecutors have to work hard if they want to move up. Besides, I've been here twice since you got home. Rumor mill says you're the one who's working ridiculous hours. And stop changing the subject."

I hooked a thumb over my shoulder to the pink package I'd put on the table behind me. "I got her an FBI dress-up kit."

Nathan nudged me. "The date? Spill!"

Cass stepped back from the cake to spin it on its turntable, inspecting it. "Her text said she's never dating again."

"Ouch! That bad?" Nathan laughed and shoved me. "So you didn't invite him home to your little palace?"

"Shut it, Miller!"

"It's funny," said Cass, adding some icing to one section of the cake. "She says it was awful, but she's blushing." She shot me an evil smirk.

I covered my cheeks. It was best not to tell them about Mr. Italy, or she'd drive me to Calabria Street and parade me around for hours. Instead, I turned to Nathan. "Is Tina coming?"

He flashed his left hand at me, wiggling his fingers. No ring.

I gasped and grabbed his arm. "Oh my god! No one told me!"

He shrugged, a practiced smile plastered on his face. "It's still pretty fresh."

Cass put the decorating spatula down and folded her arms. "So, if you didn't like Cameron—"

"Such a flake." I rolled my eyes as dramatically as I could.

"Never fear, I have another option for next weekend."

"You what?"

"Yeah, another from the dating site."

I put my hands up in front of me. "Cass, I'm done. I promised I'd be here until your treatments are finished, and I am. But me, living in Brenton isn't permanent and no dating site can change that."

"What if it goes longer or it doesn't work, Sam?"

"Don't go there." I'd stay. It was that simple. As much as I hated Brenton, I was there as long as I was needed. Even if it meant helping Kevin raise the kids.

"C'mon, Sam." Nathan leveled me with a serious look, snapping me out of a downward spiral. "Traveling from town to town every few weeks for the next storm, living out of your little RV, and only ever seeing your family on video chat is not good for you."

I rounded on him. "Sounds rehearsed. Are you here to double-team me?"

"No, that's my job," said Kevin as he joined us. "He's the triple threat."

"Jesus Christ, you three!" How many times would I hear this lecture? "I like that life! I like moving around and seeing the country! Working as an independent adjuster is freeing! And it's good money."

Cass chimed in. "You're not safe, you're alone—"

"I'm happier alone." I should have let the Italian introduce himself. No, I shouldn't. I was only in town eight months. Cass would be fine by then. She had to be.

Nathan pinched my thigh and I jumped. "Do you get treated like that when you're alone?"

"Jerk." I tried to frown at him, but his stupid grin made me laugh. "Seriously, though, I'm perfectly happy by myself. Way less stress. You guys don't understand how flustered I get around men!" The restaurant bar had been a humiliating disaster. Blushing, hands shaking, heart racing, unable to even look at him.

"You're fine around me," said Kevin.

"And me," said Nathan.

I rubbed my palms on my pants, exhaling slowly. "You two don't count. I've known you since I was like twelve. You're not 'men.'"

"Ooh, ouch!" Nathan tried to pinch me again, but I swatted his hand away.

"You need to get back on the horse some year."

"No, Cass, I don't." I kept my eyes on Nathan, in case he was trying for a third.

Instead, he winked at me. "But seriously, no dates for Sam next weekend. She's coming out with me."

Cass tilted her head slowly, looking from him to me and back again. "Oh, really now?"

"I have reservations for The Train Station. It was supposed to be an anniversary surprise, but you know...No anniversary."

"You two split up four months ago. Why didn't you cancel them?" asked Kevin.

Nathan shrugged. "I was hoping, you know."

I leaned over and gave him a quick squeeze. "Sucks, doesn't it?"

"Well, I figured I could commiserate with a fellow divorcée. Get some advice or something."

Cass and Kevin looked at each other and laughed. "From her?"

"Yeah, I'll tell you what I did after Matt and I separated, and you can do the opposite. Step one, don't sell everything you own, buy an RV, and move out of the state. I don't think the prosecutor's office would appreciate that."

Chapter 7

Samantha

"Cliff and Mike are looking for you. They'll be back in ten," said Lucy Chapman as I walked into The Pit, the office area where the adjusters worked. A thin Asian woman, she was with Foster as part of a student internship program open to MSU students after their third year. She was a mature student in her mid-twenties, having taken several years off before college.

"Thanks." I pulled my laptop out of my backpack and fired it up.

"What are you up to this morning, other than waiting for them to show?"

"Paperwork and phone calls."

"You were in the field Friday, right? It's lonely around here sometimes; you adjusters are always out in the field. Nice to see you're in the office today." Lucy talked a lot, so I knew plenty about her. Her parents were travel bloggers, and she'd been on the road her whole life. Active blog since she was twelve, studying statistics in college, planning on becoming an insurance actuary. I also knew she was adopted from China, loved cats, preferred Hubba Bubba, and typed ninety words per minute.

And she talked faster than she typed.

"That painting is the biggest single item claim we've ever had." She chewed her gum, blew a bubble, and popped it, pointing at a chart on her screen from the Business Intelligence, or BI module of the claims system, which analyzed everything we did. "I was running some queries in the BI module, and we've never paid out a property claim on a single item over eight hundred thousand dollars, except for homes and machinery. Lots of claims over a million when we're dealing with liability and legal expenses, though."

"Interesting." I sighed while I logged into the system. The tall cubicle walls surrounding our eight desks comforted me like I was in a cave. The walls kept the world out, but they couldn't protect us from Lucy's chatter.

She turned in her chair. "Very!" She popped another bubble and returned to her analysis.

"There you are!" came Cliff Anderson's gruff voice a moment later. He was a sixty-something no-nonsense beast of a man who didn't take crap from anyone. Rumor had it he once called the governor to take a strip off him for supporting some insurance regulation change, or not supporting it—the story changed every time I heard it. Either way, it always included Cliff yelling into the phone so loudly you could hear him through two closed doors.

Mike Telford was right behind him, and between the two of them, there was barely enough room for the rest of us in the Pit. Cliff threw a thumb over his shoulder and walked away, saying "Pines conference room" as he left.

• • • • •• • • • • •

Cliff pointed at Mike once we were seated in Pines. "Scott claim. Status."

Mike was a short, graying, middle-aged man on our team, who had taken on the property portion of the Chagall house claim. He stared at his paperwork. "According to the First Notice of Loss, there was a fire in the residence, contained to the living room. This included near-complete destruction of the furniture—"

Cliff snapped his fingers. "Point?"

Mike flipped to his last page, accustomed to this from Cliff. "Initial reserve at two hundred thousand. I wrote a check for three thousand for the hotel and other incidentals already. I've contacted AmLife, who carries Mr. Scott's life insurance. They're not moving until the Medical Examiner and police reports are complete, which should be fast. Police are confident it was accidental."

"Done." Cliff pointed at me next. "Sam, go."

"I think the painting's intact enough to make a comparison to the photos on file, but I have to wait for the police to release it. It'll be a total loss, though. Replacement value was set at one million dollars, assuming it passes the policy's authentication requirement, so that's our reserve."

"Done." Cliff pushed Mike's paperwork toward me, pointing to the email address. "Send them your contact information, and Mike will handle the interviews."

I nodded and pulled out my phone to send the email.

"Good. Mike, you update the system for your claim. Sam will do hers when we're done here."

Mike packed up his papers and headed out of the conference room, closing the door behind him.

"Listen, Sam, I know you're technically still employed by Thompson Claims Services as an independent adjuster, and Foster's contract with them is for standard property claims, but I have another specialty claim for you."

"No problem." Working as an IA on a daily claim contract provided me with a lot of freedom, a point of contention with my sister, but it was my preference. So long as Cliff remained happy with my performance, I could work as much or as little as I wanted. It was never the latter.

"It's another artwork claim. Hailey usually takes care of these, but your background makes you our resident expert. I've already assigned it and added Ferraro's Fine Art Restoration and Conservation as the repair vendor. We have a standing contract with them, so you can head over once you've retrieved the painting. It's a family business, and they're all about relationships. Keep that in mind."

"Will do."

"And I want you to take the intern out on some claims. Show her what adjusters do in the field."

· · · · ·· ·· · ·

Back at my desk, I logged into the claims system to review the new artwork claim. Cliff had already set the reserve, the amount the company expected to have to pay out, to the full replacement value of ten thousand dollars. The FNOL included pictures of the painting and the tear from several angles. The damage was along the grain of the underlying canvas, which would make the repair straightforward. The painting itself was a color field work, and the damaged area was a single shade of light blue without any impasto. Once the restorer had identified the correct pigments, they wouldn't have to spend a lot of time matching details. My gut told me this would be simpler than Cliff expected, so I adjusted the reserve to two thousand.

I'd worked a lot of art claims for Thompson. Between hurricanes in Florida, wildfires in California, and advising galleries in New York, I had plenty of experience with art losses. That, coupled with my passion, education, and training in art crime investigation, made me even better at it than I was at standard property claims. I wouldn't have called myself an expert, but I was pretty close.

After reviewing the photos, I called the gallery holding it to advise them I was on my way, then gave a courtesy call to Ferraro's.

"What was that?" asked Hailey Olsen, another adjuster, after I hung up the phone.

"I'm picking up a damaged painting from Mason's Art Gallery."

Hailey perked up, her eyes brightening. "And you're taking it to Ferraro's?"

I nodded.

"Need me to take it?" She looked as though she was ready to leave immediately. "I go by there on my way home."

"No, Cliff asked me to take it."

"Which one are you seeing?"

"Which one what?"

"Dr. Dom or Dr. Antonio?" Why did Hailey handle their art claims? She was an auto adjuster and didn't do property. And she was way too excited about this.

"No idea. It's an open appointment."

She laughed. "Let me give you a few tips. The owner, Dominico, is a huge flirt. I bet you twenty bucks you'll hear his 'Dom Ferraro is like Dom Perignon, but better' joke within ten minutes."

Lucy laughed from her chair, obviously not as focused on the BI work in front of her as she was pretending.

"Thanks for the warning." I chuckled at the dumb joke. Dumb jokes like Saturday night. Ferraro's was on Calabria Street, the core of Brenton's Italian neighborhood. Maybe Lucy and I could extend our visit or...No, he was from Lansing, for sure.

"Sofia's the office manager and accountant, who works the reception desk. She's Dom's oldest, quick as a whip, and she keeps the place humming. They usually have two or three other restorers working there, and then there's Antonio. If you get lucky, he'll work on your painting."

Lucy gave up the pretense and turned around. "Lucky?"

Hailey fanned herself, and Lucy and I laughed at her. "He's Dom's son, and Sofia says he's the most talented conservator there, although she may have been bragging. They act like they hate each other, but it doesn't take a genius to see it's a show."

Lucy popped a bubble. "Sounds like a good time."

I turned to her. "Well, you're in luck, Lucy."

"How's that?"

"Cliff's asked me to take you out on a few claims."

She clapped her hands. "Yay! Like today?"

I paused. The urge to say no was strong. But when I'd first started working as a claims adjuster, I'd completed several ride-a-longs until I found a mentor who taught me to excel at the job. Since then, I'd never worked with anyone in the field. I liked my alone time.

"Yes, today. You're coming with me to pick up the painting and take it to the conservator's office. Then, we'll figure things out."

"Jealous!" said Hailey.

Lucy closed her eyes for a moment. "Three hundred and sixty-eight policies, each protecting artwork over twenty thousand dollars, with an average of six claims per year. Good loss ratio on paintings."

Hailey and I gaped as she opened her eyes.

"Off the top of your head?" I asked.

"I looked it up and did some poking around after the FNOL for the burned painting came in." She shrugged like it was nothing. "It's just numbers."

"Well, I'm impressed."

"Am I dressed alright?" she asked.

I shook my head. Her Doc Martens, jeans, and Pogues T-shirt was fine for our casual office, but not for an art gallery. "I have a suit in my truck for occasions like this and I'll expect you to have a back-up if you'll be working with me."

"Got something in my car!" She leaped out of her seat and dashed down the hallway.

I frowned, while Hailey laughed and turned back to her computer. "Watch yourself around those two Ferraros, Sam. They'll hit on anything in a skirt."

Glad I packed pants.

· · · ●·●● · · ·

Climbing into my truck was a challenge for Lucy, especially in her mini skirt. She clambered onto the running boards and used the grab bar inside the door with both hands to pull herself up into the seat.

Once I started the engine, and the display screen lit up, my language training audio began, and I paused it.

"Spanish? Cool!" She leaned over to check out all the buttons on the steering wheel and pushed a couple of them. I guided her hand away before she did any damage. Unphased, she grabbed a cable from her bag and plugged her phone in to make some music selections, chewing furiously on her gum.

"I had no idea trucks could be so luxurious. My car's got nothing on this!" She settled into the leather passenger seat and adjusted the air conditioning. Seat forward, seat backward. Seat up, up, up.

Once she'd gotten the seat right and picked the music, some old school Pixies, and we'd eased out onto the road, she kept exploring. She opened the moonroof and the rear window, hit a couple more switches not connected to anything, and flipped the lid on the center console. She paused when she saw a metal container with a combination lock on it.

"Tell me that's not a gun safe!"

"Okay, that's not a gun safe."

"Seriously? You keep a loaded gun in there?"

I cast a quick glance at her. How honest should I be? "There's been more than one time I've needed to get the hell out of Dodge in a hurry. I've never resorted to personal protection, but I've been glad to have something with me."

In a surreal moment, she paused. No chewing, no bubbles, no chatter. Gun ownership could be a touchy subject.

"Can you keep a secret?" I added the gravity I felt the moment needed, and she nodded. "I was trained by the FBI, including a lot of hours at the firing range. I have my concealed carry license, and when I started traveling the country on my own, it felt like the right choice. I only take them out when I go to the range or when they need cleaning. Firearm safety is serious business."

"Holy crap! You're in the FBI?" Smart girl, stupid question.

"No, I'm a claims adjuster. I *was* in the FBI and decided it wasn't the right choice for me." Close enough to honest.

"You don't talk much. I've known you for a month now, and that's the first thing you've said not work-related. Is it me? Or are you always like that?"

"I'm a private person."

Again, she was surprisingly quiet. Maybe I'd misjudged her, based on the limited interactions we'd had.

"Me, too," she said with a grin.

I burst into laughter, and she joined me. She was growing on me already.

"To be honest, Lucy, it's a part of my past, and it isn't relevant anymore."

"Okay, fair. Speaking of irrelevant things, did you see..." She talked and talked the whole ride, and I did little more than nod. She told me about a reality TV show she was watching, about her favorite YouTuber, a trend she saw on Instagram, a new made-for-Netflix show she was excited to see, and kept going from there. It was like the comfortable background noise of television you weren't watching. When we pulled up in front of Mason's, I felt I was up to date on everything trending in the world, for the first time ever.

· · · ●· ●· · ·

Mason's Art Gallery was a small showroom in the heart of Brenton. The front window allowed a view of the interior, an open space decorated with various modern art pieces. The floor was hardwood painted white, and large stands dotted the room, holding sculptures made of plaster, stone, and metal.

I caught my reflection in the gallery door and paused for a moment. Navy suit and heels. Polished and professional, despite the butterflies swirling around my stomach. My hand tightened around the door handle, and I did a slow countdown from five. It was just a property claim, but I was on edge. The time I'd spent working art claims for Thompson hadn't affected me like this. What was different this time? Was it because I was home? One more reason I had to get out of town.

Lucy tapped me on the shoulder. "What are you doing?"

"Nothing." I rolled my shoulders and opened the door.

As we entered, a small bell rang, and a woman came to meet us.

"Samantha Caine and Lucy Chapman with Foster Mutual Insurance," I said brightly. "I'm here to get a statement on the damaged painting and take it in for repairs."

"Good afternoon. I'm the curator, Paulette Johnson." She smiled politely but gave me the weakest handshake I'd felt since the celery on Saturday, then greeted Lucy.

"We focus on local work." She led us through the first room, pointing out a few highlights. "Some of our pieces are here for sale directly from the artist. If you see anything you like, let me know."

Most of the artwork was small, no more than two feet high or wide. We admired each piece she focused on briefly but didn't linger, as we still had to get over to Ferraro's to drop the painting off.

Around a corner, a second room housed their realism collection. I gravitated toward a painting eerily similar to Monet's *Impression, Sunrise*. The colors and style were Monet's, even the brush strokes, but it wasn't a duplicate.

"It's by an artist from here in Brenton. He's quite talented; spent some time working at the Louvre last year!"

I stood closer to it, inspecting the detail, scanning for a signature. "If I'm not mistaken, it's a Monet pastiche, isn't it?"

"A Monet what?" asked Lucy.

"Pastiche." Monet had signed his in the bottom left, but there wasn't one on this painting anywhere. Roughly nineteen by twenty-five inches, same size as the original.

"I still don't understand."

I expected the curator to explain, but when she didn't, I continued. "A work of art imitating another style or another artist. This isn't a copy of a Monet, at least not one I'm familiar with but it's in his style, right down to the application of the paint."

"Interesting. Is that common?"

"Very." I stood back to take the whole thing in. "You're right, Paulette. This is good."

We made our way through a door in the back, painted to match the walls, so it didn't intrude on the flow of the gallery. The office was small and cramped, dominated by a large table at the back, while a small computer desk was nestled against the wall. She took me directly to the table where the damaged painting lay.

"It's called *Number Vee*." She flicked on a spotlight to improve the view.

"Vee?"

"Instead of Number Five, Roman numerals. I thought it was clever."

I nodded absently. It was a stretched and unframed canvas, three feet high and two wide, painted in three strips of blue, dark, medium, and light. The curator indicated the tear near the bottom, and I took a small flashlight out of my bag to take a closer look, confirming my initial impression from the photos. The tear was precisely on the grain of the canvas, and the paint was exclusively blue.

"Can you turn it over?" I asked.

Once it was face down, I pointed to the top of the tear. "See this, Lucy?"

She got in closer. "See what?"

"Ninety degree turn at the top of the tear. We couldn't see it from the front because the paint's holding it together."

"Oh, gotcha." She popped a bubble as she straightened. "You've got a good eye!"

I clenched my jaw and glared at her. She slowed her chewing, then swallowed hard.

"No, I just know what I'm looking for." I took out my phone and a measuring tape, explaining to her as I worked. "We'll take a few additional photos for the claim file, showing the measuring tape and the damage. Four inches long and one-eighth inch off to the side at the end."

Lucy remained quiet through the process. Once I was done, we applied a low-adhesive tape to the back to ensure the tear didn't expand.

The curator had witnessed the original damage—a careless visitor impaled it with a selfie stick—so she was able to answer some basic questions, sign the statement of loss, and fill out the release to allow us to take the painting.

Paulette packed the painting into a transport case. "I know Foster usually deals with Ferraro's, but I'd like to recommend a different restoration company."

I took the case from her, nodding. "We have a few restoration companies on our approved vendor list. Who did you have in mind?"

She took a business card out of her pocket and handed it to me.

"Parker's Restoration?" The card was simple, company name and phone number. I flipped it over. There was no address. Was it coincidence I'd met an artist with the last name Parker? "Does Cam-ron Parker work there?"

She scratched the back of her neck in a move telling me I was right, while shaking her head. "I don't know the names of all the people who work there, but the owner's name is Parker. He does good work."

"Fair enough." Not fair enough, actually. There was a lie in there somewhere. The question was, did it matter?

"You see, Ferraro's..." She lowered her voice, although we were the only ones there. "Their rates are too high, and they take too long."

"This painting's already booked with them, but I'll vet this company for future—"

"They got their contract with Foster Mutual years ago, but they're talentless hacks who get by on charm instead of skill."

"Really?" Cliff wouldn't recommend them if that were true. However, Cliff didn't know this industry as well as I did. I'd keep a close eye on the Ferraros. "Thanks for the warning."

CHAPTER 8

SAMANTHA

Ferraro's conservation studio was on Calabria Street, surrounded by Italian businesses, shops, and restaurants. Black lamp posts along the road held small Italian flags and flower baskets. Official maps listed it as Calabria Street, but the street signs all read *Via Calabria*, as it would have been called in Italy.

I was on alert, watching for the guy from Saturday night. But I was working, and I had Lucy with me. What would I do if I saw him? Probably run the other way.

Their office was in a white-washed building, with a black sign reading *Ferraro's* in bold letters and *Fine Art Restoration and Conservation* underneath. Two large windows along the front allowed a view inside, where a two-tiered reception desk sat off to the right side and small waiting area with black couches and a glass table balanced it on the left. A white wall, dominated with the same *Ferraro's* sign in metallic gold, separated the waiting area from the space beyond.

As Lucy and I entered through the glass front door, a sweet, floral scent struck me, from the irises on the waiting room table and the reception desk. Classical music played quietly in the background. Vivaldi's *The Four Seasons*. Sunlight beamed in from the area behind reception. My heels clicked on the floor, and the woman behind the big desk looked up from some papers to smile at me.

"Samantha Caine and Lucy Chapman from Foster Mutual." I placed the case on the floor next to me.

She stood to shake our hands. "Sofia Moretti."

A southern Italian beauty with long black hair, deep brown eyes, and olive skin, wearing a sleeveless sheath dress in emerald green which accentuated her curves. I guessed she was in her late thirties, maybe early forties, and I was suddenly self-conscious in my less than remarkable suit. Lucy's Doc Martens, mini skirt over tights, and yellow blouse stood out even more.

"Where's Hailey? She normally handles all our business with Foster."

"Not available today."

"Funny you should say that. Neither of the Drs. is here right now, either." Her eyebrow twitched slightly. She was irritated about something. "You can drop the painting off with me. I can do the intake but will require one of them to review it before I can send you the estimate." She had a faint Italian accent, betrayed by a few words here and there, as though she'd learned English early but grew up with Italian as her primary language.

"Fair enough."

She moved the flowers to the lower portion of her desk and I placed the case where they'd been. Lucy stood next to me, watching my every move. For someone normally as chatty as she was, she was silent as I worked.

I opened the case from the gallery to reveal *Number Vee* and pointed out the tear. "You can see the damage here. Four inches long, eighth of an inch slightly to the left from the end of the tear line. I applied a low-adhesive, acid-free bookbinder's tape to the back to ensure it didn't spread."

She arched an eyebrow at me. "You talk like a conservator."

"It's not the first torn painting I've dealt with." I shrugged. "The tear is on the grain of the fabric and the finish is smooth, so it should be relatively simple."

She retrieved a magnifying glass and small flashlight from a drawer in her desk and took a closer look. She nodded slowly. "You're right. The color is uniform, which will require more work to find the right shade but no texture from a heavy impasto to replicate. I doubt Dominico or Antonio will be needed for this. Are you sure about the tear taking a turn at the end?"

"Yes, but you can only see it from the back. The paint is holding it together in the front." I pulled my phone out of my bag and showed her the photos from the back. She lifted it from the side and tilted her head for a quick look.

"Hailey never uses tape." She placed the painting back down in the case.

I had no intention of going into detail on what I did and didn't tote around in my truck for art claims. All the same, I said, "I keep some on-hand for cases like this."

"Good idea." She smiled, nodding. "One of the Drs. will have to look at it, but it'll be about two weeks for the repair. Do you have anything for me to sign?"

"I do." I withdrew an envelope with the papers from a pouch inside the case, and we filled everything out. "I also have a second painting I'll be bringing in. I'm hoping on Friday."

"Let me check the schedule." She sat at her desk, hit a few keys on the computer, and hmmed to herself.

A door opened and closed in the space behind the reception wall. I couldn't see behind the wall, but I heard his voice clearly. "Sorry I'm late, Alice. Did you still need a hand?"

Deep male voice, thick Italian accent, so familiar. Surely not. But the way the sound rumbled in my core and the hairs stood on my neck—it was him.

Sofia leaned back from her desk, craning her head to see into the space. "Antonio! I need you out here!"

"Coming, Sofia!" He rounded the corner and stopped mid-step when our eyes met. He wore a pair of faded jeans and a white polo shirt hugging his biceps. The buttons were undone, low enough to provide a view of the upper slope of his pectorals. I put a hand to my hair to make sure it was in place, while I fought to keep my mouth closed. As he smiled, that perfect smile with those kissable lips I'd been trying to put out of my mind, my breath caught.

Easier to find than I'd expected. Three times in four days.

And an art conservator, not a lawyer. Wow.

Behind me, Lucy whispered, "Holy crap." She almost knocked me over as she rounded me and extended her hand. "Lucy Chapman from Foster Mutual Insurance. Dr. Antonio Ferraro, I presume?"

He dragged his eyes from me and smiled at her, shaking her hand. "You presume correctly."

"This is my partner, Samantha Caine."

He nodded to her and approached me. Strode. No, this time he stalked. I held my breath as he took an hour to reach me, running a hand through his dark brown hair, the gentle wave fanning back into place perfectly when he finished. At least he didn't trace his lips like at the restaurant.

No wonder Hailey was so eager to handle the claim.

I held out my hand, which he looked at briefly before taking, his joke clear between us.

His grip was strong yet gentle and so soft. "Ciao, Samantha Caine." His baritone added a music to my name I'd never heard before. A tingle ran up my arm, and I reflexively pulled away, but he held fast.

Sofia crossed her arms. "Antonio, I need you to—"

He ignored her, keeping his eyes on me. "It only took two days." He stepped closer, still holding my hand. Could he feel the tremble in it? He lowered his voice. "What shall it be? Dinner? Tonight?"

"Have you forgotten everything I said?" I wrenched the hand away and stepped back, clenching my jaw to keep my teeth from chattering. It was bad enough I could feel the heat in my cheeks. Let alone all the other places.

CHAPTER 9

ANTONIO

"I remember every word." I closed the distance again, wanting to remove space between us, and to keep my voice down. The gentle music in the background was just loud enough. "But, I'm stubborn."

"Antonio!" snapped Sofia. "I need you to authorize this painting."

I turned to her and gave the painting a cursory glance. "Whatever you say is right, I'm sure."

She handed me a sheet to sign, which I didn't bother reading, and she filed it away. There were more pressing matters at hand. My future was in front of me.

"So." I returned my attention to Samantha. "Where were we?"

Lucy said, "We were booking an appointment for Friday."

Not only had I found her, but she would be back soon. She still trembled but she was looking at me this time. It was progress. "And what are you coming in for?"

"I have another artwork claim. The police have the painting in custody, but I expect they'll release it any day."

"What work is required?"

"It was burned in a fire and almost completely destroyed. We need it cleaned enough to authenticate, so we can pay out the claim. No repairs needed."

"Burned how badly?"

She withdrew her phone from her bag, flipped through some pictures, and showed me. Nodding, I turned to Sofia. "Book her at nine on Friday morning. I need two hours." Before my sister could protest, I raised an eyebrow to make my point.

"Thanks," said Samantha. "We'll be back then."

"No." I leaned on Sofia's desk. "It will be very boring. I only need one of you. The one with more experience, perhaps?"

Lucy laughed. "That's you, boss."

Samantha frowned at her. "I'm not your boss, Lucy." She turned the frown on me, but it was strained. "I'll see you Friday morning."

"Bene. I look forward to it."

Once they were out the door, Sofia rounded on me. "Two hours? You never take two hours for a consult!"

"I'll have to wear something nicer Friday."

"Nicer?" She leaned back in her chair and folded her arms, narrowing her eyes. "Did you even look at the painting?"

"No. It's ridiculous I have to rubber-stamp things like this. You know the business better than I do."

She rolled her eyes, mouth tight. "Tell Papa."

"Trust me, I have." I took another look at the torn painting. "Where is he, anyway? He has been acting strangely lately."

She came around her desk, taking me by the shoulder to the reception couches. Sofia had many faces for me, usually lecturing, angry, or frustrated, but behind them all was compassion and love. She was the best big sister I could have hoped for. We sat facing each other.

"You aren't dating the dentist anymore?"

I curled a leg up on the couch. "The dentist was two months ago. You are thinking of the reporter. And no, I'm not seeing her anymore."

"You went out with her Saturday night? What happened?"

"Date number three happened." I sighed. How would Samantha feel if I had taken her to Caruther's?

She chuckled. "The restaurant test?"

"I asked her what my favorite pastime was. She didn't even bother to guess I might enjoy painting." I put an arm on the back of the couch and leaned into it. "I knew after the first date with her. She was full of herself."

"Why did you make it to date three with her?"

I shrugged. "She's pretty."

"I thought you learned your lesson."

"Sì, I did. But, you know me..."

"Stubborn." She gestured toward the front door. "And this one?"

I breathed her name out, a slow exhale. "Samantha Caine." I finally knew it.

Sofia rolled her eyes. "You obviously knew her. I thought the two of you were going to run at each other when you came around the corner. You weren't expecting her?"

"You think she likes me?"

She swatted my leg. "Obviously."

"Seeing her today was a surprise."

She leaned forward, the glare softening. "I liked her."

"Me, too." She would be back again by the end of the week. After eleven years without her, I would see her four times, at least.

"Wait!" Her eyes grew wide. "Don't tell me she's the one you called about Saturday night?"

"I may have been overzealous." But the feeling in my chest, the fullness, the tingling in my hand when we had touched. Premature, perhaps. But not overzealous.

She tipped her head forward, frowning. "You think?"

I clasped my hands together and stared at them. "She wouldn't let me introduce myself Saturday night. So I told her she would have to go out with me if fate brought us together again within a month."

"She seems clever."

"She is."

Sofia nudged my shoulder. "Especially when she turned you down."

"She did *not* turn me down. She changed the subject." Also progress.

"I thought you were out with your reporter on Saturday. Did you meet Samantha before or after you dump your last date?"

"It was fate, Sofia." I looked down to avoid her disapproving glare, suppressing my smile. "We met at the bar at Caruther's after the reporter left. Samantha's date had been worse than mine, and she needed cheering up. We only talked for fifteen minutes."

She rocked her head back in laughter. "Fifteen minutes? That led to 'I've met my wife?' You're even more ridiculous than I thought."

"There is more to tell but let me get through Friday first."

"You're planning to take her to Russo's?"

"You know me too well." Samantha would say no. She would be too nervous with me. It couldn't be a date, at least not to her. "Help me convince her to go with me."

CHAPTER 10

SAMANTHA

"Sam, Lucy," said Harry Bell, as we walked into the Special Investigations Unit's cubicle office.

"I've been by your desk about fifteen times," said Tonya Quinn, "to congratulate you on spotting Friday's ball-peen hammer damage. We found six more claims we'd already paid by the same contractor. I can't believe so many got past the team. Good job, hun." She gave me an air-high-five. She had no accent, but sometimes her turn of phrase revealed her southern background.

Harry was a retired Brenton Police officer, while Quinn was a former private investigator. Both were in their late fifties or early sixties and were Foster Mutual's last line of defense against fraudsters. When someone working a claim suspected things weren't on the up-and-up, whether we cut a check first or withheld payment, it went to them. If the system identified certain red flag items indicating possible fraud, it went to them. With their investigative experience and long list of connections, their job was to find the truth and save the company money.

Neither would stand out in a crowd, likely a benefit in their line of work. He was a couple inches shy of six feet, and she was about four inches less than Harry. Well-grayed brown hair, brown eyes, lightly bronzed complexion.

"What brings you here this afternoon?" Harry was a pleasant but serious man, always calm and collected.

"I wanted to check in with you on a claim I'm—I mean we're—handling. Lucy's shadowing me for..." I puffed out my cheeks. "Some amount of time?"

She shrugged in response. "Beats me. As long as I get the BI work finished for Cliff, I imagine until my internship ends?"

"Lucky girl." Harry gave Lucy a nod. "You'll learn a lot. She's our best."

I waved off the compliment. "I imagine you're familiar with the fire at the Scott residence last week?"

Harry clicked his pen absently. "Of course. You're handling a million-dollar portion of it."

Quinn hit a few keys on her computer and began scrolling through the catalog of photos.

"I know it was red-flagged due to its value, so I wanted to give you a quick overview."

Harry gestured to the large table in the middle of their space, and Lucy and I sat. She popped a bubble and I glared at her until she nodded and threw it in the trash.

"There are a lot of photos of this painting," commented Quinn, scanning through them all.

"Yeah. We'll likely need several of them to confirm its identity. The owners went through a process in 2015 to prove it was authentic. Up until then, it was attributed to Chagall—"

"Attributed?" interjected Lucy.

"It means they were pretty sure it was by him, but they didn't have proof. In the art world, a lot of weight is given to what we call provenance, the trail of documentation, sales, and evidence proving the painting went from the artist to person A to person B and so forth. The Scotts had gaps in the provenance trail, so it was initially insured for the price Mr. Scott paid for it, about two hundred thousand dollars.

"After Hurricane Sandy destroyed so many works of art in New York, someone recommended they have it authenticated and insured correctly. It was a big deal. Chemical analysis of the paints, ultraviolet photos, x-rays, the whole nine yards. Anything by Marc Chagall can only be authenticated by the Chagall Committee in Paris. So, the Scotts sent all the research they paid for and the broken provenance trail to Paris in 2015. Fortunately for them, the Committee confirmed it. Under French law, the Committee would have the authority to burn it otherwise."

"But he paid two hundred thousand for it!" said Lucy.

"Doesn't matter. They have the authority. You need to be confident it's authentic before you send something in for their review. Afterwards, the Scotts had it appraised by Sotheby's for a million dollars, and the Scotts called us to set the limits correctly."

"With strings," added Quinn, reading from her screen. "Policy has restrictions on it: smoke alarm connected to a central station, wall mounted professionally, and confirmation of authenticity before claim payment."

"Yeah, so like I was saying, we have all of the documentation from the authentication process which gives us a lot of options for verification. Once we're done, we can pay it out."

Harry clicked his pen a few more times and pointed it at me. "If it's the real deal."

"Exactly. However, the police took it."

Quinn suppressed a laugh. "Not surprised. Those cops think they can do anything."

Harry rolled his head back to look at her, but she kept going.

"You're the expert. What's your first step?"

I got up and stood behind Quinn. "Roll back to the first photo I added Friday." Nothing but a blackened, charred sheet of tattered canvas. "We can't authenticate it until we have it cleaned."

"Taking it to Ferraro's?" asked Harry, who had swiveled around to face us. "Watch out for them. Given the painting's state, they may try to screw you on the one-month standard contract we have with them."

This was why I was here. I dropped my hands into my pockets and pursed my lips. "Do you trust them, Harry?"

"I'm in SIU. I don't trust anyone."

"Neither should you, Sam." Quinn was back to inspecting the original photos of the Chagall. "Although that son of Dom's..."

Lucy giggled. "We were just there. He's got the hots for —"

"Lucy! Are you going to be a help or a hindrance? Because I can tell Cliff we're done with this little experiment."

She held up her hands in surrender. "Helping, promise."

Quinn chuckled at her monitor.

I ran a hand over my face and sat at the table, passing the Parker's Restoration card to Harry. "Here's the thing. Lucy and I were over at Mason's Gallery for an unrelated claim. I spoke with the curator there, and she told me we should avoid Ferraro's, recommended this company instead. They aren't on the approved vendors list. I thought we could vet them?"

Harry handed the card to Quinn, who had stopped looking at the photos. "Already done, hun. Harry says they don't make the cut."

"Really?"

He nodded. "Hailey told us about this in the spring when she picked something up from the gallery. Curator told her the Ferraros were—what was it she said, Quinn?"

"Talentless hacks."

Lucy nodded. "Who get by on their charm?"

Quinn pointed at her. "Precisely. Tell them what you found."

"The owner, Parker, is the curator's ex-husband. Divorced —"

"Fifteen years," added Quinn.

"Right. She's trying to bolster his business. The work was alright, but not up to our standards. Ferraro's remains our recommended restoration company."

"That in mind—" It was like Quinn and Harry shared a brain, the way they went back and forth, finishing each other's sentences. "—like Harry said, watch them on the one-month contract. Proving the painting's the real one or a fake should be straight-forward, given the supporting evidence we have, so Ferraro's Restoration just needs to do its job."

Harry clicked his pen a few more times at me. "I talked to a friend on the force. Said they expect their case will close quickly and the fire will be ruled accidental. What did you see when you were in the house? Did it feel accidental to you?"

I looked from Harry to Quinn and back again. My opinion on this didn't matter; it was up to the authorities.

Harry turned to Lucy. "Can you give us about ten minutes?"

Lucy furrowed her brow and checked with me. At my nod, she got up and left. What was going on?

Quinn rolled her chair closer and leaned forward, voice down. "Sam, you spot fraud like it's second nature to you. You've barely been here a month, and you've already caught five. Some adjusters go years before that happens. So, either you're involved in them, it's a coincidence, or there's more to you than meets the eye."

I tapped my finger on the table and crossed my legs. "So, you did a little digging?" My focus turned to Harry, who picked up their verbal tennis match.

"You have a masters in Criminal Justice and speak at least five languages I'm aware of. The FBI assigned you to a high-profile art crimes case in Boston. And yet—"

"Poof." Quinn flicked her fingers open. "You left to become a property claims adjuster?"

They both stared at me like I was supposed to answer—provide clarification—but it was none of their business. "You don't like not knowing things, do you?"

They both grinned.

"What's the actual question?"

"Well, hun, I'd love to pick your brain sometime. But I don't talk about my past, either, so I understand. So here it is. One, you can stop by to discuss any theories or doubts on any claim you have. Anytime. Two, I want you working with us—"

"Quinn, no recruiting."

She narrowed her eyes at him.

"Three, the system only put one red flag on this artwork claim, for its value. One flag means the adjuster needs to be cautious. We think there should have been more, but the FNOL wasn't entered correctly. The property claim listed the fatality, but the artwork claim didn't. That would have been a second flag."

Harry said, "Two flags requires Roger's approval prior to payment."

They rolled their chairs closer, in unison, Harry lowering his voice further. "Three flags would have sent it straight to us. Any thoughts on what the third flag should have been?"

I tapped my fingers on my mouth, speaking out loud as I went through possibilities. "Life insurance isn't with us. No recent mid-term changes to the policy to inflate its value. Total loss could have been it? Hard to prove the authenticity of a painting which was completely burned."

Quinn winked at me and sat back. "That's one, and—"

"There's one more. Check in when you figure it out." Harry rolled back to his desk. "You've got this, Sam. We have confidence in your work. Keep us in the loop, either in person or with your claim notes."

I nodded and stood. "Thanks for your help."

Quinn tapped me on the arm before I could leave. "And Sam, keep those claim notes private, alright?"

Private? Was someone at Foster under suspicion? "Including from Lucy?"

Lucy rounded the corner. "Ten minutes are up! Did I miss anything interesting?"

"Put this in the shredder." Harry took the Parker's Restoration card from Quinn and passed it to Lucy. "You talk a lot, Chapman. Make sure you keep your mouth shut on this claim unless Sam tells you it's alright."

· · · · ·· · · · ·

Walking back to the Pit, Lucy whispered, "Kind of intense. What were you guys talking about?"

"The Chagall claim." And so much more. I needed to mull it over and Lucy's incessant chatter wouldn't help. "How do you feel about heights?"

"Not good. I went bungee jumping once and thought about sky diving, but couldn't do it. In the 2000s, there were about two deaths a year from sky diving, although that's lower than—"

She kept going on skydiving fatality and injury data. The girl never met a statistic she didn't like, nor apparently one she didn't memorize.

When she took a breath, I interrupted, "I meant to get up on a house roof. Any problem with those heights?"

"Nah."

"Do you have sturdy shoes or sneakers?"

"Lots."

"Alright, focus on the BI system for the rest of the day and tomorrow. I'll schedule some roof inspections for Thursday and show you the ropes."

"What about Friday?" She waggled her eyebrows at me. "Can I come with you and learn from your...experience?"

I sighed, running a hand over my face. Two hours for a consult? What would I be doing? Watch him clean the painting? How boring. Or arousing. The way that shirt had circled his biceps had been amazing. And his dark, wavy hair I wanted to run my fingers through. And those jeans. I hadn't gotten a good look from behind, but—

"You're blushing!"

I nudged her. It was gentle, but her reflexes were awful, and she collided with one of the tall cubicle walls. She laughed, disarming the scowl I tried to give her.

CHAPTER 11

SAMANTHA

Wednesday was slow. Like the clock was ticking backwards slow. Two days until I'd see Dr. Antonio again, as long as the police released the Chagall to me. If they didn't, I'd have to reschedule. Good thing or a bad thing?

When my phone rang, I startled. Those big brown eyes were still distracting me. "Samantha Caine speaking."

"Heya, Sammy, it's Jimmy calling. We're done with your burned painting, so you can come and collect it anytime."

"Great, I can be there in about an hour."

He dropped his voice to a whisper. "Quick warning. You'll have to sign it out from Janelle. She's in a state over this fire and seeing you won't help. You may want to send someone else."

"Thanks for the heads up." I could do this. Things hadn't gone well with Janelle last week, but maybe I could make another attempt.

I needed to find a case to transport the Chagall but wasn't sure where to find them. Lucy was working away on the BI system, but she probably wouldn't know either. She had headphones in, bobbing her head and dancing in her seat as she typed.

None of the other adjusters were in the office, so I started dialing Hailey's cell phone. She usually handled the artwork claims, so she was my best bet.

Before I was able to finish, in my computer monitor, I caught the reflection of a man entering the Pit. The man I'd been avoiding the past month. Matt Foster. My ex-husband.

Shit. There was a reason I usually did this work in my truck.

"Sam!"

I put the phone down, took one very deep breath and turned around with the most obviously forced smile I could manage. "Hi, Matt! Long time."

He put out his arms for a hug, but I remained in my seat until he dropped them. "Where have you been?"

"Working."

Lucy shifted her attention to some paperwork on her desk, at an angle which allowed her to see us out of the corner of her eye. She'd stopped moving, so either she was focusing or her music wasn't on anymore. My money was on the latter.

"I heard! And it must be awfully hard because I've been down here at least three times a week to say hello!" He hit me teasingly on the arm. Matt was Roger's—the president of Foster Mutual Insurance—son. It was a legacy company and every generation worked there. Matt was a senior underwriter, and he was right, we never ran into each other. It had taken a lot of work on my part some days.

"I'm just heading out." I grabbed my backpack and started filling it up, desperate to get away from him. But I needed to find a case first. He'd know where they were. But then I'd have to talk to him. It had been six years. I should be over this already. We'd been friends and confidants once. Until he'd betrayed me.

"Do you have a few minutes?"

I threw the last items into my backpack and stood, hefting it onto my shoulder. "I need a transport case for a small painting. A two-by-two case would work. You know where those are?"

"Storage room downstairs. I'll show you."

"I can find it myself."

"Sam…" He scratched absently at his perfectly styled stubble.

My icy reception was making him uncomfortable. Good. I unclenched my jaw and sighed. I was being a jerk. "Yeah, okay."

He smiled, his perpetually concerned-looking eyes working overtime to calm my irritation.

We traveled the cubicle hallway and hit the stairs. We were quiet as we walked, but once in the privacy of the stairwell, he started.

"I heard Cass is sick." She'd always liked him. In fact, she'd been more torn up about our divorce than I'd been.

"Yeah. Couple months now. She got lucky. Her doctor pulled some strings to rush her diagnosis. They're thinking six rounds of chemo—she had her first early July—mastectomy, radiation, then reconstruction." I shifted the backpack, which was getting heavier by the second. "If all goes well, she'll be done by the end of March."

"March," he echoed. "Long time."

"It's pretty serious."

"Prognosis?"

"Good, but—" A lump formed in my throat. She would be alright. She had to be.

"Still scary?" He put a hand on the door at the bottom of the stairs before opening it, staring at me for a long moment.

I nodded, reaching for the door myself, to get out of the moment and put an end to the conversation.

"Are you seeing anyone?"

My hand dropped from the door. Who was he talking about? Had he heard something? The guys from the dating site? Oh my god. Did he hear something about Antonio Ferraro? Was Lucy talking?

He laughed suddenly. "Not that kind of seeing anyone." He shook his head and opened the door, ushering me ahead of him. "I meant like a therapist or anything."

I rolled my eyes.

"Oh right. Hardly the Samantha Caine way, is it? Talking to actual people and stuff." He nudged my backpack.

"Exactly."

"And how are you actually doing?" he asked, coming even with me again.

"Perfect, as always."

He cast a doubtful look at me. "Sam, you were always a terrible liar."

I let out a pained sigh. "At least one of us was." He frowned at the cheap shot.

"I thought we were past this, but you've been here over a month and this is the first time I've seen you. I know you're avoiding me."

I stared at the carpet as we walked, all its grays and browns and circles and swirls. It complimented the tall gray cubicle walls, while hideously clashing at the same time.

We walked in silence again for a moment until we made it into the storage room. It was thirty feet deep and twenty feet across. Old office equipment, computer peripherals, papers, and other junk were crammed into the back of the room. A thick layer of dust sat on those discarded piles. On a less dusty shelf on the right wall was a stack of briefcase-like boxes, the artwork transport cases.

"Thanks for showing me, Matt." I started to the shelf, but he grabbed my arm to turn me back to him.

"I said I wanted to talk to you, and that wasn't it."

"What do you want?" My jaw hurt from how tight it was. The only other option was letting the emotions out, which wouldn't happen.

"I know you're avoiding me."

"You said that already."

He rubbed his arm and looked around the room, avoiding my gaze. "I'm sorry for what I did. We. Ty was your friend, too. I don't know if it makes you feel better or worse, but he and I got married last year."

Cass had broken the news to me after it happened, so it wasn't a surprise. I'd spent a day in bed crying, then jumped out of a plane the next day. Five times. One for every year between our divorce and his remarriage.

"Are we done yet? Or do you need to get some more stuff off your chest?" Off his chest and right onto my back, ensuring I didn't forget how shitty people could be if you let them in.

"I hope you find someone who cares about you the way I should have."

I walked to the shelf. Lots of cases to choose from.

"And I have a message from Dad."

The third case was the right size.

"He wanted me to tell you directly the Scott artwork claim needs to be closed within a month."

I paused, hands frozen on the case. "What?"

"Bobby Scott was a friend of his. You know my dad. Family and friends are important, and he wants to take care of Olivia."

Alarm bells went off in my head. Would Roger bend the rules for his friends? "I need to get it authenticated before we can authorize payment."

"Yeah, and he wants it done quickly."

I nodded slowly, all the irritation with him gone. My brain started churning on the present instead of the past. I grabbed the case and made my way back to him.

"You know Ty and I are always here for you, no matter how you feel right now."

I stopped in front of him, taking in his slumped posture, his pinched face, his grimace. He missed me. Our friendship. He'd been the man I needed at the start of our relationship and I had to remember that. Putting the case down, I wrapped my arms around him. A few seconds later, I felt his muscles relax.

"Thanks, Matt."

He pulled back, smiling. "Think you could put a little less effort into avoiding me going forward?"

"Maybe twenty percent less." I grinned at him. "I need to get going, though. The police are releasing the Scott painting to me."

•••••••••••

I detoured on my way out. Knocking on the partition wall of the SIU office, Harry and Quinn looked up.

Roger and Bobby were friends, I mouthed.

She snapped her fingers and pointed at me. "I knew you'd figure it out."

That was the fourth red flag the claim should have had, but the claims tracking system only had one. This claim should have gone directly to SIU, but even knowing that, they were leaving it in my hands. Was I ready for this?

Chapter 12

Samantha

At the police station, I showed my identification and sat on one of the rigid plastic chairs to wait for Janelle.

I ran both hands over my face and leaned forward. My brain was running on overdrive. This Chagall claim was the most interesting thing I'd dealt with in years. Four red flags on the claim. Two days since seeing Antonio and two days until I saw him again. One stressful visit with Matt.

A few deep breaths to put it all aside and review my conversation with Janelle at the house. This one would go better. There was a chance for us to restart our friendship.

Good thing I'd left Lucy at the office.

"Heya, Sammy!"

I sat up with a start. "Jimmy? I thought I was seeing Janelle?"

"You will. I figured I'd come along as a buffer."

"She's that upset?" I stood, grabbed the transport case, and followed him through the secure door out of the waiting room.

He gave an ironic laugh. "You know her. If she's not upset, she's dead."

"She wasn't always like that."

"I remember. The job's jading her, I think." He led me down a short hallway to a small meeting room.

Janelle was already inside, the bagged painting in front of her. She glared at me and pushed a stack of papers in my direction. "Have a seat, Ms. Caine."

I put the case on the table and sat.

She looked over to Jimmy. "We won't be needing your services, Slater."

Jimmy pulled out a chair and lowered himself into it. "It's okay. I'm running the investigation. I'll stay."

"It's not okay." She folded her arms and shifted the glare to him. "My evidence. My meeting. If you're unclear of whose responsibility it is, read the fucking chain of custody."

The battle of wills continued for thirty seconds until Jimmy stood. "I need to work on the report anyway."

Once he was out, Janelle started without batting an eye. "We tested the painting and found it immaterial to our investigation, so we have no reason to retain it any longer." She pointed out a few items on the paperwork. "You can compare the ID of the paperwork you signed to the ID on the bag, review the condition, etcetera. Then I'll need you to sign on each line I've marked."

I stood to look over the painting under its plastic cover, pulling out my phone to review the photos I'd taken before Janelle had removed it from the Scotts' house. They'd mangled it. I flashed the images at her, more irritated than I should have been, but the negativity radiating off her triggered me. "There are obvious brush marks on the front, and it's even further torn than when we retrieved it from the house. I specifically requested no one turn it over or work on it."

"No kidding!" She stabbed a finger on the bag. "It says so right here!"

The instructions I'd asked her to pass along were written on the bag. I looked at her again. She wasn't pissed with me. She was pissed about the investigation.

I dropped back into my seat. "So, what happened?"

"This is a piece of evidence in a police investigation." She rocked her head side to side, sneering and impersonating someone. "Your concerns about further damage to it are not a top priority."

I closed my eyes and held up a hand. "I'm lost. You're angry, the painting's further damaged, and...what?"

She let out a fierce breath and leaned forward. "I talked to the officer who was checking it out and got a cock-and-bull story about how he treats evidence the way he's been trained, regardless of whether an art crimes expert provided instructions. Christ, that pushed him even further, like it was a personal insult he wasn't the expert."

"Who?"

"I can't tell you." She hooked a thumb toward the door, clear enough. Jimmy. "Suffice to say, we should be keeping it at least another week, but it's being pushed through."

"Pushed through?" This was becoming a trend. Everyone was in a hurry to wrap this up.

"This is a homicide investigation until arson is ruled out. Standard procedure. But they're pushing to close it in record speed."

"Have you talked to your superiors about it?"

She rolled her eyes. "Oh, thanks, Sam, I hadn't thought about going through official channels. I just thought I'd complain about it to you."

I balled a fist on the table. "Is this about the investigation or about us?"

She stood and walked to the narrow window with a view of the small garden and flag in front of the police department. "Both."

She put her hands on either side of the window, taking in a deep breath. "Slater's running the case, but I'm following up on a few leads he's missed. People don't die suspiciously in this town very often and million-dollar paintings don't get destroyed. The department isn't giving it the right level of attention. Fire said it looked accidental, so everyone's half-assing it."

"You never were a half-asser."

She laughed and turned around to lean on the wall. "No, I'm definitely a full-asser."

"You were always a hard worker." My instincts told me to stop there, but I had to try. "You know, I was trying to get your attention that day, not the—"

"We were supposed to go to Quantico together." She folded her arms, the lightness fading. "Instead, I lost my scholarship and had to leave school for a year to work."

"I didn't mean for any of that—"

"And you just kept going. Three degrees, a summer in London, another in Italy, then the internship with the FB..." Her eyes slid closed and she exhaled long and slow.

What could I even say to all that? She'd had her phone out during a final exam. I got her attention to put it away, but a proctor saw me. Then saw her. And it snowballed from there. There was nothing I could do but beg her forgiveness, and she was never willing to give it.

We were supposed to do all that stuff together.

"You know what?" She pushed off the wall. "I don't want to talk about what happened. Maybe some time, but not here. Right now, this case needs my full attention."

I put my fist to my mouth. Maybe sharing my own concerns about the case would help bring us back together. "I feel the same way about this claim. I'm being pushed to have it closed by the end of the month."

She stopped behind her chair, grasping it with both hands. "Is that normal?"

"For a standard claim, yeah, but this?" I gestured toward the painting. "I need to have it cleaned and authenticated before we can make a determination. The restoration company hasn't even looked at it yet. If I had a timeline from them, I could see Foster Mutual establishing a constraint, but—but not before they've looked at it."

"When do you take it in?"

"Friday. We have a thirty-day guarantee, but this is a tough job. I wouldn't be surprised if it takes longer."

"Sign the paperwork." She pulled her chair out and sat again, scribbling on a card and sliding it across the table. "Here's my private number. Give me a call if anything else —about this case—comes up."

Chapter 13

Samantha

My stomach was a jumble of knots on top of butterflies. Making my way along the sidewalk from my truck, I did a mental check. I'd chosen my most elegant Italian suit: black skinny pants and jacket, white silk blouse. All Prada. My long hair was in a messy bun at the nape of my neck. Would he like it? Was I trying too hard? Did it even matter? He'd been toying with me. There was nothing behind it. And he wore jeans on Monday. Why was I so dressed up?

When I arrived, Sofia greeted me with a smile. The scent in the air was the same, but the music was alternative rock.

"Good morning, Samantha!" She rounded her desk, air kissing my cheeks once I'd put the case down. "You look beautiful today!"

"Thanks." She was one to talk, in her tight, pale pink dress. "So do you."

"I know." She winked jokingly and returned to her desk.

"Don't let that go to your head, Sofia!" Antonio hollered from the space behind the reception wall. His heavy footfalls from the unseen space added a few extra knots to my stomach.

My brain stuttered when I saw him. Not casual. Not jeans. He wore dark gray trousers over polished black shoes. White dress shirt with the sleeves rolled up, top few buttons undone. It was halfway between casual and the sexiest thing I'd ever seen. A pair of sunglasses hung from his shirt, as though he were on his way out, rather than preparing for our meeting.

A sly smile broke across his face, and when my eyes met his smoldering gaze, it stole my breath away. He must have practiced doing that to women for many years.

I extended my hand to shake. As he took it, the same tingle from Monday ran up my arm, but I didn't withdraw, instead holding long enough for it to hit my toes. Christ, that felt good, but it wasn't exactly a good choice. I still had two hours with him.

"Ciao, Samantha."

I swallowed hard and pulled my hand away, feeling the heat rising in my cheeks. "Antonio, good to see you again."

"Good to see me?" He cocked an eyebrow. "Progress."

"I have some bad news," said Sofia.

He and I turned immediately to her.

"Dr. Dominico left suddenly this morning for two weeks, so we're down a resource. We won't be able to take your painting, but—"

Antonio's head jerked back. "Scusami? You said nothing this morning."

"—I've arranged for another restoration company in Detroit to take it on. They're very good—"

His brows knitted together, the sex-god exterior slipping slightly. "No."

"Samantha, may we have a moment?" She gestured to the reception couch and I sat. Picking up a magazine from the table, I flipped mindlessly, watching them in my periphery.

They spoke quietly in Italian, but not quietly enough, since it was a language I knew well. He stepped behind her desk as she hit a few keys and pointed at her monitor. "Antonio, look. This is the extra work you need to take care of while he's gone. Everyone else will be busier too. We don't have the time. We already gave her a two-week estimate on the other painting."

"Assign it to me, I can do it."

"You don't have the time."

"I'll make the time."

She huffed. "Fine."

I looked up as he came out from behind the desk.

"Samantha. One, I will take your painting. But, two, we have a slight problem with the schedule. Sofia was supposed to book you in at ten, not nine."

"No, I wasn't!"

"I always go to Russo's down the road at this hour and can't work until I've had my coffee. So, you have two choices. You can wait here until I return or come with me."

I stood slowly. "How long will you be?"

"Usually an hour."

"You could grab it and come back for our meeting?"

"It's a fifteen-minute walk either way. It would still be over half an hour."

Sofia rolled her eyes. "They do have the best coffee in Brenton, and cornetti to die for."

Antonio winked at me. It was suddenly stifling in their office. Or was that just me?

"Okay, I guess." I focused on Sofia, trying to appear calm, but there was a tremble in my voice. Work, this was work. I could do work.

"You guess? You owe me." He withdrew the sunglasses from his shirt and gestured to the case I'd left by Sofia's desk. "You can leave that with my sister."

"No. This painting isn't leaving my sight until we review it."

"Alright, I can carry it for you? It looks heavy."

"I can handle it."

"Like you could have handled hitting your date?" He smirked and put the sunglasses on, walking to the door. He held it open as I grabbed the case and left ahead of him, the humid air hitting me like a wall. A step behind, he ushered me to the inside of the sidewalk.

Four days ago, I'd debated searching this neighborhood for the mystery man from the restaurant, knowing I didn't have the nerve. Now here I was, on a sunny summer morning, praying I could get through the next two hours without tripping over my words or on a crack in the sidewalk.

"So, I didn't have a chance to ask the last time you were in. I thought Hailey was the only one who worked with us?"

"I have more experience than she does."

"Interesting." He paused, shaded eyes flicking around the neighborhood. "Experience with what, specifically?"

"Art claims." The case felt heavier than earlier, like I'd added three additional paintings to it. "Has anyone made progress on the color field I brought in Monday?"

He laughed. "Alice will work on it next week."

"The estimate was for two weeks."

"Sì, and she'll have it done on time, don't worry. We are exceptional at what we do." He turned to me and leaned closer with a smirk. "At everything we do."

I flinched at the innuendo, unable to control my reactions. He knew he had power over me. I could have hit him for it. "Dr. Ferraro, regardless of you finding me in a weak moment Saturday night and me agreeing to go for coffee, I'm here for a business meeting. We aren't here to talk about us or whatever the hell you're talking about."

"Oh, Samantha." The smirk didn't leave his lips. "Just tell me you're not interested, and I'll stop flirting with you."

I stopped dead in my tracks. I stared at his broad back and shoulders, his perfect ass, his graceful movement, as he continued a couple steps before stopping. He turned around slowly, taking off his sunglasses.

"I already told you Saturday night."

He put the arm of his sunglasses in his mouth and looked me up and down. "But you know me better now."

"Jesus Christ! Do you have the ability to turn that thing off?"

His smirk faltered for a moment as he stared at me, brows turning down. Like I'd hurt his feelings or something. Great.

"Listen, I'm sor—"

His lip twitched, rapidly evolving into a full laugh. His hand covered his mouth, then his heart. His laugh was infectious, but I did my best to contain my own chuckle.

"I'm sorry. Alright, I'm done. I promise." He put his sunglasses back on. "Nothing more than coffee between two old friends."

"We're business associates, not friends."

"You are a remarkable woma—business associate, Samantha. Let's make a deal. Forget about everything before this moment. No more flirting, I promise. Fresh start?"

I was rattled by my intense attraction to him, the way my heart skipped beats at his voice, how my palms sweat, and how I wanted to stare at him. I was used to being in complete control, but he could reduce me to a quivering pile of jelly with a wink.

But I had work to do. I didn't need to call Hailey and reassign the art claims to her. If nothing else, I had to prove to myself I could do it.

"Okay, fresh start and coffee. But I'm not taking my eyes off you until you review this painting."

"Not taking your eyes off me?" The smirk ratcheted up again. "If this is going to work, you can't flirt with me, either." With a wink, he turned back to Russo's and ushered me along the sidewalk.

Oh my god. This day couldn't end soon enough.

· · · ● · ● · · · ·

A green awning with *Russo's* written on it hung across the front of the Italian café down the street from the Ferraro's office. It shaded six small black metal tables with matching chairs, three of which were in use.

Antonio pulled out a chair for me and I thanked him as he pushed it in. Taking a seat for himself, he hung his sunglasses from his shirt, and I placed the painting case between my foot and the chair to make sure it didn't go wandering off anywhere. One million dollars' worth of canvas and gouache paint sitting on a random sidewalk in Brenton, Michigan.

He faced away from the door but took a quick look in the window and nodded to someone inside. A middle-aged man in a crisp white apron came out to us almost immediately, sporting a beaming smile. He threw his bar towel over his shoulder as he stopped at our table, producing a small vase with some short-stemmed roses in it.

"Buongiorno, Antonio!" The man shook Antonio's hand vigorously and clapped him on the shoulder.

Antonio gestured to me, and the man shook my hand enthusiastically. "Samantha, this is Angelo Russo. He makes the best coffee in Brenton."

"In Michigan, he means! And the best cornetti!" Angelo's accent was much thicker than Antonio's and his boisterous personality was charming.

I asked, "Chocolate hazelnut filling?"

He nodded, and I smiled, already planning to return to Russo's on my own to reminisce about my summer in Italy. Alone.

"Due caffe, per favore," Antonio said. By default, an order of two coffees meant espressos in an Italian café.

I did a quick check of my watch—9:15 a.m. "Actually, un caffe per lui e un cappuccino per me, per favore?"

Angelo nodded and made his way back into the café, straightening chairs, inquiring as to the other patrons, and wiping crumbs off tables as he went.

Antonio frowned. "You are already checking your watch? We have two hours to enjoy a coffee and review your painting. Don't be so impatient."

"No, it's—it's not that." I was suddenly conscious of the case again. "No cappuccino after ten. I was making sure it was early enough—never mind."

He exhaled, running a hand through his hair. He clasped his hands together and put them on the table. Leaning forward, he gave me a rueful smile. "Are two fresh starts more than I can ask for?"

"Don't worry about it." *Go back to the office, Sam. He doesn't care.* "I should apologize. This was a stupid idea. I'll head back to your office and wait until you're done."

I put my hands on the table to stand, but before I could, his were on top of mine. I took in a quick breath and tensed. My heart rate kicked up as the heat pooled in my core and my arms trembled. *Jesus Christ, Sam, get control of yourself.* He's just a pretty face. A *very* pretty face, but still.

"The apology is mine," he said. "Please, stay."

I pulled my hands back. It was silly but looking at him was like looking at the sun, as warmth gathered in my cheeks under his gaze. I stared at my hands now folded in my lap and let out a hesitant laugh, doing my best not to cover the blush I knew was there. I could handle any work situation, but this man had me tripping over words and feeling things I hadn't in years? Things I didn't want to feel.

"And you speak Italian?"

"Some," I said, playing down my fluency.

"Have you been to Italy, Samantha?"

I loved the way he pronounced my name. It took him twice as long to get it out as it took me, with his slow emphasis on the middle syllable, his tongue resting on his upper teeth as he breathed out *mahn* instead of *man*.

"Only once, about nine years ago. I spent a summer in Amelia, about an hour and a half north of Rome—"

"Sì, I know it well." He was leaning forward, eyes locked on me, as though every word I uttered was the most fascinating thing he'd ever heard. He sucked at not flirting.

I tried to adopt the calm and confidence he exuded, but my eyes darted over him and then moved along to anywhere else. Maybe I should get angry at him again, because I was able to look at him when I was arguing. "I spent a summer there and learned some Italian customs and practiced the language."

"From a man?"

Yes, but no. "From several men and women."

He gave me a knowing nod and wink, which caught me off guard.

"Not like that!" I spluttered, my eyes finally coming to settle on him long enough to roll my eyes. He was smirking now, toying with me again. "I did some postgrad there and boarded with a family for the summer."

"In Amelia?" He straightened, brows knit together, the smirk vanishing. "Surely not with the Association for Research into Crimes against Art?"

"Yeah, ARCA, exactly!"

"Allora..." He leaned so close his chest rested on the table. "You are a claims adjuster, with postgraduate training in art crimes and cultural heritage protection? How do you go from one to the other?"

"That's a long and uninteresting story."

"I think it would be very interesting."

No one knew the whole story, not even Cass. Some days, I wasn't sure even I understood the sharp turn my life had taken. I ran a hand along my cheek, to my neck. I should leave.

I held his gaze for an uncomfortable moment until I had to look away. He leaned back in the chair, asking rapid-fire questions, simple things like favorite food, drink, and movie. For every answer I gave, he'd share his, and we'd mull them over. Nothing earth-shattering, but it surprised me how much we had in common, like our passion for authentic Italian food, action movies, and a love of running.

Then he asked, "Who's your hero?"

I braced for his reaction when I said without shame, "Lara Croft."

His brows knit together. "From *Tomb Raider*?"

When I nodded, he threw his head back, a warm sound coming from deep in his stomach, which he held with one hand and smacked the little table with the other. The flower vase jumped, and I feared it would fall over.

"Not funny!" I couldn't contain my foolish grin. People walking along the street, the other patrons, and even some of the people inside Russo's were looking at us. "Stop!"

He wiped at his cheeks with the back of his hand to clear the tears. "She's not real! You can't pick a video game character for a hero!"

"I can!" Now I was laughing, too, my hand covering my face.

"No, no, this is how it's done." He cleared his throat, suppressing his laughter. "I choose my Nonno." He paused a moment for a few more laughs before he took a deep inhale and calmed himself. "He's my hero for the role he played in World War II."

Interesting way of putting it. "What role was that?"

"In October 1943, the Americans made their way into Napoli, and the city was in shambles. He was living in Roma at the time. He had opened the conservation company with his brother several years before the war started. When he heard about the American Monuments Officers in Napoli, helping to restore and protect the works of art and cultural heritage, he snuck through the German lines to help. The work he did there was significant. Important."

"I've heard the stories. Amazing."

He nodded, taking one of the roses out of the vase, twirling it between his fingers and pointing it at me as he spoke. "After the Allied forces made their way to Roma, and he felt Napoli was in good hands, he went home." He sniffed the flower. "Roma was luckier than Napoli had been. Much less destruction. So the shop survived, and he was a bit of a legend."

"You're right. He's a good hero."

"And you?" He offered me the rose. "You pick a video game character?"

My fingers brushed his when I took the stem, and my stomach tightened. "She's not just any video game character. Lara Croft is highly intelligent, athletic, and she'd kick your butt if you laughed at her." I hid my chuckle behind the flower.

He grinned. "You have much in common with her."

I focused on the petals but couldn't contain a smile. "She travels the world, tracking down relics and items of historical significance. I know the title of the series is *Tomb Raider*, but I prefer to focus on how she's saving those artifacts from the bad guys. Like an art protector. She inspired me to learn a lot of things, like rock climbing and survival skills."

"Survival skills? Sounds ominous."

"Not really," I said, too embarrassed to say more.

"Like my Nonno, but with more adventure?"

I smelled the rose and offered it back to him, but he declined. "Crossing German lines sounds like adventure."

He tilted his head at me, considering. "And this is why you studied with ARCA? You want to be Lara Croft?"

My jaw clenched as he made the link, and my smile faltered. I stuffed the rose back in its vase and rubbed a hand over my cheek. Nobody else had ever made that link.

He'd lowered my defenses with the conversation and the laughter. I barely knew this man, and I was revealing things I didn't share with people. What was it about him? Engaging, confident, full of life, and he understood me. The PhD was like the cherry on top. Christ, he was too good to be true.

It had been a half hour since we'd ordered, but Angelo hadn't returned. I was on the clock. I tapped the case again to make sure it was there. "Well, now I'm a claims adjuster. And I have a painting we need to discuss if the coffee ever arrives."

He tilted his head the other way, scrutinizing me. "I was wrong, Samantha. You can pick a video game character for a hero if she inspires you. In fact, she's one of my heroes now, too."

Changing the subject away from me, I said, "It's closing in on ten o'clock."

"Sì, we should get back soon." He gestured toward the window and nodded. Within a minute, Angelo had appeared with our order, plus one of his 'world-famous' cornetti.

We sipped our drinks, and I ate my treat, enjoying the sweet, flaky pastry and its rich, silky chocolate hazelnut filling. I dipped it in the foam on top of my cappuccino and tilted my face toward the sun's warmth. The food, the drink, the soft Italian voices around me; if I closed my eyes, I was back in Italy.

But unlike last time, I wasn't with a man who'd break my heart.

CHAPTER 14

ANTONIO

We finished at Russo's too soon. She asked for the bill, but I insisted. No matter what she said, we'd made a toast for a date, and this was our first. First of many, I was already sure.

She was more comfortable on the walk back to the office, although that wasn't setting the bar high. At least she had only chastised me once and we only needed two fresh starts.

"How long have you lived here? From your accent, I'm guessing you grew up in Rome?"

"I was born in Brenton." I spoke with one hand as we walked, keeping the other in my pocket. Otherwise, it would have been on her or around her, and she was obviously not as tactile as I preferred to be. "My father worked with my grandfather in the same office I work in today. My great uncle ran the original office in Roma until he died when I was five. My father moved us back to Italia to take over then."

"Why did you come back to the U.S.?"

"Family business. When my grandfather passed, my father came back to America to run the studio here. Three generations now. I hope someday my children will work here, as well."

She nodded politely.

"Do you have any?"

"Children?" She exhaled sharply. "No, they don't exactly fit my lifestyle."

What did that mean? She didn't want them? Or simply not yet? "Your lifestyle?"

"I move around a lot."

"How does that work with your job at Foster?"

"I'm an independent adjuster, so I don't work directly for them. My actual employer is more like a temp agency. Normally, they deploy me around the country wherever I'm needed—and licensed. Tornadoes, hailstorms, wildfires. And stuff." Her gaze fell to the sidewalk, the same look coming over her as the night at Caruther's.

I clasped a hand over my heart as the truth dawned on me. "And they assigned you here while your sister undergoes her treatments?"

She shrugged and nodded slightly. Before I could interrogate any further, she cleared her throat and continued. "How old were you when you moved back to the States?"

I wanted to continue asking questions and getting to know her, but the look on her face was clear: It was best to move on to lighter topics. "Old enough to start college."

"Where'd you go?"

"Michigan State—"

"Go Green!" More school spirit than I would have expected, given how quiet she had been in class.

"Go White," I laughed. "Then, back to Roma for my master's and my doctorate in Delaware."

"Delaware? What's your doctorate in?"

"Preservation Studies. I developed a new method for fresco repairs, with a lower risk of damage to the original. It's probably the least interesting thing about me."

"Really? It sounds fascinating."

"You're being polite." My free hand dug into my pocket. This was not something I enjoyed speaking about with women I was pursuing. They never found it interesting. Of course, that was part of the problem with my love life, was it not?

But her eyes lit up and she put a hand on my arm, her excitement washing over me. My stomach clenched at the touch, and I couldn't control my smile.

"I have an art history degree from MSU. My focus was on Roman through Renaissance art. Seeing the frescoes in Pompeii is at the top of my bucket list!"

I tore a hand out of my pocket and placed it on top of hers. "They are magnificent, and only a day trip from Roma." Her hand was gone faster than it had shot out to touch me, but the contact had sent a current through my body. "You didn't go the summer you were in Amelia?"

"No. Sadly, I never made it that far south."

She had said no flirting, but I couldn't contain myself. "You are a surprise, Samantha Caine. ARCA, art history, Pompeii...People don't usually surprise me. This has been a good date."

"Date?"

"Mi scusi, but you gave up on dating, did you not?"

She didn't respond, which was for the best.

· · · · ●·●· · · ·

Sofia glared at me as we stepped back into the office. "Good thing you didn't wait here, Samantha."

"Angelo sends his regards." I ignored the harassment, grinning at Sofia, and guided Samantha past the desk. "My station is at the back on the left."

Gianfranco and Alice sat at their worktables, sunshine streaming over them from the skylights. At one of the easels at the very rear of the studio, a cool spotlight shone on Zander's easel, evening out the light to better match where the painting would hang once he was finished.

A typical consult would involve a cursory review of the artwork, perhaps some time in my office to discuss her requirements, then one-on-one time with the painting before providing an estimate. Brief. Too brief for Samantha.

But perhaps I could give her a tour first. What would impress her most? The twelve-foot-high mechanized roller frame was a surprising favorite of most visitors, but she knew more than most visitors. The imaging room, most likely. However, from her sweeping gaze as we walked through the main workspace, she was already impressed.

"Why Brenton?" Her words snapped me back to the moment.

"Un momento." Vivaldi again. I returned to the reception area, leaned over Sofia, and switched to my favorite rock music stream. It was still quiet, but the energy had shifted when I returned. "Sofia is always putting on classical. No one can work with that on."

"I can!" announced Alice, and Gianfranco chuckled. I smirked at my cousin and his girlfriend, who loved to tease me.

I returned my attention to the lovely Samantha. "My Nonno and Nonna immigrated after the War—once the office in Roma was established—as many Italians did. They had friends and family who had already settled here, some with families as far back as the building of the railroad. His friends from the Monuments Officers encouraged him and became his first clients."

"But why not New York? If he was opening a branch of an art restoration company, why not a center of the art world?"

I gestured to the paintings stacked against the walls and then crossed to the storage room. She didn't follow me, so I beckoned with a finger, "Vieni qua." I opened the door and stepped out of the way to show her dozens of empty frames hanging from the walls, and over two hundred paintings in wooden slots on shelves.

"When you're the best, the people come to you. They chose where to settle, and the work started to arrive. It's that simple." I closed the door and walked her back to my station. "So, now that you're here and know you are with the best, let's look at what you've brought me."

"Antonio, please," groaned Alice. "My ears are bleeding." They laughed at me again. Our workplace was a happy space, full of people doing what they loved and enjoying each other's company.

Zander took his headphones off, heavy metal pounding out of them. "What did I miss?"

"Just Antonio's ego sucking all of the air out of the room," said Gianfranco.

"Nothing new, then." He put on his headphones and returned to work.

"They wound me." I shook my head, gripping my heart dramatically. She frowned but was suppressing a laugh. I winked at her, more instinct than anything else, which caused the frown to deepen. "Alright, let's see your painting."

She put the case in the middle of my table, unlocked it, and opened it.

"What am I looking at?" I stepped back to take it in. Shifting into professional mode, her near-constant tension, tremble, and nervousness disappeared. It was fascinating.

"The painting was in a house fire. It's insured for a lot of money, and we have to get its identity confirmed against the photos we have on file, so we can pay out the claim. However, with all the ash and soot coating it, it will be difficult to get the confirmation done."

"Why is it in a plastic bag?" I smoothed out the bag to get a better look.

"The fire's being investigated by the police, so they took the painting into custody. I thought it was better to leave it in the evidence bag, since it provided stability. The portions that didn't burn are so thin, I was afraid they'd tear if I took it out."

"Sì, smart choice." I moved the case to the side and withdrew a magnification visor from under my desk, along with two pairs of disposable gloves. One pair for her, one for me, which we donned before continuing. I put my visor on and lifted the painting from the case.

"Hold the end." I pointed to the far edge, opened the top, then reached in to take hold of the frame. Fortunately, the frame was still intact, but the canvas was in tatters. Three unburned strips crossed the middle, falling to the table as I set it down. I would have to stabilize those first. Drag marks across the front made it clear someone with no clue what they were doing had worked on it. "Tell me a woman with an art history degree didn't smear the soot into the painting?"

"That was the police." She spoke sharply, irritated. Work-Samantha was passionate about this. "I found the painting face down at the site of the fire and gave them specific instructions they didn't listen to. I gave them hell already."

"Bene, they deserved it." I positioned the magnification lenses on my visor in front of my eyes and flicked the lights on. I moved back and forth, hovering barely above the canvas. "I can't make much out. There is so much damage, but the portions under the frame may be enough to compare, if you have photos of that. It's worth quite a lot, you say. Who is the artist?"

"Chagall. It's called *Les amoureux dans le ciel.*"

I froze. This was not possible. I shut my eyes as my breath caught in my throat. What was I going to do now?

"This is what it looked like." She placed pictures on the table next to me.

I looked at them from the corner of my eye because she expected me to. But I didn't have to. I knew the painting. And this was not it.

Samantha, my clever Samantha, pointed to the edge of the burned area at the bottom right. "Looks like the signature's intact."

"Sì, you are right." I lifted the visor and touched my heart, which beat so hard it was about to break through my chest.

"Your shirt?" She pointed at the spot where the soot streaked the white dress shirt.

"Un momento, per favore." I held my breath as I walked out to the reception desk, taking off my gloves, the action hiding the tremble in my hands.

Sofia tilted her head at me when I knelt next to her, behind the desk. "You look like you've seen—"

I put a finger to my mouth and whispered in Italian. Even though Samantha could speak Italian. That had been a surprise. "Did she tell you the name of the painting she was bringing in today?"

"No. What's going—"

"*Les amoureux dans le ciel.*"

Her eyes and mouth went wide. "But that—"

"Is hanging in our parents' house, I know." I stared at her, neither of us speaking for a moment. "I must tell her this is a fake?"

"What if—what if the one at their house is the fake and this is the real one?"

I took the visor off and ran my hand through my hair. "Do I tell her the truth?"

"No, we should speak with Papa."

"You don't think he would be involved in anything illeg —"

She pointed a finger at me. "Don't go there, Antonio."

"What if he knew? About the fire, the painting, what if he's involved?"

She smacked my arm. "I said don't go there!"

"He knew the man he bought it from, Bobby Scott. Is this why he left town this morning?" I took out my phone to call him, but there was no answer. "Probably still in the air?"

Sofia nodded. "Stall her. Don't take the contract. We'll talk to Papa when he lands, then we'll figure it out."

Hanging my head, I exhaled deeply as I stood. "This is not how I dreamed today would go."

"Put on your best face."

I threw the gloves in her garbage and carried the visor back to the studio, in time to see Samantha answering a phone call. She turned to face the far wall and put a hand over her ear for privacy.

"Uncle Nathan!"

How could I lie to her? I would not. I didn't know what the truth was, however. Was this painting a fake? Was my parents' painting a fake? If I signed the paperwork taking possession of it, knowing it was not the true *Les amoureux*, would that be a crime?

"Yeah, Saturday, eight o'clock, Train Station, got it. See you then."

I stopped behind her as she hung up. "Everything alright?"

She spun around, a brilliant smile lighting up her face. "All good. And my painting?"

Hands on my hips, I braced myself. "I'm sorry, but Sofia was right. We reviewed my schedule for the next month. Given the amount of work required, combined with my father's absence, we truly can't take your painting." A lump formed in my throat, preventing me from saying more.

All the joy faded from her eyes. My fault. "You said you could make it work. Foster has a commitment from your company. Thirty days on any project."

I stared at the painting. Was it *Les amoureux* or not? "Thirty days, pending approval from my father or from me."

She elbowed her way past me, next to the desk. "You said you'd make it work." She tried to shove the painting back into the plastic bag, but the bag didn't cooperate. "Said you were the best."

"You can still take it to the company Sofia arranged." I held the bag open for her while she indelicately wrapped it and tossed it into its case, slamming it shut. I placed a hand on it to stop her from leaving. "Samantha, this is professional, not personal."

"Everything's personal with you, isn't it?" She heaved on the case, but I held fast. She looked up at me, the blush covering her cheeks, the clenched jaw, the fierce determination in her eyes. "If I'd said yes to dinner, you would have taken it, wouldn't you?"

She thought I was toying with her.

"Alright, stop. Let me see what I can do this weekend." I placed my other hand on top of hers, and she did exactly as I expected. She let go of the case, pulling her hand away from mine.

I shoved my hands into my pockets to stop reaching for her and stared at her, while she stared at the case.

"I'm being thoroughly unprofessional." She took the case from the desk, calming. "Do you expect you'll be able to arrange something?"

"Samantha, I'll do my best. I'll call you on Monday to let you know." If I couldn't figure something out, she would be gone from my life as soon as Alice finished with the gallery painting. I couldn't let that happen.

We walked to the door, and I held it open for her.

She paused before leaving, serious again. "Thank you, Dr. Ferraro. I hope you have good news for me on Monday."

"I'll be in touch." As she passed me, she smiled again. My hand took on a life of its own and touched the small of her back. She tensed but didn't look back.

· · · · ● · ● · · · ·

My shoulders slumped as she walked away, all the same grace and power she exhibited every time she left me. It was hard to reconcile the shy girl with this image of her. Russo's-Samantha compared to Work-Samantha. Samantha. I loved her name, how it rolled off my tongue, how I could taste the syllables as they flowed.

Her caramel-colored hair. How would it move as she walked, glimmering from the sun's kiss, if it hadn't been confined by the bun at her neck? Someday, I would run my mouth along that elegant neck, to her full lips with that brilliant smile. Today, she would have tasted of chocolate and hazelnuts and cappuccino.

Sofia slid an arm around my waist, and I draped mine around her shoulders.

"Pretty, isn't she?"

I kept my eyes down the road. "Stunning."

"You don't usually pick good ones for yourself."

"Fate picked her for me." I stepped closer to the front window as she got further away. "Do you remember, after Faith and I broke up, I told you about a girl from college?"

"I do. You were about ready to track her down. This one reminds you of her?"

I paused and squeezed her, warmth pooling in my chest.

She smacked my arm with her free hand. "Liar!"

"No," I sighed. "All these years later, she's come back into my life."

"Did she remember you?"

"Of course not." I chuckled. "She was always so quiet in class, sitting way up at the front. You know I was always at the back. And I look a little different now."

"A little bit." She laughed. "Do you still think you were overzealous on Saturday?"

"Would you believe she has a degree in Art History, studied with ARCA, and speaks Italian?"

"Sounds perfect for you." She shoved me with her hip.

"Sì, except..." I put a hand on the door to open it, so I could step outside and not lose sight of her, but Sofia held me back.

"Except what?"

I ripped my eyes from Samantha to glance at my sister. "She's only in Brenton for eight more months."

"It'll be a short marriage, then?" Sofia joked.

Samantha hoisted herself up into a massive vehicle.

"She drives a very large truck. How do you impress such a woman?"

"You're Dr. Antonio Ferraro. Impressing women is what you do."

"Not this one. She threw me off my game. She snapped at me, turned me down, and still I had a hard time not touching her." I sighed. "I should have told her the truth about the painting."

Samantha was finally pulling away.

"I have a feeling about this one, Sofia. I don't want to mess it up. She's nervous but fierce. If I push too hard, she'll give her claims to Hailey. I must play it slow. This is the long game, sì?"

"No, Antonio, it's not. You said she isn't staying here permanently."

I looked at her, an idea forming. "Wait. The painting she brought in Monday?"

"Yes, for Mason's Gallery. It's a small tear, should be quick. Alice will work on it next week."

I let go of her shoulder as the excitement grew. "Samantha was worried it wouldn't be done in time. I'll start the repair right now." I kissed her on the cheek and hurried back to the storage room. Small tear, easy work. I could finish it over the weekend and impress her with my restoration skills before I tried anything else.

"What was that mess?" asked Alice as I tore through the studio.

I stopped and pointed at her and Gianfranco. "Do you two have plans tomorrow evening?"

They looked at each other and nodded.

"Cancelled! Gianfranco, you are coming to dinner with me tomorrow night. Eight o'clock. Train Station."

"What?"

In the storage room, I hauled out my phone and made reservations. I had to pull some strings, but it would be worth it. I would surprise her. Quick visit, just say hello. She would be with her uncle, in a happy mood. Away from work. Away from lies and disappointments.

I pulled *Number Vee* out of its slot. This would be easy. And it would make Samantha Caine happy.

CHAPTER 15

ANTONIO

"How do I look?" I ran my hands down the black suit jacket, ensuring it would be perfect.

"Like the most handsome man here, as always." Gianfranco took a sip of his Scotch. "Why did I give up an evening with Alice for this?"

I scanned the white neoclassical-themed dining room. The crowd was elegant, and I couldn't wait to see what Samantha was wearing. It was an exclusive restaurant, but it was a family dinner, so something not too extravagant. She'd worn pants each time I saw her. Would it be the same or would she wear a dress?

My cousin and I sat at a table along the outer wall. I'd spent the last ten minutes craning my neck every way to spot her. I would locate her table, ensure I was visible, then wait. If I was lucky, she would come to say hello. Those odds were not good, given how nervous she was. The next option would be to catch her eye and wave, to see what she would do. If all else failed, I would walk over on my own.

It was perfect. I would let her know I had worked through the day to repair *Number Vee* for her. Ensure she was thinking of me. Above all, no flirting. At least, not obvious flirting.

I leaned past him to see the entrance again, and there she was. My heart stopped beating. It was a baby blue halter dress. Asymmetrical skirt, hitting at her knee. A pink pattern, maybe flowers. And her hair was down, falling past her shoulder blades. Its gentle wave reflected the light as though made of silk. It was as glorious as I'd imagined.

She slowed as she passed the paintings, modern interpretations of the Greek red-figure vase style. I would have guessed those would be her favorite decorations, given her passion for ancient art. Perfetto.

"What are you grinning at?" My cousin swiveled in his seat to follow my gaze. "Are you kidding me? We're here to stalk that claims adjuster who was yelling at you yesterday?"

"Not stalk. Surprise."

"How'd you know she'd be here?"

"She's having dinner with her family. An uncle, but I don't know how many others."

The server leading her through the dining area stopped at a table with one man. One man not old enough to be an uncle. One attractive man. My heart dropped. Her face lit up when she saw him. He stood and wrapped his arms around her, kissing her cheek. She laughed and sat with him.

Gianfranco turned back to me. "Doesn't look like family to me."

His hand on the table, hers on top of his. I kissed Sofia's cheeks all the time, but I never held her hand like that. They sat back and smiled, chatting and laughing. She nudged his leg with hers.

I couldn't rip my eyes from her. "She was on a date when I met her last weekend. Said she was never dating again."

"Then why are you stalking her?"

"It must be a friend. A good friend."

The server delivered our meals, a course at a time, and I watched as they received the same. She didn't look around the restaurant, so she didn't see me. Options one and two were a failure. Some other woman bought drinks for our table and I waved absently but didn't approach her.

After an hour of little conversation, Gianfranco was finishing his second drink. "You're the worst dinner date of all time."

"I know." Samantha's date left the table, so I stood and smoothed my jacket. Time for option three.

I hurried to her table before the man returned, forcing a smile as I walked. It was a friend or a brother. It had to be. I stopped beside her chair.

"Ciao, Samantha." It was short. And clipped. I must have sounded irritated. Perhaps I was.

Her face broke into a brilliant smile. "Antonio! Funny seeing you here!"

"Very funny."

"On a date or out with friends?"

'Waiting to see you' was not an appropriate response. I gestured across the dining room to my table. "My cousin, Frank."

Her smile faded in the awkward silence between us, and I pulled a chair over from the next table. I balanced on its edge, elbows on knees, leaning toward her. "And you? You look like you are having a good time. On a date?"

She paused, staring at me, then looking to where he had gone. All she said was "Um."

What kind of answer was 'Um?'

The crease deepened between her brows. "What are you doing?"

"I was working on *Number Vee* all day today. I finished it for you. Other than the varnish, which is drying."

"Thank you?"

"You were worried it wouldn't be done on time." I ran a hand through my hair and stared at the floor, my shoulders heaving. The irritation had left, replaced by desperation. "This is your uncle you are with?"

Her voice became smaller still. "No."

Her not-uncle returned and interrupted our conversation, polite, but an obvious challenge. "I hope you're not bothering my date." So much for 'Um.' So much for her never dating again.

I stood slowly, returning the chair, keeping my eyes on hers, the fire building in my belly. "And if I am?" I turned to him and took a step forward, stretching my height to prove I was taller. Only an inch, but I had him in height and breadth. Based on his pretty, polished appearance, I had him in experience, if it came to a fight. We stood eye-to-eye, engaged in a simple, unspoken conversation.

'She's mine.'

'No, she's mine.'

"If you're bothering her, then I'll have to ask the nice gentlemen here—" A few of the larger staff inched closer, their attention on the two of us. "To escort you out."

I kept my eyes on the competition. "Am I bothering you, Samantha?"

"No." Her voice quavered, and I wanted to hit him in his smug face for doing that to her. She was strong. Fiery. Not small.

"I came to tell her I was finished a contract I'm doing for her. Nothing more."

"Prosecutor Nathan Miller." He flashed a broad smile and extended his hand into the small gap between our chests, emphasis on his title.

I could play that game. "Doctor Antonio Ferraro." I took his hand, squeezed harder than he could, and pumped one time before letting go. "PhD."

"Yes, I know." There was a hint of superiority in his voice. "I'm...familiar with your family."

"How is that?"

"Not a concern for this evening. Now, if you don't mind, I'd like to sit back down with my date and finish our meal. I hope you'll do the same with whomever accompanied you." He smiled again, the smile of a man who had won the battle. But not the war, my friend. This woman was mine.

I turned back to her and hesitated for a moment, taking her hand, while *Prosecutor* Nathan Miller moved closer. "I'll call you Monday when you can come by for the painting." Her eyes locked on mine, those pale sea-like eyes. She put her free hand to her breast as we stared longer than we should have. I could have picked her up and taken her away right then. I couldn't be done with her on Monday. "And you can bring the Chagall at the same time. I'll take care of it for you."

I let go of her and shouldered my way past her date. Past Nathan Miller.

As I walked, my phone rang. Before I looked at it, I leaned toward one of the servers and requested my check.

It was my father. Marone, why did I agree to take the Chagall without speaking to him first? Pettiness. Jealousy. Those two never result in good choices.

"Papa, finally! Why didn't you return—"

"Antonio, my boy!" He was always so full of life and joy at the first hello.

"Did you get my message?"

"I did. I can't talk long, I'm exhausted. Missed flights and jet lag."

"Where are you?"

"Napoli! And don't ask why, it's a surprise!"

"It's the middle of the night there."

"Yes, yes. And I did receive your message. Good for you and Sofia deciding not to take that contract."

Cazzo! I squeezed my mouth shut.

"Here's what I need you to do. Take the copy of *Les amoureux* from my house and redo the authentication. You did it three months ago when we bought it, so it should be easy. I wouldn't be surprised if someone tried to pull a fast one on us and switched it at the last moment."

"Then what?"

"Then we decide what to do next based on the answer."

As I reached my cousin, I sagged into the chair. "Alright, I'll do it tomorrow and call you back."

"And whatever you do, don't let your mother know. She's terrible at keeping secrets!"

"I know."

"If ours is a fake, they'll pay for this. However, then the one Foster Mutual brought in could be the authentic one.

Let me know when you're done."

"Alright, thank you, Papa. Now get some sleep."

I hung up and put the phone on the table.

Gianfranco was on his third Scotch. "That didn't look like it went well."

"I don't think it could have gone worse unless I had punched him." I ran a hand through my hair. "The check is on its way."

"Might have made you feel better?"

"Sì, you have a good point."

Now, not only was I lying to Samantha, I had to lie to my mother. Sneak a painting out of her house, and hope it was a fake.

Chapter 16

Samantha

We watched Antonio make his way back to his table, slowly sitting as the distance between us grew. A server arrived at their table and placed a leather check holder on it, then they stood and left.

What a disaster.

I'd wanted to slap him for showing up and taking my one night of distraction away, for not letting me enjoy one evening without him invading my thoughts. At the same time, I'd wanted him to scoop me up in his arms and carry me away.

"A jealous ex I never heard about?" Nathan reached over and put a hand on my knee, his brows raised in concern.

"No, business associate." I'm sure Nathan wasn't buying that line. Antonio had been strangely intense, and the way he stared at me before he left, it was as though he was trying to say something.

He frowned. "He looked at you like you belonged to him."

I frowned back. "That's ridiculous." But wouldn't it be wonderful?

"Sam, a man typically only does that—" He waved his hands generally at where they'd stood, puffed chest to puffed chest. "—over a woman."

"You got in his face. You said we were on a date."

"Because I didn't like the way he was talking to you."

"What does it matter to you? Aren't the three of you trying to convince me to settle down in Brenton? Shouldn't you be encouraging me to find someone? Why not him?"

"Why not him?" His mouth gaped open for a moment. "Sam, he's a Ferraro!"

"So what?"

He put his hands on the table and waved mine forward. He took them and stared me square in the eyes. "They're dangerous. They're connected."

I pulled my hands away from his and rolled my eyes. "What, because they're Italian?"

"Do you swear to keep what I'm about to tell you an absolute secret?"

"Yeah."

The sound system at the restaurant was sufficient to ensure everyone's conversations were nothing but a dull murmur. However, he pulled his seat closer to mine and leaned in to whisper. "I'm working with the FBI on a smuggling ring case."

I jerked my head back to see him clearly. "You are not!"

He waved me back in. "There's a Ferraro family outside Rome with some level of involvement. I can't say more."

"What does that have to do with Antonio?"

"They're Ferraros. They're family."

"Ridiculous. Do you have any idea how many Ferraros there are in Italy?" It should have been rhetorical, but I pulled out my phone and did a web search, flashing the results at him. "Over forty thousand! That's not proof of anything. Don't make leaps like that!" Especially when it involved my love life. Wait, not my love life. I didn't date.

"Well, I didn't like the way he looked at you."

"You said that already." I shoved his shoulder and he moved his seat back. "Now, can we get back to talking about you? I think I was saying something like...you'll get over her, you'll be fine, blah, blah."

He sat back and smiled as we resumed our meal.

"I'd also say I could set you up with a friend of mine, but I don't have any. I do have a co-worker—"

"I'm not ready yet. I should stick to dinner with you whenever I'm lonely."

"As long as you're paying." I nudged his leg with my foot and he laughed.

We caught up on the last couple of years and had a great evening, although Antonio's appearance hung over me. He was all I thought about on my way home, he and Nathan sizing each other up for a fight.

Why did Antonio have to come into my life? If I were in Brenton long-term, I would have said he was perfect. It was a game, though, some macho challenge because I kept turning him down. Maybe I should go out with him, sleep with him, and be done with him. The challenge would be over, and he'd leave me alone.

I sighed. No, more likely I'd fall for him, I'd get my heart broken, and I'd want to be on my way out of town the next day. But I had to stay in town for Cass. Eight more months. Maybe I'd call Antonio for one night of bliss after her reconstruction.

That was probably the stupidest idea I'd ever had.
Or maybe the smartest.

CHAPTER 17

ANTONIO

Two steps through the back door of the studio and Sofia was hollering at me.

"Antonio, where have you been? You were due back from lunch an hour ago."

I shook my head and walked in silence to my worktable, placing the items I had brought with me to the side. The white box on top of the envelope.

Nathan Miller was Samantha's friend, her 'Um.' She had been with someone else the week before, so there was no committed relationship. She was fair game. She said no flirting, but I could be thoughtful. Thoughtful was not flirting.

Although she would be moving away in the spring. I stared at the little stack. Perhaps I should throw them out. This was stupid. There was no future with her.

"I can smell you from here!" Sofia rounded the reception wall, and everyone had a good laugh.

"Too much?" I inhaled the delicious scent of vanilla and amber. "It's wonderful."

"Everyone here is in jeans and t-shirts, Antonio. You stand out like a sore thumb." Her stilettos clicked as she stalked toward me to loosen the tie. "Exactly like Friday."

"I look good, Sofia. It's professional." I smoothed the navy jacket and straightened the pocket square.

Gianfranco peered up from his work and chimed in. "You always look good, you jackass. But there's no way you're working in that outfit."

Alice waved a hand in front of her face and joined the teasing. "The cologne is a bit strong."

"When's she coming in?" Sofia undid the jacket buttons and the top couple of the shirt. She smirked as she did it, always taunting, but always taking care of me.

"Who?" I raised an eyebrow in mock innocence.

She smacked the side of my head. "The pretty insurance adjuster." She dragged the jacket off and walked to my private office to store it. "And roll those sleeves up."

I folded my arms in protest and followed her into the office. "You said impressing women is what I do. Did you see her suit on Friday? I'm sure it was Prada. I must dress to match."

She put a hand on her hip, shifting to lecture. "Gianfranco told me about the restaurant Saturday night. I thought you would be done with her."

Shrugging, I closed the door behind us. "I'm stubborn."

"Understatement." She rolled her eyes and leaned on the desk. "Did you hear from Papa?"

As I shook my head, my phone rang. "Speak of the devil!" I placed it on the desk and answered on speaker.

"Ciao, Papa," we said together.

"Antonio, Sofia! How are you doing today, my lovely children?"

I pointed to myself, taking the lead on the call, as I sat in the seat behind the desk. "Good. Did you get my message about your painting last night?"

"I did. Excellent news! You are very fast."

"Grazie. What is the plan now? Can I tell the insurance adjuster her painting is a fake?" I picked up a pen from the desk and drew absently on the message pad.

"No."

My pen stopped and my chest tightened. I thought he would say that but hoped otherwise. "Why not?"

"She's there from Foster Mutual. Someone is claiming the insurance money for it. Assuming they know it's a fake, that's insurance fraud. Is the adjuster clever?"

I started sketching again, smiling. "Brilliant."

Sofia shoved my arm, causing a stray line across the sheet. I looked up to frown at her, which she was already doing to me.

"Then if you tell her the painting's a fake, what's the first question she'll ask?"

"How do I know?"

"And you'll tell her your parents own the original, and she'll ask..."

"So many things." Leaning back in the chair, I stared at Sofia. I should have told Samantha the truth when I first saw it. "Why did I not tell her Friday? What am I covering up? Are we involved in the fraud?"

"Exactly. And even if we aren't, any investigation could hurt the business."

I blew out a long breath.

Sofia lowered her head toward the phone slowly. "Papa? Is there something else going on we should know about?"

"There is, Sofia. I'll tell you when I get home, in person, not on the phone. But, you need to know, we can't risk this blowing up. Antonio, you need to get to the bottom of it."

"I do?" I sat up straight in the chair, looking at the flowers I'd drawn. The flowers from Samantha's dress Saturday night.

"You've authenticated *Les amoureux* twice now. You should have no problem proving hers is a fake. Go through the steps you would otherwise. Make sure the adjuster has everything she needs. Work with her to figure out who's behind this."

"Sì, Papa."

His words grew sharper, the longer he spoke. "I left Roma because of this sort of activity and I will not tolerate it in my backyard. The message will be clear. I will not have our name associated with this."

"So, you want me to continue lying to her?" The fire was building in my belly. "And not only that, spy on her investigation, telling her more lies."

Sofia put a hand on my arm.

"Yes, Antonio. This is important for our business, for our family. And Sofia—"

"Yes?"

"I already told Antonio. Not a word to your mother. I can't imagine the fury if she found someone had forged a duplicate of her anniversary gift."

"Alright, Papa." Sofia hung up and leaned next to me. "What do you think?"

"I was hoping to tell her the truth today." I stared at the silent phone. I slammed a fist on the desk, startling Sofia. "Cazzo!"

She put the hand on my arm again, but I jerked it away.

"Give me a moment alone. I need to figure something out."

She stood from the desk and headed for the door. "There are other women in the world, little brother. Women who intend to stay in Brenton, who don't turn you down, and who aren't at restaurants with other men."

I checked my watch, avoiding her glare. Samantha would be wondering why I hadn't called her yet. "It's not just that, Sofia. It's the lies. I could have explained away not telling her on Friday, and we would have been done with the deception. She would have her truth, and maybe I—"

Sofia paused at the door. "You know Papa is right."

I nodded, the pit in my stomach widening. "I know. She's too clever to accept a simple explanation."

Sofia left and closed the door behind her. She was right. How could a woman who moved around too much for children ever be right for me? I could change her mind about dating, but the rest? I added to the drawing of the flowers. And then there were the lies and the deception. What could I do? Tell her the truth anyway and deal with the consequences? There was something else going on Papa wouldn't speak about on the phone. It was bigger than this moment, bigger than my conscience.

Perhaps the police would find evidence of something sinister at the house. Arson, perhaps. If they concluded that, the claim might be denied and the authenticity of the painting would no longer matter.

The phone rang, and I startled. It was her.

A deep breath to calm myself, and I answered. "Samantha, it's good to hear from you."

"Oh, Antonio, hello!" She sounded as though she hadn't known who she was calling. Her voice calmed my nerves, as I smiled at the stilted words. "Sorry, I—you said you'd call and—I hadn't heard from you—"

"Do you have time to bring it by now?"

"Yeah, Lucy and I are at the office between appointments. We can be there in about ten minutes? If that's alright?"

Smoothing my loose tie, the smile crept further up my face. She was still nervous and excited to see me. This was good news, despite the fiasco Saturday night and the instructions from my father.

"Thanks so much for fitting it in. I know you're busy."

"Never too busy for you." Too forward?

"Oh, um, okay?"

No matter. I would be forward. "I anxiously await your arrival."

I hung up, rubbing a thumb across my lips. This would be a dangerous game. For my family, our business, for my heart.

Chapter 18

Samantha

I sat still for a moment with the phone at my ear before sliding it onto my desk. Lucy, Hailey, and Mike were all staring at me. I didn't have to turn around to confirm it.

Hailey was the first. "Well, I guess we finally know what Super Caine's weakness is."

Lucy claimed second. "So, Sam, am I coming with you, or is this another private appointment?"

Stupid. I should have called him from one of the conference rooms. *I anxiously await your arrival.* Breathing slowly while my heart came back to normal levels, I shut my laptop. "No, you're coming with me."

"Should I get changed?"

"Yeah. He's making time in his schedule for the Scotts' Chagall." I kept my gaze on my gear, as I packed up. Lucy tore out to her car for her backup clothes.

Mike went third, although he wasn't on the same path as the women. "Oh right, I forgot. The police report came in this morning on the Scott fire."

Too fast, like Janelle said. "Lucy and I need to run. Summary?"

"No arson, no foul play. Fire and death were accidents."

"That's a relief." And not unexpected.

"The son already sent in an estimate to get the repairs done to the house, and replacing the items they lost, so I sent the check request over to Cliff to authorize. My contact at AmLife told me they've already sent her the death and accidental death benefits."

The heat in my cheeks had receded, so I looked up. "Wow, everyone's moving at full throttle."

"We were all ready to go once the police department released their report. How's your claim looking?"

I shook my head. "Not as good as yours. We'll hold Ferraro's to their one-month contract, but it'll take that long to get it clean enough to make the comparisons."

"Roger won't be happy. I guess he was friends with Mr. Scott or something. Word on the street is he wanted the whole thing wrapped up fast."

"Yeah, I got the message last week. But there's nothing I can do."

Hailey chimed in, "Except visit Dr. Ant—"

I held up a hand to stop her, keeping it up as I left.

· · · ● · ● · ● · · ·

"Samantha! Lucy!" announced Sofia as we entered. She stood, walked around the desk, and greeted each of us with kisses to each cheek. "You two look beautiful!"

The classical music was playing again. "You won the battle of the bands today?"

"Antonio hates Vivaldi." She gave a wicked grin and disappeared around the reception wall as we sat.

"I love this place!" Lucy whispered.

His thick footsteps drowned out the click of Sofia's stilettos from around the corner, and I took a steadying breath. After Saturday, what should I expect? Why had he been there? What was he trying to say in that silence?

Sofia rounded the corner first. "Dr. Ferraro will see you now."

Navy blue dress pants today. Same style as Friday, plus a loose tie. Only two buttons undone at his neck. Not quite as ravishing as the black suit Saturday night, but close. Really close.

Lucy was out of her seat in a flash, while I stood slowly.

"Dr. Ferraro, Lucy Chapman." She stepped between us and shot out her hand. "We met last week? I'm Sam's partner at Foster Mutual. We're here to pick up the Mason's Gallery painting."

"Then you have come to the right place." He grinned at her and continued to me. I put out a hand to shake, but he pulled it to him, bowed slightly, and kissed it. Instinctively, I pressed my lips together to make sure my lipstick was on correctly. A brief fantasy about grabbing his tie to pull him toward me passed through my brain, but I blinked it away. Shit, I hope he didn't notice that. Or the stutter in my breath.

"Ciao, bella." Slow to release my hand, he cocked his head, and my pulse quickened. Wow, things had changed since Friday. "Your eyes, they were more like jade on Friday."

"Blue shirt." I held his gaze and, for once, the heat wasn't filling my cheeks. It was taking up residence much lower.

"Bella means beautiful, doesn't it?" asked Lucy.

I brushed it off, trying to recover my senses. "It's slang for a girl."

He narrowed his eyes at me. "It does mean beautiful." Turning to her, he continued. "But in Italia, some use it to refer to any girl."

"Well, we're not in Italy right now!" Her laugh was in my direction.

"I like her." He gestured to Lucy. "She understands me."

We walked into the studio, and Lucy gasped. "This space is amazing! It reminds me of a shop my parents took me to once in Greece, where they made books. Open, airy, big workspaces. Did you know—"

"Lucy." I put a hand on her arm before she started spouting statistics. She clammed up.

The female restorer was at the front of the room, with two of the rolling tables together, working on a painting I estimated at ten feet tall. Lucy drifted over to it, and I followed her, curious.

It was a portrait of a semi-reclined woman in a voluminous blue and purple dress, holding a sword. At her feet lay an empty plate and a whip, and she rested on a wooden wheel covered in metal studs, with a large crack through its middle.

"Saint Catherine of Alexandria," I mused. "Italian Baroque. Late sixteenth or early seventeenth century?"

The restorer nodded appreciatively. "Dead on. How do you know?"

"Saint Catherine was martyred in the fourth century in Roman Egypt because she was a Christian. She was a brilliant young woman and convinced hundreds to convert." I pointed to the elements of the painting that stood out to me. "The emperor wanted to make an example of her. First, they whipped her, but angels tended her wounds. Then they starved her, but the dove of God fed her. The emperor was frustrated his plans failed, so she was to be broken on the wheel, but it shattered when she touched it. In the end, they got out a sword and lopped her head off."

"I didn't know all of that," said the restorer. "You know your saints!"

"Not to mention your Italian Baroque." Antonio stood precariously close to me, hands casually tucked into his pockets. He leaned close enough to keep his words private. "Impressive again."

I tried ignoring him, but the air around him intruded on the air around me, and the scent of vanilla overcame me. All it would take was one step to back into him and feel his body against mine. Bad idea. But so tempting.

The restorer continued. "This was flown in from a church in France last month. I've been dying to work on it." She stood back for a moment, admiring her early progress.

Focus on the painting, Sam. "This reminds me of the one Caravaggio did of her. Just a cleaning?"

She nodded again. "My name's Alice, by the way." She gave Antonio a look. I introduced myself and Lucy, but we didn't shake since her hands were clean and under gloves. She was maybe Lucy's age, a little round at the edges, and pretty.

Antonio said, "They gave me trouble for not introducing them the last time you were here. Alice has been with us for five years. At the easel is Zander, but he wears headphones most of the time, so he'll not say hello."

He walked us over to the third restorer and introduced him. "My cousin Gianfranco, but he insists on being called

Frank." He paused, avoiding my gaze for a moment. "I was having dinner with him Saturday night."

How could I forget?

Frank, like his cousin, had the dark southern Italian hair, olive skin, and deep brown eyes, but the similarities ended there. He was my height, light on muscle, had a disfigured nose which had seen one too many fights, and his face invited you to sit and have a beer, rather than to swoon.

And the restorers were all in jeans. Antonio was the only one dressed up, aside from Lucy and me. And Sofia.

After finishing the introductions, he ushered us to his work desk, and Lucy navigated her way between us.

Number Vee sat near the middle of his desk, in all its three stripes of glory. To the side sat two manila envelopes and a small white boxboard container tied with a string. Antonio retrieved some paperwork from the top envelope and reviewed it with us.

"There was a tear four inches long exactly here." He pointed to the spot where the painting had been torn, but I couldn't see any difference between that area and the rest of the light blue stripe. "At the north end of the tear, it extended one-eighth of an inch to the painting's left side." He continued to explain the steps he'd gone through to make the repair, and we listened quietly.

Once he finished, he returned the paperwork to the envelope and slid it back into the stack. "All of the paints and the varnish are archival and fully reversible. If another repair is required, this work can be removed first." He folded his arms, clearly proud of himself. "It's perfetto, no?"

"Impressive," said Lucy. "I can't tell this was ever torn!"

I, on the other hand, excused myself to grab a flashlight and a magnifying loupe from under the desk. Time to test Dr. Ferraro's work.

I shone the light at the spot where the damage had been and got close. I looked at it directly from the front, then from each side, noticing how the brush strokes of the repair matched the original, as though the artist himself had put them there. No bumps or lines indicated where he'd patched the hole. I examined even closer with the loupe.

"Can you take it over to one of the easels?" I asked.

He picked it up, and we all went to look at it in the direct sunlight beaming in the window. Sunshine often spoiled a restoration effort, as the colors could vary under different types of light. I took another close look, using the loupe. It was perfect.

I stepped back, genuinely impressed. "This is fantastic work! The colors are right, the fill in the voids is invisible, and the texture matches the original."

"Grazie."

"Did you really do all this Saturday? And you still had time to go out for dinner?"

"I did. I'm pleased with it." He smiled at the painting but flicked his eyes at me with a smirk. "To be honest, I started Friday after you left."

"Even still, amazing work." The curator from Mason's was wrong about him being talentless hack who had to get by on charm alone. Granted, there was a lot of charm. "Alright, let's sign the paperwork and get on to the Chagall."

CHAPTER 19

ANTONIO

"Such a shame," I said as Samantha opened the case with the burned painting on my desk to withdraw the paperwork. While she found the correct pages for my signature, I slid the painting over to inspect it again. Stupid burned painting. She had done well to spot the signature at the bottom right. I knew the best place to start was with one of the strips along the middle, but perhaps I would take her recommendation. It should make her proud of her investigative skills.

"The loss of a Chagall? No kidding." She pulled out the correct sheet and handed me a pen.

"It's a good thing they have insurance." Time to begin the charade. "Many people don't properly insure their art. Who owned it? Are they local?"

"Yes, local."

"Bobby and Olivia Scott."

"Lucy—not necessary information."

"Oh, sorry." Lucy covered her mouth, embarrassed, but I was grateful for the slip. Papa had bought it from Bobby, and the fire at their house fit with the timing of this claim.

Samantha sighed and looked to me. "Now that that information is out there, I should ask if there's any conflict about this contract, given that you knew him?"

"No conflict. I only spoke with him a few times." I hesitated before signing. "However, we are very busy. I'll do my best, but we may have a problem with the thirty days."

"No." Samantha was sharp. To the point. "I'm holding you to your thirty-day contractual obligation."

"Mr. Scott died in the fire. The police are investigating, sì? Surely you won't close the claim before they finish?"

"Except the police are already done." She clamped her lips shut a moment, shaking her head. "They closed their case. Now all the insurance will pay out, except for mine."

So much for the police rescuing me. "This is upsetting you?"

"I'm behind the eight ball here, Antonio. Not a comfortable position. We need to get this done as fast as possible. I don't want to take it to Detroit or anywhere else. Your work on *Number Vee* was amazing and fast." She tapped on the paperwork, where I had not yet signed. "Can you pull off the same magic for me on this?"

Magic was not causing the knot in my stomach, but it was what I wanted to give her. I could tell her—right then and there—and still have a chance. But no. I had a duty to my father, to my family. "I'll do my best, Samantha." I signed quickly, handing the pen back to her.

"That's what I need."

Lucy grabbed the signed sheet and managed all the paperwork. "We all done?"

Samantha smiled at her and nodded.

"Thanks for everything!" Lucy squeezed in between us, shook my hand yet again with her energetic smile, and took the case for Mason's. She headed off with it, and Samantha turned with her, but I touched her arm, and she shied away from it.

As she turned, the knot in my stomach grew tighter. I lowered my voice. "I wanted to apologize about Saturday."

"No need."

"There is. I had worked for two days solid on *Number Vee* and was not quite myself."

"It's fine, really." She began to turn, but I held her arm again to stop her. This time, she faced me without breaking free.

"Could you pass my apologies on to your boyfriend?" My heart lodged itself in my throat at the prospect of her answer.

"Boyfriend? Nathan?" She wrinkled her nose, the best response possible.

"Really? He said you were his date."

"He's my stand-in big brother. And a little overprotective sometimes."

Thank heavens. I slid the white box over. Was I about to overstep my bounds? "I was thinking of you this morning. I thought you might like this." I picked it up and handed it to her.

"Oh?"

"Shall I open it for you?"

Her hands were unsteady, and she nodded. I undid the string slowly, our eyes locked. My breath became shallower, as I imagined undressing her the same way I undressed the box. She must have felt it, as well. Her pupils grew wide, and she didn't even look at what I had given her. Not my intention but wonderful.

As I finished, my hands fell to the sides of the box, covering hers. Unlike at Caruther's, this was a moment we were sharing. The slowness of time. The tilting of the axis. The rightness.

Someone in the room cleared their throat and we both immediately looked into the box. When she saw the cornetto I had brought from Russo's, she laughed so hard she almost dropped it. I winked at her, unable to contain my pleasure.

"This, as well." I handed her the thick, heavy envelope. "It's something you may want to read sometime when you are tired and can't sleep."

She slid the document out and her eyes lit when she read the cover page. "Your doctoral dissertation? Oh my god, I can't wait to read it!"

"You are trying to make me feel good, sì?"

She hugged it to her breast and shook her head. "You're so thoughtful. I needed something like this today."

"Bad day?"

"To be honest, the police closing the case bothered me more than it should."

I had withheld from comforting her so many times already, but I didn't care this time. I put my hand on her shoulder, rubbing gently with my thumb, wanting nothing more than to pull her into an embrace. Why did she have to be so perfect for me and yet so wrong at the same time?

I stepped closer, feeling her air, so close she had to look up. "Is there anything I can do to make it better?"

"You already have." She smiled softly. Without a blush for the first time.

Chapter 20

SAMANTHA

I took off work early on Wednesday afternoon after tweaking my schedule to wrap up by two o'clock. The Scott claim was weighing on me, as were the excessive hours I'd been keeping. I needed some time to relax.

Entering through the lobby of the hotel, I waved to the staff and snagged a complimentary cookie and bottle of water. Cass wanted me in an apartment, but an extended-stay hotel was furnished, had Wi-Fi, and was easier to leave at a moment's notice. And housekeeping was included.

In my room, I kicked off my boots and crashed on the couch. I reached over to the table where Antonio's dissertation lay. It was 342 pages on his method for conserving ancient frescoes, through the use of specific nanotechnology, bacteria, and short-pulse lasers. He wasn't a talentless hack—he was brilliant. I'd made it through the first hundred pages but lost focus.

I wandered aimlessly around the rooms of my little suite. Bath? Nap? Food? Read?

Motorcycle. Yes! I grabbed my leather suit, threw on a tank top and pulled on the riding pants and boots.

Soon enough, I was on the road, heading out of town leaving my cares in the dust. Out to the cornfields, apple orchards, and the long straight roads of Michigan. No plans. No goals. Just me and the motorcycle. All the time and no one to answer to.

Until my phone rang. The wake word for my headset was out of my mouth in a second. But before I could tell it to decline, it read out the caller's name. "Incoming call from Ferraro's Fine Ar—"

I hit the call button on the side of my helmet before the name was finished. "Samantha Caine speaking."

"Samantha," came the deeply accented Italian, deliberate, like he was tasting each syllable of my name. "This is Antonio Ferraro calling, from Ferraro's Fi—"

"Hi, Antonio. What can I do for you?"

"I need you to come to my office. Now."

"Hold on a minute." I slowed and pulled off the side of the highway. "Say that again?"

"I need you to come to my office," he repeated.

"Why?"

"There is something you need to see on the Chagall."

"Something?"

"Sì, this is important."

"One sec." I punched Ferraro's location into my GPS. "I'm about a half hour away."

"Can you come?"

"Yeah, I'll be there in thirty minutes," I said, and he hung up.

Was there something wrong with it? Were we back to him refusing to clean it? I was miffed at being summoned,

't entirely with him. It was more at myself for
he opportunity to see him again.

· · · · · · · · · · ·

True to the GPS' estimate, thirty minutes later, I pulled up
in front of Ferraro's. I turned the bike off and walked into
the building, pulling off my helmet once inside.

Sofia smiled at me from her chair but didn't get up.
Antonio was already there, leaning against her desk, arms
folded. How long had he been standing there? Today, he
was in pale jeans again, with a blue V-neck shirt and white
sneakers. Usually so clean and tidy, he had dark stains on his
clothes.

"You're dirtier than usual." I cringed. That sounded rude,
didn't it?

"Sì, your Chagall is filthy." He uncrossed his arms and
strode across the room to me.

"True."

But he walked right past me. "You ride a motorcycle?"
He looked out one of the large front windows. "A Ducati?"

"Yeah?"

He crossed his arms and tilted his head, smirking at me.

"What?" I asked, when we'd been staring too long.

Sofia got up and walked over to me, taking the helmet
and placing it on her desk. "Antonio, show her."

"Sì, sì! Andiamo." He beckoned me to join him. As we
walked into the studio area in the back, he explained. "As
promised, I'm doing my best. I worked on your burned
painting a couple of hours each day. It's tedious and
difficult work, and I can't focus on it longer than that."

"Thanks for starting on it so quickly." Given the pressure to rush along the claim, this news finally let me exhale. Maybe it wouldn't be such a disaster, after all.

The three restorers were working away in the studio space, barely noticing our progress through the space.

"I've been going through my father's notebooks for any references to similarly burned paintings." He waved his hands in the air. "Decades of paper."

"Did you find anything?

We rounded his desk to look at the painting. He'd stabilized the burned edges, so they wouldn't crumble when he removed the frame and stretcher. The photos I'd left with him were taped to the side of the desk and the formerly pristine white surface was covered in soot and debris.

"Only that we need to hire a summer student or something to digitize his work." He handed me a pair of disposable gloves, putting his own on, as well. "I added some canvas underneath the burned areas to give them strength. I started at the bottom right, where you pointed out the signature, dabbing with a dry sponge."

I nodded, still not understanding what was going on, but I pulled out my phone to snap a picture for the claim file.

"Then, I saw this." He held up the sponge from his table. He pointed to a small speck of black, one out of dozens.

"Saw what?"

He placed it on the table again, got out the magnifying loupe, and held it in place for me over a different speck. "Look closely. What do you see?"

I leaned down to look through the loupe and focused for a moment. "It looks like a fragment of charred wood. I found the painting under a piano; the legs had burned out from underneath it. Is that what this is?"

"Sì, now look here." He moved the loupe to the first bit of black he had shown me on the sponge.

I leaned back down to look closer. This one was different. It was smooth, not like wood at all; it looked like a tiny sweep of paint. "Some of the paint is coming off?"

"Sì!" He looked from me to the Chagall and back again, as though I should have made the same connection he obviously already had.

"Antonio, I'm sure some paint will crack off after this much damage."

"No, no, no! Hold this and look." He handed me the loupe and pointed to the spot on the canvas where the signature was barely revealed from his initial cleaning efforts.

As I watched, he took a scalpel and lifted a part of the signature. I still didn't get it. Then he ran the blade along other sections of paint in the same area. Nothing came up.

I stood and stared at him in a mix of fascination and panic. "The signature was added after the varnish?" Varnish always came last and it sealed everything in. The signature should be under the varnish, like the rest of the paint, but it was on top instead.

"Sì!"

I put one hand up slowly to my mouth, covering my gaping jaw. I looked at him and then back to it.

"Oh, shit," I whispered. "It's a fake."

CHAPTER 21

ANTONIO

"No, no, no, no." She shook her head, staring at the painting. I had given her the first piece of evidence and had to wait for her to draw the conclusions. "This painting was confirmed by the Chagall Committee in 2015. It can't be a fake. Maybe the varnish burned off in the fire?"

"The other paints are still sealed."

"Maybe he signed it after he finished it. Some artists did that, especially if they didn't like the painting."

"Sì, possibile."

She turned to me suddenly. "Computer? Do you have a computer I can use?"

I led her to my office, my daytime sanctuary. It sat in the front corner of the studio, furthest away from reception. The wall opposite the door had a row of glass windows which would have looked onto Via Calabria, were they not frosted over for privacy, and long flat drawers underneath. The walls were painted a cool blue with green undertone, a tint of manganese reflecting a foggy morning sky. Along the wall to the right, a black leather couch held decorative pillows Sofia had insisted on, and my diplomas hung above. The other wall was covered in bookshelves. Conservation manuals, art history books, historic auction guides, and a few pieces of sculpture.

But more importantly for Samantha, a desk at the center with the computer, my office chair, and two visitor chairs. I unlocked the computer as she sat. She removed her jacket and threw it on one of the spare chairs, revealing a tank top under the leather motorcycle outfit. While she frantically typed, I stood behind her, admiring.

"This is the Foster claims system. I can access everything from here." She whipped through screen after screen until she landed on a page where the photos and documentation were available for the claim. She pulled up a high-resolution photo of the painting and zoomed in as close as she could to the area of the signature. "This was taken when they sent it off to the Chagall Committee. We've got all the supporting data, which will be a huge help."

I leaned over her shoulder to get a better look, resting a hand on her back, where the tank top didn't shield her skin from me. She rolled the chair to give me a better view of the monitor, but I held steady, feeling her breath pick up.

"I don't see anything here, do you?"

Placing my hand on top of hers, I used the mouse to move the image around. Her hand was warm and surprisingly stable for how often it shook. She was getting used to me. She held her breath, staring at the screen while I leaned over her shoulder.

"Niente." There was nothing helpful on this image.

As I took my hand away from hers, she closed the image and we were left looking at a file list of attached documents. I spotted what I needed. "Open the ultraviolet photo?"

The picture I had asked for was of the painting, but the colors were all different. It had been taken under an ultraviolet light, which revealed things hidden from the naked eye.

"Zoom in on the signature," I said.

Once the section was enlarged, I gestured to a haze hanging over it. "This is an old layer of varnish. It shows up as this green; you can see it over the signature and the background. It says to me the varnish was applied after the signature paint." I stood up straight, knowing there was nothing more I needed to see.

She swiveled the chair to face me. "Can you take a similar picture of the burned one?"

"Sì, we can, but not yet." The two best photos for proof would be the x-ray or the infrared, but I hadn't cleaned enough of the debris for either of those. The corner with the signature had some promise under ultraviolet but it wouldn't be conclusive. All the same, it would show progress. "The dirt and soot would stop me from getting a good shot. I need to spend some more time with it. Then we can determine if the signature is flaking because the varnish was damaged in the fire or not."

"How much time do you think you'll need?"

"Between our backlog and committed contracts, I can only do a couple of hours a day. But I promise I'll do some every day. You will owe me after this for all the overtime I'm doing."

She rolled her eyes and turned her attention back to the file list in the claims system. "I wonder...Jimmy!"

"Jimmy?"

"An old friend of mine wrote the police report. I'll call him with some questions."

"Anything interesting?"

"Not really." She leaned back in the chair. "If it's a fake, maybe it was stolen and replaced? I'll call and ask a few questions."

As she rolled the chair back, I stood and held out a hand to help her up.

She waved it off. "I'm good. Thanks for calling."

"Prego, you are welcome."

"You know you don't have to translate for me, right?"

"Old habits."

Her eyes twinkled as she raised an eyebrow. "Like telling me I'll owe you for doing your job? You really can't turn it off, can you?"

"Oh, the lady strikes first this time." I put a dramatic hand on my chest.

"Anyway, thanks for starting on this. It's going to be a long road, isn't it?"

"I make no promises, Samantha, except to do my best."

"You already told me you're the best, right?" She smacked me gently in my chest, and her eyes lingered on the spot longer than they should have.

"I am." I winked and flashed her a provocative smirk. "You shall see soon enough."

"Alright." She rolled her eyes, making her way around the desk, toward the chair where she'd thrown her jacket. For a moment, her eyes drifted over the bookshelves, and I thought she might stop to peruse. "If there's nothing else, I'm heading out for that ride."

I followed her, taking in the dramatic view. The leather pants were breathtaking on her round ass, and my soul cried as she slid on the jacket, covering those magnificent arms. I leaned against the desk, crossing my ankles and folding my arms.

"Let me know when you've made some more progress. I'm interested in the ultraviolet results."

"Parting is such sweet sorrow," I sighed dramatically, eliciting a laugh from her.

She stopped at the door and turned to look at me, rolling her eyes. But she smiled and finished the line from *Romeo and Juliet*. "That I shall say good night till it be morrow." She bowed slightly and gave a flourish with her hand.

"You ride a motorcycle and climb rocks. Yet, you can pick out a sixteenth-century Baroque painting, and you finish my Shakespeare. You are a mystery to me, Samantha Caine."

The corner of her mouth rose slightly, launching a sea of butterflies to swirl about my stomach. She was as brilliant as she was beautiful. "I'm a pretty simple girl, in the end."

I gripped the edge of the desk to hold myself in place. "Not in the slightest, I think."

"You barely know me. Just wait, you'll see."

"I would like to. Perhaps over dinner?"

The almost-smile faded, her mouth tightening into an almost-frown. "Antonio, we talked about this. You need to stop asking."

How long could she deny our chemistry? Our similarities? The look in her eyes when she was near me? She hadn't left yet, so perhaps today was the day.

"I told you, I'm stubborn." I pushed off the desk and took a slow step toward her. "I like you, Samantha. Very much."

"I'm serious." She eased back against the door as I got closer, her breath picking up, gaze dropping to my mouth and back up again. But she was not serious. She was nervous and I could nudge her past that.

"As am I." I moistened my lips, her eyes widening and body wavering slightly toward me. Three-date rule be damned, I wanted to kiss her. Grab her, hold her close, and taste every inch of her. I leaned against the door, arm next to her head, and lowered my voice. "Just say yes."

Her jacket creaked as she placed a hand against her abdomen, the other curling around the door handle. The green of her stunning irises was practically swallowed by her pupils. "Antonio, I..."

When she paused, I took over, attempting to keep my words light. "It's not a sin to confess your interest."

Her free hand inched toward me, and I moved closer, tilting my head.

"I can't," she whispered, her fingers brushing against my stomach, a light burst of mint wafting from her mouth.

"You can."

Before our lips met, before I found paradise, she squeezed her eyes shut, clenching her fingers in my shirt. Her words tumbled out in a rapid tremolo. "I—I'm dating Nathan."

All the air rushed out of me, and I stepped away, my shirt snapping out of her grip. This couldn't be. "But you said —"

Her face pinched, and she stood there, staring. Doing nothing more than blinking and breathing. I couldn't read a single emotion. What was going through her head? 'What a pathetic fool this Antonio Ferraro is. Look at how easily he falls at my feet.'

She turned suddenly, the long braid swinging behind her, and slipped out of the office. Leaving me two steps from where she had stood, with no more of her than the scent of her leather suit on the air.

I sagged into the nearest chair. Elbows on knees, I leaned down, cradling my head. She had said he was her stand-in big brother. Wrinkled her nose at the suggestion of dating him.

She had been my anchor for eleven years. My solace each time my heart had broken.

And she was a liar, just like every other woman.

CHAPTER 22

SAMANTHA

I threw on the jacket and helmet without a word to Sofia and tore out of Ferraro's, heading for the solace of my bike.

He'd been about to kiss me. The hairs on my neck had stood up and every inch of my body gravitated toward him. All except that stupid voice in the back of my head telling me he was all wrong.

Why the hell did I tell him I was dating Nathan? What was the matter with me? Why was I so desperate to put a wall up between us? Every time Antonio got too close, I panicked.

It didn't matter. There was work to do. The Chagall Committee. They had to be correct. In 2015, they determined the painting was authentic.

I hit the highway in record time. The hum of the engine, my body cutting through the air, whizzing past the other vehicles in the passing lane.

I'd known a man like him before. Fell for him, even. Thought he was going to move here to be with me. But I was nothing more than a challenge. A conquest. One date, five dates, who knew? As soon as he had me on my back, he'd throw me away. Or string me along for months until he was tired of me. And then where would I be? Heartbroken. And still stuck in fucking Brenton, Michigan, forced to work with him unless I turned away all the claims that actually mattered to me.

I could call him. Turn around and go back. He kept asking me to dinner. Why couldn't 'yes' come out of my mouth just once? The prickles started in my fingertips as I moved from lane to lane around the slow-moving vehicles. Why was everyone going so slow? Didn't they know I needed speed to think?

I glanced at my speedometer. *Shit!* A hundred and sixty-five miles an hour. I eased off the gas and pulled the bike off the highway. Idling on the narrow shoulder, buffeted by the wind from passing vehicles, I stared at acres of corn growing under the warm summer sun.

Why would Antonio want me? A man who wanted to stay in Brenton and have his children work with him. He wanted a family. I had, too, once upon a time. Why couldn't I have met him instead of Matt all those years ago? I tore off my helmet and rubbed roughly at my eyes. It wasn't even about Antonio. It was me. Maybe it was time to assign Hailey to the Chagall claim.

That would fix everything. I wouldn't see him anymore. As much as I didn't want to say goodbye, it was my only solution. All she'd have to do was report his results back to Foster and my life would be under control again. I'd do it tomorrow.

But first, I had to figure out what I was handing over to her. Breathing deeply, I pushed him aside. We either had the genuine painting, and we were jumping to conclusions about it being fake, or sometime between 2015 and now, it was replaced.

There was a big market in copies of famous artwork, for people who couldn't afford, find, or insure the genuine article. Getting a copy done wasn't difficult if you knew where to find someone who would do it. Something as current as a Chagall wouldn't be done by someone on the up-and-up. Copyrights on his artwork would still be active for seventy years after his death, which had been in the '80s.

Option A, it was stolen, a copy put up in its place so the Scotts wouldn't know. Option B, the original was swapped out for a fake by one of the Scotts or someone else with access to the home.

Either option ended with the painting in the hands of someone we'd never find, either a thief or a secret buyer. So, forget about finding the original and focus on proving the Scotts' painting wasn't it. That was the first goal.

I grabbed my phone and called the Brenton PD, asking for Jimmy.

"Heya, Sammy! What can I do ya for?"

"You just wrapped up the investigation on the Scott case, right?"

"Yup."

"No findings of arson or foul play, right?"

"Right again."

"Any chance you can do me a favor?"

"Depends. Whaddya need?"

"Could you see if any break-ins were reported at the Scotts' house since 2014?"

"You know I can't." If I'd asked before he'd submitted the final report, I bet he would have looked it up.

"Yeah, never mind. I'll talk to you later."

I put down the kickstand and stopped the motor, got off, and walked toward the ditch. Would Janelle help me? Had our relationship improved enough for me to get a favor? Doubtful. I had a friend and a half on the force, but I didn't have any pull. But I did have pull at Foster.

I called Lucy next.

"Hi, Sam!" She sounded overly excited. "You'll never guess what I found out from—"

"Lucy, is it important?"

"Not even close."

"Okay, I need you to query some stuff in the claims system."

"You got it! Give me one sec." I heard her fingers moving over the keyboard.

"Tell her you're on your way out," came Mike's voice in the background.

"Tell Mike he needs to get off his butt and go work some claims, or I'll beat him this month on my closure ratio."

Lucy laughed but didn't convey the message. "Sam, the odds of him catching you are a quadrillion to one. Okay, I'm in, what do you need?"

"Search all claims reported by last name Scott. Filter the results for first name Olivia, Robert, Bobby, or David."

"Scott, Scott, Scott," she muttered as she went through the results. "We've got the open painting claim, Mike's claim for the fire, and three more. Looking for anything in particular?"

"Property claims only, does that help?"

"Two of them were auto claims. Want me to open the other?"

"What's the date of occurrence?"

"December 12, 2015."

Bingo! "Cause of loss is theft, isn't it?"

"Nope, ice damage to the roof."

"Dammit!" I paced on the side of the highway, as cars and trucks whizzed by me. I couldn't let go of this case until I had answers, but all I was finding was more questions.

"Aren't you done for the day?"

"Yeah, I'm—I'm still frustrated about this thing. Never mind me, I need to get going anyway. Thanks for the help."

Chapter 23

Samantha

The next morning, my phone rang with a call from Lucy. "There's a police officer who wants to see you, an Officer Williams."

My jaw clenched. "What does she want?"

"I don't know. Said it's police business, and you can either talk to her at our office or at the police station."

"Unbelievable." I rolled my eyes, staring at the laptop in my mobile office. After my encounter with Antonio the day before, I didn't have the energy for anything outside my job. I hadn't even been to the office yet. I shut everything down, knowing I'd have to hurry to talk to Janelle and still make my next appointment.

"I put her in the Pines. How far away are you?"

"Fifteen minutes."

Once I arrived at the office, I headed straight to the Pines. I counted back from five, took a slow breath, and opened the door. She was in uniform, pacing, a thick folder in her hands, not bothering to stop when I came in.

"What's up, Janelle?"

"Did you read the report Slater put together?" She slammed the folder on the table. "It's a load of horseshit!"

"No?"

"Your company paid the damn claim out, Sam! How can you not have read the report?"

"I only have the artwork portion of the claim."

"And you told me you were getting pressure on it, right?"

"Right, but the restoration company only started on it Monday."

She ran both her hands over her close-cropped hair, just like she used to, even when she'd had long hair. She stopped pacing, opened the folder, flipped through a few pages, and stabbed at it with her finger. "Read this page."

I frowned, irritated to be called in for this tirade when I had so much other work to do. But she was looking for help, despite her attitude, and I wanted to make amends.

I leaned over the page to read. It was a summary of findings, listing the highest-level details:

• In preparation for the room being painted, the canvas tarp had been spread over the couches, floor, and other furniture in the living room.

• Before the painters could get started, Mrs. Scott told them to leave because she had an emergency to deal with.

• They left the tarp, their paints, and tools in the living room, as they would be back the next day.

I looked up from the report, at Janelle. If the art claim had been valid, I would have run this down further, in case we had action based on one of the policy conditions not being fulfilled during their remodeling. But I put it aside because my gut told me the painting was a fake, so that remained my focus.

Janelle was pacing again, and I shot her a quizzical look. I sat and continued reading:

- At the same time, someone from their security alarm company was in the process of upgrading their system.

- The installer had removed the original control panel, which severed the connection to the central station.

- That was the point when Mrs. Scott told him to leave as well.

- The fire had started in the living room when Mr. Scott fell and dropped a cigarette on the painters' tarp.

- With the security system disconnected, the fire burned for an estimated twenty minutes before a neighbor reported it.

"Jimmy told me they didn't find any evidence of arson?"

"Right. We had an accelerant dog check the place, and he didn't find anything beyond the painters' paints and tools. Arson investigator didn't find anything, either." She stopped pacing and sat at the table.

"And no evidence of foul play?"

"Right again. Looks like an accident."

"So...what do you want from me?"

"Do you buy it?"

I tapped my finger a few times on the table and finally shook my head. "Sounds suspicious. Too coincidental. Painters and security installer both leaving at the precise moment they're set up for the perfect fire?"

"Exactly!" She exploded out of her chair. "At least someone's with me!"

"Why's the case closed?"

"Slater's a moron." Hands on hips, she huffed. "And like I told you already, the evidence bears it out. But I don't like coincidences."

"Here's what I'd be asking: One, what was her emergency? Two, why not let the painters either clean up their stuff or work while she was out? A family like that wouldn't hire unbonded workers. Three, same question for the security installer."

"Again!" She sat suddenly. "Exactly!"

"So, why are you here talking to me about this?"

She blew out some steam and pursed her lips. "Because I don't have any other option. I know something went on in that house. I can feel it in my bones. But the evidence points to an accident, so the Chief won't authorize money or manpower for any additional investigation. AmLife and Foster have closed their claims, based on our report. That leaves you."

I tilted my head, narrowing my eyes. "Leaves me for what?" But I already knew the answer.

"To figure this out. Why hasn't your claim closed yet?"

"Due diligence."

"Details?"

"You remember what the painting looked like when we found it? It was insured for a million dollars. To pay it out, we have to compare the remnants to the photos we have on file. It's a time-consuming process."

She nodded slowly. "So you were pissed about how our guys handled it?"

"Yeah. I have someone working on it, but he estimated it would take a month."

"So, we have until the end of August."

"We?"

"Okay, you." She balled her fists on the table. "I can't touch it or the Chief will have my hide. I'll leave the full report with you, but my recommendation would be to start with—"

"The painters, the security guy, and Mrs. Scott. Yeah, I know."

As she stood to leave, I stopped her. "Hold on, I have something else. There's a possibility the painting may be a fake."

She sat, lifting an eyebrow, looking for more.

"I don't know for sure yet. We have more tests to do. Either way, let's assume it's a fake. It was authenticated in 2015. So, I'm wondering if it had been stolen and the Scotts didn't know. What you can help with, is—"

"Break-ins reported at their house. Jimmy said you'd called. I didn't understand where you were coming from, but it makes sense now. I'll look. I should be able to get away with that much, at least. Did you look for theft claims in your system here?"

"I did, but no hits. If anything was stolen from their house then, they didn't go through us for it."

"Any other insurance?"

"I'll check around. I'll book the appointments and visit the neighbor who called it in, too. Maybe something she saw would help."

Janelle nodded.

"Momentary truce?" I asked.

"Don't get ahead of yourself." Contrary to her words, she patted me on the arm, and headed out.

I ran a hand over my face. As if my own curiosity would have let me hand this over to Hailey, I certainly couldn't now. Janelle had given me something important, and I had to keep it if I wanted a chance to earn my friend back.

Chapter 24

Samantha

With Janelle gone, I wanted to scan through the police report further, but I had scheduled site visits. I grabbed the folder and started out to my truck. I didn't make it to the exit before Cliff's booming voice echoed through the office while he strode down the hall toward me. "Caine! Back here!"

"Yeah?"

"David and Olivia Scott are here," he said, once he'd caught up with me.

Did no one realize I spent most of my time out of the office? Did they not own phones to find out if I was available?

"I have an appointment in—" Quick check of my watch. "—forty minutes, and it's a thirty-minute drive."

"Mike," he hollered. "You here?"

"Yeah, boss." The response came from the direction of the Pit.

"With me." He headed to the Pit without checking I was behind him.

Per usual, Lucy was there, popping gum and doing something incomprehensible on her computer. Hailey was also there, updating the notes on a claim.

Cliff waved Mike out of the seat and sat, switching the claims system to his manager's dashboard. A couple mouse clicks later, and the full adjuster schedule was in front of us. He filtered the results down to Mike and me. Mike's was empty, and mine had three appointments showing for the afternoon.

"Mike, you're taking Sam's next appointment." He switched the appointment details in the system. "Get off your ass and get going. It's in—" He paused and pointed at me.

Watch check. "In thirty-six minutes, and it's a thirty-minute drive."

Mike's brow furrowed. "I haven't had lunch yet."

"Grab it and go. You're also taking her last appointment of the day." He switched the assignments.

"Cliff—" I held up my hands to stop him from taking my claims away, but he kept going. He removed the filter for Mike's appointments and added Hailey's. Also, an empty afternoon.

"Hailey." He flipped my other appointment over to her. "You're taking Sam's other claim this afternoon. It's in an hour and a half."

"But she doesn't do prop—"

"Will do." Hailey switched to her outstanding list to take a peek at the details and distance.

"Lucy," he barked as he logged out of the claims system and turned around to look at us. "Go with her. Keep your mouth shut."

Then he turned to me. "They're in the Oaks conference room. Wow them with customer service, and when you're done, go sit on Ferraro until he's finished. The old man's watching this one closely, and you're running out of time."

"Cliff, it hasn't even been two weeks. This is ridiculous!"

"Sam, go."

"Lucy, I need some printouts. Policy dec, high-value artwork endorsement, and the photo when I grabbed the painting from their house. Got it?"

She gave me a thumbs up and I slapped the cubicle wall before dashing outside to my truck to grab my laptop. Lucy joined me on my way to Oaks, a large conference room with a meeting table for twenty and eighty-inch screen on the wall.

Olivia was a refined older woman with gray hair, dressed in a black jacket topped with a string of pearls and a black silk flower pin on her lapel. A dahlia, a symbol of elegance and dignity. She was thin, but not frail, and stared blankly at the tissue in her hands. I couldn't imagine the sorrow after losing her husband of forty-eight years.

David was in his mid-forties, with thin blond hair combed back to emphasize his large nose and forehead. He leveled Lucy and me with a cold gaze as we sat, his light brown eyes showing far less sadness than his mother's. He drummed his fingers, telegraphing his irritation.

"Mrs. Scott—" I began, but David interrupted.

"You're the art claims expert?"

I placed the interruption aside and put one of my business cards on the table. "My name is Samantha Caine, and this is my colleague, Lucy Chapman. And yes, I am."

Lucy looked over at me, notepad in her hands. I nodded to one of the seats, and she sat, as did I. While we talked, I got my laptop up and running and logged into the claims system.

"First, I'd like to express our condolences on your loss. I met your husband once, about twenty years ago, and he was a kind man. I assume you're here to discuss the progress of your Chagall claim—"

David interrupted again, forceful, but not losing his cool. "The other claims have already closed. AmLife and Foster have already paid everything out. Why is this part taking so long?"

"I understand this is a difficult time for you, but we should review the process."

"What process?"

"The Chagall painting was insured for a lot of money."

I opened the folder Lucy had given me and showed him the photo I'd asked her for. Olivia looked up at it and blinked away tears.

"You can see from the burn pattern the fire spread from the right side and there are still strips remaining through the middle. I regret to say it's a total loss, so we'll be paying out the full replacement value of one million dollars." I pushed a copy of the policy declaration to him and pointed to the insured value.

"Are you doing that today?" he asked. Olivia had stopped crying but was still staring at her hands.

"I'm afraid not, David. The coverage is specific for artwork valued over one hundred thousand. Any total loss from damage, like fire or water damage, requires confirmation the painting is the one listed on the policy." I pushed another sheet of paper to him, explaining the specifics.

He looked at the photo again, seeing the painting was basically a mass of black fabric now, with no discernible colors left. "How do you do that?"

"We have a professional taking care of it. They'll clean the soot off, take it out of the frame, and find areas we can confirm against the photos we have on file."

"That seems reasonable," he said begrudgingly. "How long will it take?"

"Roughly a month—"

"A month?" He hit the table with a fist.

"It's a delicate process. We have the best in the business taking care of it—"

"David," whispered Olivia, "please calm down. It will take what time it takes. It won't bring him back."

Her comments seemed to work on him. He took a few deep breaths, as I waited. Lucy was about to say something, so I tapped her leg with mine to get her attention and shook my head.

"Have you logged into the insured's web portal?" I asked, referring to the website where our policyholders could access information about their claims.

"No."

"I added an update yesterday. You should have received an email. Either way, I'll pull it up now, and we can look."

I hit a button in the middle of the conference table, and the big screen lit up, mirroring the image I'd brought up on my laptop. "This photo was taken last Wednesday when I retrieved it from the police station. It was covered in a layer of soot, but you can see how little of it remains. As you can imagine, it will be difficult to prove this was the insured painting."

"So how will it be done, then?"

I brought up the photo I'd added to the claim the day before. "This photo was yesterday, after the larger sections of debris had been removed. The conservator added some stabilizing fabric behind the tears to keep them from ripping further and made some progress on cleaning the bottom right. I asked him to start there since it's the most stable and contains the signature."

"How much needs to be cleaned before you can wrap up the claim?"

"It's more of a wait-and-see sort of thing. He'll do some work, we'll review it, and discuss the next steps. I'm afraid it may take the full month."

He nodded, while Olivia continued to stare at her hands. "That's a lot of progress in a week. I'd like another update before the week is done."

"Absolutely." I sounded confident, but the pit in my stomach argued it. "I want to make sure you and your mother are being taken care of. I do also have a couple questions. I'll be brief; it should only be another five minutes."

He nodded.

"First, do you or your mother have any other insurance which may cover the painting? Like a contents-only coverage at another company, additional coverage for moving it, or showing it at a gallery?"

Olivia shook her head and answered quietly. "No, none."

"Second, was it ever loaned to a gallery or to a friend? If there are discrepancies in our review, I'll need to talk to those people, in case the painting was damaged in their possession."

"Yes. My father loaned it to Mason's Art Gallery a year ago. It was on display for about six months, I think? Mother, do you remember?"

Her shoulders heaved a few times and she dabbed at her eyes.

"It's alright," I said, not wanting to upset her further. "Mason's has short-term coverage with us for loans, so it would have been covered there. Do you recall the dates?"

"Dad always handled those details."

"Don't worry about it, I'll talk to Mason's. They would have what I'm looking for. That's all I had, thanks for your patience."

"Thank you for bringing us up to speed. Can we have the contact information for the company cleaning it?"

"Take my card. Feel free to call me anytime you have questions. I'm available twenty-four-seven."

David slipped my card into his pocket, and he and his mother stood to shake our hands.

"Thank you, dear." Olivia patted my hand. "I appreciate what you're doing for us."

David put his arm around her, escorting her out of the building.

Lucy grabbed a piece of gum from her pocket and stuffed it in her mouth. "What's with the extra questions?"

I grinned at her. "Not much gets by you, does it? Antonio found something odd with the painting, so he's doing some more investigation."

"Not simply more cleaning?"

"Yes and no. More cleaning, so he can do some additional tests."

"More time with Dr. Ferraro can't be a bad thing." She winked at me.

Yesterday morning, I would have agreed with her. Instead, I regretted promising to get a status update for David. I wasn't ready to see him again.

CHAPTER 25

SAMANTHA

"Sam, Lucy," said Harry Bell as we walked into the Special Investigations Unit's cubicle office. "What can we do for you this afternoon?"

I sat in a chair at their large table, putting the police file down. "It's the Scott claim again. We've learned a few more things I wanted to review with you. I spoke with a police officer with suspicions about the whole event."

Harry sat forward, a gleam in his eye. "Summary."

"First and foremost, Harry. Your friend was right about the police closing this case fast. It was wrapped up yesterday." I tapped the folder in front of me.

I updated them on the salient points of the case, including the police ruling it an accident, everything we'd discovered through Antonio's work, and my suspicions the painting was a fake. Lucy added a few colorful details but mostly listened, and Quinn flipped through the police report while I spoke. Once I was done, Harry reached for a piece of paper and placed it on the table.

"What do you have planned so far?" he asked.

I counted interviews on my fingers, and he wrote as I spoke. "I've scheduled with the neighbor who reported the fire, the security system installer, and the painter."

"What about the insured?"

"I just talked to her, so I think we're good there. Mike relied on the police report instead of interviewing the other parties, so I'll make sure someone from Foster talks to everyone involved."

"Circle back to the insured after you've got all your other information in hand. What else?"

He was leading me somewhere. I didn't have anything else planned, but he was patient, pen hovering over the paper while he waited. I rubbed a hand over my face. "If the painting's a fake, we need to prove it. I'm pretty sure it is, but that's primarily in Antonio's hands right now."

"How's that going for you?" Quinn raised an eyebrow.

Lucy giggled, until I nudged her under the table.

"Quinn, stop," interrupted Harry, pen still hovering.

I did my best to ignore them while trying to figure it out. "So, I need to find...intent to defraud? If any of the surviving insureds knew the painting was a fake, they should have alerted us of the change in value. I need to find out if anyone knew."

"Exactly." Harry wrote a few more things on the sheet. "If it's a fake, we don't pay. If the insured didn't know, then they're not at fault, and we potentially have a theft claim to deal with instead. If they did know, though..."

Quinn picked up his line of thought. "There are a lot of other places this investigation can go. For now, focus on the intent to defraud, but keep an eye out for anything else. If you find something material, the police will reopen the case and investigate the rest. Don't get too far in over your head."

Harry asked, "What happened with Ferraro's? Did they try anything fishy with the one-month contract?"

"Yes and no. Dominico left town last Friday, when I was supposed to bring it in—"

"What's that?" asked Quinn. "He left town the day you were bringing in a million-dollar painting you suspect may have been either stolen or forged?"

Harry eyed her. "Our town's foremost expert..."

My first instinct was to defend Antonio's family. They wouldn't be involved in this, would they? My second instinct was to listen to Harry's advice. Don't trust anyone.

"They're down a resource. Antonio is working overtime to clean and authenticate this one."

Quinn and Lucy shared a glance, overselling it to be sure I noticed.

"Is it possible," interjected Harry, "the fraud was on the underwriting side? A lie or fraudulent documents when they added the coverage for the painting?"

"No." I looked back at them, finally having a question I knew the answer to. "Their supporting evidence was impeccable. I believe the painting was replaced sometime between 2015 and now."

"Could they be keeping the original in a safe?" asked Harry.

That hadn't occurred to me, although it was common for high-value artwork. "I expect someone would have mentioned it?"

"Assume everyone's either omitting or lying about something, Sam."

"I could pass it over to SIU?" I suggested.

"Teach a person to fish," said Harry, winking at me as he handed over the sheet with his notes. "Get it on the go, Sam. We'll do an ISO search for you, in case there are any other claims which could be related, whether through Foster or any other insurance company. The system would have done that automatically for fraud flags, but we all know how well that went, so we may spot something it didn't."

"You've got a nose for this, hun," added Quinn. "Maybe you should leave claims and join our department."

"I warned you, Quinn." Harry frowned at her. "Cut it out."

Chapter 26

Samantha

I hesitated, hand on the door to the Ferraro's office. I'd promised David an update on the Chagall by end of the week. Friday at five o'clock was last-minute, but perfect. Surely Antonio wouldn't be there at that hour.

Sofia looked up from behind her two-tier desk as I stepped through the door. She flicked her eyes back to the studio, then quickly smiled as she came around to give me cheek kisses and led me to the waiting area. Not a word. The music today was opera. My heart ached at the sorrow in the soprano's voice.

"I know it's late. I was hoping to get a status update on my Chagall."

"Let me check with Antonio. I'll be right back."

Shit. He was there.

She returned a moment later and ushered me to the couches. She sat next to me, putting an arm on the back, forcing a casual air. "He'll be about fifteen minutes. He needs to finish what he's doing and get your painting out of the storage room."

"Thanks." I reached for one of the magazines on the table, but she didn't leave the couch.

"What have you been up to since Wednesday?"

"Work." I shrugged, holding the magazine on my lap. Always the same answer to that question. "I've been busy."

"And why the surprise visit?"

I rubbed a palm across my pants. "I promised the policyholder an update by the end of the week. So, here I am. End of the week."

She nodded.

"I was expecting Antonio would already have left by now." I looked down at the magazine.

"Then why come if you didn't think he'd be here?"

I shrugged again, gripping the magazine so I wouldn't start rubbing my face. "I thought someone else would be able to show it to me."

"Everyone else left an hour ago. He and I are the only ones left."

Oh no.

Antonio poked his head around the waiting room wall long enough to speak. "I have the painting out. You can come back to the studio."

Putting on my best professional smile, I stood, while my stomach tied in knots.

Sofia touched me lightly on the arm. "Samantha, I have to leave soon. Would your boyfriend be alright with you being here alone with him? If not, I understand, and I'll stay."

"I don't have a boyfriend." What was I walking into? Would it be flirtatious Antonio? Professional Antonio?

· · · · ●·●· · ·

The painting lay on one of the worktables. He was again in faded jeans and a gray t-shirt, which moved like it was made of silk, highlighting his muscled shoulders and chest.

"I've made some progress on cleaning the bottom right corner." He was cool, not looking at me. "Based on the original design, I also cleaned the strip which remains across the middle of the canvas. It should be the next place we look if the signature doesn't work. Please take whatever pictures you need." He stood back to give me room, forcing his hands into his pockets.

It was the first time I'd felt out of place in his office. Awkward and nervous, sure, but this was different. And the music was making it worse.

"Sofia sure picked a depressing soundtrack today, didn't she?" I turned back to him, but his jaw clenched, and I groaned inside. Poor choice of words.

"Take your pictures. I'll be right back."

He left the studio to speak with Sofia, and I took photos with my phone. They spoke in hushed tones, rapidly in Italian, but I couldn't make out any details.

The music stopped abruptly.

When he returned, he slid the painting into its protective sheath and took it to the storage room, engaging the lock when he finished. Silent the whole time.

I asked, "How close are you to the ultraviolet pictures?"

"Another week, perhaps."

"A week?" Stunned, I stared at him, desperate to shake him out of this mood. "It looked so close to being ready. Is there really that much more you need to do?"

"I can only work on it so much in any day. I have other commitments." He ran a hand through his hair and blew out a rough breath. "And I'm exhausted."

"But you said you were the best."

"I suppose my best is not enough for you, is it?" His lip curled up with his harsh tone. This was a side of him I'd never seen before.

"I didn't mean—" I couldn't hide the tremble in my voice, but I folded my arms tight against my chest to control their shaking.

"You have your pictures. The painting is locked away. I'm going. Sofia will see you out."

I nodded, feeling as though I'd been slapped, and he walked out of the studio. I followed a few paces behind and turned the corner as he left. I stopped inside the door as he headed along the sidewalk, eyes down. Why did my heart feel like it was breaking over a man I'd never even been on a date with?

"Some days," mused Sofia, standing behind her desk, causing me to jump. "He's the most brilliant man I've ever met. And other days, he's the stupidest."

"Thanks for squeezing me in, Sofia. I'll be back in a week or so."

"Hold on," she said. "Are you familiar with the Children's Hospital Charity Gala?"

"No." Odd question.

"They're holding an auction for some paintings this year. My father had his eye on two of them but wanted to see them in person to choose which one to bid on. Papa and I had planned to go together, but he's out of town. Antonio was supposed to go in his place, but he has been in such a mood he canceled. Now, here I am, with two tickets to the gala, and no one to go with me."

"Take your husband?"

"He knows nothing about art, Samantha."

"Frank?"

She rolled her eyes. "I couldn't spend an entire evening with him. However, it's dawned on me I know someone familiar with the art world whom I would enjoy spending an evening with."

I raised an eyebrow, suspicious of where this was going.

She retrieved a large black envelope from her desk and handed it to me. I opened it and withdrew an invitation to the gala, gold imprint on black paper. The event was the next day at the Lansing Convention Center.

"Short notice, I know. I like you, Samantha. And from the look on your face, you need a girls' night out."

Strange offer. I'd been back in Brenton for a couple months, and my social life revolved around my family. Cass would say I should branch out. Maybe she'd even leave me alone about dating someone if I struck up some female friendships.

"You know what?" I nodded, sinking into the idea of going with her. "Yeah, I think that'd be fun."

"Wonderful!" She spoke rapidly. "It's black tie. Wear something blue, it lights up your face. Something elegant you can dance in. Show some cleavage and leave your hair down."

Noting the wary look on my face, she put her hands on her hips and frowned. "I'm not coming on to you. My date needs to be the second most beautiful woman there! After me, of course!"

I laughed at her feigned conceit. "Will do. Want me to pick you up?"

"No, no. Take a cab. The tasting bar will be worth it. Are you familiar with the Convention Center in Lansing?"

"Yeah."

"Good. There's a boardwalk between the Center and the river with a fountain that lights up at night. We'll meet at the gazebo down there at seven o'clock."

CHAPTER 27

ANTONIO

Sofia's arms were already folded as I stepped through the front door, her lecturing face on. "Yes, she's gone, if you're wondering."

"I know." Good riddance. I had watched her climb into her giant truck and drive off. But her scent clung to the air, taunting me, like citrus and a warm Mediterranean breeze.

Standing slowly, Sofia kept her eyes on me. "You spend all this time and effort looking for the right woman, and when she's standing right in front of you, you walk away! What were you—"

"I told you. She's dating someone."

She slapped the desk as she rounded it, her voice grating. "I asked her, and she said she doesn't have a boyfriend!"

"She's a liar! Just like every other woman! Said she was not dating Miller, then admits she is! Stringing me along this whole time, while she was with another man!"

"You are so full of yourself!" Sofia poked me in the chest. "She didn't string you along! She turned you down!"

I swatted the finger aside and walked around her, into the studio to collect my things, but she followed me.

"She's not Faith! Stop treating her like she owes you something."

I wanted to throw one of the chairs. "This idea of finding the right woman is stupid. I should go back to screwing everything in sight. I was happy then."

She smacked the side of my head. "Drop the macho act. You're looking for a family, Antonio, not a harem."

"Che cazzata!"

"You know what your problem is? You're very adept at romancing your way into a woman's underwear—"

I glared at her, not giving her the satisfaction of a response.

"But what you need is to romance your way into a woman's heart. When was the last time you tried that?"

A woman's heart. Samantha's heart was full of nothing but lies and deception. Beautiful woman like her, playing hard to get with me. Miller was probably an old flame, and she thought she could use me to make him jealous. And I fell right into her trap.

"Sofia, leave me alone. Let me clean up my things in peace."

She stormed off to her desk, while I packed my tools in silence. Damn burned painting. What to do with it now? I had to finish cleaning it enough to prove it wasn't the real thing, and I had to continue seeing her. How could I spy on her when the sight of her drove me mad?

I could tell her the truth about the painting. That would put an end to things.

But it was not what I wanted.

What I wanted was Nathan Miller out of the picture. And for her to never leave Brenton. How could fate give me someone so perfect and yet so wrong for me at the same time?

Snatching a paintbrush from under my desk, I squeezed until the handle snapped. I stared at its broken halves for a moment, the bitterness fading. I stretched out my jaw, releasing the pain from clenching it so long.

Samantha had been standing there less than an hour ago, arms wrapped around herself as she trembled. And I walked away from her because of a lie. But which was her lie? Her eyes when I opened the box or her words about *him*? And was it as bad as the ones I had been telling her?

"Sofia, I hate this."

She returned to my desk, tight-lipped. "Done ranting?"

"She makes me feel like I'm twenty again, when I didn't know how to talk to women." I threw the broken paintbrush in the trash. "I've held her in my heart for so long."

"You're in love with an ideal that only exists in your head."

I exhaled, long and slow. "I know."

She softened, placing a hand on my arm. "You barely know her. Move on from this ridiculous obsession."

"I'm not obsessed."

"Did you forget about the restaurant already?" The kind hand switched rapidly to a smack. "Here's my advice: Find someone you can be friends with first."

"What do you think I've been doing all this time?"

"I have no idea. I've watched you for years, moving from one woman to the next, never getting close to any of them. Always stopping after your magical third date, before you risk any real connection. You compare every one of them to a figment of your imagination, so of course none of them stack up. And now here you are, angry with Samantha because she didn't live up to your ideal of Samantha."

"I—"

She held up the lecture hand to stop me. "Sure, you two got along well at Russo's, but all you've done since then is flash your smile at her and treat her like a trophy for some testosterone-induced competition. Women don't get to say no to the great Dr. Antonio Ferraro, do they? You keep pushing her, because you want to win, but all you're doing is making her uncomfortable."

I straightened my shirt. "I am not." Sofia didn't understand. The constant trembles, moving away from me, not looking at me, those were nerves because Samantha was attracted to me. She was not uncomfortable. Or was she?

"And on a professional level, your behavior with her today was an embarrassment. Get some self-control. You'll run this office someday, which won't work if you behave like that every time a pretty face walks through the door."

"She's more than a pretty face." She was brilliant, engaging, and challenging.

"So are you. Start acting like it."

"What does that mean?"

"It means I'm done with this conversation."

"Fine." With a sigh, I kissed her cheeks. "I'm going to the gym."

"Again?"

"Either that or I go to Russo's and eat everything Angelo has on display." I patted her arm and headed for the back door. "See you tomorrow."

"Change of plans. Pietro can't pick me up after the gala, so I'll need you to drive me home."

I rested a hand on the door as my shoulders sagged. "I'm taking a cab." The charity gala was the last place I wanted to be. I wanted to continue being angry. But maybe the free alcohol and time with familiar faces would help lift me out of this mood. Maybe I would even find someone new to take my mind off Samantha. Someone I could be friends with. Anything was worth a shot at this point.

"No, you are taking your car and driving me home. No drunken wallowing."

"Very funny."

"Meet me at the gazebo by the river. I'll be there at six-thirty."

There was no arguing with Sofia when she took that tone, but I turned around with a wry smile. She was never on time. "I'll be there at seven o'clock, then. Try not to be any later." I winked, expecting an eye roll in return.

But she grinned at me instead. "Seven o'clock it is, little brother. It should be a memorable evening."

CHAPTER 28

SAMANTHA

My sister drove too slowly. Always had and always would. But I appreciated the ride to the charity gala all the same.

We'd spent the day together. She'd helped me find the perfect dress—pale blue silk chiffon with wrapped bodice and full skirt which billowed as I walked—and paired it with crystal-studded heels and clutch to match. We'd gone to a movie, and she'd done my hair and makeup. It was the perfect girls' day, which I'd be following with the perfect girls' night.

It was time to turn a corner, and this evening was the first step. I'd have a carefree evening, eat way more than I should, and definitely drink more than I should. There would be handsome men to dance with who wouldn't expect anything after the gala was over.

"Thanks for everything today, Cass." I closed my eyes and turned my face to the sun, feeling its warmth on my face.

"C'mon, you gave up your life to come home and help me. This is the least I can do!" The fabric of her headscarf rustled as she fiddled with it.

Keeping my eyes shut, I reached over to squeeze her arm.

"You don't understand how much it means to me. Seriously, you've had some big-time growth."

Opening one eye, I cast a sidelong glance at her. "This conversation is getting too serious, Cass."

"I've been thinking about this a lot lately, Sam. When was the last time you stuck around through the tough times?"

"This is why you told Kevin to stay with the kids while you drove me? Another lecture?"

"Not at all! Think about it! After Mom died, you should have been living your FBI dream, but you quit instead. After your divorce from Matt, you sold everything and moved out of the state. Christ, when Dad left, you ran away from home, and you were only five!"

"What the hell?"

She slowed in front of the Convention Center, pulling over near the top of the stairs. Dozens of well-dressed people milled about the main doors of the two-story gray concrete building, and even more were heading down to the riverside.

She shifted the car into park and turned to me. "I'm not making my point clearly. Thing is, I'm proud of you. I know it's hard for you to be here, but you're here anyway. It means more than I can say."

"You have kind of a shitty way of saying it."

"This cancer thing's given me some real perspective, Sam. I'm not immortal. None of us are. And I worry about you."

I resisted running a hand over my perfect makeup and took a deep breath. "Do we have to go over this again? Right now?"

"No, I'm sorry." Her lips tightened, and she looked away from me. "Nathan came by last night. I should have talked to you about this earlier, but he's worried about you."

"Worried?"

"You may not be safe. He thinks you have a stalker."

I shook my head. I must have misunderstood. "Did you say a stalker?"

"If he's there tonight, that Italian guy from The Train Station, I want you to call me. Or better yet, one of your cop friends." She put a hand on my knee.

"You're kidding me, right?"

"Nathan said he almost got into a fistfight protecting you in the most exclusive restaurant in town."

I put up a hand to stop her. "First of all, his name's Antonio and he's working on a claim with me. He came by to say hello while Nathan was talking to the kitchen about dessert. We were having a simple discussion." Complete lie, but she didn't need to hear the details. "Second, Nathan was the one who got in his face. He wasn't protecting me. Do you seriously think I need protection from anyone?"

"Maybe."

"Cass, I can kick the ass of pretty much any man I meet. You understand that, right? And as for those two, there was enough testosterone coming off the pair of them they could have fueled a small city."

"Sam, I know you're strong. But you remember Vincenzo? You let him get away with—"

"Tell you what. If you see Nathan again before I do, tell him to keep his nose out of my fucking business." I shoved the car door open and got out.

"Sweetie—"

And slammed it behind me.

What did they think? I was some dainty little princess who needed to be bubble-wrapped?

My ankle-length skirt floated behind me as I made my way down the stairs. Cass didn't come after me, so she must have left. I stopped halfway and squeezed the railing so tight my fingers hurt. Vin was nine years ago. Why did she have to bring that up? We met in Amelia during postgrad and I fell for him too hard and too fast. He'd pledged his undying devotion, and I'd fallen for every line of it. Seeing through a man's need to prove his virility was probably the most important lesson I'd learned while I was there.

The fountain in the river let out a great spray, and colored lights danced in the water. The green wrought-iron fence at the water's edge was decorated with white balloons and a large crowd of people in tuxedos and gowns filled the area.

As for Antonio? He wasn't a stalker. He was charming, thoughtful, and intelligent. He made me feel special. More beautiful than I'd felt since the day I left Amelia. He...he... he what?

He was Brenton, and I was the road. He was family, and I was solitude. I stared at the fountain, seeing only the blur of water and lights. He was all wrong for me. He was playing a game and nothing more. I had to put him out of my mind.

Easier said than done.

I continued to the gazebo. It was large enough to squeeze at least thirty people underneath, but there were only four, deep in conversation. A fifth leaned against an upright, facing the fountain. Sofia wasn't one of them. I pulled my phone out of my clutch and checked the time. Seven o'clock on the dot.

Maybe I'd watch the fountain while I waited for her. As I passed the gazebo, I looked again at the man standing apart from the small group. His back was to me, tall, broad shoulders, and then he ran his hand through his hair. And it hit me.

I froze and my instincts told me to call Cass to pick me up. But running home to her wasn't what I wanted.

I wanted *him*. And it was damn-well time I did something about it. Screw Cass and Nathan's warning. Screw my own doubts.

"Antonio?" I asked, my voice unsteady.

He turned his head. "Samantha!" His mouth fell open, and he immediately straightened. He wore a black one-button tuxedo with satin lapels and good god, he was gorgeous. "I didn't expect to see you here."

"Sofia said you cancel—" My fingertips began to tingle. Was this his doing or hers? "I think we've been set up."

The surprise on his face flashed to irritation, as he muttered Sofia's name. It contorted further into anger. He tore his ticket from his pocket and held it out to me. "My sister can be persistent. You should call your boyfriend. I'm sure a *pretty* man like him has a tuxedo lying around."

I rubbed my fingers together to get the blood flowing and summoned all my courage. "I'm sorry."

He continued to offer the invitation. "No need to apologize for my sister's meddling. Take my ticket. Have a good evening."

I was setting myself up for failure. For once, I didn't care. "No, I mean, I'm sorry I told you I'm dating him, because

I'm not."

His hand dropped, the invitation still in it. The fountain exploded in color, and the crowd oohed over it, while he stared at me, eyes narrowed. "You said you were. You lied?"

My heart was thundering and all my instincts told me to stop. Instead, I nodded my head.

"Why?"

"Because you wouldn't take no for an answer, and I panicked."

"That is the stupidest thing I have ever heard." His face was softening, the anger fading.

"You're right." I blinked at him several times, my fingertips regaining feeling. "Why were you at The Train Station last Saturday?"

He ran a hand through his hair again, looking back to the water, his shoulders sagging. "I heard you on the phone with him when you were picking up the repair. I thought I would surprise you away from the studio."

I swallowed hard, pushing down the lump in my throat. "Why?"

"You turn me down every time I ask. I thought seeing me away from work would make a difference." He looked down at the ornate brickwork around the gazebo, silent. Through all our other meetings, all the faces I'd seen from him, the constant had been overwhelming confidence. This shy, quiet side pulled at my heart.

I touched his arm, and he looked back up at me.

Taking my hand gently and kissing it, he whispered, "You're the most beautiful woman I've ever seen."

The lump moved south, taking residence in my lungs, which started to heave.

"Would you finally say yes tonight?"

"Well, I guess our assigned seats are together?" I couldn't just say *yes*, could I? I had to make a lame joke.

"Samantha." He rolled the syllables of my name again, extending the crook of his elbow to me, the last of my resistance melting away. "Please? Or must I beg?"

I slid my arm through his, attempting to remain calm while he held it against his warm body. *Him*? Begging for *me*?

• • • ● • ● ● • • •

"Sofia believes I've made you uncomfortable." He shook his head while we leaned on the railing and watched the fountain. "That was not my goal."

"Well, I haven't hit you yet, so it hasn't been that bad." I chuckled, hiding the truth of how uncomfortable he made me. Not in a bad way, but I couldn't exactly tell him.

"That wouldn't end up well for me, I expect. You are quite strong." He trailed a finger along the slope of my arm, up to my shoulder. When I pulled away, he put his hand in his pocket. "I'm making you uncomfortable again."

"I've finished half your dissertation." I studied the river, the sun's reflection dancing across the surface.

"And? Did it put you to sleep?"

I suppressed a laugh, shaking my head. "And it's fascinating. I'm at the part where you're identifying the particular strains of bacteria you wanted to focus on, viability for vertical surface applications, and possible long-term risks."

He leaned closer to me, eyes wide. "You are actually reading it?"

"Of course I am!"

"Perhaps someday we'll go to Pompeii, and I'll show you how it's done for real. Would you like that?" He looked serious, but it was obviously a ridiculous joke, so I frowned and rolled my eyes. He laughed and leaned his shoulder against mine. "You did say it was at the top of your bucket list."

"I did, but if I were going to go, I'd travel with a friend instead of someone I barely know."

"Come now, Samantha. I thought we were becoming friends. Was I wrong?"

Friends. I maintained my focus on the fountain. "Do you usually tell your friends they're the most beautiful woman in the world?"

He waved a dismissive hand. "No, not usually."

I exhaled sharply and hung my head.

"Oh, Samantha." He placed an arm around my shoulder and gave it a quick squeeze before I could wriggle out of it. "You are too serious."

"You know, I've heard that once or twice."

"But if *I* may take a moment to be serious?" He leaned against me again. "I would like to be clear on two things. One, my date is the most beautiful woman here. And two, a wise person told me friendship should come first."

"First?" Heat rose in my cheeks. I kept my focus on the fountain while he continued smiling at me.

"Uncomfortable again. I shall have to work on that." He straightened, offering his elbow. "Come, let's go to the auction room. There are two paintings my father wants me to choose between, and I would appreciate your opinion on them."

· · · ● · ● · ● · · ·

The expansive dining area contained over a hundred tables set for twelve apiece. White fabric draped across the ceiling, below the level of the dimmed lights, casting a million shadows around the subdued room. The tables were set with black cloth, gold plates, and simple crystal stemware, crowned with bouquets of white roses and hydrangea. Soft string music carried through the room from speakers hidden behind the decorations.

During dinner, we kept our heads together. We barely touched the food, as we worked on learning as much as we could about each other. On becoming friends. When the meal was over, the music shifted and the DJ took charge.

"That's interesting," I said. "I expected a live band."

"They used to have one but changed two years ago and it was a success. She's an up-and-comer, but you won't see her truly shine until the after-party at midnight."

After-party? I wasn't an after-party kind of person. But I'd be willing to stay out all night with Antonio, talking, smiling, and laughing until my sides hurt. This was much better than rejecting his invitations.

I watched the crowd dancing but remained focused on the man next to me. When a slow song started, Antonio stood, straightened his jacket, and held out a hand. "May I have the honor of this dance?"

"You know," I said, placing my shaking hand in his. "I'm kind of fond of dancing."

"As am I. Do you know this song?"

"No."

He chuckled over his shoulder as he towed me to the dance floor. "'Perfect Symphony' by Ed Sheeran and Andrea Bocelli. I'll be covered in goosebumps in precisely one minute."

He'd held my hand to kiss it earlier, but as we walked— him clutching my hand near his back—this kind of intimacy caused butterflies to swirl in my stomach. He guided me to the middle of the crowd and pulled me into the starting position. I looked around at the other couples, checking if we were surrounded by experienced dancers. We were. He pivoted my chin, so I faced him.

"I'm the only one here, bella."

Unexpectedly, he lowered his hand from my shoulder to the small of my back and pulled me in against him. My hand on his arm instinctively slid to his neck, and his cologne hit me like a wave, notes of amber and vanilla. I felt every inch of his hard, muscled body against mine like we were designed for each other, and my body tingled with desperation at the full-body touch I'd wanted since the first moment I saw him.

"Wait for it." He looked at me, the corner of his mouth lifting. We stood in the middle of the floor, stationary, as other couples swirled around us. When the Italian tenor's voice layered into the song, his deep vibrato penetrating us, goosebumps shot up my arms.

"You, too?" He beamed as he broke our grip and ran a hand lightly over my arm, guiding my hand to his chest, to his heart, which echoed my thundering beat. He shook his wrist so his sleeve rose high enough I could glimpse his goosebumps. He dipped his forehead toward mine, closing his eyes. "I have no words for this moment, Samantha."

His mouth was so close, I could feel his hot, wine-tinged breath on my cheek, as rapid as my own. I closed my eyes and bit my lip, not sure how I'd survive much longer without combusting. If *friends* was this all-consuming, what would *more* be like?

His hand swept along the length of my arm as we began to sway, and his temple met mine. He sang the Italian lyrics, his lips close to my ear so only I could hear, in a voice so deep, it reverberated all the way down to my toes. I kept my eyes shut tightly, willing the moment to never end.

When he pulled his head away, I opened my eyes, and he was staring right back, still so close, as he sang the final Italian lyrics: *Because you are perfect for me.* It was just a song, but a shudder ran through me. He knew I spoke Italian. What was he doing?

This was too much. Too fast. It wasn't real.

"Um, thanks." I removed my hand from his chest and stepped away. "For the dance, I mean."

He didn't release my waist. Instead, he drew me against him so forcefully I gasped, and he whispered, "We are not done dancing."

Gone were the smiles, the smirks, the pleasantries. Replaced by an intensity that made my body ache, like he was about to devour me. And I wanted him to. I swallowed hard, the tightness in my chest traveling south and taking residence between my thighs.

When he licked his bottom lip, I had to fight against my instincts to run. Replaced immediately by a new instinct to kiss those lips and discover if they were truly as soft as they felt on the back of my hand. I ignored it all.

As the next song started, he pushed against me, and I stepped back, to the side, forward and again, as we fell into a waltz.

"You dance beautifully," he said as he led us across the floor.

I couldn't rip my eyes from him, from the way he kept staring at me, as if he were memorizing my face. It was like I was drowning, everyone else a blur outside the little bubble we shared. "Took lessons."

"Bene. Do you know the tango?" He spoke slowly, every word a weight between us.

"Um, yeah, all the standards."

"I doubt we'll have the opportunity here, but I would very much like to tango with you." The way his eyes scanned my face, lingering on my lips as they parted under his gaze, I was pretty sure he didn't mean the dance. "After all, it is the dance of..."

He paused, releasing his hold on my waist to spin me slowly, then pulled me back against him, impossibly tighter than before. The hand at the small of my back inched to my tailbone, and the tightness escalated. It was the most closed closed-position I'd ever danced in.

"Argentina?" I said, unable to utter the words he was suggesting, like love, passion, or desire, and not so sure I could handle hearing them from him.

The spell was broken. He tried not to laugh, but once I started, he was done for. He spun me again, the laughter continuing.

"You are too clever, bella," he said, the gentle smile returning. He curled his lead hand to his chest, taking mine with it, rubbing his thumb over my knuckles and then along my arm.

When the music switched tempo, the couples separated. More people joined the crowd, but we remained, in the middle of the dance floor, still in each other's arms.

"Grazie." He kissed me on the cheek, and we stepped apart while dozens of people around us started enjoying the high-energy music. I would have called it a chaste kiss, but my body was begging for him so vehemently the word wouldn't fit in my vocabulary.

He retook my hand and led me toward our table. On the way there, he was interrupted by a man who wanted to speak with him, and I excused myself to the dessert buffet. Being away from him gave me a moment to clear my head. It was hard to imagine I'd planned to spend the evening with his sister.

At the buffet, while a staff worker explained the selections, a woman sidled up beside me and offered her hand in greeting.

"Hi, I'm July." In her free hand was at least a double of rum.

"Nice to meet you, I'm—" I raised my hand to shake in greeting, but she interrupted.

"You're August." She shook my hand, her tone condescending. She probably wasn't on her first glass.

"Samantha Caine, actually."

"August is so much easier to remember." She raised her drink in my general direction and put an arm around my shoulders. "Welcome to the Calendar Club, honey."

"I'm sorry, I think you have me confus—"

"I saw you on the dance floor with Dr. Antonio. Sorry to break it to you, but he's a serial womanizer. He'll wine you and dine you, make you think you're the most beautiful and interesting woman in the world, and then he'll be gone. On to the next one. You'll show up somewhere next month and meet his flavor of September."

"What are you—"

She pointed to a couple of women at a table nearby. "That's May and sitting next to her is October. From last year." The two of them snickered and waved. "You wanna know the worst thing?"

I didn't respond. She was talking to hear herself and didn't care what I had to say. She was grabbing my attention, though.

"He's such a fucking gentleman," she sighed dreamily. "I never even got to see that luscious body naked."

She quickly withdrew her arm from around me and stood back, looking over my shoulder with an evil grin. Antonio stood there, glaring at her.

"You have had too much to drink, Victoria." He didn't take his eyes off her, while mine rested on him. "You should go home before you embarrass yourself. I'll call you a cab."

"Yeah, you're probably right, but I'm good." She looked at her glass, downed it, and headed off to the table where May and October sat, casting me a backward glance.

"Mi scusi." He approached, sliding a hand to the small of my back. "Let's go outside and get some fresh air. The fountain lights will be beautiful."

My head was swimming. I'd crashed hard from the high I'd felt from our dance, after her little revelation. I wanted to be there with him but felt cheap and on-display. Was he really no different than Vincenzo? Was it all an act? Carefully crafted words and actions?

Being around him numbed my brain. My fingers prickled, and I shivered, moving away from him. "I'm tired. I'll call my cab early. Good luck with the auction."

He took my hand. "Stay. Please. I'm not ready for goodbye."

"I'd love to, but I need to go."

"Let me drive you home."

I pulled the hand, but he held fast. "No, you have to stay for the auction."

"I can arrange for a proxy bid."

My first instinct was to say no, to avoid the awkward feeling inside of me, to avoid talking about what happened, to avoid the moment when he dropped me off. Despite it all, I craved more time with him. So, I accepted.

CHAPTER 29

ANTONIO

I shook hands with the woman who had taken the auction proxy for my father. Before searching for my date, I pulled out my phone and texted my sneaky sister.

Thank you

She replied, *Made any friends yet ;)*

Working on it

I put the phone away and spotted Samantha as effortlessly as a compass finding north. She stood in front of one of the paintings on display for the auction. She was a vision. An absolute vision. The dress highlighted every aspect of her miraculous body, and her luxurious hair fell down her back in long, loose waves. She tilted her head, speaking with a shorter man, who pointed to elements of the artwork. Her lips were tight, eyes narrowed. It was not the face of someone absorbing the art, it was the face of someone appraising it.

As I neared her, the man evaluated me. I glanced at him while placing a hand on the small of her back, staking my claim. Giving an almost imperceptible nod, he moved to the next piece. She, however, didn't react.

I leaned close enough to whisper, her citrusy scent heightening my desire. "You seem taken by this painting. You've been staring at it for ten minutes. Would you like to stay for the auction, and I can bid on it for you?"

She rolled her head toward me slowly. "The last thing I need is stuff. Especially stuff with a starting bid of ten thousand dollars."

I suppressed my smile, only letting it rise to a smirk. I had never heard such a wonderful answer. She wouldn't want me for my money. "It's a charity auction. It will likely go for far more, despite it being in such desperate need of a cleaning."

She narrowed her eyes again and shook her head. "And that's not why I'm staring at it. I recognize this piece but can't seem to place it. It's driving me batty."

This was why she hadn't reacted to my touch. This was Work-Samantha, even more intense than I had seen before. "Gallery? Museum?"

"I don't know." She flagged down one of the attendants. "Do you have the provenance for this painting?"

The woman nodded and returned a moment later with a tablet, showing the history of possession. I took it from her, and we scrolled through the short list.

"Private residence for the last twenty years. You must be mistaken, bella. Unless it was on loan somewhere you visited?"

"No. Not it." She bowed her head and covered her eyes with a hand, squeezing her temples.

I returned the tablet to the attendant and waited while she thought. After five minutes, I put the hand to her back again. "Are you alright?"

"I can almost see it. The memory has white space around it. White wall? Was it a photo, maybe?" She started muttering to herself. "C'mon, Sam. Think. Think. Where did you—"

The hand shot away from her face and she snapped her fingers. Pulling her phone out of her clutch, she whipped the small bag under her arm. Her fingers sped across the tiny keyboard.

"What are you doing?"

She looked up at me suddenly, as though she had forgotten where she was. She lowered her phone and stepped toward me, her chest against mine, and I inclined my ear to her mouth. "I think it's stolen. I'm looking it up."

"But the provenance?"

"Gimme a sec." She rotated her body, using mine as a shield against prying eyes. She scrolled quickly, performing one search after another, on the FBI's Stolen Art website. "Dammit, it's not here."

"Perhaps you are wrong?"

Her eyes shot from her phone to meet mine, a wicked grin on her face. "You doubt me, Dr. Ferraro?"

Who was this woman? She had so much more confidence than I was used to seeing in Samantha. This was a woman in her element.

"I would never, Ms. Caine. But, if it's not there, what next?"

"PSYCHE, of course." She snapped her fingers at an attendant walking by. "I need a laptop!"

"Sorry, ma'am, but we don't provide that service here."

As she became more focused on the work, she became far less personable.

I put my hand on her back again and gave her a wink. "Give me a moment." I strode across the room to an attendant. A young blond, pretty, who paused when I smiled at her.

"Buongiorno. I'm in need of a laptop. Can you provide such a thing?"

"I'm sorry, sir, but I can't."

I leaned closer. "I tell you what. Go and speak with Margaret over there." I pointed to the woman who had taken my father's proxy bid, one of the auction's coordinators. "Ask her if it's alright for me to borrow one for a few minutes."

Given the size of my father's bid, I was not surprised for the young woman to return within a few minutes with what I needed. A laptop and a slip of paper with the login information.

"Grazie. I'll return it soon, I promise."

Tucking it under my arm, I returned to Samantha, who was squinting at her phone, using the site anyway.

"You get more flies with honey, bella, than you do with snapping fingers and sharp voices." I held the laptop up to show her, and she shot me a teasing sneer.

She evaluated the room and found a table allowing her to keep her back to the wall. I pulled up next to her, draping my arm around her chair as she logged in.

"So, what is this?"

"You should know." Eyes down, her fingers flew while she spoke. "Protection System for Cultural Heritage. Interpol. The Italian Carabinieri—" She nudged me with her leg without skipping a beat in her words or her fingers. "—

partnered with a ton of other countries to create this massive database of stolen cultural heritage items."

"How do you have a login to an Interpol website for stolen artwork?" A series of thoughts flew through my brain. Everything she had told me about ARCA, Lara Croft, and things she had said about her ability to handle herself physically. There was a side to this woman I didn't know, yet wanted to desperately.

But, if she were so intent on tracking this random piece down, what would she do if she found out my secret about her burned painting?

"Long story." She performed search after search, convinced she would find something, like a woman possessed. I took out my phone and tried my own web search. Three sites later, and I couldn't contain my pride in her.

"You are brilliant, Samantha." I showed her the results on my phone. A news article about the painting being stolen twelve months ago. She snatched it from me and shot out of her seat.

"Goddammit! I knew it I'd seen it somewhere!" She smacked my shoulder. "I could kiss you!"

Before I could react, tell her she should or tease her— saying I was not interested— she was gone. With my phone. Waving a finger for me to take care of the laptop. I returned it and joined her, as she was showing our information to the coordinator.

"The provenance documents were faked," she was saying, leaning around the coordinator's laptop and pointing at the screen. When Margaret saw me, she paled.

"Dr. Ferraro, I'm so sorry. I assure you this is not the type of—"

I held up a hand. "Don't worry. I understand. We are all lucky Ms. Caine was here this evening."

Watching the two of them discuss the painting, seeing the intensity in Samantha's eyes, I fell harder for her. She didn't simply understand my world, she was part of it. Papa would love her.

Once they had finished, one of the attendants removed the painting from its display, and they contacted the authorities.

"Impressive again." I offered her my elbow, which she took. She clutched my arm; however, a darkness had fallen over her features.

Once we were back in the ballroom, she finally spoke. "You know what pisses me off the most? It was in the news, the police were involved, but for some unknown reason, it didn't make it into one of those databases."

"Why does that make you so angry?"

"Because the team in there would have checked. Those things exist for a reason." She huffed, squeezing my arm tighter. "Or not. Maybe they wouldn't have. This gala was a small enough auction."

I stopped and turned to look at her. "But you found it. This is a good thing. You should be proud."

"You know what's even worse?"

I shook my head.

"The coordinator's screen said the painting's appearance here was arranged by Mason's Gallery."

"Why is that worse?"

"They had the burned Chagall last year. If there's something sketchy going on with Mason's Gallery..." She trailed off, mouth hanging open, while she stared at me. "I need to interview them. Remember I told you my theory on *Les amoureux* being stolen and replaced? What if that happened while it was at Mason's? What if this isn't a one-time thing?"

My stomach dropped. My parents had first seen it at Mason's. What if she found out it had been purchased? My lie would be revealed.

Her eyes continued darting back and forth and she tapped a finger on her clutch, lost in thought.

I tucked the arm she held tight against my side to get her attention, and her eyes snapped back to me. "Are you in a better mood now? We can stay?"

She shook her head. "I'm tired. I'll take that drive home now?"

· · · ● ● ● ● ● · ·

On our way out, there were too many hands to shake and embraces to make to keep up with Samantha. I had neglected many friends in favor of her and heard the complaints many times over but couldn't care less. Other than Victoria, it had been a miraculous evening. And I was about to drive the most amazing woman in the world home.

This was our second date. No kisses until the third. I had a strict code. Unless the evening at Caruther's was a date? We had shared a toast. But no food. Not a table. That was not a date. I would continue to be the gentleman. Sofia was right. I had to win her heart first. Her underwear would come later.

"What are you smirking about over there?"

I squeezed her arm against me again. "Have you met me before? This is my resting face."

Her laughter was so sudden, a couple nearby turned in surprise. She was still irritated, but at least it was not with me. A good thing, given her reaction to Victoria. We navigated row after row in the warm, dark night, lit gently by the moon and light poles, until we reached my car.

Her brows knitted together for the briefest instant when I unlocked it. Most women oohed and ahhed over my Maserati convertible, but Samantha 'The last thing I need is stuff' Caine remained silent. I opened the passenger door for her and held her hand while she sank into the buttery-soft leather.

I slid into the driver's seat, started the engine, and put the top down as we pulled out onto the road. "Alone, at last." My chest tightened at those stupid words. That line was nothing more than habit. What would come afterwards?

She entered an address into the GPS and turned her face out the side window. "I appreciate the ride."

A layer of frost. That was what would follow my stupid words. We were back to square one, with her avoiding me. Her hands didn't shake, but she rubbed them together. This was not the painting. It was Victoria again, and my words had triggered it.

"Please tell me what Victoria said to you?"

She shook her head slightly but remained silent.

"Samantha, I don't know what she said, but it wouldn't have been kind. She's not a good person." I looked at her briefly as she kept her eyes out the side.

She sighed, not looking back at me. "Let's talk about something more interesting."

I could work with that. "Bene! I do love listening to you. Let me see...if you knew you were to die tomorrow, what would you do with the time you have left?"

"Gee, easy question." Her eyes were undoubtedly rolling. "What time tomorrow?"

"Sì, good question."

She was thawing. The evening was not ruined.

"Let's say tomorrow at noon. It will be sudden, and you can do anything between now and then."

"Fourteen hours?" She hummed quietly for a moment. "Drive to Detroit and hop on a plane to New York. Eat pizza in Times Square, take in the view of the city from the top of the Empire State in the middle of the night, watch the sunrise from the Brooklyn Bridge, and spend the morning at the Cloisters. And that's where I'd die."

I nodded slowly, aching at her solitude.

"What about you?" she asked.

"So sad. To die alone, far from home."

"It's not sad. I like being by myself. It would be peaceful."

"And as you die, what do you regret?"

She paused, quiet for a moment. When she answered, it was sharp, not from her heart. "Not saving enough money to leave to my sister, to pay her bills while she's getting treatment."

"Why do you not spend your last day with her?"

"Because she has enough sadness in her life right now. She doesn't need to watch me die."

"What if there was only tonight? No airplane, no travel, two hours. What do you do with the last two hours?" I would have pulled the car over and made love to her in the back seat. If she would have me.

"I'd write a letter to her and the kids, then probably pick up a bottle of wine and head home."

Again, the shallow answer. She was more irritated than I had thought. This was my moment to share, though. My moment for as much honesty as I could give. "I would spend the time with my family, with those I love. I would give them all the time they need to say everything they want to say, so there are no regrets for them when I'm gone."

"Well—"

"Life is about love." I smiled, a warmth spreading through my chest, imagining a future with her, spending my last two hours with her. Sofia would tell me to slow down, but I didn't care. "Without love, what is the value of life?"

"You can love yourself."

"And do you love yourself enough for two people?" I snuck a brief sidelong glance as she turned her face to the window again.

She was quiet for several minutes. "What do you look for in love?"

A surprisingly open question, coming from her.

"Someone who chooses time with me when they have two hours left. And you?"

"I don't know," she whispered, shaking her head slightly. "I have a shitty track record."

"We have that in common." I patted her thigh. I had meant it as a sign of empathy, but all the blood in my body lurched to my core, and I had to resist pulling the car over. Had to resist sliding my hand under her dress, between her legs. I rubbed slowly with my thumb, a reel of images flashing through my brain as her body tensed the same way mine had.

This was only date two. Control. Friends first. I returned the hand to the steering wheel and gave her a smile, shaking my head.

"I prefer to see you happy than sad, bella." I started asking simple, small questions, designed to get to know her. The same conversations I had had with a hundred different women, trying to find the needle in the haystack.

All too soon, we reached the address in the GPS. No house, no apartment. It was a hotel. "I think you entered the wrong address."

"Pull up to the front door."

"You live..."

"In a hotel, yeah. Extended stay." The blush crept up her cheeks again and she reached for the door handle once I had pulled into a space by the door.

"No, wait." I rounded to her side and opened the car door, offering a hand to help her up. As she stood, I stepped back and enveloped her hand with both of mine. I bowed my head to it and kissed the back, my lips lingering on her flesh, imagining for a brief moment it was other parts of her body. When I couldn't stand it any longer, I brought her hand to my chest, so she could feel the strong muscles and my racing heart. So she would know it was not just words.

"This was a special night for me, and I thank you, Samantha Caine. You have enchanted me, and I hope to see you again soon."

My brain knew it was date two, but the rest of my body protested.

"I guess you'd better hurry up with the painting, so there's a reason for me to come back to your office!" She blurted out, likely uncomfortable with her hand on me, but she didn't try to move it.

I laughed softly, time losing all meaning. I released her hand with one of mine and touched her glorious cheek, brushing it lightly with my thumb. I leaned in and touched my cheek to hers and then to the other, kissing the air instead of her. It was a casual gesture, something I did with family and friends, but it was different with her. Different than it had been with any other woman. I thought to remove her hand from my chest, so she wouldn't know the impact she had on me. But I left it there, allowing her to feel how her presence caused the blood to surge through my body. Feel my desire for her. My longing.

I traced her jawline as I finished and let go of her hand on my chest. She held it there a moment longer, staring at it, her own breath becoming deeper.

She was already mine.

But I had to focus on her heart. Gathering all my willpower, I took her hand and escorted her to the entrance. The glass doors slid open as we approached.

"Goodnight," she breathed, holding my gaze.

"Sogni d'oro, bella." I cupped the back of her neck and pulled closer, placing a tender kiss on her cheek. She inhaled sharply, and I closed my eyes, wanting more. As I withdrew, her mouth turned toward mine, but she was slow and I was stubborn.

"Sweet dreams to you, too." She stared a moment longer, her eyes on my mouth, then she turned on her heel and entered the hotel.

Once she was inside the building, she waved to the staff at the front desk, stopping to pick some envelopes up from them. Before vanishing farther into the building, she turned to face me. She hesitated, chewing on her lower lip. Was she going to come back outside? Ask for that kiss? Invite me in? How stubborn could I be if any of that happened?

Heat and hardness settled in my core as I stared at her, neither of us moving, but clearly wanting to. Not very stubborn, it would appear. I took a step and the front doors slid open, ushering me forward.

She startled and looked at her small clutch, ripping her phone out of it to answer. Her whole body deflated. The moment had passed, at least for her. One final glance back at me, a wave, and she continued along her path inside, away from me.

I watched after her, the doors forgetting about me and closing of their own volition. Reminding me that she was out of my reach. That I had decided to win her heart first, no matter how much I wanted the rest.

But what would that accomplish? She had said she was only in Brenton for the short term, but I hadn't thought she was this dedicated to keeping it short term.

A hotel?

No lease to break, nothing to sell?

She could leave at a moment's notice, whisking my heart away to whatever corner of the country she left for.

Fate was a cruel mistress.

CHAPTER 30

SAMANTHA

Monday morning, I walked into the break room at Foster Mutual to grab coffee before heading to my desk. It was a small room off the hallway with a kitchenette, a couple of round tables in the middle with seating, and copies of local and national newspapers. Cliff was there, making a fresh pot, so I leaned over the papers to scan the headlines while I waited.

When I pulled the *Brenton Times* out from under one of the national papers, I gasped.

Cliff poured a cup for each of us and stifled a laugh. "When I told you to sit on him until he was done with the Scott painting, that wasn't what I meant!"

The headline read 'Children's Hospital Gala a Success.' There was a half-page article about the event, and the picture, taking up a third of the article, was of the dance floor. Antonio and I dead center. The caption under the photo read, 'Dr. Antonio Ferraro, Brenton's most eligible bachelor, attends Children's Hospital Charity Gala. Ferraro's company contributed over one million dollars to the charity, helping make it the gala's most successful year.'

There was nothing about me in the article, but there was plenty about Dr. Dominico's million-dollar bid on the painting Antonio and I had chosen and a tiny paragraph about the stolen painting. But why that picture? When I read the byline—Victoria Meyers—the easy guess was she was none other than Miss July.

After tearing off the front page and stuffing it in my pocket so no one else would see it, I grabbed the coffee and headed to the Pit.

A sly look from Lucy as I arrived told me I was too late. "Good weekend?"

I shot her a sidelong glance and greeted Matt, who was waiting for us with printouts of the Scotts' prior insurance policies. As a senior underwriter for the company, I had asked him to review them with us, in case he could find something abnormal.

"The replacement value on their home increased at the standard rate every renewal," said Matt, comparing the policy declarations for each year. "New coverages were added as we introduced them, like cyber risk, but nothing out of the ordinary. No changes in liability coverage. A couple of minor changes to remove lesser-value paintings and jewelry, but nothing material.

"I remember reviewing the increase when they sent it in 2015. It was a big deal around here. We had to get a special acceptance from our reinsurance company and put some stipulations on the policy. Dad signed off on it directly."

I frowned, which Matt picked up on immediately.

"Is there something going on I should know about?"

"Nothing," I lied. "I've been talking to Harry and Quinn. They have me seeing shadows everywhere."

"Yeah, they can do that." He was tentative but continued to review the paperwork. I'd never been able to lie to him, so either I was getting better, or he was giving me the benefit of the doubt. Or enough rope to hang myself with. "There's nothing out of the ordinary here. We retain seven years' worth of documents in the main system, but they've been with us for ten. If you want anything from their first three years, you'll have to talk to IT about archived documents." He stood and stacked all the papers together. "Can I talk to you for a quick sec before I go?"

We stepped outside of the Pit far enough our voices wouldn't carry but kept our conversation at a whisper.

"Sam, I wanted to tell you I'm happy for you."

"For what?"

He tilted his always-furrowed brow toward me. "We all saw the article in the paper. I'm glad you're dating. You looked happy with him."

So much for tearing the picture out. "I'm not dating him."

"You sure? The photo looked pretty serious."

It had felt serious in the moment. There had been highs and lows Saturday evening. I folded my arms to prevent my hand from travelling to my cheek to touch the spot he'd kissed.

"Was that all?"

"Yeah." He touched my arm lightly. "If you need me to look at anything else, from a work standpoint or a friend standpoint, you know where to find me."

I thanked him as he left and returned to the Pit.

Lucy was sliding the declarations into an envelope. "To the IT department?" With advanced warning on wearing something professional, Lucy had cleaned up well. Black slacks and a loose white top. Doc Martens still, but surprisingly, no gum.

"You got it."

. . . .

The Information Technology department, full of programmers, testers, and business analysts, was on the second floor of the building. They were responsible for the Foster Mutual software programs including the policy and claims management systems. The rest of the Foster building was partitioned with cubicle walls, but the IT department was a large open space with desks on wheels. Power poles dotted the room so team members could move around and park their desks wherever they felt and plug into a pole. They were an odd bunch, solitary, and liked their large office darker than the rest of the company, so half the lights were always off.

"Who are we looking for?" asked Lucy.

I walked purposefully through the room until I spied Cass' husband, Kevin, who worked as a senior software developer. If the information was anywhere in the system, he'd be able to find it for me.

He was at a standing desk, an over-sized pair of headphones tuning out the world. I knocked on his desk and he startled and pulled the headphones down around his neck.

"Sammy! You scared the shit outta me! What are you doing here?"

"This is Lucy," I said, to be polite. "She's the intern I told you about."

"Yeah, I remember." He nodded at her. "Oh, hey, I got a text from Cassie. Something about you in the newspaper?"

"No comment." I glowered at Lucy, who looked excited to share. "We're looking for old policy information. Lucy, tell him what we need." If nothing else, getting her talking about work would stave off the newspaper discussion.

"We're researching a claim and we need some policy docs. Here's the policy number." She wrote it in his notebook. "We can only get seven years from the main system, but we need ten. Matt Foster said there's an archive somewhere. Can you pull anything out to help us? Ideally, we're looking for their original policy declarations."

I added, "And, if possible, an original copy of their application questionnaire."

"Yeah, we populate an archive on a seven-year cycle. Gimme two minutes to check in this code I'm working on, and I'll get to it."

His desk was a mess, which surprised me because he was so neat and tidy at home. There were stacks of notebooks, dirty glass and plate, a bowl of candy, two Detroit Tigers bobbleheads, and six pens in a 'World's Best Dad' mug.

"Alrighty then." His fingers flew over the keyboard as screen after screen of colorful text flashed past him. He typed almost as fast as Lucy did and none of it made sense to me. Before I knew it, he flipped to another window with a copy of the reports and he flicked one of the bobbleheads. "I've got the original application for you and all the decs. Want me to print them?"

"You're kidding! That seemed way too easy."

"It's rare to need anything this old, but sometimes, especially with personal injury claims, they can go back a long time. You're hardly the first person to make a request like this."

We retrieved the documents once they finished printing. When someone applied for insurance, there was a standard set of questions the company asked, which was the first thing Kevin printed for us. I flipped through it to the end, and skimmed until—

Lucy beat me to it. "Prior insurance with AmLife."

"Hmm."

"Good or bad hmm?" asked Kevin.

I nodded absently as I looked through the first three years of policy documents. They all looked the same as the first one we'd gone over with Matt, so I threw them in the shredder box. I stared at the application. Prior insurance with AmLife. Their life insurance was still there.

"Thanks, Kevin." I pointed Lucy toward the exit of the IT department. "Let's talk to Mike, get him to check with his contact to find out if they carry insurance at AmLife other than their life insurance."

"Sure, but why?"

I rubbed a hand over my face. "There's something fishy with this claim, so we're looking for any clues. Harry and Quinn said to focus on intent to defraud, but I'm wondering if the painting was stolen and they didn't know. Olivia doesn't strike me as the type of woman to intentionally defraud a company run by a friend. The Brenton PD hasn't answered my questions about theft..."

I sighed. "I've got to be honest, Lucy. I'm kind of grasping at straws here."

"Harry and Quinn are the experts, right?" she asked, and I nodded. "Why do you think they wouldn't take it over?"

"I have a sneaking suspicion this is a test."

•••••••••••

"Yeah, that red flag doesn't belong. Click here...and here..."

"What's—" Lucy protested when I stopped her from entering the Pit. We were looking for Mike, but Hailey's voice caught my attention.

"Aren't they supposed to be approved by Cliff?" asked Mike.

"Only when they're valid," said Hailey.

"If you say so." Mike's voice was uncertain.

They stopped, so Lucy and I entered the space.

"Hey you two." I kept my eyes on Hailey. "What are you doing?"

"She was showing me how to clear red flags. Did you know we could do that?"

"No. Common practice?"

She shrugged with a smile. "Want me to show you?"

"No, I prefer to play by the rules." I narrowed my eyes at her, but she snorted.

"Software lets me do it, so it's by the rules."

"Did you ever think it was a system bug you should be reporting to IT?"

"And not be able to do it anymore? Not likely!" They were getting too used to my attitude. It wasn't working on them anymore. Either way, I'd tell Kevin about it.

"Mike, I need a favor."

"Sure, Princess. What do you need?"

Hailey stifled a laugh. Apparently, both of them had seen the paper.

"So jealous." Hailey waved before heading out. "If I didn't know you better, I'd ask for details."

I rolled my eyes and turned my focus back to Mike. "Can you ask your contact at AmLife and find out if the Scotts had any coverage over there, other than life insurance. If so, any claims since 2014 or 2015, particularly break-ins or theft."

"Why?" He spun his chair around to look at us.

"Just a little extra digging."

"I don't think so. That's not normal digging, Sam. Something's up?"

"Can you do it for me? Message me anything you get back."

He sat there, unwavering, arms crossed.

"Otherwise, I'll stop taking Lucy out with me, and I'll encourage her to tell you about every single YouTube cat video she's ever watched." I crossed my arms right back at him and gave him an eyebrow raise for good measure.

"That's cruel and unusual punishment." He unfolded his arms and turned back to his laptop.

"Hey!" said Lucy indignantly.

"I'll call him later this morning."

I patted him on the back. "Thanks, big man, I knew I could count on you."

· · ● ● ●● ● ● ● · ·

Once the truck's engine was roaring, my phone rang. The audio system announced Antonio's name, and my heart fluttered. Lucy's face lit up. Prepare for humiliation.

She reached over and hit the call button on the steering wheel. "Hi, Antonio! It's Lucy and Sam!"

"Two beautiful women on one phone call. I'm a lucky man!"

Lucy giggled, while I rolled my eyes. But that voice. Those soft lips. His thumb rubbing my thigh. The curve of his muscles under my hand.

"Antonio. What do you want?"

"Lucy, it sounds as though Samantha is in a mood today. You are keeping her out of trouble, I hope?"

Yes, humiliating.

She kept laughing, though. "That's a two-person job, at least."

"Sì, you have a good point. Did she tell you about the auction on Saturday?"

I had to put an end to this. "Enough. Why are you calling?"

"Oh, bella, you're no fun today."

As much as I tried to be serious, I could feel the smile creeping up my face. He was too charming for his own good. For my own good. But how much of it was real and how much was everything Victoria Meyers had said? Was he wining and dining me? Did we share a moment outside my hotel or was it all a game to him?

And was it a good thing or a bad thing that Cass had called and interrupted me before I pulled him into my hotel room? That would have been a mind-blowing night.

"Two things, and I would appreciate if you wait until I'm done. One, I would like to see you today."

Lucy's jaw dropped and she tried to poke my arm, but I dodged it.

"Two, I was thinking about what you said about *Les amoureux* being at Mason's Gallery last year, and thought perhaps I could join you when you speak with them? If I know you at all, you will be going today? No time wasted."

My first instinct was to say no. I wouldn't be able to concentrate on my job with him and his hands and his lips and his voice there. My second instinct was that another art expert might help with the conversation. Plus, he'd been a big help Saturday. He was honey to my vinegar.

Lucy chimed in. "We're on our way there right now."

"Perfetto! I'll see you in ten minutes."

As he hung up, I shook my head at Lucy. "You need to keep your mouth shut sometimes."

She blew a bubble at me, from gum I hadn't known she had in her mouth. "Not my strong suit."

Chapter 31

Antonio

I paused with my hand on the gallery's door. Samantha was explaining something to Lucy about an abstract piece, while the two of them laughed. She used her hands to describe the movement, her whole body involved in the story. As though she were art all on her own.

Saturday had been a miracle. This amazing woman had spent the evening with me, danced with me, let me hold her. She was open to becoming friends and hopefully more.

How could I spy on her? No. I was ensuring she had all the information she needed for her claim. I was helping her. Taking a deep breath, I entered the gallery, the chime of the bell over the door announcing my arrival. The women turned to see me, two very different smiles on their faces.

Lucy was giddy. She wore her excitement on her sleeve. It was charming.

Samantha, on the other hand. What was her smile? Forced, for certain. But was she forcing it up or forcing it down? Regardless, I approached her first.

"Ciao, bella." I took her hand to kiss, but she restrained it. Was she embarrassed around Lucy? I bit my lip and took the guess. "If you are uncomfortable about me kissing this hand in a professional setting, I could kiss Lucy's, as well."

She frowned at me. Not the playful frown, but a genuine one.

I moved on to Lucy and gestured at the artwork on the walls. "So, how do you feel about abstract art?"

"Sam was trying to explain, but I don't get it." She squinted at one of the paintings, tilting her head.

Samantha nodded at her protégé. "It takes some time to absorb. Come to the next room, I think you'll find what you like there." Leaving the front room, we made our way around the corner to the second, where the landscapes and portraits hung.

"This is more me." Lucy wandered from painting to painting, admiring the sculptures.

Samantha remained at the entrance to the room, watching her, leaning against the wall. I slid my hand into place at the small of her back, but she shifted her weight away from me.

I moved close to keep my words private. "Are you upset I'm here?"

She shook her head slightly, keeping her eyes on Lucy.

"Would you be more comfortable at dinner tonight?"

She chuckled, which evolved into a smile. "I'm working until eight tonight, and you have a Chagall to clean."

"Will you ever say yes when I ask you out?"

She turned to me with a twinkle in her eye. "Probably not. I don't date, remember?"

I leaned closer, my mouth next to her ear. "So I'll have to wait for you to ask me out? Is that the plan?" She shook her head, but with the smirk this time. She pushed off the wall and followed Lucy into the room.

"Which one's your favorite?"

Lucy stopped in front of one resembling Monet's *Impression, Sunrise*, pointing.

"Mine, too," said Samantha. Perhaps I would buy it for her if she liked it. Or paint one of my own. Sì, I would paint this for her. Mine would be a better copy than this.

"It's for sale if you'd like to buy it," came a woman's voice from behind us. As we turned, Rhonda Wells, owner of the gallery, joined us. A sharply dressed woman in her mid-sixties, she spiked her short white hair, and always wore red glasses and black clothes.

"Dr. Ferraro." She gave me an appreciative smile, shaking my hand. "Scouting for your father?'

My smile faltered, but I snapped back in place quickly. "It's good to see you again, Rhonda. Have you met Samantha Caine and Lucy Chapman from Foster Mutual Insurance?"

Rhonda shook with each of them and addressed Samantha. "You handled the *Number Vee* repair, didn't you?"

"I did. It's a beautiful painting."

"It's crap!" She sniffed. "The artist is my curator's son, so I had to include it. He's sold a few pieces from here. Thinks he's God's gift to the art world. I told him it's Brenton, for Christ's sake, but he thinks he's the next Mark Rothko."

"That's his junk over there, too." She pointed to a drip painting in the first room. "Rothko said he wished to bring people to tears with his depth of emotion. *Number Vee* inspires the wrong sort of sorrow."

Lucy looked fit to burst. She laughed a lot; I liked her. Perhaps I would introduce her to my younger brother, Lorenzo.

Rhonda guided us to the back of the gallery, into her small office. She sat in the chair behind her desk, inviting Lucy and Samantha to sit opposite her, while I stood.

"Dr. Ferraro. I have an appointment with these ladies..." Rhonda let the words hang, an unspoken request for me to leave.

Samantha gestured to me. "I invited Dr. Ferraro to join us, Ms. Wells."

Rhonda glared at me for a moment over her glasses. Her comment about scouting for my father had my guard up. My father offered to buy *Les amoureux* while it was here, however the Scotts didn't sell it until afterward. Papa went directly to Bobby Scott for the sale, so Rhonda may have been in the dark. But would she make the guess? Would she let it slip he had made the offers?

There was little I would learn here. I would, however, ensure Papa's secret remained. My secret now.

She hit a few buttons on her computer and tilted her head back to look at the screen through the bottom half of her bifocals.

"So we're all here about *Les amoureux dans le ciel*? The Chagall?" She hit a few keys and moved the mouse.

Samantha said, "Yes, could you tell us exactly when it was on display?"

"Hmm..." Rhonda kept her eyes on the monitor. "June 13 through December 18 of last year. It was quite the coup. Most of our work is local; we rarely get something so high profile." She tilted her head down to look at us over the top rim of her glasses. "We had a tremendous uptick in foot traffic and purchases when it was here. Even had a few offers to buy it."

"Really?"

"All from the same gentleman. He was insistent he had to have it." She looked at me briefly before turning back to the computer, tilting her head again to read the screen. "Five offers, actually. Sotheby's valued it at one million. He offered them a hundred thousand more, but the owner refused to sell."

Lucy's eyes widened. "Big offer! Why would they turn that down?"

Papa had said Bobby Scott was greedy and wanted more.

"Said it wasn't about the money, it was about their pride in proving the attribution. I suggested they sell it. Substantial return on their investment."

"Could you tell us a bit about your security system here?" Samantha asked.

Rhonda turned back to her, narrowing her eyes. "Why?"

"We carry the insurance on that painting and several others in your gallery. We need to be sure you're protecting our investments."

Rhonda pursed her lips, unconvinced, but turned her monitor to face us when she pulled up the display from her security cameras. "We have multiple cameras, including each gallery room, in the storage room in the back, in my office, and at each door." I leaned in to get a clearer look as she clicked through the images, showing us no part of the gallery went unrecorded.

"Ever had a break-in?"

"Two, yes." She turned the monitor away from us again.

"When were they?"

"If I understand you, you only want to know if either break-in was when *Les amoureux* was in the gallery?" Rhonda looked at Samantha over her glasses again and received a nod in return.

She returned to her computer. "Hmm...No, one was before, and one was after."

"Can you tell us who put in the offers on the painting?" asked Lucy.

I gripped the back of Samantha's chair, staring at Rhonda. She couldn't answer that question. If she did, it would be the last time my family spent any money here.

Rhonda directed a cool glare at Lucy. "You're new to this, young lady, aren't you?"

Lucy nodded, shaken.

I chimed in, speaking slowly to keep my voice level. I directed it all to the gallery owner. "Private sales are treated with the utmost discretion. It's a well-understood rule within the art world, particularly as the prices grow. Buyers will use brokers or intermediaries to make offers, often specifically to remain anonymous."

"Why?"

Before I could continue, Samantha took over, with her own slant. "Because more than half of all stolen artwork is taken from private homes or organizations. If no one knows you have a multi-million-dollar collection, no one will try to steal it. Someone offering that much for a painting is in that group."

Before Saturday, her words would have surprised me. But, given our little investigation, it merely heightened my need to discover her true self.

Rhonda grinned at Samantha. "You're not new to this business."

"Not really." Her tone was light, but it masked so much more.

Past my greatest worry for the meeting, my grip on her chair weakened, and I placed a proud hand on her shoulder. "Samantha spotted the stolen artwork at the charity auction."

"Stolen what?" asked Lucy.

"It was a favor." Rhonda pressed her lips together. "My curator said it had come through another restoration company—"

Samantha leaned forward, out of my grip. "Parker's?"

"Yes, exactly."

"She tried steering us away from Ferraro's. Told us Parker's was much better, but Foster wouldn't approve them as a vendor."

Rhonda's frown deepened. "She's normally a better judge of character."

Lucy cocked her head. "I don't understand. Why put a stolen painting up for auction? A sale, I'd understand, so you can get money for something you didn't buy. But why an auction?"

"Legitimacy," said Samantha. "They run the painting through a small, reputable auction. Muck it up a little—" She touched her shoulder, where my hand had been. "—so the starting bid can be lower and fewer people are interested. Someone involved in the whole thing buys it for a low price."

"Still not getting it, Sam," Lucy said.

"You remember I told you about provenance? They can wipe out a period on the provenance and start it back up as a legal purchase at an auction. It looks legal, and they can sell it to an unsuspecting private buyer. Odds are, that buyer would confirm the last step in the provenance, not the ones before it. But if a buyer tries to go back further, they renege on the sale and the seller finds someone else."

"Or," said Lucy tentatively. "They'd already sold it, and the party donating it had no idea it was stolen?"

"Also possible." Samantha nodded to Lucy and turned back to Rhonda. "Sorry, one last question. Any staff let go during the time the painting was here or after?"

"Sweetheart, I run a small and honest gallery, no matter what happened Saturday. Me, my curator, and my daughter. That's it. Anyone who comes in to do any work here, including cleaners, only does it when one of us is here. I take the responsibility of this gallery and its contents seriously."

"Thank you, Rhonda, that's all we needed."

"I have one question for you, though. I heard the owner of *Les amoureux* passed in a fire last month. Are your questions related?"

Samantha tilted her head.

"I'm guessing you're here because the widow's looking to sell it, and needs to verify nothing happened to it for the six months it was out of her possession?"

My lip twitched; I felt it. I breathed through it to keep my body steady. Rhonda didn't know about Papa's purchase.

"We may be." Samantha sat back and steepled her fingers. Not a flinch at the deception. Smoother than I had expected, after how nervous she had been with me initially.

"I guarantee you nothing happened while it was here. If she wants to sell it, I can contact the man who made the offer last year." Her eyes flicked to me, narrowed, sending a message to Papa which didn't need to be sent. She would have made a sound commission. "He won't likely go over the Sotheby's price now if the widow's coming to him, but he'll make a fair offer."

"Thanks, we'll keep that in mind," said Samantha. I gave a subtle nod to Rhonda, seating myself in the lie.

They all stood, shaking hands. Rhonda walked us out and asked again if Samantha was interested in the *Impression, Sunrise* copy.

"You mean the pastiche?"

I put my hands behind my back and approached the painting. I had replicated Monet's masterpieces before, creating copies from the originals, and I recognized the brush strokes. It was an excellent imitation of his style. "Pastiche? Are you sure?"

"Well, it's not a copy." She placed a hand on my back. "It isn't signed, there's too many smokestacks, missing a person in the front rowboat, masts on this ship are at the wrong angle..." She paused, clasping her hands in front of her, her gaze falling. "Sorry, old habits."

Old habits? Before I could ask further, Rhonda clapped slowly, three times. "Good eye, Ms. Caine. I'm pleased so many of our paintings are covered by someone who understands this world. If you ever want to change careers, though, I'd love to have someone as sharp as you. I may be in need of a new curator soon, depending on how this whole auction debacle unfolds."

"I'm good, thanks."

Sì, she was good. Very good. My stomach was unsettled as I flipped back and forth from admiration to fear that I couldn't fool her forever.

CHAPTER 32

SAMANTHA

We congregated on the sidewalk outside the gallery before splitting to our respective vehicles. He'd held the door for us, the consummate gentleman. Just like Victoria had said. Her voice kept popping into my head at inconvenient moments. Especially at the gallery when he was complimenting me.

Every time he touched me, I wanted to sink into him, but it was business. Maybe he was just touchy-feely in general. No, it was me. Offering to kiss Lucy's hand if it made me feel better. So charming. I closed my eyes and leaned toward the sun, absorbing its heat.

Why was he even there? He got nothing of value out of that. Hadn't even asked any useful questions.

Lucy was happy, though. "Dr. Ferraro, thanks for coming. I'd love to get more of your take on abstract art sometime."

I shook with the chuckle, trying to hold it in. Her lack of social boundaries had irritated me when I'd first met her, but it was growing on me. Like a fungus.

"I would love to. However—" He paused, that deep, accented voice running chills up and down my spine. "—it would appear you already have an expert with you."

"Hardly." *He'll make you think you're the most interesting woman in the world.*

"Don't sell yourself short. I was impressed."

I tore my face away from the sun's warmth and serenity to frown at him. "You're impressed easily."

Lucy spluttered a laugh.

"That was more than an art history degree and a summer with ARCA. How do you know so much?" He touched my back again. It was innocent, but every time he did it brought back memories of our dance, the look in his eyes, and the invitation I'd almost given him.

I shifted away from him, my body protesting the whole time. If only it would listen to my brain. My brain knew I had to be careful around sexy men with their smooth words and ready smiles. "I told you already. Long and uninteresting story."

"Over dinner would be an excellent time to tell me."

"Do you listen to anything I say? Or are you running your own little narrative through your head for me?" I marched back to the truck and turned, reminding Lucy it was time to go. Goddamn Victoria Meyers and her fucking Calendar Club. I make one decision to follow my heart instead of my head and this happens.

Behind the wheel, I watched the two of them chatting. He smirked, she laughed, they shook hands, and she walked to the truck with a grin.

"My word was moody." Lucy hoisted herself into the truck and pulled the heavy door shut. "His were fierce and determined. Then I suggested stubborn, but he said you weren't as stubborn as him."

"Lucy, enough."

"Then, he told me I was supposed to convince you to go out with him again." She shoved me playfully while she laughed. He hadn't moved from the front of the gallery and stood there watching me with an exasperatingly sexy smirk I felt all the way in my toes.

When Lucy gave him a thumbs up, he waved and headed to his car.

"How are you saying no to that? I mean, seriously! You two are so cute together. He obviously likes you a lot."

"No, Lucy, he obviously likes *women* a lot."

"Didn't kiss my hand when he came in."

"Cut it out!" My phone rang, and I answered. "Saman—"

"What the literal fuck, Sam?" Great. My sister.

Lucy's eyes popped as I disconnected the phone from the audio system and held it to my ear.

"Cass, I've got someone in the truck—"

"If you tell me it's him—" I had to pull the phone away from my ear. "—I will lose it!"

"It's that intern I'm mentoring. I'm working. I'll call you later."

"You were supposed to call me Saturday night if he showed up!"

Antonio drove off, his music thudding so loud my rearview mirror shook. I turned the engine off and slid out of the truck, mouthing *one sec* to Lucy.

"Cass, I'll say this one more time, then I'm done: I'm a grown woman."

"Nathan said—"

"Stop!" I rubbed a hand over my face and took in a deep breath, let it out loudly enough she heard it. "I seriously need to get back to work. But I love you, so I'll give you the quick and dirty version. You going to listen until I'm done?"

Grudgingly, she agreed.

"Alright. Sofia, the woman I was supposed to be going with, is his sister. She set us up. He and I both thought we were going with her. But, I had a great evening with him. I like him, Cass. A lot. Enough it's freaking me out. And you guys coming down on me isn't helping."

"Really?" Her agitation faded into surprise.

"Yeah, really."

"What about The Train Station?"

The hand over my face dropped as I stared in the direction he'd driven off. "I can't tell you how many times he asked me out and I said no. So, yeah, he heard me talking to Nathan about going there and he showed up, hoping to make a good impression on my family."

"Family?"

"Yeah." I laughed; it sounded so stupid. "I called him Uncle Nathan on the phone. Listen, I'm working all evening tonight, but I'll come over tomorrow after work, okay? Give you the full details?"

"You sure he's safe?"

"Yeah." For everything but my heart.

"What about the near fistfight?"

"Seriously, Cass." I put my hand on the truck door. "You know how Nathan is. He started it."

She sighed heavily. "I don't want you to get hurt again, sweetie."

"Me, either. But sometimes you need to take a chance, right? I haven't since Matt. Isn't that what you were trying to convince me to do?"

"Alright. I'll reserve judgement for now."

I hung up and climbed back into the truck.

Lucy put a hand on the center console. "She one of the reasons you said no to him?"

"My sister's a bit much."

"Do you want to talk about it?" she asked, doubtful.

I grinned and turned on the engine, appreciating she knew the answer.

"What do you think?" Lucy leaned on the center console as we pulled out for the short drive back to Foster Mutual. "A secret buyer wanting to pay that much money was interesting."

"Yeah, someone out there with a lot of money wanted it. Badly. It's possible the Scotts found out who was offering the money for it and sold it after it left the gallery to keep the sale secret. Or someone had the resources to steal the original and leave a copy—"

My phone rang again. Janelle. I ran it through the truck's audio system.

"Hey, Janelle. It's Sam and my partner Lucy. Got anything for me on break-ins at the Scott residence?"

"You know your stuff, Sam. Yes, they had a break-in and theft in July 2015—"

I hit the steering wheel. "Dammit!"

"What?"

Lucy said, "The painting was still in Paris in July."

"That the only break-in you've got, Janelle?"

"Yeah, sorry, Sam. You have any other news on your end?"

"Did you hear about the auction on Saturday?"

She laughed. "I'm assuming you're talking about the stolen painting they found?" At least one person didn't bring up the photo, although the implication was in her laugh.

"That's the one."

"Yeah, I heard. Rumor has it a couple FBI agents are arriving in Lansing next week. Rumor also says a tall woman in a blue dress and long brown hair caught it. Some sort of art claims—I mean art crimes—expert. Did you see anyone there who fit that description?"

"Nope. Not a one." I grinned, while Lucy poked my arm. "Thanks for the info anyway, Janelle. We'll be conducting interviews this week. If we find anything, we'll be in touch."

As I hung up, Lucy said, "Why does everyone know about this thing Saturday except me?"

"It's something Antonio and I stumbled over."

"You're not going to tell me the details?" When I shook my head, she continued. "Alright, so if the only break-in the police have was when the Chagall wasn't at the Scott house, are we done with the theory it was stolen?"

"Probably, but I want to double-check with Mike and Quinn first."

Lucy initiated the call to Mike.

"Hey Mike, this is Sam and Lucy. Did you hear back from your contact at AmLife?"

"I did. Exactly what you expected. The Scotts had a Business Owners policy with them. Theft claim in 2015. My guy sent me the full details—"

"Mike, stop. Was it July 2015?"

"Yeah, I forwarded—"

I pulled the truck over as my mood plummeted. "Thanks, Mike, I appreciate you looking into it for me."

"You owe me one!" he said as he hung up.

Shifting the truck into park, I sat back and folded my arms.

Lucy popped a bubble. "What next? Quinn?"

I nodded slowly, and she made the call.

"Good day, Sam. I just finished pulling some bad news for you."

"Thanks, Quinn. Lucy's with me, by the way. Would the bad news be the Scott claim in July 2015, by any chance?"

"Indeed it was. You already tracked it down?"

"It was a bit of an adventure," said Lucy.

"How'd ya find it?"

The pride in her voice had me sitting a little taller after the disappointment. "Matt Foster to IT to Mike in claims to AmLife. With a detour talking to someone at the Brenton PD. Probably would have been easier to get it from you."

"Like I said, you've got a nose, girl. So, if you already knew, why are you calling me?"

I tapped a finger on my arm. "I need your opinion. One of my running theories was about it being stolen and replaced without the Scotts knowing. We talked to the owner at Mason's Gallery. The Chagall was there for six months last year, and I feel pretty confident it wasn't stolen while it was there. From the results I got from the police and this Business Owners policy claim, I'm not feeling it being stolen from their house, either. What do you think? Should I drop the theft angle?"

"Depends. Question is, why are you so convinced it was stolen and replaced with a fake?"

I looked at Lucy, as though she could answer the question for me, but she shrugged. "Faith in Bobby Scott? Faith he wouldn't have hung a forgery in his house intentionally?"

Quinn's voice softened. "Faith in humanity is admirable, but not part of your job description, Sam."

CHAPTER 33

SAMANTHA

Lucy and I sat around a table in Kathy Becker's cramped kitchen, having tea in mismatched cups. The modest house with flowered wallpaper was a far cry from the Scotts' large one next door. The police had already interviewed her and we'd read their report, but I wanted to take care of some due diligence.

Kathy was a woman in her seventies with bottle-blond hair and a loud geometric-print blue dress, which clashed with her wallpaper. Wide-eyed with a broad smile, she said she was more than happy to answer my questions.

My phone sat in the middle of the table, recording our conversation. "Can you explain what happened before you called the fire department on July 31st of this year?"

"Yes, I was in the kitchen, cleaning carrots from my garden." She gestured out the back door. "I smelled some smoke and ignored it until the scent got so strong, I went out front to check what was going on. That's when I saw the smoke coming from Olivia's house!" Her hand trembled as she reached for her teacup.

Before Lucy could ask another question, I gave her a quick look, reminding her to be patient.

"She and I used to have tea every Saturday, you know. I'd go over to her house, and we'd have a cup and talk about everything and nothing."

"Kathy, you were saying about the fire?" I reminded her gently.

"Oh, yes!" She took a steadier sip of her tea and continued. "Sorry, it's been a trying time for everyone in the neighborhood. Anyway, yes, I hurried over to see if Olivia or Bobby needed help. They have an alarm system, so I thought the fire department would already be on their way. But when I got over there, the alarm wasn't going off. I rushed back to my house and called 9-1-1, and they sent a truck right away."

"Can we see your garden?" Interesting, Lucy. That hadn't been one of the questions we'd rehearsed.

"Why, yes!" She stood quickly and ushered us outside. The backyard was as immaculate as her hair. Perfectly flat lawn with precisely edged flower beds and a vegetable garden in full swing.

A five-foot high oak fence ran the perimeter, with a gate allowing access to the Scotts' yard. She led us to the garden and explained how she managed it, until Lucy interrupted.

"Are you married, Kathy?" she asked.

"Oh, no, my husband passed away almost ten years ago. This yard was his prize. I miss him terribly." She paused and picked a carrot out of the garden, absently brushing the dirt off. "I wonder if Olivia misses Bobby as much."

"I imagine she misses him a lot."

"I doubt it." Kathy tore off the stem. "They used to argue a lot."

"About what?"

"His business, his friends, money. I heard them talking about selling something to cover some business debts. I didn't understand what it was, but it sounded like he said they should sell the 'seagull,' and she said they couldn't. Big fight over that one."

Lucy didn't make the connection. "They argued about selling a seagull?"

"I'm sorry. I spend a lot of time out here, and their voices carried. I didn't mean to eavesdrop." Her eyes widened.

"Of course not." I nodded gravely. "Did you hear anything out of the ordinary the morning of the fire?"

"A couple of vans had been there earlier, but I think they were having some work done."

Lucy said, "We know about a security company and a painting company. Was that it?"

"Could be. They left in a hurry, though, with Olivia yelling at them, and then she drove off, as well. It seemed a little fishy if you ask me."

While they spoke, I snapped a photo of the Scotts' house, capturing the boarded-up windows and dark stains on the roof, then walked to the gate. Time to get a closer look.

"If you'll excuse us for a moment, Kathy." I beckoned Lucy to follow. Kathy was about to protest, but I smiled warmly and went anyway.

Lucy was right behind me, and we made our way to the back of the Scotts' house. "What's up?"

I gave her a motion to be quiet. We rounded the house to the concrete driveway at the front. I looked out toward the street but couldn't see anything. I tried a few different angles, took some pictures, but the house was completely concealed. I repeated my checks and photos at the back of the property, where the fence separated it from the main road and the river beyond.

When I was done, we made our way through the gate, closed it behind us, and I asked, "Were you close to Olivia?"

"We had tea weekly, if you consider that close."

"And what about her husband?" Lucy asked.

She gasped, putting a hand on her chest. "I don't know what you're implying, young woman, but—"

I leaned between Lucy and Kathy holding my hand up. "We didn't mean to imply anything. It was a standard question. I think we're done, though. Thanks, Kathy."

·· • • •·• • • ··

I pulled a block down the road, so we weren't lingering in front of Kathy's house, then Lucy and I hopped to the back seat. I fired up the laptop and started a private note on the claim system, tagging Lucy so she'd have access to it.

"What did we learn?" I asked as I typed.

"She was either interested in or having an affair with Bobby." Lucy began tentatively but grew more confident when I nodded. "I don't think she and Olivia are as friendly as she said. And the comments about them arguing a lot, about money, specifically. That was interesting."

"I agree. Remember Matt pointed out they'd sold several other paintings and jewelry? Sounds like they were having financial problems. And I'm betting what reminded her of a seagull was the Chagall; close to how Cliff pronounced it. Rhonda said they didn't want to sell it, maybe that was because they knew it was a fake?" I paused, glaring at my phone for a moment, willing Antonio to call with some news. "*If* it's a fake. We still haven't proven it yet."

"Why were we sneaking around the house like that?"

I typed while we continued. "I was looking for a line of sight for any cameras, but it was a no go out front and in back."

Lucy nodded.

"Also, the Scotts' house is still boarded up. We cut them a check last week for the repairs. Considering how insistent David Scott was about the claim, I would have expected repairs to start right away."

"Are we getting anywhere with this claim, Sam?"

"We're close, Lucy, I can feel it." I checked my phone again. "When Antonio proves the painting's a fake—"

"Or proves it's authentic."

I tapped a finger on my keyboard. Why hadn't he called yet? Maybe he was too busy charming some other client to work on my—*Stop, Sam.*

"You're blushing."

"Lucy, zip it."

CHAPTER 34

ANTONIO

I sat in my office at the studio, hand on the three photos. It was enough evidence to justify calling her. Two days since the gallery, four days since the gala. I hadn't heard from her. She would have said she was busy if I had asked, likely working. She would tell me to work on her burned painting. But the more distant she was, the surer I was that Victoria was behind it all.

She wanted to see the ultraviolet results, and I had them. So, I called, running a thumb across my lips, imagining so much more than a business meeting.

"Hi, Antonio, hold on a sec." She became muffled. "Lucy, stay there. I'll be up as soon as I'm off the phone." And clear again. "Sorry. What's up?"

"Ciao, bella. I have some news on your burned Chagall. Can you come to my office?"

"I'm working out of town all day. How about tomorrow morning?" She spoke quickly, clearly busy.

"No, no, today. I can bring everything to you."

"Antonio, I'm an hour out of town." She thought a little barrier would stop me?

"Perfetto, I need to go out and grab lunch anyway. It will be a nice drive. Have you eaten yet?"

"No."

"I have the ultraviolet photos of the signature. I think you will want to see this. Do you have time?"

She gasped.

I had her.

"Yes! I have a half hour between appointments at 1:30. I can send you GPS coordinates for where to meet."

Another adventure with my Samantha. "Bene, I'll bring lunch. See you then."

· · · · ●·●· · ·

Her coordinates led me to a rural road in the middle of southern Michigan, the pavement cracked and in need of repair. It was barely wide enough for two-way traffic, and the shoulder was a narrow strip of grass and weeds that barely fit her giant truck. The cornfield across the road waved in the gentle wind, and the sun was high in the sky. The drive had been magnificent.

I shifted the car into park and grinned, lust filling every inch of me. Kings of Leon screeched out "Sex on Fire" through the stereo system. Was it making an impression? Did it make her think of all the things I thought of?

No reaction.

Did she even recognize the song?

She sat on the tailgate of her truck, unlike I had ever seen her. Gone were the suits and formal wear, replaced by thick-soled work boots, black cargo pants, and a stained pink polo shirt. And a ball cap, confining her luxurious hair. This was the rock climber, the woman who trekked to the top of mountains, who owned the exquisite arms I had been fantasizing about since the night at the restaurant.

I wanted to touch her, taste her, make her smile like she had before Victoria had inserted herself.

I turned the car off and got out, my freshly polished shoes already coated with dirt. No matter. I would walk through fire for her, so what was a little dirt? The black dress pants and button-down had done their job already. She had scanned the length of me and bit her lip.

Smoothing my tie and shirt, as well as the fall of my pants, I kept my eyes on her. The seduction had begun. This was date number three, after all. I grabbed the two containers from Russo's and approached her.

"What did you bring me?" she asked casually.

"Ciao, bella." Balancing the two containers, I took her hand, her surprisingly soft but strong hand, and brought it to my lips. I savored her, thinking again of how much I had wanted to kiss her Saturday night. She had obviously wanted the same.

"Antipasti from Russo's!" I bowed to present her container. It was cheesy, but she would like it.

"Looks great, thanks." She opened it briefly, glanced inside, and placed it next to where she sat. "About the ultraviolet pictures, though?"

"Speaking of things which look great. I like your look today. Very rugged." Rugged? Was that a compliment?

"This is my fieldwork look. And speaking of work—about those pictures?"

I retreated to my car and leaned a hip on it, waving a dismissive hand. "No work until we've eaten."

"I only have—" She checked her watch. "—twenty-six minutes before I need to go."

"Then, we eat fast." I smirked, but she must not have been feeling playful.

She didn't pick up her container; instead she narrowed her eyes and tightened her mouth. I approached and placed my food next to hers, settling my hands on either side of her, touching her thighs. I looked directly into her eyes, pale green today, less than a foot away from her. She wouldn't be able to avoid the conversation this time.

"You are still bothered by Victoria, sì?"

The blush climbed up her cheeks, and she broke my gaze. "Yeah."

"Tell me." I pulled her face back to mine. "What did she say?"

She pulled her face from my grip, and I jumped up on the tailgate to sit next to her, the width of the small containers between us. She withdrew a newspaper clipping from her back pocket and handed it to me.

As I unfolded it, I nodded. As I had expected. Victoria Meyers. "I would guess she told you we dated."

"Last month." There was a tremor in her voice. Not nervous, but angry.

"Sì."

"She called me August."

"Scusi?"

"She said you date a different woman each month, so I was the flavor of the month for August, and she had been July."

The Calendar Club. That was what she had meant. "We went on three dates and had nothing in common. She was not happy when I told her I was not interested in continuing to see her."

She was quiet, picking up her container and moving the food around.

I folded the paper gently and slipped it into my shirt pocket. I sighed and gripped the tailgate. "How much time before you have to go?"

"Twenty-three minutes." She acted calm, but her whole body was tense. "Is it true?"

I couldn't lie about this, as well. I had to be honest with her. This was important. "Sì, it is."

She bowed her head and gave a bitter laugh. "Then I think we should look at the pictures you brought. We don't have more to talk about."

The sun was blazing. I looked exceptional in black, but it was a poor choice for this meeting. I loosened the tie and undid a few buttons, rolling up the sleeves. The leaves on the corn fluttered in the breeze, and I took a deep breath. She needed to know why I did what I did. And hopefully, she would understand.

"My Nonna always said to me, 'Antonio, mangia! Eat! You are too skinny!' and she would stuff me with meatballs and cannoli."

Samantha picked up a piece of parmigiana but remained silent.

"I was a...big boy. My friends called me Fat Tony. I spent most of my life that way, and the girls had no time for me. I flirted, I had crushes, but only had a couple of girlfriends. When I moved back to Italia for my master's degree, I lived with one of my cousins, who taught me how to exercise and eat well. After a couple of years..." I flourished my hand, indicating the product of too many hours at the gym.

"Then, the girls were all over you?"

"Sì, exactly." I nudged the food around in my own container, but ate nothing. "I moved back to America for my doctorate and met a beautiful woman who wanted to spend every moment with me."

My heart hurt just thinking of her. The greatest heartbreak of my life. "Her name was Faith. We were engaged and planning a family. We had fun together, and I loved her very much. I thought. But all she loved was my wallet and how she looked on my arm. I took a trip to Napoli for my research and was gone for three weeks. I missed her so much I came home early to surprise her."

I took one of the olives from my container, stalling. The story was difficult, even after all those years. Samantha didn't hurry me––she simply listened. But my time was running out. I looked at her, hanging on my every word.

"Do you know what I found in our apartment?"

She shook her head.

The lump formed in my throat, making it hard to go on. "I could still smell dinner in the air. Lasagna. Two plates in the sink and two wine glasses on the counter."

Samantha gasped and put a hand on my arm. "Oh, no."

"Sì." I nodded slowly. "I walked in on them in our bed. *Our* bed. And I...I left. She tried to make excuses, but I was done with her."

"I can't blame you."

I swallowed hard, needing to finish. "After I got over the surprise, the shock, I spent a lot of time talking it over with my family, especially Sofia. I figured out one critical thing.

If I went back in time and looked at our first three dates, without lust, without the marvel such a beautiful woman would want to be with me, I knew Faith was not the right one. I wasted all that time on a shell of a person who was beautiful on the outside only."

I shook my head slowly. "So, I made a decision: Three dates. If I don't find what I'm looking for in a woman by the time we have had three dates, then she's not the right one."

Samantha withdrew her hand from my arm. "That seems harsh."

"No, it's practical."

"Since when was love ever practical?"

I closed my eyes. How many women had come and gone since then, none of them passing the third date? "For aught that I could ever read, could ever hear by tale or history…"

"The course of true love never did run smooth."

"Sì, exactly."

"It's ironic. That caused you to date more women. My divorce caused me to stop dating altogether."

I jerked my head back. "You were married? When?"

"After my mom died. I'd been dating Matt for a year. I'd never expected anything to come of it. Hell, I moved away for half that time with no intention of coming back. He was like a placeholder. But when she died…" She stopped, closing her eyes for a moment and exhaling. It was a day for honesty. "When she died, my world fell apart. He was there for me and we dove into it without thinking. The marriage didn't last a year."

"That is very short. What happened?"

She popped an olive in her mouth, laughing to herself. "Turned out he was gay."

"Marone! I didn't see that coming!"

"Yeah, me, either. We'd started drifting apart before the honeymoon was even over. I don't know when he finally came to terms with it, but we spent most of our marriage just co-existing. We split amicably enough, but I figured I was happier by myself. That's when I left town."

"But you didn't move on from how he hurt you. You shut yourself off to love."

She straightened, curling her lip. "No different than you. You've let your love life be determined by what she did to you. Aren't you bothered by the reputation you've gotten?"

I waved it off. "Most people spend too much time worrying about what others think of them and not enough time doing what is best for themselves."

"Not afraid your reputation will scare off the right one?"

"Have I scared you off?" I smiled, but a knot tied tight in my stomach.

She stared back at me, mouth twitching as though to say something, but nothing came out. She didn't say 'yes,' at least.

Tentatively, I reached for her. Traced the line of her jaw with my thumb. "Let me help you figure that out." My chest felt light, and my blood stirred as I wrapped my hand behind her elegant neck. I leaned toward her, tilting my head to avoid the brim of her hat. Her lips parted for me. As my mouth sought hers, I whispered, "This is our third date, after all."

She leaned away immediately. "This isn't a date!"

I let go of her neck and sat up straight, laughing. "Sì, of course, it is! I bought lunch for us, and now we are talking over food. This is a lunch date."

"No, it's not. This is a business meeting! You brought pictures for me for a case we're working on. And even if it were, it would only be our second, anyway!"

I counted them on my fingers. "Russo's, the gala, and today. That makes three."

"Russo's wasn't a date, either!"

"Sì, it was. We went together, we had coffee, you ate, we told each other many things about ourselves, and then I paid. That was a date. I even said it was a date as we walked back to my office."

"Well, today's not a date, regardless," she insisted stubbornly.

"As you like." I winked and nudged her arm. "That way, I won't have to make a choice about whether to see you again."

She tried hard not to smile at me, but the truth was all over her body. "Do I get a say in this matter? What if I don't want to see you?"

"Don't be so silly." I waved it off, teasingly. "Of course, you do!"

I leaned toward her once more, but she avoided my mouth, shaking her head. "No kissing during business meetings. Now, I have—" She checked her watch. "—fifteen minutes before I have to go. Show me the pictures."

"Sì, if it is to be a business meeting, we must do some business!" I edged off the tailgate and retrieved an envelope with three large pictures from the car. She hopped down, and I laid them out next to each other. Each was a different close-up of the signature on the burned painting.

"That's it? Three photos?"

"Sì."

"You could have emailed them to me."

"True, but I thought it was a good excuse to see you." I smirked and brushed the back of my knuckles across her cheek. She knocked my hand away with a mocking sidelong glance and focused on the photos.

"What am I looking at?"

"Nothing. No haze."

"No haze means...what?"

"Remember the green haze from the old varnish? It's not here. It's not anywhere."

"So, it's definitely a fake, then?" She grabbed my arm tightly, shaking me.

"It's possible the varnish was affected by the fire. The temperature could have made it more soluble, then that, combined with the water could cause it to fluoresce differently. Doubtful, but—"

"Possible." Her grip released as the wind left her sails. "So, this is proof of nothing."

"Not definitive proof yet. Do you have access to more photos of the painting from here?"

"I do." She rounded to the back seat of her truck where her laptop was set up. She hopped in, leaving the door open. I stood next to the truck, resting my arms on the top of the door frame, watching the screen. The pose would highlight the shape of my torso, my broad chest, and muscular arms. She would have to notice.

As her laptop started, I had to take care of the regrettable part of my visit. "How is the rest of the investigation going?"

Like at the gala, she typed while she spoke. "Ups and downs. We've dropped the theory it could have been stolen."

Thank heavens. It wouldn't hurt me either way, but if justice were to be served, she would have to find the actual guilty parties.

"I talked to the neighbor who reported the fire and have more interviews set up this afternoon. Alright—I'm in. What do you want to see?" She paused at the list of pictures, focused on her screen.

I leaned in to get a closer look, close enough my cheek almost touched hers. "The x-ray. Open that one."

I knew what I was looking for before it was open. I had already started on that section of the painting, anticipating the ultraviolet being insufficient. I paused the appropriate amount of time to pretend I was analyzing the image, then pointed at the center of the painting. "This will help. You can tell Chagall changed his mind on what he was doing. The red flower in the middle of the bouquet was originally down lower. He painted over it and re-added it higher. I think the place where it originally was is on the strip across the middle which survived the fire. If I can clean up some of the damage to that area, an x-ray should tell us for sure. Send it to me. And there is an infrared photo in the list— send that as well."

She emailed the photos, closed the laptop, and turned to get out of the truck, but I didn't move. This was date number three. We had taken care of our business. We had shared our heartbreaks. Every fiber of my being told me she wanted me as much as I wanted her. But her heart, her fears, were in the way. It was on her face when she spoke of her mother and her ex-husband.

We stared at each other, our shared desire thick in the air. She rubbed her fingers along her palm and bit her lip. Still so scared.

"Samantha, I don't want my heart broken again any more than you do."

She closed her eyes. She was going to say no. Again. But I could be patient. I had to be if I wanted her in my life. Before I could tell her, ensure her she was safe in my hands, she opened her eyes and took hold of my tie. She pulled me to her, slowly, eyes fixed on mine, moistening her lips in anticipation.

"I've wanted to taste your lips from the day we met." I slid a hand to the back of her neck and tilted my head to avoid the brim of her hat. When I pressed my lips to hers, my eyes slid closed. The blood pounded in my ears, drowning out the songbirds outside the truck and the gentle breeze rustling the corn.

As the pressure increased, our lips parted together, and my tongue met hers. Olives. She tasted of olives. I smiled in the kiss, while she moaned, low and guttural. My tongue pushed into her mouth, sliding along hers. We pulled apart slightly, then met again, her tongue sweeping along mine.

Warmth spread through my chest, a happiness invading my very soul. I put a foot on the running board for balance and my free hand on the outside of her thigh, caressing her strong leg.

She suddenly broke away. The tie was still in her hand, but she leaned slowly back, eyes wide, brows turning down. "Oh my god, I shouldn't have done that. I'm so sorr—"

"Yes, you should have." I leaned in, meeting her lips, and slid her toward me.

She had a moment of hesitation, until she moaned again and rolled her fist around the tie to pull herself closer to me. Her tongue moved around mine in hungry circles and she grabbed my hand on her thigh, moving it to cup her ass. The blood pounding in my ears started traveling lower.

Her watch pinged. She jumped, releasing my tie and hitting her elbow on her laptop. "Shit!" She slammed a hand on her watch to silence her alarm. "I'm late! I need to grab Lucy!"

Shoving me out of the way, she launched herself out of the truck.

"Lucy?"

"Yeah, I dropped her off at a diner for lunch." She ran to the back of the truck, grabbed the photos and Russo's containers, then passed me again to throw them in the back seat. "We've got more claims this afternoon and interviews."

"Bella, we should have a third date, you and I."

"Yeah, sure." She raced back to slam the tailgate shut.

I stepped in the way before she reached the driver's door, catching her. "I want to meet the real Samantha. You plan everything?"

Her muscles were tight from the sudden panic and her breath was even more rapid than when we'd kissed, but she stood in front of me, chewing on her lip. "Can you play hooky tomorrow morning?"

"Hooky?"

"Unless tomorrow's too soon?"

I ran a hand across her cheek. "Five minutes from now wouldn't be too soon."

"I don't have any appointments until two o'clock. I'll pick you up at your office at seven."

"In the morning?"

Her panic dissolved as a smile spread across her face. "We're going hiking. I know just the spot."

"Hiking?"

"You want to know the real me? That's as real as it gets on short notice."

"It had better be a good hike." I winked at her and planted a quick kiss on her cheek. "I have decisions to make after all!"

CHAPTER 35

SAMANTHA

Josh Irons, the lead painter at the Scotts' house on the day of the fire, was a tall man with short, dark brown hair. He looked strong, but not athletic, likely from years in his profession. He had slightly crooked teeth and a yellow tinge on the thumb and index finger of his left hand, identifying him as a smoker.

We were in the Pines conference room at Foster Mutual, the last place on Earth I wanted to be. Maybe not the last, but it wasn't the first. That would have been anywhere Antonio and his lips were. And his scent. He smelled so much better than the stench of stale cigarettes emanating from Mr. Irons...*Work. Focus on work.*

Earlier, we'd interviewed the security system installer. As expected, he told us about disabling the security system and being kicked out of the house before connecting the new one. He also told us about an argument between Olivia and Josh Irons the morning of the fire, which wasn't mentioned in the police report. I'd asked Lucy to start the interview with Irons, then I'd intended to handle a few questions about the dispute.

After he sat and we'd finished the date and name routine, Lucy dove in. "Can you go over what happened when you arrived?"

"Yeah." He leaned back in his chair like he didn't care to be there. "We arrived, talked to Mrs. Scott, she showed us where we would be working. The room was almost all wood, including the ceiling, not much to paint, so we didn't need all three of us. Seemed like a waste of money and time. So, we talk it over, she makes sure we know what we're doing, and we get to work.

"Step one, move the furniture to the middle of the room since we were only gonna be painting the walls. Step two, take the dressing off the walls, paintings, light switches, you know. Step three, tape the edges. Step four, throw down a tarp to cover the furniture and floors, so nothing gets splattered. Step five, we paint. It ain't rocket surgery."

"Did you get to step five?"

"Hell, no. Mrs. Scott threw us out before we started. I'd opened a couple paint cans to get going and barely had time to seal 'em back up before she flipped." He shook his head and tapped on the chair with his fingers.

"Flipped?"

"Yeah, she was fucking rude. She got a phone call, then told us she had to leave immediately so she could deal with it. I told her we were bonded, not to mention honest working men, so we could stay, but she forced us out. Like we would steal her stuff or something."

"Did you argue with her?"

"Argue?" He rubbed the armrest. "I tried, but she wasn't having it. Like I said, I just got the cans resealed. They

woulda dried up sittin' there uncovered. Waste of money!"
He rocked in his chair, growing fidgety.

"Did you argue about anything else?"

"Hell, yeah!" He leaned forward in his seat, putting his
hands on the table, talking with them slightly. "We were
moving the paintings into the office. Standard stuff. I take
this one off the wall, and she goes ape. Yelling at me to put it
down, like I was some little kid. Fuck. She said her son
would move it. Said it was worth five times our lives.
Arrogant bitch. Seriously, who says shit like that to people?
Just because they've got money, they look down on people
like me."

He leaned back in his chair again, shaking his head. "Ya
know, sometimes those rich dicks get what they deserve.
Divine justice. Everyone's the same when they get to the
pearly gates, ya know?"

He flexed his left hand a couple times, agitated and
itching for a cigarette. Time for me to jump in.

"Which painting were you moving that got her so
upset?"

"Damned if I know. Some weird-ass painting with
floating heads and flowers."

"Did you go back to their house later?" I clasped my
hands together on the table and leaned forward.

"Do what?"

"You know, did you go back to talk to her about it?
Maybe have a few drinks then go back to tell her what you
thought of her?"

"No! Why would I do that?"

"I don't know. You were angry? Thought you'd call her a
few names to her face?"

"No way. I planned to send some other guys the next day to do the painting. I wasn't going back there. I'm a professional and the supervisor. I got plenty of work without dealin' with that kind of bullshit."

"You knew the security system was disabled." I narrowed my eyes, lowering my voice. "Maybe go back and take that painting she said was worth more than your life?"

He leaned forward to match me. "You accusing me of something?"

"Start a little fire for revenge?"

His lips pulled back as he bared his teeth. "Fuck. You."

"So, that's a no?"

He slammed his fist on the table and toppled his chair while he stood. "You're not the police. I don't need to put up with this shit."

I sat back in my chair while he stalked out of the room.

"Sam, what was that?" Lucy asked.

I shrugged. "Trying to work him up. He was acting like he was guilty of something the whole time he was sitting there."

"How?"

"The constant movement, tapping his foot, brushing the chair, making the fist. I figured I'd turn up the heat a bit and see if anything slipped."

"Did it?"

"Nope. The only time he wasn't acting guilty was when I asked him if he went back to tell her off." I laughed. "He was pissed."

"No kidding!" Lucy collapsed in the chair next to me. "So, what did we learn from this? Olivia Scott's mean?"

"Yeah, that surprised me. She seemed so sweet and kind when we met her. He was obviously talking about moving the Chagall, but if she knew the painting was a fake, why flip out on him for handling it?

"Oh, and he's a smoker. Fire started from a cigarette. Could be something..." I flipped through the police report and found the autopsy results, scanning them quickly. "Mr. Scott was a smoker, too. The level of nicotine in his blood indicates he'd been smoking shortly before he died."

"So, it may be nothing."

CHAPTER 36

SAMANTHA

When I pulled up at Antonio's office Thursday morning, he was in black shorts, gray T-shirt, and new trail running shoes. He'd bought an outfit for our hike. Good sign. Maybe early morning hiking wasn't such a terrible idea for a date after all. He wore a lightweight backpack with a water reservoir and carried a little white box tied with a string.

The straps of his backpack highlighted how broad his chest and shoulders were. Gorgeous. I'd seen his thick biceps several times in T-shirts and had admired the way his pants had cupped his rear on more than one occasion, but this was the first time I'd seen his legs. They were muscular, with calves like rocks. God, what did the rest of him look like under those clothes? A shiver ran through my core.

As he got into the truck, I said, "Please, let that be what I think it is!"

He smiled and put the box on the center console, leaning over for a kiss, but I backed away. Stupid reaction. It was instinct. Habit.

Unphased, he laughed and withdrew two travel mugs from his backpack, deposited them in the cup holders, and threw the surprisingly full pack into the rear seat next to mine. He opened the box and showed me two cornetti.

"E un cappuccino!" He tapped the travel mug on my side.

"You're too good to me." I pulled the truck out onto the road. "This feels kind of weird."

"Being here with me?"

Yeah. "No, it's my sister's chemo day. I normally spend the morning with her."

He placed a gentle hand on my arm. "We can reschedule."

"As long as I'm there during the infusion, she's okay." She'd been upset, but I told her I had mandatory work training. I was such a bad sister.

"I usually start work at ten, so this will push me back a few hours. Since we are spending time together this morning, I can't complain I have to work through prime dating hours in the evening."

The weird feeling subsided, replaced by a flutter in my stomach. Change the subject. "How's my Chagall coming?"

He took a sip of his coffee. "Quite well. It will be out of the frame this afternoon and I'll try the infrared photo tomorrow. There's likely too much organic content still present, but we have the equipment, so I may as well try. If that doesn't work, my next test will be the x-ray. It could be ready as early as Monday or Tuesday, if I work through the weekend."

"Do you think you'll have time?"

"I was hoping to be busy." He nudged my arm.

This was happening so fast. The kiss had been magnificent, but where did it lead? I was still leaving in the spring. Wasn't I? Could I be chained to one town? To Brenton? Again? I was getting ahead of myself. Although I did shove condoms into the bottom of my backpack. Why did I do that? It had just been one kiss.

"I had some interviews yesterday for the Chagall claim. I think I told you?"

"Sì, you mentioned. Anything interesting?"

"Can you keep a secret?"

"I'm very good at that."

"Turns out Olivia Scott—the woman who owned the painting—is a bitch."

He laughed and pulled his cornetto out of the box, a light dusting of powdered sugar falling on his shirt as he took a bite.

"That looks delicious."

"The food or me?"

My body reacted before my brain did, pulling in air and tightening between my thighs. I didn't look at him to see his smirk. Didn't have to. "You're ridiculous." But so right. "Anyway, there were painters setting up in the house the morning of the fire. They were taking everything off the walls, and when he took the Chagall down, she went ballistic. Told him it was worth more than his life."

"Quite rude."

"So now I'm confused. If she knew it was a fake, why would she freak out about its value?"

He took another sip of his coffee, then spoke slowly. "Perhaps her husband was the one who sold it and had the forgery done without telling her?"

"I've been discounting Bobby Scott as a guilty party, since he died in the fire." And who he'd been to me. "But you aren't the first person to remind me I need to stop doing that."

"You never did say how you knew him?"

I hit the phone link on my steering wheel. "Call Lucy Chap—"

He reached over and ended the call request.

"What are you doing? I want Lucy to dig in to this theory."

"Tell her later. This morning is for us."

My heart skipped. "Us?"

He turned around, looking in the back seat. Opened the glove box and pulled down the visor. "No one else here I can see. Unless you're planning on meeting someone else on our hike?"

I'd never run into anyone there before. What part of my brain had planned that? Probably the part reacting to his sugar-coated chest and hiding things under my first aid kit.

"You know, bella, this is the first time I have ever been driven by my date. I don't think I like this."

"I was stunned you drove a Maserati out on those rural roads Wednesday. I expected you to call and say your car had died."

"Never underestimate the power of an Italian engine." His perpetual smirk ratcheted up from flirtatious to suggestive. Yeah, that was the part of my brain that made this plan.

I shook my head. "Trust me, the road we're hitting would chew your car up and spit it out."

"Sì, and where is that?"

I opened the large moonroof and put on my sunglasses. "You know, Michigan's a state of water. No matter where you are, you're never more than six miles from some lake or river. There's a trail about fifty miles west of Brenton that leads to an old fishing spot on the Grand River with a little sandy beach on it. Problem is—no vehicle access. It's a three-mile hike after a four-mile drive over terrain that's difficult even for my truck."

"How do you know it?"

"I was working a claim out near there last year when I was in town for a big hail deployment. Another adjuster I worked with told me, and I've been three times so far. It's my favorite spot."

"Sounds like an adventure."

"So much of an adventure, we aren't going on a date today."

"Scusi?"

Eyes on the road, I made my triumphant announcement. "This is Survival Training 101!"

"You are kidding me?"

"Nope."

"You are a clever woman." He grabbed his travel mug and took another sip of coffee. "Perhaps too clever for me."

"There's a distinct possibility you're right."

CHAPTER 37

ANTONIO

"It's beautiful here." I gazed in awe at the trees and plants, listening to the squirrels chattering in the trees and the birds flitting about. How had I never done this before?

"Yeah, peaceful." She closed her eyes briefly as we walked along the narrow path, barely wide enough for the two of us.

Pursuing Samantha was a delicate balance. Push hard enough to find her boundary, go slightly beyond, then step back and wait for her to become comfortable. Like a waltz. Our kiss had been a substantial push, and she was not yet comfortable with it. Although she brought me somewhere special to her. She was almost there.

"So, what shall we talk about today, bella?"

"What's your idea of a perfect day?"

"Easy question. Spending the day in bed with a beautiful woman."

"Sleeping?" She rolled her eyes almost as often as my sister did.

"Breakfast in bed, making love, reading, making love, watching a movie, mak—"

"Let me guess."

Ducking under an overhanging branch, I laughed. "You don't think that would be a wonderful day?"

"Watch your step." She put a hand on my forearm, pointing to a small snake slithering across the trail.

"Good eye. Survival training was an excellent idea. I like seeing you in your element instead of only hearing you talk about it."

"You've never gone for a hike before?"

"Not like this. I think I've been missing out on a lot." We resumed our pace, and I continued pushing. "So, if making love is not part of your perfect day—"

"Hold on, I never said that. I just rolled my eyes at you listing it as every second event of the day."

"That tells me you have not been made love to properly."

She laughed me off, but the thought was in her head, as firmly as it was in mine. Her shorts and tank top revealed much of her lovely, strong body, and I couldn't wait to see more of it.

"Well, this is my idea of a perfect day. Hot summer morning, out in the middle of nowhere, listening to the birds and the wind."

"Did you and your ex-husband hike?"

She veered far off the trail, making her way around trees and over rocks. "No, never."

"Why not?"

"He was too urban for me. Didn't like getting dirty, except in the kitchen." She kept her eyes on the uneven ground in front of her. "Cities have a lot to offer but there has to be a balance."

"Come back to the trail with me." I beckoned her closer. "My survival instructor can't teach me anything from so far away. I may be eaten by a snake."

She paused and looked at me, chewing on her bottom lip. "No."

This was a test. One I would pass. I made my way around the branches edging the main trail and headed after her.

"Thanks for being a good sport about this. I wasn't sure you'd come out here." She stopped at a large tree which had fallen over and hopped up to walk atop it.

"I want to meet the real you. I can tell by your smile this is it." I walked on the ground next to the tree, taking her hand when she reached out for balance.

She stopped suddenly again. "Shhh." She knelt slowly, straddled the tree trunk, and searched for something. "Over there, do you see it?"

Nothing. Her arm raised, pointing to a spot in the distance. I looked in the direction she indicated, toward a rustling noise, but I couldn't spot the source. I placed my face next to hers, focused along the length of her arm. Her finger moved slowly, until I finally saw the small red fox she'd been tracking.

"I do now." I put an arm behind her while we watched it trot through the woods. We were close enough that her citrusy scent mingled with the wet earth and leaves surrounding us. Moving closer, my cheek touched hers, eyes remaining on the wildlife. I whispered, for fear of scaring away the fox or her, "How beautiful."

The fox disappeared, and she placed her hands on the tree to stand again. She was not getting away from me so soon. I dragged her off, placing her in front of me, body to body, holding her against me by her hips. "I love how confident you are here."

She blinked up at me, resting her hands against my chest. I reached behind her to pluck an errant leaf from the top of her backpack, brushing my fingertips across her shoulder as I pulled the hand back. Her eyelids eased closed and she tilted her head, allowing me access to run the fingers along her lovely neck. As I began to lean forward for a kiss, she slipped away, winding her way back to the main trail.

Keep pushing.

"I don't understand," I said after we'd walked quietly for a while.

"What's that?"

"How could you marry a man who didn't share your greatest passion?"

"Long, boring story."

"You say that a lot."

She looked at me, but her eyes fell to the trail. "What are the most important traits in a relationship to you?"

"You avoid many important questions, you know?"

"Now, you're avoiding mine."

"It depends. Are we speaking of romantic relationships?"

"Yeah." Her eyes remained down, but there was a hint of a smile on her lovely lips. We were speaking of us. For all her nerves and her protests, she had *us* in mind.

I said, "Friendship and respect. And you?"

She hooked her thumbs in the shoulder straps of her heavy pack. "Honesty and loyalty. Knowing the person you're with will be there through everything, they'd never lie or keep something important from you, and they'd hold you to those same standards."

It was like she knew my secret, testing me further. What would she say if I confessed the truth, that I knew the location of the true Chagall and had all along? It would be a relief to tell her everything. But complete honesty would ruin this budding relationship. "Have you ever had that?"

"I thought I had it with Matt. I mean, he's a fantastic man, and I could trust him with most things. Part of my heart will always be with him, but we should have just been friends."

"As I said, friendship comes first. Usually, that's as far as it should go." Her relationship with her ex-husband was a fascinating one. So much pain, yet it was clear he meant a great deal to her still. "Have you come close with anyone else?"

"Geez, are you writing a biography or something?" She nudged me when the trail became too narrow for us to walk side-by-side, and she took the lead. "You ask a lot of questions."

"You and I have a great deal in common, bella. Talking about the pain helps you move past it and on to something new."

"Talking about things is overrated."

I laughed and took a sip from the water reservoir in my pack, watching her long stride. Her legs went on forever, and the outlines of the muscles enthralled me. Her ass looked almost as good in the shorts as it had in the leather pants. "The view is fantastic. I particularly like this narrow path."

Choking on her laughter, she stepped into the bushes at the edge of the trail and ushered me ahead of her. "You're pathetic."

I winked as I passed, and she fell into step behind me. "Is the view any better from back there?"

She laughed rather than answer, but she didn't say no.

"It was the same after Faith and I broke up. I don't think she ever truly loved me, but it's hard to trust again, all the same."

She patted the side of my pack. "Well, you can trust me."

"I hope so." I cast a glance over my shoulder, and we shared a smile. "That leaves honesty. So, tell me a secret."

"Don't have any."

"Liar."

"Yeah, complete lie. But I don't have interesting ones. What about you?"

"Oh, bella, I have some big ones. But I would have to kill you if I told you."

"Perfect. This would be a great place to hide a dead body. No one ever comes out here."

I paused as the trail became wide enough for us to walk next to each other again. "So, we are all alone, just the two of us?"

"Yeah. You, me, the snake, and that red fox."

"In that case, I think this is my second most perfect day." I moved closer to her, eliminating the space between us, the back of my hand finding the back of hers.

My fingers slipped into her palm, and she took in a slow breath, goosebumps creeping up her arm. I caressed the arm to admire the result of my touch and slid the hand back down to interlace my fingers with hers. I had held her hand many times—to shake, to kiss, to lead her through a crowd —but that moment was special. She smiled at the ground, accepting me as more than a friend.

We chatted as we walked, hand-in-hand, until we arrived at the river. The trees were thick on the other bank, but our side had a small beach. It was only deep enough to lie down on, sand dotted with rocks and pebbles, but the river was wide enough for a swim. A swim would be a wonderful nudge.

"This is remarkable. I didn't know there were places like this on the Grand."

She let go of my hand, sitting on the sand to open her pack, and pulled out several small bags. "Pick your poison. I've got trail mix, banana chips, and astronaut ice cream."

"As much as I want to know what astronaut ice cream is..." I knelt next to her, placing my pack on the sand and pulling out a picnic blanket, which I spread for us to sit on. "And I know I told you to plan everything..." Next, I withdrew three stainless food containers and forks.

She lifted her bags of snacks, as if to complain that her menu was superior. "Couldn't help yourself, could you?"

"Bella, you packed for survival training. I, however—" I withdrew a small bottle of wine with two plastic glasses. "—packed for a date."

A frown creased her lovely face momentarily, as was her way, until a smile broke free. "More antipasti or more sweets?"

I opened each box, showing her the modest feast. "Pane e prosciutto with pesto, farro salad with tomatoes and pecorino cheese, and pears with gorgonzola."

"And Chianti?" She settled next to me, picking up the glasses so I could pour the wine. "I haven't tasted a bite, but I'm pretty sure this is going to be the best meal I've ever had hiking."

We chatted and laughed over the food, as she rattled off each type of tree around us and pointed out different species of birds. Once we finished, we packed the boxes away, enjoying the last sips of our wine. She leaned back on her elbows, face up to the sun shining through the break in the trees.

I did the same. What a moment. Sitting on a private beach with my Samantha. Nothing more complicated, until a trickle of sweat ran down my back. Time to push her again.

"You know what we are missing in survival training?" I stood and pulled my shirt off. She hadn't expected that, but the sharp intake of breath and wide eyes told me it was a good choice. I unbuttoned my shorts and pulled them off, stripping to my underwear. "Swimming!"

Her hand covered her cheek, hiding the blush yet again. "I was only planning to come out here for the scenery, not for a swim."

"Now, there is more scenery." I waded into the water while she stared. "However, I think my survival instructor needs to join me or I may drown."

CHAPTER 38

SAMANTHA

I froze and swallowed hard. His body was perfection. From his muscled shoulders to his washboard abs to the sharp angles of his astonishing hipbones, perfection.

He reached the middle of the river and dove under. If I'd seen this unfold for two other people, I would have called whoever was stuck on the beach a fool for not following him. But I just sat there, staring. If I went in after him, where else would it go? And was I ready for that?

For once, I let my first instinct win and stripped down to my sports bra and underwear, wading in and diving underneath. When I surfaced, he splashed me, a beaming smile lighting up his face. We swam together, chatting and joking for a half hour, cooling off from the hot mid-August day. When we returned to the beach, the sand stuck to everything, so we sat to air dry before getting dressed. I looked up at the trees and laid back, so happy he'd brought the blanket.

He lay next to me, and I squinted my eyes open, shading them from the sun. He propped his head on one arm, leaning toward me. The pose accentuated his muscled body, looking like he was sculpted by Michelangelo himself. We were all alone. No timer counting down the last few minutes of my lunch break.

His voice dropped to a low rumble. "Have you changed your mind yet, bella?"

My breath picked up at the depth of his voice, the words irrelevant. "About what?"

He reached a hand over to my face, running it along my cheek. My heart quickened at his touch, and I closed my eyes, focusing on his caress. And on not bolting.

"About never dating again."

'Yes,' was on the tip of my tongue. But when I opened my eyes, they locked with his. The word wasn't necessary.

"I'm a lucky man." He brushed a wet hair back from my face, leaned over and paused, his hand still on my cheek. The corner of his mouth, no more than an inch from mine, twitched slightly. "But there's no kissing in survival training, is there?"

I breathed with him, in and out, as he hovered there, and I stared into his big brown eyes. How did we go from him cheering me up after a bad date to...this? From me wanting to spend the rest of my days alone to him taking up space in my life?

I grabbed the back of his neck. He grinned and met me, our tongues sliding over each other's, greedily, desperately, still tasting like the wine. Even better than our kiss in my truck. I wrapped my other arm around his back, delighting in the smooth lines of muscle and sealing my eyes to focus on every sensation. On the water splashing in the river, the heat of the sun, the sound of his low moans.

An intense hunger pulsed between my thighs; the same one I felt every time I was close to him as if his body were calling to mine. I'd imagined touching him but doubted it would actually happen, let alone be this incredible. I launched a leg over the small of his back, hooked it, and pulled him on top of me. Fluidly, he had himself between my legs, forcing me open, grinding his growing erection against my underwear. I lifted my hips to meet him, needing to remove the space between us.

One hand snuck under my bra, and he kneaded my breast as our mouths grew more urgent. When he squeezed so hard I whimpered, I felt him smirk.

"Molto bene, bella." His voice reverberated in my chest, as though he was already inside me in more than a physical way. His hand explored along my belly, to the waistband of my underwear, and he ran a fingertip along it. "May I?"

What was I doing? I wasn't the girl who lost her head over some guy, but here I was. Losing myself. But not just some guy. The right guy?

"Yes." I lifted to his mouth and my hand on his back slid under his boxer briefs, assuming the same permission I'd given him. I needed him, his skin, his pressure, his friction.

His finger teased at my waistband, and he pushed up, so I could see him clearly. A sheen covered his brow, and his face was flushed. "In case I was not clear enough yesterday, I need you to know I'm not looking for something casual. No matter what my reputation may be, I want more out of life."

I stared up at him, unsure what to say to that. My heart pounded harder and faster, the prickling taking over my fingertips.

"To be honest—" He leaned in to kiss my cheek, then lifted again. "—I didn't expect this. I hoped to kiss you again, but to touch you? Feel you move against me?"

The words stuck in my throat. *I was hoping for this, too.*

"I'm unprepared. But, I think, we can make do..." He eased himself down my body, mouth trailing along my neck, across my chest. A brush against my breasts. Tongue tracing along my abdomen, circling my belly button. He folded his fingers under my waistband, his hungry eyes sending a charge through me. "If you will allow me?"

I nodded, squeezing my eyes shut and bridging slightly so he could inch my underwear off, down my legs, his hot breath following inch by inch. He nudged my knee on his way up, folding it to nestle his face between my legs.

"Yes," he whispered, blowing softly so I clenched. "I think we can make do quite nicely."

His tongue, gentle and firm found my clit, and I sucked in a sharp breath. The numbness traveled up my fingers through my hands, as his tongue danced over me.

I opened my eyes, watching him focus on my pleasure, gaze fixed on my sex as his head moved, taking in every angle. I moaned, clutching at his hair. "You know, survival training requires you to be prepared for anything."

He looked up at me, taking the barest pause. "Anything, you say?"

"I, um—" I sucked in a long breath as his finger eased inside me, and I lifted against his face. The crinkles around his eyes told me there was a smile down there. "—I may have packed condoms."

"This is good news." He sealed his mouth around my clit and sucked, flicking across it as he released, making my muscles tense around his finger, which continued exploring inside me.

Tightness spread out from my core, coursing through every cell of my body, in reaction to each twist and swirl of his tongue and fingers. I looked up at the clear summer sky, the trees waving slowly in the wind, the birds flying overhead.

What the hell was going on? I barely knew this guy, and I was about to have sex with him on a riverbank in the middle of the woods. I closed my eyes again. My whole body was throbbing, craving him, but the voices churned in my head. *Miss August. Serial womanizer. He'll break your heart. Three dates.*

Don't just be about sex. Please, don't just be about sex.

No, he said it wasn't just sex. He said so. Was he being honest? He didn't bring the condoms, I did. So why was I doubting him? Vincenzo's voice echoed in my head, 'I'll be there next month.' Matt's voice, 'Tyler and I are in love.'

Focus, Sam.

My emotions were going haywire, and tears welled in my eyes. Antonio wasn't either of them. He was different. He was so...so...what? So perfect? For me? But there was no future for us. I was leaving Brenton in eight months.

But what he was doing felt so good. Could I do just sex? Even if it wasn't what he wanted?

Maybe he felt my doubts, maybe not, but he stopped what he was doing and crawled up my body. Pushed my hands to either side of my head, pinning me, interlacing our fingers. We kissed slowly, twirling our tongues around each other's. The warning voices in my head quieted as he squeezed my hands, but my body continued to tremble.

What if I didn't move away? What if I gave this a chance?

"Antonio," I murmured, testing his grip on my hands. There was significant strength behind his muscles; they weren't just for show. There were still ways I could get out, but I didn't want to. Just needed to know I could.

He paused, his voice soft despite the hunger in it. "Do you want me to let go?"

I shook my head. I needed this. Needed him. This was exactly where I wanted to be.

"Then tell me what you like," he whispered, squeezing my hands again.

"You said I'd never been made love to properly." I groaned as he stroked his constrained length against my flesh. "Show me."

He grinned devilishly and released one of my hands, skimming his touch down my body, leaving a trail of fire. Two fingers slipped back inside me, his thumb teasing the most sensitive spot. "I believe you enjoy this."

"Mm-hmm." My leg came to rest on his hips, and we started to move in rhythm, pulsing as though more than his fingers were inside me. It was like our first dance at the gala, our bodies instinctively knowing how to move together. Like they were designed for each other.

His face nuzzled against my neck, more of his weight settling on me. "Samantha, you will have me?"

I threaded my fingers into his damp hair, flexing the hand he hadn't let go of. The moment was right. Surprisingly right. "Oh my god, Antonio. Yes."

He pushed up, smiling down at me with tender eyes, their gold flecks dancing. "You said you brought—"

"What the hell?" came a stranger's voice, surprisingly close.

"Get a room," came another's.

We immediately separated—Antonio tossing a side of the blanket to cover me up—and I rolled to see a group of five young men with fishing poles coming down the end of the path. No, no, no, no, no. They were far enough away they likely didn't see my half-nakedness, but they definitely saw enough. The heat flushing through my body traveled into my cheeks.

This was the first time I'd ever run into anyone else at this beach. Worst. Timing. Ever.

"Eyes, gentlemen." Antonio stood, exhaling in frustration, not hiding his blatant erection as it slowly faded. "I'll give you two hundred dollars to head back to where you came from."

The guys kept their eyes on him, as he stood with folded arms between them and me. "We walked two hours to go fishing. We're not going anywhere for forty bucks each!"

Antonio looked back to me and shook his head, barely phased by being caught with his pants down. "That's all the cash I have. Do you have any with you?"

I clutched the blanket around me, mortified. "No!"

• • • ● • ● ● • • •

We dressed quickly and headed back along the trail. Once we were far enough away we couldn't hear the intruders anymore, he took my hand. "I would still very much like to make love to you."

"Yeah, well, we'll have to find somewhere a bit more private."

"It's alright. I've waited for you this long."

The air ran out of my lungs in a rush. "'This long?' You're kidding me?" I pulled my hand out of his and stopped. It had all been a game, after all. "We've known each other two and a half weeks!"

His eyes went wide, and he threw his hands up between us. "Samantha, that was—"

"Victoria was right! You're the kind of guy who—"

"I'm not! Per favore, give me a moment."

The pained look on his face made me pause, but I folded my arms to prevent myself from punching him. "You've got five minutes."

He sighed and ran a hand through his hair, taking most of those minutes in silence. Planning an excuse. "My feelings for you started much longer than two and a half weeks ago. We went to college together."

"No, we didn't."

"We did. You took Roman Art and Archaeology?"

"Yes."

"The last week, you did a presentation on the section of Trajan's column with the female torturers." He took a step toward me, but I backed away.

I shook my head, remembering the presentation, but unable to recall him. Was Nathan right about him being a stalker?

"You were brilliant, beautiful, and possessed a clear passion for things that mattered to me. I have carried that memory with me..." He closed the distance between us and took one of my hands, holding it to his heart. "Here. I've been looking for a woman with those traits ever since."

"You didn't even know me." My hand trembled, but I didn't pull it away.

"Imagine my surprise—" He lifted the hand to his lips and kissed it. "—when you came back into my life and I had the opportunity to get to know the real you."

"Why didn't you say anything?"

"I worried it would scare you off."

I took the hand off his chest and clenched it. "Honesty and trust. If we don't have those, we don't have anything."

"We? So, there's still a chance for a we?"

I rubbed at my face, like I could find the truth there. Was my pounding heart warning me about his secrets or telling me to make love to him right here? He wanted me, but did he want the real me or some ideal of me he'd created out of thin air more than a decade ago?

"What other secrets are you keeping?"

"Oh, bella." He put his arms around me and shook his head. "I'm sorry. I should have told you the truth." His mouth opened and closed, as though he was going to say more, but I couldn't handle more.

"Stop. I need to think." My brain had a brief argument with my heart and some other parts of my body, and I stepped out of the embrace. "I don't know what to do with this."

He exhaled slowly, taking me by the shoulders and looking me square in the eyes. "I understand. I'll give you all the time you need. But let me be clear. My attraction to you started a long time ago, but it was the real you who captured my heart."

This wasn't what I'd been expecting. The beach wasn't it. My breath became shallow as the reality hit me; this wasn't about flirtation or sex or three dates. My heart was pounding so hard and fast I could barely hear myself think.

I could, however, hear the voice in my head...*Don't let him in, Sam. He'll just break your heart.*

CHAPTER 39

SAMANTHA

I sat in the Pines, door shut, eyes closed, trying to review the Scott claim. I couldn't focus at my desk, with Lucy's gum popping, Mike's breathing, and the buzz of the lights. I couldn't think in the conference room because my brain was on Antonio. After what almost happened on the beach and his confession about college, I thought I'd needed space. What I needed was him. To let him prove it was about more than his memory of me. But what if it wasn't?

There were so many questions remaining about the claim, I had to narrow my focus.

My first goal was to decide if the Scotts should be paid for the painting. The lack of varnish over the signature hinted that the charred painting was a fake. As soon as I could prove it, the claim would be denied. If it had been stolen, we could shift to a theft claim, but there was no evidence, so the consensus was to drop it.

My second goal, assuming it was a fake, was to determine whether there was an intent to defraud Foster Mutual. Based on Olivia's reaction to the painter moving *Les amoureux*, I could eliminate her. I had to stop assuming

Bobby was innocent, so that left him and David. And did the missing red flags have any role?

My third goal was to help Janelle figure out what happened. Quinn warned me about getting too deep in this claim. The offers to purchase the painting while it was at Mason's, the Scotts' financial problems, Bobby's possible affair, the angry painter, the house still being boarded up. If Janelle hadn't asked me to investigate, I would have dropped it all.

My fourth goal? Figure out Dr. Antonio Ferraro. Not my priority and yet my priority. Last night, after three hours of staring at the ceiling, I remembered him from that class. A tall, chubby, bushy-haired guy who always sat at the back of class, laughing with his buddies. But that only answered a single question.

Deep breath. His lips. My fingers in his hair. The taste of his tongue carrying a hint of the wine, mingled with—

Focus, Sam.

I needed to talk the claim through with someone, so I opened the door and stepped out.

"Caine! Chapman!" Cliff's booming voice echoed down the hall. Standing at the end of the hallway, in front of the conference rooms, he pointed at the floor in front of him. This was the Cliff I'd heard stories about. "What the hell are you doing?"

Before I could get a word out, he lowered his voice. "David Scott's in the Oaks with the old man. I think he's demanding you be removed from his claim. I've read all your notes on it—"

"They were—"

"Yeah, private. I'm the head of the claims department. I have access to those." He shook his head at me, keeping his voice low. "You're handling this exactly right. I haven't filled Roger in yet, because he's thinking with his heart. He won't listen. I'll have your back if he tries to pull you, but you need to get this thing tied up soon."

I leaned in to keep my voice down, as well. "Don't you think it's odd how he's pushing to close this claim so quickly? It's only been three weeks and it's a million dollars, Cliff. I've got due diligence to finish. What happens with the reinsurance if we don't have the authentication?" Just like insurance companies provided coverage to individuals and businesses, reinsurers provided coverage for insurance companies. They were critical to providing the services our insureds needed. "It's not like Foster has enough money sitting around to pay that off without the reinsurer kicking in some of the loss."

"You're right. It's odd."

"So, what's your move? Other than feeding me to the wolves?"

"Nothing yet. I was hoping Roger was just mourning, but that should be over by now."

"I don't like this."

"I understand." He raised his voice again, our private discussion over. "Just get your ass in the Oaks, Caine!"

Lucy arrived once Cliff was done. I snapped at her and pointed to the conference room. "David Scott's there, and he's looking for us. Roger Foster's with him." Her eyes went wide. Her summer internship was almost over, and she needed a glowing review to secure a position after graduation. I had to keep this on me.

I put a hand on her shoulder. "Keep your mouth shut. I've got this."

"Samantha, Lucy." Roger smiled as we entered. We were close enough to Cliff's tirade they would have heard it.

David Scott, without his mother, sat next to Roger at the middle of the large table. Neither of them looked happy.

Roger was in his late sixties, tall, thick, and showing his age. His once-dark hair was entirely gray, but he was as commanding as ever. After Matt and I divorced, he'd blamed me for his son coming out of the closet; apparently, being a 'bad wife' did that to a man.

"Mr. Foster, Mr. Scott, good to see you both." I smiled politely as Lucy and I sat.

"My dear friend Bobby Scott passed away three weeks ago. I've done everything in my power to ensure his family receives what our company promised them. Olivia wants to pick up the shattered pieces of her life and move on, not continue to be reminded of her loss. It's been ten days since we paid out the claim for the damage to their house, and David tells me the repairs are already in progress."

Lucy and I focused on Roger, but she flicked a look in my direction at the mention of the repairs being in progress. That eliminated the theory Olivia had pocketed the repair money.

"But you—" Roger pointed at me. "You have put up roadblocks at every opportunity. Why shouldn't I take you off this claim and simply tell Cliff to pay it out?"

That was the question, wasn't it? If it had been the original, this claim would be closed already. I didn't have proof it was a fake, and Cliff had been clear enough to stay quiet until I did. I shifted my focus to David. Did he know the truth?

"My apologies, Mr. Foster, Mr. Scott, but confirming this painting as the original is a reinsurance requirement, and it's taking longer than expected. The conservator has had some unexpected scheduling delays—"

"Perhaps—" Roger's voice was cold and measured. "—if my adjuster and the man cleaning the painting were spending more time focused on this claim, and less on traipsing about town in pretty clothes, it would be done already."

My smile faltered for a moment, but I glued it back in place. Fucking Victoria and her newspaper article. At least Lucy was in the clear; this was about me, and it was personal.

"I assure you, the conservator has been spending evenings and weekends working on the painting. I've expressed the level of urgency to him several times."

Roger turned to David, the irritation flipping to empathy. "David, Ms. Caine will have your claim closed within a week, or I'll contact our reinsurer directly and advise them the authentication was not possible given the damage. Either way, it will be finished and we'll pay you and your mother any money you are owed. That's my guarantee."

Dammit.

David Scott thanked him and walked out, with no more thought to Lucy and me than the smug look he flashed while standing. The whole thing had likely been rehearsed before we arrived.

Roger turned back to me. "Got that? One week."

"Yes, sir."

"And keep your profile down. Cliff tells me you've done a great job the last couple of months, so I'll spare you the lecture about how each of us represents Foster Mutual." He stood, giving me one last scowl at the door. "I shouldn't have let you come back."

The door slammed behind him, and Lucy finally exhaled.

"Well, that sucked," I said, sagging in the chair.

"Why didn't you tell him your suspicions?"

"We can't say anything until we have proof. The Scotts are personal friends of Mr. Foster." I'd kept Lucy out of the red flag discussions and my discomfort with the claim being hurried along. She didn't need to get caught in the cross fire.

"He doesn't like you."

"No kidding." I rubbed my face and tried to settle myself. Normally, work was a piece of cake, and my personal life was a mess. Things had somehow switched on me, and it was unfamiliar territory.

When I didn't say anything more, she suggested, "Trip to Ferraro's?"

Nodding, I pulled out my phone and texted Antonio. *You available?*

For you, always

Your office?

I have other ideas...

I shook my head and texted him back, *Lucy's with me*

Dump her at a diner? ;)

We need to talk about the painting

Okay. See you in 10?

Give me 30

"Ferraro's it is. Thirty minutes. But before we go, I've got a few other stops. Wait for me in the Pit."

• • • • • • • • • • •

I knocked on the wall at SIU and Harry and Quinn waved me in to sit at their working table. Motioning them both close, I kept my voice at a whisper.

"I can trust you two, right?"

Neither of them nodded. It would depend on what I was about to tell them.

"I have a feeling the missing red flags aren't actually missing. I'm heading up to IT to have someone check into it. Someone I absolutely trust."

Harry and Quinn looked at each other, and he responded. "What's changed since we talked about this?"

"It started with the Scott claim. I'm getting a lot of pressure to close it quickly, whether it's the authentic painting or not. I mean, who pushes through a million-dollar claim? Then, look at all those ball-peen hammer claims. Quinn, you said it yourself. You were surprised so many got through. Maybe it's a coincidence, but—"

"Which of us believe in coincidences?" asked Harry.

Quinn shook her head. "None of us."

"Tell you what, Sam. Go put in your request with IT. If there's anything there, have them print the results off and bring them directly to one of us. No email system."

I nodded and hurried upstairs to see Kevin. If Cliff wasn't doing anything, I was.

• • • • • • • • • • •

The desks were all moved around again, but I found my brother-in-law quickly. "Hey, Kevin. How's Cass doing?"

He stood back from his tall desk. "Good. Tired. You're bringing dinner tonight?"

"I am, but listen—" I lowered my voice and moved closer. "I need a favor and I need you to keep it quiet. Does the system track red flags being removed from claims?"

"It does..."

"Could you print out a report for the last two years, showing all of them? Not like approvals from Cliff, but when they're deleted?"

"What's going on, Sam?"

"And when you get that list, print it out and hand-deliver it to Harry or Quinn in Special Investigations. You can do that, right?"

"I can."

"Don't tell anyone but SIU."

CHAPTER 40

SAMANTHA

"Samantha!" Sofia stood and rushed over to me as Lucy and I entered. "It's been too long!"

"Only one week, sneaky."

She smiled broadly and gave me cheek kisses and a hug. "Antonio's on a call in his office. He's expecting you. Should only be a minute or two."

"Can someone get the Chagall out of the storage room, so we can make it quick?"

"He already did. Is something wrong?"

"Just a rough day at the office, Sofia."

She nodded, told us to sit, and disappeared around the waiting room wall. I heard a knock and then Italian voices from the back.

His voice had me out of my seat, hand on my stomach to calm myself. Lucy took my lead and stood, as well. I sat back down. Wait for him. Patience.

"You're a mess. Mr. Foster really rattled you."

"He did." And so much I couldn't tell her.

My stomach churned and my heart wouldn't calm down. I was imagining it all. Too much time with SIU. But what if Roger Foster was doing something he shouldn't? Or Cliff?

Cliff had access to everything, and he hadn't answered my question about the reinsurance. What if I was confiding in the person behind it all? What about Hailey? Taking on those property and art claims instead of sticking to the auto claims she was supposed to adjust, knowing how to remove red flags? I was going to be sick.

But then, like the sun coming out on a cloudy day, everything was suddenly right. He walked around the corner into the waiting room and marched right to me. I was back on my feet in a second. He looked exhausted.

"Ciao, bella." He took my hand and kissed it gently, coming close enough to keep his words at a whisper. "Mi sei mancato molto."

I tried not to swoon as he told me how much he'd missed me, smelling him, feeling his presence. I wanted to grab him, kiss him again, feel his tongue against mine, touch his body, but kept my wits about me and frowned playfully. "It's only been twenty-four hours."

He grinned mischievously, about to strike back, when Lucy interrupted.

"Listen, Sam got completely reamed over how long the Chagall's taking. We need an update for the claim file today. We have one week to wrap it up, or they'd pay it out regardless."

"Sì? Is this true?"

"Yeah. Straight from the president of the company."

He put his hands in his pockets and stared at me for a moment. He darted to Sofia's desk, taking advantage of her absence, and the music changed from Vivaldi to rock.

"Antonio!" she shouted from the studio.

"Andiamo!" A wink and he beckoned us back to the studio, to his desk, where the burned painting lay. It was finally out of its frame, the edges which had been protected from the fire in surprisingly good condition.

I smiled and gave a little wave to Alice and Frank, who were at their desks working away. Zander sat in the back at an easel and didn't budge. I took a quick picture of his progress with my phone.

"Our next step is to check here." He pointed at the strip of surviving canvas across the middle. "The x-ray sent to the Committee showed a flower here before Chagall painted over it with the leaves. I took it out of its frame and tried the infrared photography last night, but that picks up carbon-based materials, so it lit up with all the soot. So, we are back to the x-ray. I planned that for Monday, but we are on a tight schedule, sì?"

"Do you have the equipment here?" Lucy asked.

"Has Samantha not told you we are the best?" He acted hurt. "Of course, we do! It will take thirty or forty minutes to produce the images. I make no guarantees. I had wanted to clean the damage more before we took this step."

He yawned.

"Late night?" I asked.

"I arrived at work late yesterday." He winked privately at me. "I was working on it until three in the morning and back at seven."

His cousin laughed. "He's never started work at seven."

"How about Lucy and I run to Russo's while you're doing the x-ray. I'll grab you a coffee. You look like you need it."

"You are too good to me." He gave my arm a quick squeeze, and I smiled broadly as Lucy and I left.

I told Lucy about Via Calabria as we walked and complimented her on taking charge when Antonio had arrived. She teased me about flirting with him. We tried a few samples before choosing a selection of pastries, and forty minutes later, we returned with coffee for the office and the treats, topped with Angelo's well-wishes.

"Done?" Lucy asked Antonio, once he'd had a sip of the coffee we'd brought.

He checked his watch. "Sì, it should be done now. Let me get it from the imaging room."

He stepped in and then quickly came back out of the first room at the right, behind Sofia's desk, holding a life-size printout of the x-ray image. He took it back to his table, where he lay it next to the painting. The debris from the fire, which still covered most of it, was evident throughout the image, but a few things stood out. It clearly showed the outline of the burned areas and the ghost-like outline of the table and violin at the bottom, which were still covered in soot.

Antonio pointed to the middle of the x-ray, to the strip where the original flower should have been. "No extra flower."

I logged into the mobile version of the Foster claims system and opened the x-ray image from 2015. I frowned.

"Computer?" he suggested.

"Yeah, this image is too small."

The three of us headed into his office. He went in first, unlocked the computer, and held the chair for me. I pulled up the 2015 x-ray.

"Can you print it?" asked Lucy.

He leaned over me and pressed a few buttons. "Imaging room." He headed out to retrieve it, while Lucy and I walked back to his desk. With the image of the original x-ray next to the new one, it was clear. This was not the original painting.

Lucy was the first to speak. "This is a fake. Even I can tell that."

"Sì." Antonio yawned again.

"What's this?" I got in close to the new x-ray. There was a darker area in the middle of the canvas, not from the painting or the soot. We'd been so focused on the flower we almost missed it. It looked like an intentional shape, maybe a portion of text. As it dawned on me, I turned slowly to Antonio, who nodded. "Copyist."

Lucy asked, "What's a copyist?"

"A person who makes copies of famous works. They typically add a mark on the canvas to show it's not an original," I said.

"So, it's a forgery?"

"Not necessarily. Any auction house or museum would do tests like this to prove authenticity, so a copyist adds a mark or signature, to ensure others aren't fooled."

Antonio continued. "Artists have been copying the masters to learn the trade for centuries. But no honest copyist would make an exact duplicate of an artist's work until the copyright has expired, which it has not for Chagall. I've done many myself."

"Have you?" My attention shifted to him.

"Sì, the best hang together at my parents' house."

"Okay, so back to our painting for a minute." Lucy returned us to the issue at hand. "What does this mean for us?"

"We know it's not the original," I said. "There's no debate anymore. I'd like to talk to the copyist if we can trace that mark."

"I'll do some research this weekend." Antonio put a hand on the x-ray and looked at it again. "Come by on Monday afternoon. I'll have a full report for you by then, including the images we have done. If I'm lucky with my search, I may have the copyist's name and contact for you by then."

"That's excellent," said Lucy.

I smiled at him, a mixture of relief over the progress on this claim and pride in his work.

He yawned again. "I need to get home and get some sleep."

"Okay, I'll see you..."

He'd said he was hoping to be busy this weekend. He meant with me, right? The words stuck in my throat as my mind played through how to finish the question, and I felt stupid for having started.

"Can we talk for a moment?" He added over my shoulder, to Lucy, "In private."

Lucy headed to the reception area as Antonio ushered me into his office. When I turned around, he was standing with his hands on the doorknob.

His eyes narrowed and a sly grin spread across his delicious lips as he locked the door. "Have you had enough time to think, bella?"

"I have."

His chest puffed and his head inclined toward me, like a bull about to charge. "And?"

"You went by Tony."

A hand flew to his chest, the bull vanishing. "You remember me?"

"You sat at the back of class and laughed a lot. A lot! You were very loud, and you irritated the crap out of me, because I was trying to pay attention."

Two strides and he'd wrapped his strong arms around me, picking me up. "Sì, that was me."

"But you always had the right answers when the prof called on you. That irritated me even more. You were outgoing and high energy. Not the kind of person I ever would have hung out with."

"You were very clear about that!"

With a chuckle, I said, "You asked me out once."

He bit down on his lip, but a smile burst free. "Do you remember what you said?"

I shook my head instead of answering, remembering only that I'd turned him down.

"I'm so happy we became close now instead of then." He kissed my cheek and held me tight. "You forgive me for not telling you sooner?"

Pulling my arms out of his grip, I wrapped them around his neck and kissed him quickly. "I do, but promise you won't do that again?"

"I promise I'll never again not tell you we shared a class in college."

I yanked on a chunk of his hair. "It's partly my fault. I should have remembered you. It was so clear when it finally came to me last night."

"Marone, I weighed a hundred pounds more than I do now. And my curly hair? Terrible. I would have been stunned if you had recognized me."

I tried to separate from him, but he refused to let go. "Alright, did you need to talk to me, or was that it? You know there's no kissing and hugging and stuff at business meetings."

"My father's returning tonight. His trip was apparently a success. My parents are throwing a party tomorrow at their house for a big announcement."

"Business trip?"

"Sì, to Napoli. For our third and possibly final date," he said, feigning gravity. "I would like you to come to the party with me."

Oh, god. "At your parents' house? Wouldn't that be more appropriate for a fourth date?"

If he'd told me Dr. Dominico would be in the office on Monday, so come in and talk about art, I'd be all over that. This was 'choosing to stay in Brenton' serious.

"Sofia will be there, as will her husband, Pietro, my brother Lorenzo, and some of my parents' friends. There will be food and wine, and we can stay as long or as short as you want."

Saying yes meant I was choosing him, for as long as this would last. Not leaving as soon as Cass was well enough. My brain had a tough time keeping up. My heart, on the other hand, was almost there already.

"Yeah, I'll come."

CHAPTER 41

ANTONIO

I drove fast and took the corners tight on our way to my parents' house. This was not the time for a quiet, reflective drive like when I drove her home from the gala. This was horsepower and testosterone. And that evening, with Samantha in the passenger seat, it was foreplay.

When we arrived, she showed me a map on her phone. "You took thirty minutes. This says my place is forty-five minutes from here."

"You love your adrenaline sports. Did it turn you on?" I pulled down my sunglasses and raised an eyebrow. "We could use the extra fifteen minutes to—"

She put up a hand. "It took me almost an hour to do my hair and makeup. You are not messing them up!"

"Your loss, bella." I squeezed her thigh and she smacked my hand away.

The large wrought-iron gate with decorative shields was open for the guests. It separated the property from the main road and led us to the driveway of burnt umber paving stones. We drove around the marble fountain in front of the house and parked on the side. Their house was a red brick monstrosity, two stories in front with colonnades and an immense balcony above the main doors.

She breathed it in. "You didn't do it justice."

"Sì, it's a bit garish."

"How many rooms?"

"I don't actually know."

"How many bedrooms?"

"Good question." I winked at her as I dropped my sunglasses into the center console.

She laughed me off. "As a basis of size."

"Seven, I think?

"Really?"

"Shall we go in, or would you like to estimate the square footage next?" I rounded the car to open her door and held out a hand.

"I'd say twenty thousand?"

"You are stalling."

As she stood, she placed a hand on her stomach. "I don't know if I'm ready for this. I mean, you have a big decision to make after this date, after all. It would be pretty awkward to come by your office on Monday if you've decided to end it at three dates."

I met her sarcasm with my own. "Then you had better put your best face on." When she didn't smile, I kissed her cheek and wrapped my arms around her. "You realize I've already made my decision, sì? You are playing with me?"

"Yeah, I know." She blushed, failing at a smile.

"Don't worry, bella." I kissed her cheek again. "You are perfect, and they will love you."

We walked up the end of the driveway, up the marble steps to the house. I opened one of the large wooden doors.

The bright marble foyer and walls were a warm shade of cream. The wide spiraling staircase led both upstairs and down and the chandelier dangled on its long chain from the ceiling far above us.

Her eyes scanned the room, likely measuring distances and estimating values. When they arrived at the two-story windows of the sitting room opposite the foyer, she leaned forward, drawn to the view.

"Antonio, my boy!" My father's head popped up from one of the high-backed chairs in the sitting room. The whole crowd stood and approached us. Samantha's grip on my hand tightened.

She would be fine. Sofia adored her already. My father would fawn over her, her intelligence, and her passion for art crimes. My mother was simply excited I was finally introducing them to a woman after so many years. They all swore they would be nice to her.

My father was shorter than her in her high heels, but his personality more than made up for it. He grabbed her hand from me and kissed it three times.

"Please, Antonio!" He didn't take his eyes off her. "Tell me this is not your Samantha. She's too beautiful for you. I must take her away for myself!"

"Sì, Papa, this is Samantha. She's too smart for me, as well, so be careful."

"Then my heart is broken. If she's too smart for you, then she's far too smart for me!"

She chuckled at him. "It's a pleasure to finally meet you, Dr. Ferraro."

"Dom! You must call me Dom! Dom Ferraro. Like Dom Perignon, but better, because it's Italian!"

She stifled a laugh, which quickly broke free. He used that joke on everyone he met, and it was especially effective on the women.

My mother glided into the foyer with us, looking as elegant as ever.

"Samantha." Papa patted her hand, which he still held. "Please meet the treasure of my life, my Valentina."

Mamma put one graceful hand on Papa's, and he let go of Samantha. They greeted each other with kisses at the cheeks. Mamma shared only the faintest of smiles, though. When she greeted me, I gave her a look which begged a question. What was going on? She patted me on the cheek and retreated to the sitting room. Very serious. Very unlike my mother.

The rest of the family greeted us, Sofia and her husband, Pietro, Frank and Alice, and my younger brother Lorenzo. Samantha was a model of grace and courtesy, even when my brother and brother-in-law flirted with her. She held my hand every moment she could, which I squeezed when she tensed.

"Mamma, Papa, I would like to take Samantha for a tour of the gardens while the sun is still up, before the guests arrive."

"Yes!" Papa turned to her and shooed us away. "You will love the gardens! Just be sure to come back!"

We walked through the sitting room opposite the foyer. Tried to, at least. There were many paintings and decorations through the room, and she slowed at each.

"We can look at all of this tonight." I ushered her out the glass-paneled door to the back patio with its large flagstones. We made our way down the brick staircases between the three levels, to the terraced gardens. The wisteria covering the pergola at the base of the stairs was still in bloom, despite it being late in the season.

We strolled the gardens, chatting and laughing. How could my world be any better? It was a miracle she had come back into my life, and I knew she would stay with me. She didn't care about my money, we had much in common, we enjoyed spending time together, and we were almost done with the burned painting. The lie would be over soon.

She became quiet for a moment, uncomfortable. When I squeezed her hand, she blurted, "Does a conservator really make this much money?"

It surprised me, but I recovered quickly. "Bankers."

"Bankers?"

"It's old money. The men of my father's family have been bankers since the days of the Medici. My brother and I are named after Cosimo's brothers, in fact. The Medici patronized the arts, so did the Ferraro family, and many of us became artists, as well."

"Oh." She stared at the grass. "That's fascinating, but I apologize; it was too personal."

I squeezed her hand again. "There is nothing too personal, bella."

"Then why me?"

"What do you mean?"

"You're brilliant and talented. You're the most handsome man I've ever met. You're—" She floundered, waving her free hand around us. "—wealthy. You could have any woman on the planet. Why me? I'm just a boring claims adjuster from Brenton, Michigan."

How did this remarkable woman think so little of herself?

I stopped and took her hands, warmth spreading through my chest, unable to control my smile. "As soon as I saw you at Caruther's, I knew you were beautiful. That part was simple. It was the moment you dropped your hand from your face that I recognized you from college, and it was like a flash of lightning to have my second chance with you.

"I enjoyed your company at Russo's so much; you were funny and charming, and we had a great deal in common. But, when you told Alice about the St. Catherine painting, I was in awe of your intelligence and knowledge of my world. That was the moment I knew I wanted you more than I've ever wanted another woman. And then, the auction. Marone, it was amazing. Would you like me to continue? Because I can."

She smiled, but it faded quickly, and she tried to withdraw her hands, likely to rub them over her face or create a barrier between us. "Maybe?"

I kissed each hand, holding tight. "I want the woman who can finish my Shakespeare, who dances like an angel, and who gives up her life when someone she loves is sick."

She blew out a deep breath and her muscles began to relax.

I pulled her closer, placing her arms around my neck while I wrapped mine around her waist. "After my fiancée, I decided to find the right woman, not play around anymore, no matter how it looks from the outside. And I think I've found her."

She stared back at me, rubbing her nervous fingers behind my neck. A warm summer breeze blew past, bringing her citrusy scent to me, and I inhaled her deeply.

"You are my dream, Samantha."

Her hand cradled the back of my neck, and her thumb rubbed behind my ear. Words were difficult for her, but that touch said everything I needed. I was her dream, as well.

"Tonight, I intend to show you." I leaned closer to her, my cheek against hers, whispering through the lust thickening my throat. "I will make love to you until the sun comes up and has gone back down again."

She tensed, the hand on my neck grasping tight. Her breasts pressed against me, swelling with her deep breaths. She was so willing. "That'll definitely mess up my hair and makeup."

I touched my forehead to hers, chuckling. "You are the most charming and ridiculous woman I've ever met."

She smiled and we kissed, sealing a promise to each other for later. Before we got too carried away, soft voices began to carry from the patio.

She looked to the house. "Time to be social?"

I nodded and we made our way back to the patios and the other guests. My arm around her shoulders, hers around my waist, I introduced her as my girlfriend. She jerked her head at me the first time, but she squeezed me when I winked at her, so it was done. We chatted over drinks and antipasti, while I introduced her to everyone.

The white-jacketed caterers ushered us in for dinner. Again, I had to nudge her along with a promise of everything I would show her after dinner.

The dining room regularly sat fourteen, but an additional table was set to accommodate eight extra diners.

Papa was at the head of the dining table, with me and Samantha to his left, while Mamma sat at the other end. By the time the meal started, dusk was nearing, so the chandeliers and candles were lit, casting a soft glow through the room.

Bottles of red wine, made from their vineyard, were brought up from the wine cellar, and the glasses were filled liberally. Samantha and I drank little, small touches and glances a reminder of our intentions for later.

After four amazing courses and two hours of conversation, Papa stood at the end of the table and tapped his fork to his glass as he raised it. "Friends, family! I asked you all here to celebrate! But none of you know why. Are there any guesses?"

"Because you don't need a good excuse for a party?" suggested one of his friends, and everyone laughed.

"So true!" Papa's broad smile was even wider than usual. "But no, there's a special reason for tonight! You know I was gone to Napoli for two weeks, yes?"

He looked around and heads nodded.

"My son, Antonio, earned his doctorate degree for a groundbreaking method of conserving ancient frescoes, so they will last a thousand more years. I'm so proud of him for this research."

I shook my head, rolling my eyes. A thousand years. Samantha reached over to hold my hand under the table.

"Since then, he has been working at the studio with me, making no use of this. So, I went to Napoli to talk to the archaeologists in charge of the excavations of Pompeii. I told them about this new method. And can you guess what they said?"

Again, he stopped for effect, but my excited smile had already started. Goosebumps covered my arms and I looked back to Samantha, who was hanging on Papa's every word. My mother had tears in her eyes.

Papa looked at me, holding his wine glass up with one hand and placing the other on my shoulder. "They will use his new method for the restoration of the newly excavated *Casa di Marte.*"

The group applauded, some obviously understanding the significance of it. My jaw dropped and I squeezed Samantha's hand.

"Oh my god, Antonio! That's amazing!" She kissed my cheek. "I'm so proud of you!"

I placed my other hand on my father's, blinking away the tears forming in my eyes. This truly was the best evening of my life.

Papa hadn't yet taken a drink and continued once the applause stopped. "And you, Antonio, will be there for four months to train them. You leave for Napoli on Tuesday!"

What? No, no, no. My grip on Samantha's hand faltered, and it was her turn to squeeze to reassure me. I looked back to her, my smile gone. Her smile gone. She had just come back into my life. I couldn't lose her already.

"To my son, Antonio!" declared Papa. "Trainer of the Pompeii conservators!" He raised his glass and drank as everyone cheered.

Everyone except for Samantha and me.

CHAPTER 42

SAMANTHA

"Congratulations." I pasted on a smile but all I wanted to do was cry. He shook his head and pressed his lips to my hand. It had been a surprise to him, as well.

With the group still applauding and offering congratulations to Dom and Antonio, plates of tiramisu were placed in front of each person.

"Where's the bathroom?" I needed to get out of that space. He was leaving for four months. I hadn't even known him three full weeks yet, and he'd be gone for four months. In three days.

He pointed down the hall, recommending a private one past the foyer. I got up, shaky on my feet. Four months. The house was a blur as I walked, tears welling in my eyes. When I arrived, I collapsed on the edge of the large tub, smacked it a couple times, and cried. I was Miss August, after all.

Our future was so clear now. Four months would turn into eight, then a year, and I'd never see him again. Our three weeks together couldn't compare with this opportunity. No, he'd promise to come back, then never would.

I lost track of time as I wallowed until there was a light knock on the door.

"Are you alright, dear?"

"One sec." I grabbed some tissue to blot at my eyes, did a quick check in the mirror to tidy my make-up, and opened the door. Valentina.

"I told Dom surprising him was a stupid idea. I told him, Antonio is bringing the first girl home to meet us in years, you don't tell him out of the blue he'll be leaving her for four months."

I pressed my lips together tightly, trying to stem a fresh flow of tears. Then she stepped in and hugged me tightly.

"I wanted to make a good impression," I whimpered as she rubbed my back gently.

She pulled away, her hands on my shoulders. "And you did, Samantha. All I needed to see was the look on his face whenever you were near him."

"I'm sorry for—"

"No apologies. I remember what young love is like." She stroked my cheek and smiled warmly. "Come, let's go back for dessert. He's worried about you."

"Thanks."

We walked out together, into the hallway lined with paintings I'd been too distraught to look at on my way past earlier. The one immediately across from the bathroom was Botticelli's *Venus*. Next to it was Vermeer's *Girl with a Pearl Earring*, and on the other side, da Vinci's *Lady with an Ermine*.

She paused and turned to me when I didn't keep step with her.

"Valentina." I counted nine classics of the Old Masters. "Antonio told me his best copies all hang together in your house."

"He told me you had a good eye. Yes, these are his. Some painted from books, others while in museums." She gestured to the obvious place where a tenth should be hanging. "He's written about thirty letters to the Louvre to convince them to let him do the *Mona Lisa*, but they don't let any of their copyists near her."

There was something off about *Venus*. "She has your eyes."

"He made each of them as a gift to me." She smiled proudly, the resemblance deepening. "This one was the first, but I told him not to ruin their perfection by putting me in their faces. So instead—" She pointed to a line in the *Girl*'s turban. "—he hides my name in them."

"That's beautiful." I looked closer at each one, admiring his talent, and trying to find the hidden name in each.

She tilted her head slightly. "Samantha, Dom will kill me for this, but would you like to see our private collection?"

I gasped, which she took for a yes.

"He says it's for family only, but I have a feeling you're close enough." She led me to a stairway at the end of the hall. "But it's private, no word to anyone on what we own."

"Absolutely!" I was over the moon for the opportunity to see their private collection. But, 'close enough' to family? What did that mean?

She opened a door at the top of the stairs, into a room darkened by heavy curtains. She flicked on the light to illuminate an octagonal room with a small round couch in the middle. She directed me to the right, to a painting I didn't recognize, but immediately knew the artist.

"Toulouse-Lautrec?" I named the famed French painter, who loved his dancing girls at the Moulin Rouge.

She looked at me, impressed. "Yes, very good!"

"Original?" Stupid question. I knew that.

"Yes, all of these are original. All purchased anonymously for our family only. They are special to us."

I followed the curve of the room to the next, a small framed piece of yellowed parchment with ink drawings. I gasped. "This isn't a set of da Vinci sketches, is it?"

She looked closer. "How did you pick that out?"

"It's his style, it's distinctive. And, to be honest, I assumed if it was here, it was something extraordinary."

I turned to look at her, to smile, to make things right with Antonio's mother. She smiled back, as we shared a moment, art lover to art lover.

But then my eyes caught something behind her.

Vibrant blue background.

"Oh!" she said, following my gaze.

Vase of red and yellow flowers on the right side.

"My Dom bought it for me a few months ago."

Two floating heads in the top left.

"He'd been trying to buy it for over a year."

Table, bowl of fruit, violin.

"It's by—"

"Chagall," I whispered, and my legs gave out. She steadied me as I lowered to the round couch in the middle of the room.

"Yes." She sat next to me, concerned.

In my mind, I was ten years old again, looking at it for the first time. Thirty and staring at photographs of it with Antonio. But my reality? Standing in front of it with his mother.

"Are you alright?"

My heart had stopped, and I couldn't fill my lungs. "No, I don't feel well. Could you get Antonio for me, please?" My fingers were already numb.

"Yes, sweetheart, you sit here for a minute. I'll be right back." She patted my hand and headed out of the room at a clip.

All originals, she'd said. They'd bought it a few months ago. The first day in the studio with Antonio, he'd paused and rushed out to Sofia when I told him the name of the burned painting I'd brought to him. He'd known all along.

Well, at least one mystery was solved—I knew where the real Chagall was.

I got out my phone and made a quick call.

A couple of minutes later, two sets of footsteps approached, and I heard her voice first. "I thought you would be happy. We were bonding over the art."

Then his worried voice. "Mamma, family only, you know that!"

He came into the room and immediately knelt in front of me, grabbing my hands folded in my lap.

"Is she pregnant?" whispered Valentina.

"Mamma, no, please." The worry was thick in his voice, and he waved her away.

As soon as her footsteps faded, I pulled my hands away from his. He touched my knees, and I bristled, clenching my fists against my need to hit him. "Don't touch me."

"Bella, please, let me—"

"Explain? Is that what you were going to say?" I tried to stay steady, knowing my voice was shaking. My whole body was shaking. "It's been a lie, this whole time. From the second I told you the name of that painting, you knew the truth! And you've been playing me for a fool this whole time!"

"No, please, let me—"

"I want to go home."

"Please, bella—"

"I already called Nathan. He's picking me up in town. I don't want to embarrass you on your big night, so make whatever excuses you need."

"It was a private sale. It was secret!" He ran his fingers through his hair in desperation.

"You couldn't have told me it was a fake without saying anything more?"

"I wanted to, but—but you would have asked how I knew. I saw how you worked at the auction. You don't let things go."

"You dragged out cleaning it for three weeks, knowing the pressure I was under!" I fumed. "All the little tests you ran on it? Snapping your fingers, so I'd come running like a little lap dog? Is that what I was to you? Nothing more than a fucking challenge? You're all alike!"

He clenched his jaw. "I didn't want to let you go so quickly."

"You could have asked me on a fucking date instead of playing this stupid game!"

"I did. You said no!" His voice broke as his tears fell. "Over and over again! I needed something to hold onto you with."

"Well, guess what." I didn't need to say more. He knew. I looked at him—at the tears in his eyes. The need to slap him was strong. He'd ruined everything.

He hung his head and reached for my hands again.

I stood and wiped my eyes roughly. "We need to go. Nathan will be waiting for me."

We headed back downstairs together and we kept up appearances. I let him put an arm around my waist as his family came to say goodbye. We walked out like that, and he helped me into the car. I programmed the GPS and turned away from him, ignoring him the whole way.

When we arrived at the gas station where I'd arranged to meet Nathan, Antonio hurried to open my door, but I didn't wait for him. Unfortunately, he got there in time to close it for me, taking away my chance to slam it.

"You know what hurts the most, Antonio? How many times we talked about the importance of honesty and trust, and the people who betrayed us. All the while, you were lying to me."

He grabbed my hand and fell to his knees. "Samantha, one more fresh start, please."

"Enjoy Naples." I wrenched my hand free, not looking back. "Four months should net you four girlfriends. Should be fun."

As I approached the car, Nathan met me, wrapping his arms around me. "Did he hurt you? Did he touch you?"

I shook my head, unable to speak. I had to get away. I could break down in the car.

"Samantha!" Antonio pleaded one more time.

Nathan moved around me. "Leave her the fuck alone, you asshole. Haven't you done enough?"

I turned to see them. Antonio was up, Nathan stalking toward him. But Antonio's eyes stayed on me, and he didn't see the right hook coming until it connected with his cheek.

I let out a strangled sob. "Stop! Take me home!"

Antonio's head jerked back up, eyes still locked on me. "I am so sorry!"

Nathan growled at him, not budging. "Get lost. She doesn't want to see you anymore."

"Go home, Antonio. Just go home." I turned back to Nathan's car, collapsed into the passenger seat, and fell apart.

CHAPTER 43

SAMANTHA

Nathan refused to take me to my hotel. Instead, we went to Cass and Kevin's. I slept in their guest room and he slept on the couch. She'd tried to get me to open up about what happened, but I just wanted to be by myself. The way I should have stayed. Antonio was too good to be true. I shouldn't have let him in.

When I woke the next morning, I peeked at my phone. Twenty texts from Antonio. Five calls. Two emails. All apologies and excuses. I read the first few and almost caved, then mass-deleted everything.

By the time I came downstairs, everyone was gathered for breakfast. After eating their fill, while I pushed food around my plate, the kids got dressed and ran out back to play on their swing set. I helped Nathan clean up the dishes when Cass tried again to get me to talk.

"It's time."

I continued with the dishes.

"You need to talk about it," she pressed.

I paused in placing plates in the dishwasher. "No, I don't."

"What happened?"

"Sam," said Nathan, taking the plate from my hands.

My lungs tightened as the words formed in my head, my breath coming in quick spurts. "He lied," was all I got out before the lump blocked my throat again and the first tears came.

"About what?" Kevin asked. "Something important?"

Cass gaped at him. "You're kidding me? Important?"

"What? Did he lie about wearing brown shoes and actually wore black, or did he lie about being single and he was actually married? The size of the lie matters."

"It's a long and stupid story," I said.

Cass returned her focus to me. "We don't have anywhere to be."

I leaned against the counter to catch my breath, closing my eyes, replaying it. His words in the garden, being introduced as his girlfriend, Dom's news, Valentina's kindness. And Antonio's face when he came into the private gallery. That gorgeous face streaked with tears. Just a pretty face, hiding a lying soul.

"We were working on a claim together. We had a million-dollar policy on a burned painting we had to authenticate. We'd been working on it for weeks and finally proved it was a fake." I stopped, inhaling deeply when the tears started again. "But, he'd known it was a fake from the first day."

They were silent, until Kevin asked hesitantly, "That's it?"

My eyes burst open in shock. "What do you mean, 'That's it?'"

He shrugged. "Doesn't seem like a big deal. He knew it was a fake and helped you prove it."

"He lied, Kevin! Every time I went to see him—every single time—was one more lie. He manipulated me. Pretended he cared but he was probably laughing at me the whole time, like a pathetic fool who jumped whenever he said, 'Come here, Sa-mahn-tha.' Pulling strings like I was a little puppet. I took crap from Matt's dad over it." I rubbed my hands over my face roughly, trying to block it all out, but I couldn't.

"I thought I'd found someone special," I sobbed, covering my face. "Someone right for me."

Cass's arms wrapped around me. As I cried into her shoulder, she whispered, "You love him, don't you?"

"No. I could never love someone who lies to me."

"The lie isn't the problem." She smoothed my hair, speaking softly. "You're scared shitless you might be honest to goodness in love with someone."

"It doesn't even matter anyway. He's moving to Naples on Tuesday."

"Good," grumbled Nathan.

"That makes even more sense." She pulled back and lifted my chin so I was looking at her through the tears. "You're running away from him before he can run away from you."

I pushed away and turned to Nathan. "I want to go home now."

He touched my arm but shook his head.

"We talked about this, sweetie." Cass counted them off on her fingers. "Dad, Mom, Vincenzo, Matt. They all left you."

"It's not the same!"

She still had her fingers up and counted her thumb. "Now, Antonio, and yes, it is."

I buried my face in my hands again, ignoring her when she spoke with Nathan.

"I'd hoped you were wrong."

"I punched the asshole. No one does that to my Sam."

"Good for you," said Cass.

CHAPTER 44

ANTONIO

I froze outside the front door to the office, my heart unsure whether it should accelerate or just surrender and stop beating. Samantha stood on the other side of the large window, speaking with Sofia. Samantha's face was tense; she was still so angry.

But she was here. She hadn't sent Lucy alone. I had one more opportunity to see her before I left. Before I moved a half a world away from her. No chances to make it up to her, to win her back, to see her anywhere. This would be it. I had found the copyist who had created the fake version of *Les amoureux dans le ciel*, so perhaps she could forgive me? Not likely, though.

I balanced two trays of coffee from Russo's, the bag of cornetti hanging from my elbow. When I reached for the door, Lucy saw me and opened it. She was always so kind and cheerful, full of smiles.

"Wow, what happened to you?" She craned her neck to get a look at the side of my face.

It was still tender and the bruise dark enough to get attention. Angelo had laughed it must have been over a woman, and I told him he should have seen the other guy.

Except the other guy was fine. He had taken her home. The night she should have been with me.

Samantha turned, and our eyes locked. Dark circles clung under her jade-green eyes, and the corners of her mouth were hard. Not the faintest of smiles for me.

"Lucy," she snapped.

Her protégé moved to her side abruptly. "We're here to pick up the burned painting and your report."

"I brought coffee and pastries for our meeting." My voice was weak, and I didn't step further into the office.

"Thanks!" Lucy took the coffees to Sofia's desk, and my sister took the bag. Samantha would have to deal with me now.

We stared at each other, the same conversation rolling between us as on Saturday.

Liar.

Sorry.

Honesty and trust.

Forgive me.

Her jaw flexed several times and she blinked slowly. "Quite the bruise."

"It was the least I deserved."

Sofia and Lucy stopped talking and looked at each other, an awkward silence blanketing the room.

"The painting?" she said through gritted teeth.

I took a shaky breath and approached her. I reached for her hand, hoping her resolve was weak. I tried to push her boundary one more time, but she withdrew it too quickly.

"Lucy, I've got this. Stay here." She watched me like she expected further deception at every move. "Let's go."

The painting's case lay closed on my desk. We signed the paperwork in silence, and I slid it into the thick envelope with my report.

"So, I've been wondering." Her voice was so cold. "Are you sure the one at your parents' house is the real one?"

I nodded slowly.

"You authenticated it, didn't you?"

"When you brought this one in, it was the first thing I did. Please know, my mother was not aware of any of this. She was taken with you."

"So, let me guess. Your father and sister knew the whole time?"

I ran a hand through my hair, rather than fall to my knees and beg for forgiveness. "I found the copyist. His information is in there."

"It wasn't you? That would be perfect."

"No, Samantha, it was not me."

"I guess all those interviews I did, I could've asked you all along." She folded her arms, Work-Samantha in control. "Who did your parents buy it from?"

"Bobby Scott."

"Right. So, Thursday, in the truck, when you suggested Bobby had sold it and had the forgery done without telling his wife..." She clenched her jaw and squeezed her eyes shut, a tear forming in the corner of her eye. My heart broke yet again. I never should have lied to her.

"Samantha, I'm so sor—" I took her hand, but she tore it away, dragging it across her cheek.

"And Mason's. Why were you there?"

"I wanted to see you again—"

"No." She picked up the case and the envelope. "You were protecting yourself, weren't you? Making sure Rhonda didn't reveal your little secret, because your father was the one who offered on it while it was there?"

"I'm sorry for all—"

"What I want to know most, though, is did you ever actually care about me, or was it all—" Her lip curled and she turned to leave.

My throat hurt and I swallowed hard to get the words out. "Mi piange il cuore."

"Bene." She faced me, pushing the knife deeper as her voice quavered. "So does mine."

A wide-eyed Sofia stood at the dividing wall with Lucy, whispering to her. Samantha collected her, thanked Sofia for everything, and left.

My anchor was gone.

Sofia waved me into my office at the back.

"I have to go home and pack." I had argued and argued with Papa not to send me. Or postpone the trip. But this was a Ferraro responsibility now. He had convinced them to take me, so I had to go, or our name would be tarnished.

"Are you alright?"

"I shouldn't have lied to her. I knew it, but I did it anyway."

"I'm sure she'll forgive you eventually, little brother." She put her arms around me. "Did you write her that note we talked about?"

"It's with the report."

"I hope it works. Call me if you need anything."

I nodded and left through the back. In my car, I dialed her number, just in case, but it stopped on the first ring.

CHAPTER 45

SAMANTHA

Lucy climbed into the passenger seat next to me. "My heart weeps."

"What?"

"Sofia told me that's what he said to you. 'My heart weeps.' What's going on?"

"I don't want to talk about it."

"Did you hit him? Looked like a pretty nasty—"

I put up a hand and she stopped. The charred remains of the Chagall copy were secured in the back seat, and I pulled the report out of the envelope, flipping to the summation.

"Dammit!" I seriously debated smashing my head into the steering wheel.

"What?"

"The copyist." I covered my face with the paperwork.

"Again, what?"

I shook my head and took a few breaths. "I know him. And I'm in just the fucking mood to talk to him."

I tossed the papers to Lucy to put back in the envelope, hit the ignition, and programmed the address Antonio had provided into my GPS.

"Sam." She fumbled with the papers. "There's something in here."

A hand-written note. Addressed to me. Not a chance I was reading it. I stuffed it in my purse before Lucy got any ideas.

When my phone rang, and I saw his number, my breath caught. I immediately declined the call.

"You know you can block his number, right?"

I'd done that Sunday morning, then undid it. Probably ten times, back and forth. Maybe I was a glutton for punishment, maybe I wanted to hold onto my anger so I wouldn't forgive him.

· · · · ·· · ·· · ·

I knocked on the door, Lucy at my side. She carried Antonio's report and the painting case. I was fired up and ready for a fight. I rang the doorbell when no one arrived immediately, then knocked again.

The door opened, and the curator from Mason's Gallery greeted us, a flicker of recognition crossing her face.

"I'm sorry. I must have the wrong address. I'm looking for Cam-ron Parker. I was told this was his residence?"

"Why are you looking for him?" She was apprehensive but obviously knew him.

"My name is Samantha Caine." I held out my hand to shake. "And this is Lucy Chapman. We're with Foster Mutual Insurance."

"Paulette Johnson—Oh, wait, I remember you! You took care of fixing *Number Vee* for him!" She broke into a smile. "Cam-ron's my son, he lives downstairs."

No wonder she'd thought that stupid painting was so clever. He'd painted *Number Vee.*

"Is he home? We have a few methodology questions about another piece he did."

"Oh, he loves talking about his artwork." She beamed with pride. Pride in her thirty-plus-year-old son who lived in her basement and who alienated women at restaurants because he was an asshole. Yeah, lots of pride to be had there.

She showed us to her dining room table and went to get him. The house was covered with artwork, likely all his. She returned to let us know he'd be right up, as he was putting the finishing touches on a new piece, then left to get us some water.

"How are we playing this?" asked Lucy when we were alone again.

"I've got it. You sit back and don't learn anything from me on this one. This will be the least professional you've ever seen me." I rolled my shoulders and blew out a deep breath.

When Cam-ron appeared in the dining room entry, I stood, with a wicked smile for him. Unlike his mother, he recognized me immediately.

"Hi, Cam-ron." I grabbed for his wilted celery handshake. "Please, have a seat."

His dirty blond hair was unkempt as though he'd rolled out of bed when we arrived. Finishing something up, my ass. He wore the same torn jeans and "Stay calm and paint on" T-shirt as when we'd first met.

The night I made the toast with Antonio.

But I didn't linger on the memory.

I had work to do.

"You may not remember me, but my name is Sam. We met at Caruther's about three weeks ago. If you recall, I'm an insurance adjuster, and I'm here on official business." I took out my phone and hit record. "Mr. Cam-ron Parker, do you acknowledge this conversation is being recorded?"

"Yeah."

"Good, let's get to it."

"What's going on?" He spoke slowly, his eyes not fully awake yet. His mother returned with a glass of water for each of us and stood over him to smooth his hair.

"This is my colleague, Lucy Chapman." Lucy gave a little wave. "Lucy, please open the case. Cam-ron, we don't want to be here any longer than necessary, so here it is. You painted this copy of Chagall's *Les amoureux dans le ciel*, correct?"

"It's burned?"

"Yes, to a crisp." I tried to smile but was likely baring my teeth. "But you can make enough out to tell that's what it is?"

"Yeah?"

"Thank you. I'm sure you're aware it's illegal to create an exact replica of a painting done by any artist who has been dead less than seventy years and try to pass it off as an original?"

"Uh, yeah?"

"Good, and you understand Marc Chagall, whose painting this is a copy of, died in 1985? Do you know when the copyright on his work expires?"

"No?"

"2055, Cam-ron. Is it 2055 yet?"

"No?"

"Do you normally create forgeries like this?"

"No!" He looked at his mother for help, but she was as nervous as he was.

"Then why did you forge this painting?"

His mouth gaped open and closed like a fish.

"Cam-ron, are you aware that any person in the state of Michigan who commits a fraudulent act is guilty of a felony punishable by imprisonment up to four years or a fine up to fifty thousand dollars, or both? My next stop will be the Brenton Police Department unless you give us the information we need to keep you out of prison."

It was a bluff. Those were laws for insurance fraud, but he wouldn't know any better, so I went with it.

"She offered me double my regular fee!" he blurted out, shaking. "She said it needed to be perfect! I put my mark on it, and I didn't sign it, so it isn't a forgery. It was a lot of money! And she paid in cash." His mother rubbed his shoulders and consoled him, calming him.

"Who is she?" I asked, leaning forward.

"I don't remember her name." He looked back at his mother again. "Mom?"

"I'll get it, sweetie." She bustled off. His mom took care of his business, too?

"Am I going to jail?"

Time to play nice, to get his cooperation. "Not if I can help it."

"I didn't know it was against the law. I thought it was a code of ethics thing, you know, a recommendation?"

While she was gone, the suspicious voice in my head reminded me of a bonus question. "Are you familiar with

Parker's Restoration?"

"That's, uh, my dad's company."

"Do you work for him?"

"No. He had to let a bunch of people—"

His mother returned with the invoice, interrupting. "Olivia Scott."

One more lie from Antonio. It hadn't been Bobby. Or maybe he'd been guessing Thursday. No, it was most likely a lie. I turned to Lucy, whose jaw went slack.

"Could you say that clearly for the recording, please? Who commissioned Cam-ron to create an exact copy of Marc Chagall's *Les amoureux dans le ciel*?"

"Olivia Scott did, Ms. Caine. She paid Cam-ron twenty thousand dollars for a duplicate of the painting you named. The order specified the dimensions and that there be no obvious differences between the original and the copy." She offered the invoice to Lucy, who took pictures of it.

I continued, "That didn't seem at all suspicious to you?"

"Suspicious? No. She said they were putting the original into storage and wanted the copy to keep on their walls. Something about insurance costs."

It was a fair answer. The practice was common. But they hadn't called Foster to reduce their rates, so it was clearly another lie.

CHAPTER 46

SAMANTHA

Lucy climbed inside the truck, but I sank onto the running board. Antonio's face that morning. The deep purple bruise marring half his cheek, the red-rimmed eyes, the slump in his normally perfect posture. The weight on my chest made it hard to breathe. I leaned my head back on the door, closing my eyes and pointing my face to the sun.

My heart weeps. Oh god, so did mine. Everything was so perfect, right up until his father's announcement. Life was coming together. I could have had a future in Brenton, watched my niece and nephew grow up, and built something with Antonio.

Instead, all I wanted to do was leave. Pack up the RV, hitch it to the truck, and I was gone. I wouldn't be here when he got back. I'd move on. He'd move on.

But I couldn't. I had to stay for Cass. All I wanted to do was run from everything, but for once, I couldn't.

· · · · · · ● · · · ·

"So, Olivia Scott paid for an exact duplicate of the painting to be made," said Lucy when I joined her in the truck cab. "That proves she knows it's a fake. She didn't alert Foster before the claim, or after. So, that's insurance fraud. Case closed. Right?"

"Right! Cam-Ron didn't put a signature on it, so I'm betting one of the Scotts did. Let's take this to Janelle, then we'll show Cliff."

Once the truck's engine was roaring, my phone rang, and I put it through the truck's audio system.

"Sam! It's Mike from work. I need a favor." He sounded like he was in a hurry.

"What's going on?"

"I'm running behind on my site visits today. Cliff said your schedule was open. Can you help a guy out?"

I grinned at Lucy. Mike did leave the office on occasion, after all. "Yeah, what do you need?"

"Hold on." His footsteps stopped, and my phone buzzed. "Can you make that address in a half hour?"

I checked the GPS on my phone. "Yeah, we can."

"Vandalism at a property on the river. I'll assign it over to you. Thanks."

"No problem." I hung up and frowned. "I guess we'll head to the police after this."

I turned the truck off, and we moved to the backseat office to log into the claims system. I read the highlights of the First Notice of Loss to Lucy. "House on the river... paintball splatters on the steps and small dock...Seems pretty simple. We'll take care of that, then head to the police station."

I printed out the claim documents, and Lucy collected them, tucking them in a folder from the filing box at her feet.

· · · · ●· ●· · ·

A half hour later, we rang the doorbell and waited. The house was like many in the area, older homes which had taken up riverfront property a half-century ago. The neighborhood was mostly brick and vinyl houses and a lot of new roofs and upgrades from the original designs. The yards were well-maintained, with neatly cut grass and blossoming gardens.

A young woman came to the door, and I smiled politely.

"Hello, my name is Samantha Caine, and this is my partner, Lucy Chapman. We're with Foster Mutual Insurance."

She extended a hand to shake. "Nancy Shaeffer. Nice to meet you. I was expecting a man, though?"

"Mike Telford was supposed to come, but he had something come up. He asked us to come by regarding your vandalism claim. Can we take a look at the damage?"

"Sure." She slipped some shoes on and led us through a gate at the side, into the small backyard. It was fully fenced with a shed at the rear, and the Grand River ran along behind, only thirty feet across at this point. Nancy walked us through a gate to her dock.

"We have a couple of jet skis we take out on the river. They're in the shed. No damage to them. It's all down here." She pointed out the green paint splatters. I took a few photos to add to the file. From the dispersion pattern, it was clear they had been fired from the river.

"I don't suppose you have any idea who did it?" I asked, on a lark.

"No, but we have a security camera." She pointed at the back of the house. "We had some drunk guys land on the dock last year, so we installed it. They didn't do any damage or anything, but it scared us."

"The deck has a poly surface, and the concrete steps are painted, so it could simply be a matter of getting it all cleaned, maybe some touch-ups. Your deductible is..." I paused while Lucy flipped through the policy documents.

"Five hundred dollars."

"It's possible it will cost less. But, it's also possible we can find the people who did it and recoup the cost from them."

"Okay," said Nancy. "You want to see the video?"

"Yes, please."

We entered through the back door, and Nancy led us to her home office. She loaded the video from the afternoon the paintballs were fired at their dock. The camera was trained on the river, and the video clearly showed three men on jet skis, firing their paintball guns as they went by. They weren't wearing helmets, masks, or even life jackets. She paused the video, and I was sure the police would be able to use it.

"That's fantastic." I was impressed with the quality of the image. I gave Nancy my email address so she could send me a copy of the files. "Given the video, I'll forward it to the police department. They may want to handle this legally."

"But we'll get the dock and stairs cleaned up, right?"

"Absolutely."

If only all claims were this straightforward. I looked at the backyard in the video, the clear faces of the men on the jet skis, the river, and the road on the other side. And the blurry house beyond the road. I leaned in closer.

I grabbed my phone and pulled up a satellite map, checking if we were where I thought we were. I zoomed out to the full width of the river and then zoomed back in on the property directly across from us.

"Lucy." I turned my phone to her slowly to show her the map.

"Yeah?"

"Do you know what that is?"

Her eyes went wide as it dawned on her, too.

Nancy craned her neck around to look at the phone.

"How many days to you keep the files for?" Lucy asked.

"I don't know. My husband deletes them when we run out of space."

I offered a little prayer and crossed my fingers. "Do you have a file from the morning of July 31st?"

"Let me check." Nancy closed the current video and scrolled through the file list. She highlighted three files. "These three are from midnight to noon that morning."

Was this the 'keep an eye out' Quinn had suggested? I inclined my head to the chair while I looked at Lucy, who reacted.

"Can I sit?" She took the seat from Nancy, who seemed uncomfortable, but not enough to decline any of our requests.

"Play the one covering ten that morning," I told her.

"On it, boss." She cued up the video. The timestamp read 8:00 a.m. and nothing was happening.

"Fast forward to when the fire starts."

She dragged the progress bar slowly forward, until I saw it.

I grabbed her shoulder. "Stop! Back it up!"

She was already doing it. 10:22 a.m. The fire wasn't yet visible. But something else was. Lucy gaped. My stomach did a cartwheel.

Nancy slammed a hand over her mouth. "Is that what I think it is?"

"It sure is. Do we have your permission to forward these to Foster Mutual and then Brenton PD?"

Nancy nodded slowly, taking the seat back from Lucy.

CHAPTER 47

SAMANTHA

I forwarded the security video to Janelle with the subject line, *Merry Christmas—I'll be at the station in 15 minutes.* When we arrived, she was waiting on the front steps. Good sign.

"What's this?" she demanded.

"You watch it yet?" I took the steps two at a time.

"Of course not." She frowned at me. "Sounded like a virus."

My shoulders dropped. "C'mon, we need a big screen to watch it." I grabbed her arm.

"Why?" She removed my hand and didn't budge from her spot in front of the doors.

"Evidence on the Scott claim." I rubbed my hands together. "You're gonna love this!"

Janelle looked over at a still exhausted Lucy. "What's her problem?"

"She's out of shape. C'mon, let's go."

She signed us in with visitor's badges, and we headed toward one of their meeting rooms. As we walked, she hollered, "Slater!" and Jimmy's head popped up. "Let's go!"

We were all sitting in the room when Jimmy arrived, carefree as always. "Heya, Sammy!"

Janelle gave him one of her customary glares as she started up the computer locked to the meeting room desk. She logged in and called up her email account, grabbed the video file, and hit play on the big screen.

"So what is it, Sam?"

"Security camera footage from a house across the river." I could barely sit still, waiting to see her reaction. "We were working a vandalism claim, and we stumbled across it."

Lucy instructed her to fast forward to 10:20. Janelle advanced it and hit play again. A couple of minutes later, we all saw it, grainy and fuzzy, but obvious.

A figure emerged from the back of the house, dressed in black from head to foot. It stopped briefly and then walked across the back yard and through the door in the fence to Kathy Becker's house. We kept watching until the flames were visible in the windows, and the smoke started seeping out of the living room.

Her eyes grew wide as she watched the figure and the fire.

"I knew it!" She pounded the table and launched herself up to get closer to the screen. "Goddamnit, I knew it! Jimmy, get the Chief!"

She stayed on her feet while the video continued playing, the flames getting higher and higher. She gave me a big high-five. "Merry fucking Christmas, Sam!"

Jimmy returned a few minutes later with an older gentleman, who I assumed was the Chief of the Brenton Police Department. They played the video for him, and he nodded slowly.

"Slater, get this to IT and have them bump up the quality. Then we'll see if we can figure out who this person is and tie them directly to the fire."

"Tie them directly to the fire?" interjected Lucy. "Looks pretty direct to me."

He smiled condescendingly. "The legal system needs proof. Not guesses, assumptions, or hunches. Proof." He stood, thanked us for our contribution, and left without another word, Jimmy hot on his heels.

I felt deflated, and Lucy must have, too, but Janelle still had a massive smile on her face.

"We do have something else," I said to Janelle.

"As good as this?"

"No, but pretty good. You remember when I said there was a possibility the burned painting was a fake?"

She nodded.

"We have confirmation it wasn't the original, including the invoice Olivia Scott signed to commission a duplicate. The copy burned in the fire. Lucy, email Janelle the invoice pictures."

Janelle wrote her address out for Lucy. "Insurance fraud?"

I nodded.

"And likely arson," she added, looking back to the video. "I'm reopening this goddamn investigation and I'll be damned if Slater runs it this time."

Lucy and I were escorted out of the police department with several more thank yous from Janelle. She was ready and raring to go, but the justice system worked slower than we mere mortals.

"Olivia Scott has screwed up my life long enough," I said to Lucy once we were in the truck. "I'm taking her down."

"Shouldn't we let the police do that?"

"Fuck 'em."

Her eyebrows shot up. "What?"

"You heard the Chief. They'll act after they know who it is." I tapped my finger quickly on the center console, itching for another fight. "Do you know who it is?"

"I think it's Olivia."

"But do you know?" I challenged her, and she shook her head. "Exactly. A figure wearing black. Maybe a man, maybe a woman. It could be anyone, but my bet's on Olivia. I'll print that picture out and shove it under her nose. See if that gets us an admission of guilt."

"It could also clear her?"

"On an arson count, sure. Then we leave it to the police. No matter what, she committed insurance fraud, so we have her on that."

· · ● ●· ● ● ··

When I got to my hotel room, I emptied my purse onto the nightstand. As I poured out the contents, the letter drifted gently to the table. I looked at it, lying there, folded in thirds, daring me to read it.

I left it and went out to the sitting room to watch something. I'd taken a lot of my rage out on Cam-ron and was emotionally depleted. I grabbed for the remote, which was sitting on Antonio's dissertation. I'd read the whole thing and concluded he was even more brilliant than he was charming and handsome.

Too bad he was an even better liar.

I walked back to the bedroom and sat on the bed, staring at the stupid letter. I picked it up slowly, a gaping wound opening in the pit of my stomach. I unfolded it, the elegant script taunting me:

My dearest Samantha,

If I were to die tomorrow, lying to you would be my greatest regret. I was wrong, and I cannot apologize enough. I wanted to build a future with you, but a lie is no foundation to begin upon. I ask for a second chance, to show you my heart is true.

You told me Pompeii was the place you most wanted to see in the world. Please, come visit me in Napoli, and let me show it to you. If you cannot, I beg you to wait for me, until I come home. I will spend all the time it takes to regain your trust in me.

I am yours. There will be no other women. I promise you.

All my heart,

Antonio

I threw the letter back on the table, crying before I'd gotten to the end of my name. I shouldn't have read it. I should have thrown it out like I'd deleted his texts. I wanted to call him, text him, tell him I forgave him. But, if he lied about the painting for so long, and so convincingly, what else would he lie about?

I was better off alone.

Chapter 48

Samantha

"This should be fun." Lucy grinned while I collected my laptop and paperwork as we left the Pit for our confrontation with Olivia.

"Fun isn't the word I'd use." Actually, it was the exact word.

"Can you believe it's my last day of my internship?" She paused as we walked, taking in a deep breath. "During my first couple months here, hardly anyone paid attention to me. You taught me a lot over the last month, and I appreciate it."

"You're a quick study." I clapped her on the shoulder. "Actuarial's lucky to get you."

"As much as you hate people, you're going to miss me." She nudged me, which I let happen for once.

"Hardly." I nudged her back. "I don't suppose you've ever considered rock climbing?"

"Oh my god! I would love to! I was watching a video about—"

I put up a hand as we rounded the corner into the SIU office. Quinn's back was to us, working on a laptop with a privacy screen, which she closed when Harry greeted us.

"Lucy and I are on our way to a meeting, but I wanted to check if you got that info from IT?"

Quinn turned slowly. "Yes, we did." The look on her face generated a lot of questions.

"Find anything?"

Harry narrowed his eyes. "Like Quinn's said, you've got a good nose. Leave it at that. No need for more digging."

They were always mysterious but shutting me down was unlike them. "You found something."

Quinn's mouth twitched. "We did. Harry and I have a lot of work to do." She waved us away.

"What's with them?" asked Lucy as we reached the conference room.

I shrugged, grabbing a chair from the next room and setting it outside the door.

As we entered, I smiled politely, but my gloves were already off. Olivia's black outfit, hair, and makeup were as impeccable as her posture. She was an example of grace. David, on the other hand, made a show of checking his watch.

I held the door open, carefully controlling my pleasure. "David, would you mind waiting outside, please? We'd like to speak with your mother for a moment."

"I have every right to be here."

"You're right, but there's a chair outside for you."

Olivia put a hand on his arm, nodding slowly, and he stormed out.

"It's been a while, Mrs. Scott. How've you been?"

"Olivia, please." Her brow creased as she sighed. "It's been a difficult few weeks."

"I can't imagine. I hope Foster Mutual has been able to help through this trying time."

"Oh, yes. You have all been so helpful."

"This is a status update, but I'll record the session for the claim file. Do you mind?"

"Not at all."

I hit the record button on my phone. "Olivia, we're here to discuss the insurance claim for your painting *Les amoureux dans le ciel*, by Marc Chagall, which was burned in the fire at your residence on July 31st. According to the policy documentation, the painting has a valuation of one million dollars, and you are claiming the full amount." I paused to give her one last chance to advise us of the change. Nothing.

"We had the painting cleaned to compare against photographs on file with our office. During that process, we discovered the painting was a copy, worth twenty thousand dollars."

I put Cam-ron's invoice in front of her. Her shoulders sagged slightly, but in the blink of an eye, she resumed her dignified pose. The reaction was so subtle I almost missed it. I had her, and she knew it.

"We believe you sold the original painting in a private sale and replaced it with a copy. Your contractual obligation to our company required you advise us the painting was no longer in your possession. While that could have been an oversight, we've also discovered you've been experiencing financial difficulties. Given those two facts, I believe you intended to recover an additional million from our company, on top of the money already paid out for the fire."

Silence.

"And in case you aren't aware, insurance fraud is a felony in the state of Michigan, including withholding known facts from your insurance company. So, Olivia, would you like to dispute anything I've said?"

She put her hands on the table, interlacing her fingers. She closed her eyes and inhaled deeply. As she exhaled, she started talking.

"Thank you for insisting my son remain outside." She flexed her fingers a few times, staring at the invoice. "Yes, everything you said was accurate. We sold the painting three months ago for less than it was worth. We hung a copy so none of our friends would know. When you first spoke with us after the fire, all I was thinking about was losing Bobby—" She blinked away a few tears. "I didn't even hear the conversation we had. After that, David insisted he handle everything, but he didn't know the truth."

"I spoke with a painter who was at your house the morning of the fire. I understand you became quite irate when he moved it. If you were aware of its true value, why react to him that way? He said you told him it was worth more than his life."

"He was a rude cretin."

"Well, here's the thing." I opened my laptop and retrieved the security video. "The fire was set intentionally, and I believe you knew that. In fact, I believe you started the fire—"

"No!" She lurched forward and gripped the table's edge.

"—with the intention of burning the painting and defrauding our company. The house and property claim would cover any repairs but adding the million-dollar art claim would cover a lot of debts. And yelling at him about moving that painting would ensure he could attest to it being there."

"No!" She stood suddenly.

"Mrs. Scott, please sit."

She sank into her chair. "I didn't start the fire! Bobby died in that fire!" Lucy grabbed a tissue from a box at the end of the table and sat next to her. Olivia took the offered tissue and dabbed at her eyes.

I turned the laptop to her and hit play. "This video shows the back of your house, minutes before the fire becomes visible. You can see a figure leaving from the back and crossing the yard."

She watched quietly until the smoke and fire appeared, her mouth widening.

"Now, Olivia, would you like to tell me anything? I'm not the police, you don't have to, but the authorities always look kindly upon those who cooperate—"

She stared silently as the flames grew higher.

"—or confess."

I shut the laptop and placed a printed photo from the video in front of her, showing the hooded figure.

"I don't own a jacket like that," she whispered.

"Pardon?"

She looked at me, eyes intense and focused. "That's Kathy Becker!"

"Your neighbor?"

Olivia's eyes narrowed, the sad widow replaced by the woman the painter had told me about. "That witch was after my husband for years! Came to the house every week for tea and to flirt with him!"

Out of the corner of my eye, I saw Lucy smiling. She'd have to learn to control herself.

"You're right, we were having financial problems. Kathy told you, didn't she? Always listening at that fence, eavesdropping on us. Waiting for me to go out, so she could sneak over and try to seduce Bobby!"

She stabbed a finger on the photo. "That little whore showed up in this jacket one day. Just as I was getting home, she pranced up the driveway in the jacket and nothing else!"

I folded my arms, not trusting her as far as I could throw her. "Are you sure, Olivia?"

"I've never been so sure of anything in my life!"

As her voice grew louder, David barged in. "Mother?"

Olivia turned to face him, flipping the photo upside down in such a fluid movement, David didn't see it. "David, I'm fine. Please wait outside."

"I heard—"

"Outside, David." His puffed chest collapsed, and he skulked out, sitting so hard I felt it. She was not the misty-eyed widow. And David was not the strong, forceful one.

"Did they have an affair?"

Olivia remained quiet for a few seconds before responding. "Yes. He swore it didn't last long."

She flipped the photo to look at it again. "She heard us talking about selling the Chagall. After he died, she threatened me. Give her fifty thousand dollars or she'd tell everyone about…" She paused again, tight-lipped, and blinked rapidly. "About the affair."

"What did you say?" The tightness started behind my eyes, as though tears were on their way. As guilty as she was and as much as she'd lied, she was heart-broken, just like me.

"No matter what happened, I loved Bobby, and I will not allow her to smear his good name. Even if he tarnished it himself. I told her I'd pay her."

"Olivia, do you think Kathy could be responsible for the fire?"

"Yes, I do."

"And do you think it's possible she killed your husband?"

Olivia gasped and put both hands to her mouth. "Not if she thought she could have him. But if he'd broken her heart--"

"Love makes people do strange things." My voice broke for a moment. I peeked at my watch. What time was Antonio's flight leaving? Was it too late to change my mind?

I forced an even tone, trying to maintain my upper hand. "Alright, Olivia. You committed insurance fraud. That's a felony. Your best bet at this point would be to help the police catch the person who started the fire at your house."

Chapter 49

Antonio

I stood at the top of the escalator, past security at the airport. Looking down at the crowd of loved ones, every hug, kiss, and tearful goodbye broke my heart a little more. I kept watching. Maybe she would come running after me, like at the end of a movie.

It wouldn't happen, but there was still hope. She hadn't returned a single call, text, or email. Likely blocked my number. All that was left was the chance she had read my letter and believed me. Believed my apology, my request she wait for me.

Did I even deserve it?

A lie. Just as she had said. There had been a lie between us since the day she handed over the burned painting. And so many lies after that day. No argument, except with myself. I could hardly blame Papa or Sofia. I should have told her the truth. I had ruined my chance with the woman I was meant to be with. Eleven long years of her being my companion when my heart broke and now I was alone.

The minutes passed while I waited, stretching into an hour, until my flight was called.

I could be the one to play out the movie scene and chase after her, on my knees again to beg for forgiveness, but it wouldn't end with happily ever after. She would tell me to leave her alone. She would remind me about honesty and trust. All I would accomplish would be missing my flight.

I watched.

I waited.

She didn't come.

My name was called for the flight. I was late.

I pulled the newspaper clipping from my back pocket and unfolded it, looking at the image of us on the dance floor. The only picture I had of us together. Throat thick with the tears I refused to shed in public, I whispered to her for the hundredth time. "I am so sorry."

Dropping my head to the paper, I said a silent prayer she would contact me once I was in Napoli. I folded it and put it away, then pulled out my phone.

One last text, then I would go.

I love you

No, that was not it. She wouldn't believe me.

I'll miss you

No, she wouldn't care.

Forgive me

No, it was not enough. Apologies didn't matter. But the words came to me at last and I sent her my final text.

It was up to her now.

Chapter 50

SAMANTHA

Olivia had elected to tell her story without a lawyer, and the group of us sat in an interview room at the Brenton Police Department Tuesday afternoon. Olivia and David Scott, Janelle and Jimmy representing Brenton PD, and me. Lucy sat outside.

"My husband, Bobby Scott, left for work early in the morning." She clutched her tissue. "We had some upgrades planned for the house, and the workers arrived around eight in the morning. Sometime around nine thirty, I received a phone call from my neighbor, Kathy Becker, who told me she was downtown and had seen Bobby get into a car accident. The two of them had just ended..." She paused and looked to her son. "David, I'm so sorry you have to find out this way, but the two of them had just ended an affair."

David's eyes bulged, but a gentle hand from his mother kept him quiet.

"She'd been obsessed with him for years, ever since her husband died. I was afraid she'd done something to him. I was in a panic, so I forced the workers out and sped off to where she said the accident had been. There was nothing. I spent a good half hour looking around the area, in case she'd given me the wrong address. Then, I went to the bookstore to check if he was there."

"And was he?" asked Janelle.

"No, he'd left about an hour earlier. His employee didn't know why or where he'd gone. I thought maybe he'd forgotten something at home, so I headed back. When I arrived, the house was in flames, and the firefighters were already there." She stopped to press the tissue to her eyes. "And I found out my Bobby had been inside."

Jimmy placed a photo in front of her, a blown-up image of the figure behind the house. The team at the police station had been able to magnify and sharpen the photo, so additional details were visible in this copy. Other than revealing some blond hair, I couldn't make anything out well enough for an identification.

"Do you recognize the person in this photo?" asked Jimmy.

"I do." Her face hardened. "Kathy Becker. Can we talk about the blackmail now?"

"Yes," said Janelle. "Please tell us about that."

"She called me two days ago, demanding I pay her fifty thousand dollars. She said I'd had a windfall since his death. She told me she would tell everyone about the affair unless I paid her."

"Did she tell you when and where she wants you to deliver the money?"

"Yes." Olivia smoothed her jacket. "Thursday morning at The Haberdasher Café, downtown."

"Would you be willing to help us catch her?"

"Absolutely."

"Good, now let's talk about the painting."

"I don't see how that's any of your business."

"It appears to be insurance fraud, Mrs. Scott."

"I forgot." Olivia's eyes narrowed at Janelle. "My husband of almost fifty years died, and I forgot to tell the insurance company about the change we'd made with the painting. I wasn't thinking clearly."

"Mother?" David leaned toward her, speaking for the first time.

"It's nothing. We sold the Chagall a few months ago, and your father—" She sneered. "—didn't call Foster to tell them about it."

"But it was still hanging in—"

"That was a copy, David."

He sat back in his chair at a look from Olivia.

"I'll speak with Roger to clear the whole matter up."

Janelle nodded, and they returned to the blackmail exchange. No. This whole thing was about the painting, the fraudulent painting, and they were glossing over it like it didn't matter.

"Wait a minute!" I blurted. "We're letting her get away with defrauding Foster Mutual?"

Olivia smiled at me, mock compassion on her face. *Poor, silly little girl,* it said. That's why she'd insisted Janelle let me watch the interview. Payback.

Janelle asked coolly, "Has she accepted any money or signed anything confirming the value of the painting, concerning this claim?"

"Signed? No." Dammit. She had me.

"Then it's up to Foster Mutual, Sam." Janelle turned back to Olivia to continue their discussion, leaving me floundering for words. Olivia had won.

· · · ● · ● · ● · · ·

Once the interview was done, and the plan in place, Olivia and David left.

Janelle took the chair next to me. "Sam, you did great. Whether we nail her for the fraud or not, you and Lucy led us to an arsonist, a blackmailer, and possibly a murderer. I know it's a blow to your pride, but—"

"Pride? That's not what this is about!"

I needed to hit something. Preferably that witch, with her condescending smile. She was as guilty as the day was long, but it was in Roger's hands now, not mine, and not the legal system.

I stomped out of the room, Lucy scrambling to join me when I passed her.

The worst part about this claim was supposed to be Bobby's death. I was supposed to mourn him in private and move on. No fraud, no arson, no lies. No falling in—

My phone buzzed as I reached the truck, and my heart dropped. Another text from Antonio.

I hope to have my friend back someday

I grabbed the door handle for balance and leaned my head against it, my chest constricting. I should have left him blocked.

Lucy took the phone from me and deleted the message. "You like him a lot, don't you?"

"Yeah, I do—I mean, did."

"Is it something you can forgive him for?" She handed back my phone.

I straightened and let out a long breath. "Doesn't matter. He's gone and I'm leaving in the spring anyway."

"You won't even be at Foster when I come back?"

"No, I'm going on the road."

She looked down and gave a small nod, before heading to the passenger side. "Do you ever keep any of your friends?"

CHAPTER 51

SAMANTHA

"He did what?" I launched from my seat in the Pines conference room, hollering at Cliff.

He sat calmly with his hands clasped over his stomach. "Roger accepted the invoice you found and paid Olivia yesterday afternoon."

I dragged my hands over my face in disbelief.

"She owned a twenty-thousand-dollar painting that burned in the fire, so he paid her fair market value for it."

I hit the table. "Goddammit!"

"And he wanted me to pass along his thanks—"

"His what?"

"—for saving the company nine hundred eighty thousand dollars."

"I can't believe you're this calm, Cliff! That was fraud!"

He stood slowly with a sigh. "Bobby Scott was his friend. You know how he is."

"Fuck!"

"Watch your volume, Sam, or you'll get a reputation like mine," he said with a smirk.

"Did they at least cancel her policy?"

He shook his head and patted me on the back. I stormed out of the conference room, slamming the door for good measure. There was nothing more I could do. Back to my stupid, fucking, boring property claims.

Before I turned the corner to the Pit, a commotion by the front doors caught my attention.

"Am I under arrest? No! So don't touch me!" Roger walked down the hall and shot me a venomous look as he headed out the front doors. Escorted by two officers, Matt hot on his heels. Janelle, Harry, and a man I hadn't seen in years had been following them but approached me instead of leaving.

"Elliot?"

Janelle looked from me to him. "You know Special Agent Skinner?"

"It's been too long, Sam." He stood a few inches taller than me with skin almost as dark as Janelle's and short black hair, gleaming FBI shield at his waist.

"What's someone from Art Crimes doing here?"

"So, you haven't forgotten me? Just ignoring my calls?" He shook my hand and grinned. "I was already in Lansing, thanks to you."

"Let's go to a conference room." Harry led us to the Oaks, and we sat. Quinn slipped in out of nowhere to join her partner. Why were we all here? Together?

Everyone at the table sported some level of a smile. Except me. "What the hell? Those officers were taking Roger—"

Janelle held up a hand. "Get comfortable, Sam. This will be a bumpy ride."

She opened the folder she'd been carrying under her arm and flipped through photos as she spoke. "Everything went down at the Haberdasher Café exactly like we planned. Olivia was right. We have Kathy Becker on surveillance admitting to the blackmail, to being in the Scott residence with the intention of setting the fire, and to witnessing Bobby Scott fall and hit his head. And leaving him to burn."

"Oh my—"

Harry picked up from her, beaming like a proud father. "Good idea getting IT involved on the red flag report. We found a few that had been removed by Cliff, Hailey, and Mike, but we've spoken to them and put an end to that. However, over the last two years, we found sixty-three instances of Roger removing red flags from claims. So, Quinn tailed him yesterday. We expected it would take a while to get to the bottom of this, but—"

Quinn pulled a photo out of Janelle's folder. Roger and Olivia on a sidewalk downtown, kissing. "Looks like we missed a fifth red flag on the claim, hun. An affair."

My jaw dropped.

"Harry and I took this and the red flag report straight to the Brenton PD."

Janelle tapped on the photo, on a box in Roger's hand. "Olivia used a gift box with her own money for the blackmail sting at the Café. We're fairly certain this is the same one."

Harry said, "We suspect Roger's involved with a group of contractors who aren't on the up-and-up. He removes red flags so SIU doesn't get involved in their claims, they get paid, and so does he. And yes, that includes the ball peen hammer claims. Our reinsurers have been notified and may press fraud charges against him. The police are questioning him now, but I expect he'll be locked up before the day's out."

Oh, no. I got my ex-father-in-law arrested. "Wait a second. So Olivia promised to pay Roger off to get the claim pushed through?"

Quinn said, "I'm not sure if she was paying him or if they were just splitting everything. My bet is that Roger was in on the whole thing."

"What whole thing?"

Janelle grinned, her eyes twinkling. "This morning, Kathy Becker met with her lawyer on a plea bargain. She's claiming her call to Olivia was planned. Wait until the security system was offline and the painters had everything set up for the perfect fire. Pre-arranged signal, phone call, and bam. Everyone's out of the house at the right time."

"I was right about the painter!" I pounded a fist on the table. "Her argument with him was to bring his attention to the painting!"

Quinn and Harry grinned at each other.

"Oh my god." I jumped out of my seat, shaking my head, as the final pieces fell into place. "Explains how Olivia ID'ed Kathy in the blurry video. She already knew who it was."

"And it gets better." Janelle counted off on her fingers. "One, Olivia's cell phone records show she called her husband as soon as she was off with Kathy. Likely to have him rush home. Not sure yet the plan there, but we'll figure it out. Two, no one's seen Olivia or David since Roger cut them the twenty-thousand-dollar check yesterday. Three, she cashed all the insurance checks and hasn't paid any repair contractors. She's got over a million in cash on her."

"Holy shit!" I *was* right about her not getting the repairs started.

"We expect they're already out of the state, if not the country, so Special Agent Skinner's liaising with us. We're doing a press conference tomorrow morning at 10:00 a.m. We owe a lot of this to you, so we'd like you to be there, if you could say a few words?"

I sank back into my chair. What a whirlwind. "Yeah, of course. Absolutely."

Elliot finally spoke. "Now that Sam's up-to-date, can she and I have the room a moment?"

Once the rest were gone, he leaned back in his chair, folding his arms across his chest. "You know, your badge and creds are still waiting for you."

"You were already in Lansing because of the stolen painting at the charity auction?"

"Precisely. The team had Dr. Ferraro's name, and we tracked it back to you. Can't say I was surprised, except to see you back in Michigan. Good news for me, I'm hoping?"

"Was anyone by the name of Paulette Johnson or Cam-ron Parker involved?"

"I can't go into the details, but those names aren't on our list. It's still early days."

I nodded, relieved. Cam-ron was clueless and an ass, but he hadn't struck me as a criminal mastermind.

"I was hoping to speak with Dr. Ferraro—the younger, of course—while I was here. Do you think you could arrange that for me?"

My stomach lurched. "He's in Naples."

"Any thoughts on when he'll be back? I'd like to shake hands with the man who helped you at the auction and with this case."

"Sometime around Christmas?"

"Interesting." He paused a moment, then plowed on. "Listen, speaking of Italy—I have a team shipping out next week to work with the Carabinieri, tracking down some leads on an artwork smuggling ring—"

"Hold on. Is Nathan Miller working with you?"

"You know him?"

"Old friend. He mentioned he was working with the FBI on a smuggling case. I was sure he made it up."

"He's part of the task force."

"And is Antonio implicated?" It didn't matter. I was done with him. He was in Italy for four months and I was done. But my throat closed over anyway. My stupid throat. And my stupid heart.

Elliot betrayed no emotion, other than a slight twitch of his eyebrow. Maybe I imagined it. "Why would you think he was involved?"

"Nathan said he was." Was it just a ploy to keep me away from Antonio?

He nodded slowly, waiting for my reaction which didn't come. "Well, if you aren't ready for the full commitment, I could pull a few strings to get you on as a contractor."

Every time I saw Elliot, he asked the same thing. When was I coming back to the FBI? I'd been running away so long I didn't know how to stop and be in one place anymore. The week before, stopping seemed like it was finally a choice.

I rubbed a hand over my face. "Rejoining the FBI has been on my mind a lot lately, especially after the auction. I have commitments here until the spring, but I'll let you know after that."

As he left, Janelle returned and leaned on the table. "Amazing work, Sam."

"From fraud to arson to murder."

"Unbelievable."

I leaned next to her. Things had improved between the two of us over the last month. But, with the case wrapping up, it might be my last chance to talk to her. "You know I couldn't lie to them about what I saw. You had your phone out during a final exam."

"You could've lied." She flexed her jaw and focused on the floor. "But, if you had, I would have lost all respect for you."

"Rock and a hard place." I looked at her, while she kept her gaze down.

"I wasn't cheating, you know."

"Then what were you—"

"I'm sorry I wasn't there for you. Your mom's accident, whatever happened with the FBI, your divorce..." She ran a hand over her head. "I'm a pretty bad friend, too."

I gripped the edge of the table so she wouldn't see my hands shaking. Were we finally making up? "We always were two peas in a pod."

Patting me gently on the leg before she left, she smiled. "I'll see you tomorrow morning. Maybe we can grab that coffee after."

What a roller coaster. If only Antonio was there to see it unfold. I couldn't have done it without him. Yes, I could have, if he'd told me the truth. But if he had, we would have simply declined the claim. We wouldn't have done the x-ray and found the copy mark or the fraud. Wouldn't have found the blackmail, the arson, or the murder. Or Roger. Or the stolen painting at the gala. Or had a second chance with Janelle.

His one little lie had led to so much good.

But he was still a liar. Just like Olivia. Just like Roger.

So much for the Professional Lie Detector.

CHAPTER 52

SAMANTHA

I sat on a short stone wall along the edge of a garden at the Metropolitan's Cloisters Museum. The medieval monastery-style building was peaceful and inspiring, even with hundreds of people walking past me. The open courtyard was bordered by stone walkways topped with terracotta roof tiles, while flowering plants and ornamental trees surrounded the center fountain.

Antonio's voice echoed in my head. *If you knew you were to die tomorrow, what would you do with the time you have left?* A fourteen-hour trip to New York City, I'd said, ending at The Cloisters. I sighed and checked the timer on my watch. I'd made all my stops and still had over two hours left to sit and pretend it was as wonderful as I'd told him it would be, while the pit in my stomach kept reminding me it wasn't.

What would his favorite part of the museum be? Would he like the art or the sculpture? The stained glass or the architecture?

I breathed deeply. *Stop, Sam, just stop.*

I pulled out my phone and called Cass, covering my face with a hand, trying to find some privacy in the crowd.

"Hey, sweetie, what's up?" She was having a good day with lots of energy, which made me smile for a second.

"Cass, I'm sorry, but I have to cancel girls' night tonight."

"Seriously? I was looking forward to it!"

"Well, I'm sort of in New York."

"You're what?"

"I flew out early this—"

"Shit! You're not—"

"I'm not on the run, Cass, calm down." I rubbed my cheek, staring at the small pink bricks at my feet, scuffing my shoe against one that stuck up. "I needed some alone time."

"Bullshit." She huffed. "He's an asshole, Sam. Don't let him do this to you."

My throat closed over for the millionth time, and I clenched my jaw to stave off the threatening tears. I should have thrown myself into work instead of coming here. Putting him out of my mind while I wrapped up the Scott case was easy compared to this.

"It hasn't even been a week, Sam. It'll get easier."

I rested my chin on my hand, focused on the daylily in front of me. "I don't know how long I'll stay. I cleared some time with work, though. My boss said I earned it with that painting claim."

"Sam—"

"I'll be home for your next chemo, I promise." I sniffled, but she remained silent. "I gotta go, Cass. Love you."

I hung up and leaned forward, staring at my phone. I had Janelle back, Lucy and I were becoming friends, and the odds were in Cass's favor. Roger was in custody, the Scott case was in the FBI's hands, and Elliot told me they still wanted me. I had every reason to feel positive about my future.

But I felt empty. *You are my dream, Samantha.* I pulled up the Ferraro's website, selected Antonio's bio, and stared at his smiling face.

I should have taken pictures of us together, so I had something more personal than a website. No, I shouldn't have, that would make it worse. My finger hovered over his photo, my brain telling me to close it, but my heart aching to remember the moments we'd shared. I hit *Contact Us* and the phone rang. It was Saturday; no one would be there, but maybe his voice would be on the recording.

Before it went to message, Sofia answered, and my heart dropped. I put the phone tentatively to my ear.

"Hi, Sofia. It's, um, Sam Caine calling. I thought you'd be closed."

"Samantha! What—what can I do for you?"

I had no idea what she could do for me. No idea why I'd called, other than to punish myself. *I wanted to build a future with you.*

"Samantha, you two belong together."

My throat was too tight to say anything.

"Call him. He's heartbroken, and you must be, too, or you wouldn't be calling me." Her pace increased and her words ran together. "He told me everything. I'm so sorry! Papa and I told him to keep the secret."

"Sofia, I—"

"You're perfect for each other! Call him! I have his number right here. I'll give it to you. Please! Don't punish him for our mistake!"

"Sofia," I snapped. "He's a grown man. He makes his own decisions."

"He loves you!"

Exhaling, I covered my face again. "I shouldn't have called. I'm sorry."

I hung up before she could get another word in, blinking away tears as I paused the timer on my watch. Why was I even timing it? What was I trying to prove? My phone buzzed with a text message from Sofia. His phone number and address in Naples.

I decided to find the right woman for me. And I think I've found her.

He terrified me. No, my feelings for him terrified me. If I gave him my heart, he'd break it. But it was too late. Instead of giving him a chance, I broke it for him. *My heart weeps.* And his heart had been caught in the crossfire.

I shut the phone off. *Because you are perfect for me.* Then I turned it on again. And off.

Grabbing my backpack, I swung my legs over the cloisters' half-wall, into the covered walkway, and made my way toward the exit. Janelle had forgiven me, I'd forgiven Matt, but I couldn't forgive Antonio. Was Cass right? Was it nothing more than an excuse? Was I running away from him before he could run away from me?

I looked at my watch. The timer was paused on two hours.

What do you look for in love? I'd asked him.

Someone who chooses time with me when they have two hours left, he'd responded.

I started to run.

Chapter 53

Samantha

The plane landed at the small airport, and I jostled for position. I rushed through baggage claim and out the doors to the waiting line of taxis, hiring one and handing over the address. It took an hour through winding streets and highways, my head spinning the whole way. I was exhausted. It had been a long day and a long flight. This was either the smartest thing I'd ever done or the stupidest.

To my right, the bay was clogged with ships of all sizes; to my left, Mount Vesuvius loomed over the city. As we slowed, I put the window down and inhaled the peppery scent of an olive grove on the warm salty air. The car turned a corner into a side street and came to a stop. I paid the driver and asked him to wait for ten minutes, in case.

I approached a tall, narrow metal gate, leading to a stone courtyard and a three-story white stucco villa. The dark wooden doors were open, and a score of windows faced the water. My heart was pounding so hard and my hands shook.

Please, just please.

A familiar-looking man stood in the courtyard, cleaning a motorcycle. Tall and muscular, with broad shoulders and dark hair, but it wasn't him. As I pushed open the gate, it creaked, and he turned to give me a once-over. His face reminded me of Antonio's so much. This was the right house.

"Buongiorno, bellisima," he purred, stalking over to me.

"Is Antonio here?" My nerves were such a jumble, I'd spoken in English.

"Antonio?" He scoffed, in a thick Italian accent. "He doesn't see the pretty tourists. But I do." He bit his lip to make his intentions clear. "I'm Mario, his far sexier cousin."

I stood frozen, backpack over one shoulder, unsure what else to say.

He came closer, tilting his head, taking in every angle of me. Suddenly he paused, pursing his lips. "Un momento...I know this face. You're his Samantha?"

"I hope so."

"Good you are here. My cousin talks about you." He smirked, so much like Antonio's smile that my heart skipped. "A lot. He has been very boring."

My breath caught when I heard bare footsteps on the tile inside the doorway. Antonio appeared, in dark gray lounge pants, nothing else, arms folded. No smile, no *bella* greeting, and he stopped before he reached the courtyard. The bruise had faded to yellow, but still covered half his cheek. His posture was defensive, but his cousin's words...Maybe this wasn't a mistake.

"Mario, leave her alone."

The cousin winked at me and disappeared into the villa.

"What are you doing here?" Such sorrow in his eyes.

I could have run to him and been done with it, if he still wanted me. But there was so much I had to say. "You remember when you asked what I'd do if I knew I would die the next day? And you told me how sad my answer was?"

His brows knit together. "Sì."

"I had to prove you wrong, prove I was right about everything. I was better off by myself, without you."

"So, you come here to break my heart all over again?" His normally confident, full voice was strained.

"You gave me fourteen hours. So, I got on my bike Friday morning, rode to Detroit, and caught the first plane to New York. I did everything I told you I would." My words were coming out sharp, but it was the only way I could speak. "I walked across the Brooklyn Bridge, went to the top of the Empire State Building, ate pizza in Times Square, and went to the Cloisters. And it was peaceful and beautiful, exactly like I said it would be."

He sighed and hung his head, turning away to walk out of my life for good.

"But." My voice broke and the tears started. "All I could think about was that you weren't there with me. Holding my hand, making me laugh, asking me a million questions."

He stopped and faced me, arms still crossed, but listening.

"The whole thing took twelve hours." I showed him my watch with the paused timer like it meant something. "I had two left, Antonio. Then Sofia sent me your address. I went back to the airport and paid a ridiculous amount of money to get on a plane to come here. Because I want to spend those two hours with you. I don't want to be anywhere else in the world, unless you're there with me."

He unfolded his arms, the pain slipping from his eyes.

I was sobbing, but I had to finish. It was too important not to. "I want you to forgive me for being so stubborn that I couldn't forgive you. I couldn't believe someone as miraculous as you would want me. I was scared to fall for you, but now, I'm terrified I've lost you. I don't care if you tell me to get back on a plane after those two hours are up, I just want to be with you right now."

He closed the distance to me, his dark eyes soft.

"I don't want your heart to weep anymore," I choked out, as he took my hand and kissed it gently.

"You have come back to me. What can my heart do now but sing with joy?"

"I want this relationship to work, Antonio. More than anything I've ever wanted."

"But how?" He pressed his forehead to mine and wiped my tears away with his thumbs. "You'll be gone three months after I get home."

I dropped my backpack and slid my arms around him, unable to control my tremble. "I started looking at apartment websites when I was at the airport."

He took in a shaky breath. "You're staying in Brenton? To be with me?"

As I nodded, he pulled me closer, hugging me tightly. I buried my face in his neck, pressing my cheek against his skin. This was where I belonged. With him.

"Again, I'm a lucky man." He leaned back to look at me, brushing his knuckles along my cheek, tears welling in his eyes. "Oh, Samantha, I love you."

I squeezed my eyes shut. It was on the tip of my tongue, but I couldn't return the words he wanted. I'd come so far. But not that far. Not yet.

He put a hand under my chin, tilting my face up. "Do you love me?"

"I don't know." I could barely get the words out. "But I do know this is the first time I've ever run toward something that could hurt so much."

"I swear, on my life, I will never hurt you again."

He took my face in both his gentle hands and kissed me as I'd never been kissed before. Full of tenderness and of devotion. And of passion. It was everything. I pulled myself closer to him, our bodies fitting together perfectly. The exhaustion of the last couple of days faded, replaced by the burning desire I'd felt on the beach.

"There is only one problem left, bella." A delicious grin spread across his lips, as he picked me up and I wrapped my legs around him. "I need far more than two hours to make love to you properly."

I kissed him again and laughed, brushing away my final tears. "I have a week and a half. Is that enough?"

"That's not much time. We must get started right away."

I sealed my mouth to his as he carried me inside, all my instincts telling me to never let him go again.

• • • • •• • • • •

THE END

• • • • •• • • • •

Thank you for reading *Burning Caine*. I hope you enjoyed reading it as much as I enjoyed writing it. If you did, please consider leaving a rating or a review. Reviews help readers discover new books and authors—and I'd really appreciate it!

If you want more Sam and Antonio, I've got something special for you! You can join my newsletter (scan the QR code below or visit https://janetoppedisano.com/) for access to *Meeting Caine*. This short story shows what happened the day they met in college. It didn't go so well for him!

The newsletter also includes access to behind-the-scenes details (like my inspirations and research), news on my upcoming releases, and photos of my ridiculously adorable dog.

And if your need for more Sam and Antonio still isn't quenched, check out book two. *Chasing Caine* picks up where *Burning Caine* ends and follows Sam and Antonio during her time in Naples. There's more heat plus an art crime to be solved!

Thanks again,
Janet

ACKNOWLEDGEMENTS

When I started writing *Burning Caine*, the intention was to write a mystery. Samantha was mostly the same, but Antonio? He was the bad guy. The book was going to be in her point-of-view, she was going to fall for him, and we wouldn't find out until near the end that he was actually in on the whole fraud. Then he would have ended up in jail or something.

But the more I wrote, the more time Sam and Antonio spent together, the more I realized I just couldn't do that to them. They had too much chemistry. With each revision, their need to be together intensified, and the book gradually shifted from mystery to romantic suspense.

There are so many people I'd like to thank for helping me make this book, my debut, a reality! Pardon my overly analytical brain, but I'm going to thank them in chronological order, based on when they came into my book-life!

First and foremost, I'd like to thank my husband and son for their patience and support. Writing is a labor of love and it takes an inordinate amount of time to finish a book. I've abandoned them for many hours while I sneak off to the writing cave, but I've also spent a lot of hours while in the car and in cold rinks, writing while my son practices hockey.

Then there are my alpha readers, Paula and Patricia. They've read every draft of every novel I've written...and didn't like Antonio from day one. It took a few revisions to win them over, but they were enthusiastic and gobbled up every iteration. And they helped make the character stronger in the process.

Next up, my beta readers: Cassie, Dianna, Gayle, Kim, Patty, Robbie, Sharron, Tracy, and Vivian. These wonderful ladies provided such valuable feedback and enthusiasm, I wouldn't have kept going without them.

I can't say enough about how important having a crew around you is. For me, that's my Pit Squirrels. My what? During the lead-up to the 2020 #RevPit contest on Twitter, I met an amazing group of women (Amelia, Ariana, Beck, Katrina, Kim, Kira, Liv, Melissa, Noreen, and Rose) who became my writerly besties. They're always there, for the highs of agent signings, publications, and contest or award wins; to the lows of rejection letters, query letters, and imposter syndrome. They pick me up and inspire me every day, and I'm lucky to be able to do the same for them.

On top of all that, there's my #FridayKiss family. We share snippets of our romance works-in-progress every Friday over on Twitter (and Instagram, Facebook, and TikTok!). I've met an amazing group of romance writers who've cheered me on and shown the love, all in 280 characters or less.

In May 2020, things got *real* with *Burning Caine.* I was selected as a winner in the #RevPit contest by the indomitable editor Miranda Darrow. She hacked and slashed that manuscript that everyone loved to absolute pieces. But like the phoenix emerging from the ashes, the story evolved into a real, actual romance! It was an overwhelming experience, and just the distraction I needed from the state of the world. We were such a fantastic match, when I decided to publish my books, I (did my due diligence and spoke with other editors, but) knew she was the one I wanted to entrust my words to.

As a follow-up to that, I'd also like to make a shout-out to the entire Revise & Resub community. The editors provide such a depth of support and knowledge for authors and their contests (both the annual RevPit and the smaller mini-events) are absolutely top-notch.

And finally, I'd like to thank you, my reader. Without you, I'd just be typing in my basement (or at my dining room table or in a hockey rink or in the car) for nothing. Knowing someone out there is going to read my words and find a little bit of enjoyment or an escape for a few hours means the world to me. So yeah, thanks again.

ABOUT THE AUTHOR

Janet Oppedisano hails from Canada's East Coast and has lived in five provinces, from the Maritimes to the Prairies. Growing up with a Mountie for a father and marrying a Navy diver, it's no surprise she writes romance with a hint of danger and mystery in it. Not to mention strong heroes and equally strong heroines.

Prior to publishing her debut novel, she won awards for two of her unpublished works. *Burning Caine* (hey, that's this book!) won the 2020 #RevPit contest and the Romance Writers of America's 2021 Vivian Award for Most Anticipated Romance. *The Reaper's Gambit* (coming out in 2023) won the Georgia Romance Writers' PrePublished Maggie Award for Best Paranormal Romance.

When not writing, you can find her...thinking about writing. And indulging in her favorite pastimes, like baking, traveling, hiking, playing with her dog, and watching her hockey goalie son on the ice.

Oh, and it's pronounced oh-ped-ih-SAH-no. Exactly the way it's spelled. Honest!

• • • • • • • • • •

Follow Janet:

facebook.com/JanetOppedisanoAuthor/

twitter.com/JanetOppedisano

bookbub.com/authors/janet-oppedisano

instagram.com/janet_oppedisano/

Made in the USA
Middletown, DE
05 February 2022